The Golden Road

The Golden Road

MARINA OLIVER

PAN BOOKS

First published 1996 by Penguin Books

First published in paperback 2000 by Pan Books
an imprint of Pan Macmillan Ltd
Pan Macmillan, 20 New Wharf Road, London N1 9RR
Basingstoke and Oxford
Associated companies throughout the world
www.panmacmillan.com

ISBN 0 330 39681 1

3 5 7 9 10 8 6 4 2

Printed and bound in Great Britain by
Mackays of Chatham plc, Chatham, Kent

For Cindy, Duncan and family, not forgetting Jezebel.
They appreciate veterans.

Acknowledgements

After my husband and I had driven a leisurely 2,000 miles in summer in a modern car over part of the Monte Carlo Rally route, my admiration for the Rally crews, covering 2,500 miles in January in a hundred hours in their often open cars, soared stratospherically. I read many of their accounts, and apart from my two imaginary crews and their adventures, all the incidents referred to are true.

As usual the librarians in Birmingham and at the Bodleian provided an invaluable service, and I am also indebted to many other people for help and encouragement. The Hockley Jewellery Quarter Discovery Centre, my mother- and father-in-law, Frances and Brookes Oliver, the staff at the Motor Heritage Museum at Gaydon, and the librarians at the Bibliothèque Louis Notari in Monaco all supplied information. I am particularly grateful to Christine Bissett-Powell, Bert Hammond's granddaughter, for lending me some of his mementoes, and the committee and members of the Lagonda Club for showing me their marvellous cars. My agent Sarah Molloy and my editor Richenda Todd were supportive as ever, and I owe them much.

Prologue

JOSIE Shaw, feeling desperately large and awkward in her new black clothes, stood dutifully beside her diminutive mother and scowled at the assembled mourners. How could they look so cheerful, even laugh out loud, when they had just attended the burial of her stepfather, one of the kindest, most generous of men? Even her mother had thrown back the ostentatiously heavy veils she'd worn at the church over her fair hair, and though she clutched a black lace handkerchief in her hand, her eyes were dry and she was talking volubly.

Josie glared round. She wished they'd all go away. Then she saw one man who wasn't enjoying the funeral feast. Leo Bradley stood alone, black hair overlong and untidy, as it had always been when she'd seen him as a boy. But he was far more handsome now, his good looks and clean-cut profile were the first thing you noticed about him. He held a glass of sherry but seemed oblivious of everything but his own thoughts. His deep-set eyes were shaded, his square jaw jutted pugnaciously, his attention was clearly far away. The mourners tactfully side-stepped his tall, broad figure, leaving him a barrier of space as unscalable as a high wall. After all, it was his father they had buried and Leo, she'd been told, though only twelve at the time, had quarrelled bitterly with his father when George Bradley had married the recently widowed Dora Shaw. He'd never accepted them, never visited them willingly despite George's urging.

Leo suddenly became aware of Josie's gaze, and stared at her in some surprise. It was a year since they'd last met, when she'd been a leggy, gangling schoolgirl who, he'd thought, ought to have been a boy, she was so vital and strong. Joseph Shaw must have been a big man, like George. Josie was quite unlike her delicate mother, tall and with strong features that softened into a different kind of beauty from Dora's Dresden shepherdess fragility. Black suited her, with her pale skin, green eyes and vivid auburn hair, while it made Dora look ill, even haggard. He raised one eyebrow slightly and inclined his head, then slipped through a doorway into the lush overgrown conservatory. Two minutes later Josie entered from the garden.

'I – wanted to say how sorry I am,' she said softly. 'I loved Papa George very much.'

'He thought of you as his daughter,' Leo said curtly. 'You probably knew him better than I did.'

Josie glanced at him curiously. So he still resented his father's second marriage. 'Did you feel I'd pushed you out?' she asked bluntly.

'I never blamed you. You were only a baby. Two, weren't you? Josie, let's walk in the garden. It's so hot in here, and I'd appreciate it – if you feel you can talk about it – if you could tell me how it happened. You were there, they said, but I wasn't told much else.'

She led the way across the smoothly mown grass and through an opening in the yew hedge. This surrounded a formally planted rose-garden, and the rich scent filled the hot, still air. 'It was dreadful. I was on the opposite hill, and I saw it, but I – there was nothing I could do.'

'Sit down.' Leo pushed her towards an ornately carved bench and sat beside her. 'You don't have to tell me, not if it upsets you.'

'No, I'd like to talk about it. Mother couldn't bear to listen. I haven't told anyone yet. They didn't want to upset me, they said.' She paused and gathered her thoughts. 'Mother wasn't in the best of moods. She had been saying that she wanted to go to the French Riviera, but we couldn't afford it. The weather had brought on a headache. Papa George went out for a breath of fresh air, he said. It was terribly hot, like today. I'd hoped he would take me with him and teach me more about driving, but he'd gone by the time I'd helped Mother to bed, so I decided to climb up the hill behind the house. Do you know Church Stretton? It's all hills. It was so peaceful, the woods, and fields with ripe corn, and animals grazing. I was looking at all the timbered buildings, and wishing I could walk in the Welsh hills. There was a train coming, I could see the smoke and hear it chugging, but it was so far away I could still hear the skylarks and the bees. I was so happy on my own. I was planning what I'd do when I left school. Women can do all sorts of things now. We have the vote at twenty-one; there's even been a woman cabinet minister. I want a career, not to be like my mother, dependent on a man.'

For the first time Leo smiled. 'Did my father bring you up a suffragette?'

Josie glanced at him and shook her head. A single tear glistened on her surprisingly dark eyelashes. 'No, but he understood,' she said with a slight quaver in her voice. 'He talked to me about important things – the Nazis in Germany, and the General Strike a few years ago, and India becoming a dominion, as well as the new television experiments the BBC is working on. But he didn't talk to me about why Wall Street is so important.'

'I expect he thought you wouldn't understand about the stock market.'

'I can't understand why people trust others to make their money for them like Papa George did rather than opening their own business.'

'It's called investment.'

'I'll work for my money when I have a business. I won't depend on anyone else and risk being let down by them.'

'Women shouldn't have businesses. They're better off at home.'

'Oh come on, Leo. It's 1930, not 1830. Women run shops, become doctors – they even fly aeroplanes. I won't depend on a man like my mother did. It's not done her much good.'

Her voice wavered and Leo stretched out and took her hand in his. 'Stop, if it upsets you.'

Josie gritted her teeth. 'No, I want to tell you. I heard a car, an odd, high-pitched tone which didn't seem normal. Yet the engine noise was familiar. Bentleys have a distinctive whine. He loved that car. Even when he lost so much money he wouldn't sell it. It was on the hill opposite, coming down a very narrow steep road, and it was travelling fast, much too fast. It was coasting out of gear; that was the odd sound. Something must have gone wrong.' She shuddered, reliving those terrifying moments, and Leo hugged her comfortingly. Josie took a deep breath. 'He didn't have a chance. The car smashed into a stone wall. It was thrown into the air and landed upside down on some rocks. It burst into flames and just fell apart. They said – they said he was dead or unconscious before the fire. I hope so. Oh, Leo, I do hope so.'

'My poor Josephine,' Dora whispered. 'She can't bear even to look at a motor car now. We had to come home by train, you know, after George was taken from me.'

Josie, entering the room quietly, almost exclaimed out loud when she overheard these words. Leo grinned at the look of indignation on her face and hastily seized her hand.

'Come and have some food,' he ordered, and dragged her across to where a buffet had been laid out.

'It's not true, though!' Josie protested. 'It was Mother who said she'd never again go in a motor car. She'll never agree to let me have one, and Papa George had promised. She's starting to believe her own fairy stories,' she hissed angrily at Leo, impatiently shaking her head as he offered her a plateful of ham. 'I

4

can't eat. How can people seem so happy at a funeral and guzzle food?'

'I didn't feel like eating before I'd talked to you. Now, it's odd, but I'm ready to say goodbye to my father.'

'Well, I still don't! I want to drive out in a car just to show her,' she added petulantly.

'Can you drive? You're only – what – fifteen?'

'I'll be sixteen in October. And Papa George taught me to drive, though he only let me practise on private roads. But the Bentley's gone. Leo, you have a car, don't you?'

'Yes. Josie, come back. You can't drive my car!'

Josie grinned mischievously over her shoulder and ran from the room. By the time he caught up with her she was wrenching open the door of his small car. He grasped her shoulder and spun her round, then shook her angrily.

'You madcap! You're not old enough, and even if you were I wouldn't let you drive my Midget.'

'Why not? I could,' she challenged. 'Are you afraid I'd smash it into the nearest ditch?'

He reached over and removed the ignition key. 'I'm not letting you try. Women can't drive.'

'Oh! What a load of rubbish. How about the women who drive in rallies and even at Brooklands? Mrs Bruce was placed two years running in the Monte Carlo Rally. And she flies aeroplanes and –'

'And you want to emulate her?'

'And what about Amy Johnson? If she can fly to Australia on her own I don't see why I can't drive a tiny little car.'

'Don't be silly. Do you want another funeral?'

Josie went white and her head drooped. Leo, afraid he'd hurt her, began to try and explain but she turned and ran away round the side of the house. He shrugged. She was just a naughty child, sulking at a deserved reprimand. He'd leave her to herself. At least she couldn't now steal his car, and he doubted whether she would be idiotic enough to take one belonging to another guest. He walked slowly back towards the house, and for a few seconds didn't associate the new sounds he heard with Josie. Then he leapt hastily aside as she appeared astride a small motorcycle, waving gleefully before roaring off towards Redditch.

'Josie, you devil, bring me bike back!' A thin, sandy-haired young man gesticulating wildly cannoned into Leo as he raced after Josie.

'Come on!' Leo grabbed him. 'My car,' he explained tersely as he thrust the fuming young man into the passenger seat and fumbled for his key. The Midget shot out of the driveway, terrifying a huge draught-horse pulling a passing coal waggon, and set off in pursuit.

'You're old George Bradley's son, ain't yer?' the young man asked when he'd recovered his breath. Leo nodded. 'Me sister Lizzie said so. Me name's Freddy Preece, I'm Josie's cousin. Ma an' Aunt Dora are sisters.'

'Is she always this crazy?' Leo asked. He'd just seen Josie in the distance and relaxed slightly.

'Dunno. We don't see a lot of our posh relations,' Freddy replied. 'Only came to the funeral 'cause Ma said we 'ad to show respect. Aunt Dora likes us ter keep out of 'er swanky friends' way. We're not respectable enough. Think yer'll catch 'er?'

'Yes, she's going quite slowly, and I can get over sixty in this little baby.'

'Blimey!' Freddy was impressed.

By now they'd passed all the houses of Moseley and were out in the winding country lanes. Josie had to slow down but Leo, laughing suddenly at the thought that Josie's bright beacon of hair was helping him keep her in sight, barely slowed his headlong pace. Freddy grabbed at the door when Leo slid round one bend on two wheels, then was thrown forward on to the dashboard as Leo braked abruptly. When he'd disentangled himself he found Leo furiously berating a defiant Josie. Freddy clambered out of the car, an appreciative grin on his face.

Josie swung round. 'You utter cretin!' she blazed at Freddy. 'Your stupid machine's run out of petrol. I'd have got away if you kept the tank decently full.'

Freddy gave a crow of laughter. 'I can't afford petrol fer thieves that pinch me bike. An' if yer've damaged it, young Josie, yer'll pay.'

'I know better than to damage it,' she flared.

'Yer, but 'ow'm I gonna get it 'ome?'

'There's a spare can in my car,' Leo said, amused. 'You, Josie, are coming home with me.'

'No! I won't! I'd rather walk!'

She stalked off, watched in exasperated amusement by Leo. Freddy, busy squeezing the last possible drop of petrol into the motorcycle tank, laughed.

'Carrots an' temper,' he explained. 'Gals with red 'air are a menace. I always steer clear of 'em meself.'

He replaced the petrol can, and gave a cheerful wave, shouting his thanks as he rode past Josie with a nonchalant flourish. She ignored him, as she ignored Leo when, having turned the car in a convenient field gateway, he drove slowly alongside her and civilly offered her a lift.

'It's several miles,' he pointed out. 'Your mother will be frantic.' She turned her head away. 'There are matters to discuss with the solicitors. Don't you want to be there?' Silence. 'Perhaps you're too young to be consulted.' That brought him a glare of fury. 'Or perhaps they wouldn't listen to a girl anyway. This is men's business, after all.' Josie's mouth opened, then she recollected herself and her nose went up in the air. Leo chuckled. 'Oh, don't be a little ass! Excuse me while I let the pony and trap overtake me.'

He drew forward a few yards and halted, the side of the car hard against the hedge. The trap driver, with a curious glance at them, raised his whip in acknowledgement and trotted on. Leo waited. Josie had to come on his side of the car. She hesitated, and then, as he opened the door and stepped out, turned and began to run back the way they'd come. He sprinted in pursuit.

'Let me go!' she panted, struggling in his grasp. She was big and strong, but Leo was much bigger and stronger, and within half a minute was carrying her back to the car, dumping her unceremoniously into the passenger seat and blocking her escape as he climbed in after her.

'You'll stay there!' he commanded briskly, and before Josie caught her breath the car was bowling along at a speed which precluded any thought of jumping out.

Josie fumed impotently and began to plan revenge. Before she could devise anything sufficiently awful they'd reached her home, and he virtually frogmarched her into the dining room where Dora was talking to George's solicitor.

'You mean I'll have to sell this house?' Dora was saying angrily. 'Leo — there you are. Tell him it's nonsense. George said he'd always take care of me,' she went on accusingly. 'He was a wonderful husband, but why on earth he had to gamble on foolish schemes to build silly gadgets for cars, I don't know. I blame that dreadful man Scott.'

'It is in no way Mr Scott's fault,' the solicitor said wearily. 'I have explained. Mr Bradley was no longer a partner in his business. William Scott did all he was legally bound to do when he repaid the investment, as Mr Bradley asked. He has no further obligation towards you.'

'But his business is flourishing now, and it was George's money that helped him get started.'

'That makes no difference,' the solicitor began, but Dora went on angrily.

'It was only because William Scott didn't keep his word and make that fortune he said he would that George put money into those American companies, and when that beastly Wall Street crashed and he lost it he was so distraught that he drove carelessly.'

The solicitor sighed. He knew she had not accepted the verdict of suicide. Now was not the time to discuss it. 'In any case there are many debts, and to meet them this house must be

8

sold. As yet I can't say what will be left, if anything. Fortunately Miss Josephine's school fees have been paid for next year, but I strongly advise you to prepare yourself to take a job after that,' he added, turning to Josie and smiling encouragingly at her.

'I want a job. I'll take one now, if it will help.'

'No, that would be premature. The school fees are not refundable, so it would be a pity to waste them, and in a year you will be better qualified. With two million people unemployed you need qualifications. I suggest you spend some time learning to typewrite. It is a genteel occupation, better than working in a factory.'

Dora was affronted. 'My Josephine work in a dirty filthy factory! How can you even think of such a thing?'

'I don't, Mrs Bradley. Now we must make arrangements for you to move. You could rent a couple of rooms, just until we see what money is left, when perhaps you might be able to afford a small house in one of the new suburbs. Three hundred pounds would buy quite a pleasant house.'

'A tiny house in a *suburb*?' Dora exclaimed. 'Nonsense. George knew that I don't understand money. He's left it to Leo. You'll take care of us, won't you?' she asked, turning to Leo who was leaning against the marble mantelpiece.

'It's not my affair,' Leo said shortly. 'He left me nothing apart from my mother's jewels, for he knew I have enough with what my uncle left me. I won't keep you in idleness when you must have plenty of money of your own, from what my father gave you when he was alive.'

Dora raged, saying it was his duty to look after his father's wife and her daughter, and Josie writhed inwardly. After a while Leo, icily calm, simply turned and left the room. The solicitor gazed after him enviously, but remained seated. Josie, though still smarting from the humiliating way he'd forced her to come home, swiftly followed him.

'I'm sorry,' she said awkwardly.

She'd always felt obscurely guilty about Leo, who had been

9

brought up by his aunt and uncle after his own mother died. Josie had seen him rarely, Dora being unwilling to become responsible for a stepson only seven years younger than she was. She'd been sixteen when she married Joseph Shaw just before the Great War. Josie had been born the following year, days before her father had been killed in the trenches. Two years later, George Bradley, a much older widower, had fallen for Dora's fragile and helpless air and married her.

'Leo won't want to leave his aunt and uncle or his friends, will he?' Dora said to George a week after she'd met the boy. 'He's so big and noisy and energetic, climbing trees or doing other dangerous things. I thought the house was collapsing round us when he came down the stairs on that tin tray. I adore little children, but I couldn't manage him. Besides, your brother and his wife can't have children and he owns a very good business. He'll want Leo to go into it with him later.'

The infatuated George, though disappointed, recalled the intemperate criticisms his son had made of his future stepmother after their first meeting and agreed it might be unwise to force them to live together. He'd contented himself with the thought that he would at least have a daughter, and perhaps he and Dora might have more children. Thereafter, Leo had seen his father infrequently, and even less of Josie. She had heard talk that he'd inherited his uncle's jewellery business and the house in Handsworth, but knew little about his life.

Leo turned to acknowledge Josie's apology for her mother's behaviour. 'I've broad shoulders,' he grinned, 'but no obligations to your mother. My father regularly put money for her in special accounts. Even though his investments went she ought to have ample, even if she has to sell this house. You don't need a place this size anyway.'

'I don't think she has any money of her own,' Josie said doubtfully. 'Papa George always paid her bills.'

'She must have plenty. Women don't understand business. But if all else fails I'll give you a job in my factory.' Leo smiled goodbye as he drove away, leaving Josie alone with a cloud of dust.

Back at the house, Dora raged and wept and swore that she would never suffer the indignity of renting rooms in someone else's house. Eventually she was put to bed by her sister, Phoebe.

'Good job I stayed to 'elp the maid clear up,' Aunt Phoebe said, when they eventually left Dora asleep.

'But what can I do?' Josie asked. 'Where do I start to look for rooms? And how much should I pay?'

Phoebe patted her hand. 'Don't worry. Tell you what, I could let you 'ave a pair of rooms; I've got a house far too big for just me and Freddy, Lizzie and Ann. It won't be for long, maybe. Aston's not what yer ma's used to and she'll throw a fit at her loose-living sister helpin' 'er with 'er wages of sin.'

Josie grinned. 'Just because you and Lizzie's dad weren't married? But he loved you, and he gave you that house.'

'Luckily fer me and Doris! Oops! Better not call her that, she thinks it's common. You could 'ave two of the rooms on the first floor, the big front one as a sitting room so's you're independent, and share the back bedroom. Dora could bring any furniture she wanted to keep.'

Josie hugged her. 'Aunt Phoebe, you're a brick!'

Phoebe laughed. 'A cushion more like, with my figure!' Josie grinned. Aunt Phoebe was blonde and buxom, with red cheeks and merry blue eyes. 'I'll find a man to move the furniture tomorrow, and we'll have Doris there before she thinks of too many objections.'

Chapter One

J OSIE sprawled on Lizzie's bed, resting her chin in her hands as she watched her cousin putting on her new matching frock and coat. Lizzie was humming the latest dance tune she'd heard when she and her new boyfriend had been at the Tower ballroom. Idly Josie wondered what it would be like to have a man kiss her. Lizzie had confided that although she'd only been out with Matthew Horobin a few times he'd kissed her already, but then Lizzie was small and dark and pretty.

'What's Matthew like?'

'He's terribly handsome,' Lizzie said dreamily. 'And tall, I only come up to his shoulder even in my highest heels. He's got dark curly hair, a deeper brown than mine, but it will never stay flat however much brilliantine he uses. His eyes are dark brown too, and his lips so soft!'

Josie giggled. 'He sounds like Rudolph Valentino.'

Lizzie blushed. 'He is,' she declared. 'But his chin's firmer, he's more rugged. He's fascinated by machinery.'

'Yes, you said he preferred mending the ones in the factory to helping his father deal with customers. But why doesn't he want his father to know you're going out together? Is he ashamed of you? I wouldn't even speak to a man like that.'

'Of course he's not. It could just be awkward for us.'

'You mean the other girls would be jealous of you going out with the boss's son?'

'They might not be so friendly. They'd be bound to think I'd tell him what they said, perhaps spy on them.'

'That's ridiculous!'

'I know we live in a good house in a nice road. But they could easily drag up the old scandal about Mom and Dad not being married. A couple of the girls could be really nasty, they've got their own eyes on him.'

'Well, his father does own a big jewellery firm.'

'That's not why I like him. But it would be nice if they saw me in his new car,' Lizzie added wistfully. 'He might put that money from his uncle in a business to do with motor cars. I'm so glad you said you'd come to the rally today and try out the new car he's thinking of buying.'

Josie pushed herself up. 'If I'm going to make a four-some with the car's owner I'd better go and say goodbye to Mother.'

As Lizzie went downstairs, Freddy intercepted her on the landing. 'Goin' out with Matthew?' he asked.

'Yes. Why?' she demanded suspiciously.

'I've 'eard of a real good thing, and I thought yer might mention it to 'im. After all, what's the use of a sister courtin' one of the nobs if she can't do a chap a favour?' he went on ingratiatingly.

'Oh yes? Not making enough as a bookie's runner?' Lizzie asked scornfully. 'I'm not asking Matthew to put money into one of your mad schemes.'

'It's not a mad scheme. It's a cert. Me pal, Sid, 'im as works at the stadium, 'e's got the chance of a pup that's the best thing 'e's ever seen. Nothin' else will be able to catch this little beggar once 'e's full grown and trained. 'E'll be even better than Mick the Miller.'

'A pup? A greyhound, you mean? Have you gone mad?'

'Come on, Sis, a good dog's worth 'undreds a year. But the owner wants a fancy price. Then there's all the expenses of trainin' before yer gets anything back.'

"If you ever get anything! Freddy, get a proper job.'

'Workin' for nothin' when there's money to be made out of mugs? Catch me! All I need's a start, a backer. If Matthew's willin' to invest a couple hundred quid –'

'You must be crazy. You can buy a greyhound for a few pounds. Two hundred pounds just for a dog?'

'There's food an' trainin' and so on. And it's a very special dog, Lizzie. It'll make 'im lots more'n that.'

'With prize money? Don't be daft!'

Freddy winked broadly at her. 'Not just prizes, Sis. You're too innocent. There's more ways of skinnin' a cat – or dog, as the case may be.'

'I won't ask him.' Lizzie's tone was uncompromising, her blue eyes icy.

'A hundred? Fifty then,' Freddy tried to persuade her.

'No. And don't you dare speak to Matthew about it either, or I'll – I'll report you to the police!'

Freddy glared. She wouldn't give away his minor infringements of the law, he knew, so he wasn't worried. He had hoped to persuade Matthew to lend him some cash. He needed spares for his motorcycle, too. Even his ingenuity couldn't always keep it going. He sighed. He hadn't been able to touch Aunt Dora, either. In the year she and Josie had lived with them he'd had nothing but a tie for Christmas and some handkerchiefs for his birthday. Much good it was having rich relations! Lizzie was his best hope, but it might be better to wait until she had actually landed a wealthy husband. Then an impecunious brother-in-law might reasonably expect sympathy. Either that or he'd have to think of a scheme more acceptable to Miss High and Mighty Elizabeth Preece. He left the house, racking his brains for a foolproof scheme for making money, but admitted with a rueful grin that strict legality and making a fast fortune didn't often go hand in hand, not in this world anyway. But Freddy had unbounded confidence. He'd find a plan, eventually.

Outside he encountered Wilf Edwards lounging on a garden

wall opposite. Freddy joined him, and resisted the suggestion that they went to Wilf's house for a drink.

'Me sister's posh man friend's comin',' he explained. 'I want ter spy out the land.'

'What for?'

'Money fer the dog, of course.'

'Yow do' even know the feller; yow car' goo up an' ask 'im fer a couple 'undred quid!'

'Not yet, I can't, but when they're spliced 'e'll cough up. 'Sides, 'oo knows wot we might see?' he added, nudging Wilf in the ribs and winking heavily at him.

Wilf frowned uncomprehending and Freddy sighed. Wilf was strong and fearless, good with his fists, always ready to join in any fight without asking what it was about, but he had nothing between the ears. Freddy sometimes wished he had a pal who would appreciate his brilliant schemes, might even contribute to them. It was wearing having to think of every detail himself as well as imagining what calamities there might be if his henchman got hold of the wrong end of the stick. Since Wilf was prone to do this, Freddy spent a lot of time trying to avoid unnecessary catastrophes.

They waited, not speaking except for commenting loudly on the charms of every girl they saw. Most ignored them; some gave them furious glances which only made the two young men laugh; only one damsel, for Freer Road was a respectable neighbourhood, stopped to bandy insults. Wilf was all for following up this promising introduction but Freddy grabbed his arm as he slid from the wall.

'Not now! Look, this is probably 'im.'

'Bloody 'ell!'

Even Wilf was impressed with the vehicle which swept round from Hampton Road and drew up with a flourish. The bodywork in two shades of blue sparkled, two spare wheels perched at the back, and the black leather upholstery shone as did all the metal components, the wire wheels, headlamps and radiator grille. Two young men in dark blue blazers and caps got out, the driver, who was slightly shorter than his passenger, gesticulating. The passenger nodded eagerly, then went to knock on Phoebe's door while the other man opened the bonnet and began to adjust something.

Lizzie opened the door. Freddy could see his mother hovering in the hall and the net curtains at one window of Dora's sitting room twitched. Freddy wondered how Josie had deterred her mother from insisting on meeting the young men.

Matthew introduced the girls to his friend, they were assisted into the small back seat, and then Matthew took the wheel. As he drove away Freddy felt a wave of furious envy shake him. He wanted a car like that. He'd wanted one ever since he'd been to Brooklands, and knew that, given the chance, he could race with the best of them, though he rarely had an opportunity to drive. He couldn't even afford to repair his motorcycle. Moodily Freddy ignored Wilf's salacious speculations about Lizzie and rich young men. He wanted an even better car, but there was no job he could think of that would earn him enough money before he was too old to enjoy it.

It was the first time Josie had been in a car since George's funeral, and she revelled in it, though she was a little disappointed to discover the rally wasn't a race as such, just a series of timed stages. They drove north through Tamworth and Lichfield, finishing at Beacon Hill for a late picnic lunch before the speed climbing competition began. The girls unpacked the hamper Matthew had brought, and they sat on bright tartan rugs on the side of the steep hill, gazing across the vast untidy sprawl of the Black Country as they ate the picnic food. Josie tried not to think of the last time she'd been sitting on the side of a hill, watching George die. At least there was no hill opposite today.

'On weekdays the smoke is so thick you can't see the few miles to Walsall, let alone beyond Wolverhampton,' Matthew said. 'If they still used these hilltops to light beacon fires it might be difficult to see them.'

'No need, now we've got radio and the telephone,' William Scott replied. He was a chunky, solid sort, his grey eyes always seemingly focused on some distant prospect, and he became animated only when he was talking about cars or other scientific marvels. 'Soon we'll be able to transmit pictures too so we can see what enemy is attacking us,' he explained.

Lizzie shivered. 'Surely there won't be another war? Wasn't it supposed to be the war that ended all wars?'

'There have been plenty of little ones since, in Turkey and the Middle East for instance,' Matthew pointed out.

'I meant in Europe.'

'We stopped occupying Germany last year,' Josie said.

'But the Germans are still aggrieved over the huge reparations they simply can't afford to pay. Their whole economy is in a mess, and over a hundred National Socialists were elected to the Reichstag last year. There will be more trouble,' William predicted.

'Can't we refuse to trade with them?' Josie asked. 'Papa George said we could put pressure on difficult governments that way.'

William shrugged. 'We trade where we must, even when we don't approve of someone.' Josie saw him glance at Matthew and narrow his eyes. Was he making a comment, or was it an accidental glance, she wondered.

She regard him curiously. When he'd been introduced she'd realized he was Papa George Bradley's former partner. George had provided most of the money, William the expertise. Together they were going to adapt motor cars to include William's inventive devices designed to make motoring easier and more comfortable. Two years ago, when George lost the rest of his money in the Wall Street crash he'd asked William Scott to buy him out. Despite having to borrow heavily Scott had complied, and almost immediately had begun his string of rally victories. This had led to a huge demand for his motor cars, specially adapted versions of several popular marques. He now employed a hundred men, had a new and large workshop, and was clearly prosperous. William was Josie's own height, broad-shouldered and deep-chested. The grey eyes, usually abstracted, now held an amused twinkle, and although he had spoken with easy familiarity about new scientific advances he was dismissive of his own engineering skill.

'Just good luck,' he'd said as Matthew tried to explain to the girls the technical modifications that had assisted William's swift rise to racing success. 'I happened to think of a few changes which worked before anyone else did. I was fortunate, but that doesn't mean I'll continue to be.'

'I liked the look of those new springs I saw in your factory,' Matthew commented.

'Don't talk about them,' William said swiftly. 'So far it's only an idea, but if I can make it work I'll have a winner. They'll improve the suspension enormously.'

'Are you going to win today?' Lizzie wanted to know.

'Matthew's driving. His main competition is Leo Bradley.'

'Leo?' Josie asked. 'Where? I haven't seen him.'

'He started first, was well ahead of us at all the checkpoints. He's over there with that blonde who looks like Bebe Daniels.'

Matthew grinned. 'Leo always picks real beauties, but they never last for long. He's got those film-star looks that have the girls swooning. He's left a whole crop of broken hearts round Birmingham. But come on, we must get ready.'

They gathered up the remains of the picnic. 'Where should we stand for the best view?' Josie asked.

'Near the top. I'll take you up now and show you a very good place while Matthew gets the car ready. After all, he's driving today, he can do the hard work.'

Josie folded the rug. 'Do you want everything back in the car? Won't the extra weight be a disadvantage?'

'We'll leave everything here,' Matthew said as he began to take the spare wheels off the car. 'We even take the back seat out. Pass me the rug, I can put the seat on it.'

Josie glanced to where race officials were already busy at the top of the hill. The excitement was beginning to infect her. 'I wonder what it feels like in a car instead of standing watching?' she asked wistfully.

'One day you'll know,' said William. 'Plenty of women compete. Maybe you'd like to come as my passenger next time?'

Lizzie was enthusiastic. 'And I'll go with Matthew. What fun!' she exclaimed. 'Why are you letting down the tyres?' she added.

'Only part-way. It's for greater traction. You'll have to learn the technicalities as well as look glamorous if you want to race,' Matthew told her, grinning.

Lizzie wrinkled up her nose. 'I'm hopeless with machines. It's my limit to press the right buttons on the polisher at work. Come on, Josie, let's get to the top.'

Leo studied the course. It was steep, containing several hairpin bends and one long deceptive curve where the edge sloped away unexpectedly sharply. The first few competitors reached the top safely, though in slow times. Then the next driver lost control at one of the bends and ploughed into the bank. There was a pause while his vehicle was towed away. Leo glanced about him. His gaze travelled slowly over the crowd and he stiffened. How did Josie Shaw come to be at this hill climb? She was with another girl, smaller and plumper, who was clinging to her with one arm and chattering excitedly. There was a family likeness in the shape of their faces, the curve of the cheek, the slightly tip-tilted nose, the firm chin. He suddenly remembered she'd been at his father's funeral, one of Josie's cousins.

Leo set himself to recall what he knew about Josie's family. It was little enough. As a boy he hadn't been interested in a stepmother he rarely saw. Their dislike had been mutual. Dora's father had been rector of a small Warwickshire parish, but her parents died before she married Joseph Shaw. There had been a sister, and a brother who had died during the war as had Dora's first husband. Both had daughters. He forced his attention back to the track. The next competitor made the best time so far. He glanced across at Josie and her companion, clutching one another and shouting in excitement. Even from a distance Leo could see Josie's eyes gleaming, and her perfect white teeth biting on her lip as she watched. He recognized the next driver, Matthew Horobin, the son of another jewellery manufacturer. Leo knew him from school, though Matthew was a couple of years younger. Beside him sat William Scott.

Matthew did well. He went fast into the bends, slewing round and losing the least possible time before accelerating up the next slope. Only on the deceptive curve did he falter, struggling to keep the car straight when it wanted to ease over to the outer edge. He managed to control it and roared up the final straight to a burst of cheering. Then it was Leo's turn. By now the track was rutted and it was more difficult to make a good time, but Leo got off to a very fast start and took the first bend at a speed which made the crowd gasp. The burst of acceleration along the short straight stretch had his passenger flung back into the seat squabs, and Leo was conscious that she was squeaking with fear. He grinned. She'd certainly have her eyes closed tightly, and would be of no help to him at all, but she was decorative and that was all he wanted of a woman. He took the next sharp bend perilously on two wheels, and reached the top to a burst of excited cheering.

Matthew and William were stripping off their leather helmets and gauntlets. The stewards called for silence and announced the result. Leo had won, with Matthew third. Leo saw Josie's friend fling her arms about his neck as Matthew laughed and lifted her into the air, swinging her round gleefully. Leo looked towards Josie and wondered how she came to be with William Scott. Why had Dora condoned it when she blamed him for George's financial losses? Leo stepped forward to offer his commiserations.

'Better luck next time, perhaps. You drove really well.'

'Thanks,' Matthew said. 'William, it's a great car! I'm definitely buying it before I decide where to put the rest of Uncle John's money. Perhaps I'll buy a garage.'

Leo nodded to William. 'Another sale?'

'Matthew has a bargain,' William declared. 'Leo, you know Josie, and this is her cousin Miss Elizabeth Preece.'

Leo smiled at Josie, then introduced his own companion as Pearl Gregory. 'We met last year,' he said to Lizzie.

The talk soon turned to future rallies. Matthew was planning to enter the next half-day trial, and Lizzie would go with him.

William turned to Josie. 'Then you can come with me.'

'It would be fun to do the two-day one as well,' Matthew said eagerly. 'How about it, Lizzie with me and Josie with William? And you, Leo?'

Pearl, who had barely said a word, became animated. 'That would be tremendous fun, Leo darling. Do let's go.'

'My mother wouldn't let us go,' Lizzie said regretfully.

Pearl raised her eyebrows disbelievingly. 'Golly, how antiquated.'

Leo was shaking his head. 'I may not have time. My clerk wants to retire, and unless I can replace him quickly I'll have too much to do at work. I'll do my best though – it should be a good couple of days.'

Josie was weary of tramping the streets, being told they wanted someone with experience, someone older, or the vacancy was filled. By the time she found a job, she thought ruefully, the cheap but smart navy skirt in serviceable serge, with inverted pleats and a longer length than she had ever before worn, and the white poplin blouse with its new wider shoulders and close-fitting sleeves would be worn out.

The hundred pounds with which Dora had been left after selling the house and settling her late husband's debts was woefully inadequate to purchase them new accommodation away from Freer Road. Remembering the solicitor's suggestion, Josie had taken typewriting lessons after school, and spent the fortnight since the end of term looking for a job.

She emerged from yet another fruitless call where the only vacancy had been for a press operator. She wouldn't accept that yet and waste the money spent on typewriting lessons. Perhaps she'd meet Lizzie from her job as a polisher at Matthew's father's factory in Hockley and they could walk home together. It would save the tram fare. She was feeling inadequate. Lizzie, a year older, had been working for two years and Ann, a year younger, had just moved from her first job in a laundry to be chambermaid at Endersby's hotel in the Hagley Road. Her mother and George had known the hotel well and Dora, in a rare mood of generosity, had recommended Ann to the owner, Marigold Endersby. She'd rejected Josie's suggestion that she might apply there too, saying that if her child had to take a job, and she still didn't think it necessary, it would not be a menial one. Josie stopped suddenly. Leo Bradley had promised her a job, and at the rally last week he'd mentioned that his clerk was leaving. Even if he didn't mean it, she must at least ask. It had been embarrassing meeting him again after the ignominious way he'd chased after her when she'd stolen Freddy's motorcycle, and she'd resented the supercilious manner his glamorous companion had adopted towards her, but she must ignore that.

Josie soon found his factory and was directed up steep, wooden stairs to the office. She knocked nervously, and took a deep breath at the impatient invitation to come in. Then she opened the door and stepped inside.

Leo was sitting behind a big, cluttered desk. He glanced up and a look of stunned surprise came into his eyes. Josie marvelled at their intense blueness, and wondered how he could be so tanned when he spent all his time inside this small, badly lit and dingy office. He dragged a hand through his hair, making it even more untidy, but didn't speak. Josie cleared her throat, her mouth dry with apprehension.

'I – you offered me a job,' she stated baldly, and Leo suddenly grinned.

'So I did. Wasn't that foolish of me? But I forget my manners, come and sit down, Miss Shaw.' He rose to his feet and Josie thought he looked even taller than she remembered.

He moved a chair to the side of the desk, dusted it with his handkerchief, and gestured to Josie to sit.

Nervously she complied. 'I've learned to typewrite, and I can do shorthand and simple bookkeeping,' she said hurriedly. 'I – I'm neat and tidy' – she couldn't prevent herself from glancing at the mound of papers and ledgers on his desk – 'and my handwriting is clear. And I need a job.'

He suppressed a grin, and regarded her seriously. 'And what makes you think I have a job to offer?'

'You said your clerk was leaving, last week. And you did promise me one, and I need something! I'd rather be a secretary, but I'd work in the factory if necessary.'

'I don't need a secretary. I prefer a male clerk.'

'You're still angry with me for trying to drive your car!' Josie said bitterly. 'I shouldn't have come. I'll go.'

A slight cough from behind her made her jump, and she swung to see a gnarled old man emerging from behind a screen. He carried a tray with a pot of tea and two cups. 'Perhaps the young lady would like a cuppa,' he suggested, and pushed the papers on the desk aside to clear a space for the tray. 'Mr Leo, could I 'ave a word?'

Leo followed him out, and Josie told herself she'd been a fool to come here. He hadn't meant it, and there was no vacancy. She'd leave as soon as she could, but after the old man, presumably Leo's clerk, had made the tea, it would be churlish to refuse.

It was some time before Leo returned and he was looking grim. Perhaps he'd had bad news. But he smiled at her briefly and asked her to pour. 'Why are you in such need of a job? Your mother should have plenty in her savings accounts. I know how much my father deposited for her.'

'No, it's all gone. She didn't understand it wasn't meant as part of her ordinary allowance.'

'And you blame my father for not knowing this?'

'Of course I'm not blaming Papa George for anything! He was so desperately worried when things began to go wrong. He thought he'd failed my mother and it was that, I believe, rather than losing all his money, that made him – give in. He'd have happily started again but he couldn't face asking her to live in poverty.'

'Killing himself hardly prevented that.'

She shook her head swiftly. 'Didn't you know? He took out an enormous life-assurance policy, but because of the suicide verdict the policy was invalid. He thought he'd provided for us.'

Leo looked at her with suddenly narrowed eyes. 'So that was it. He never did have good judgement,' he said softly, 'though if he'd waited and not insisted on having his money back the scheme with William Scott would have shown a profit soon.'

'Well, that hardly helps now, does it? I must find a job. If you can't help me I'll go – it was foolish of me to come. I'm sorry if I've wasted your time.'

'Hold on a minute. Why are you always in such a hurry to get away from me? You're right, Bert is going to retire soon, and since I've already invested in a typewriter I suppose I ought to employ someone who can use it when he leaves. I'll give you a trial here in the office.'

Josie hadn't anticipated quite the frenzy of horror and dismay she would provoke. Dora had complained about the drab, plain, cheap, uninteresting and unflattering garments she had bought, saying they made her look like a beanpole. She had called Josie wicked to ruin her one claim to attractiveness when she cropped her hair. Unfortunate though the colour was, Dora said, the hair had been thick and long and glossy. Now it was just the same as any other silly little girl's. Her rage on being told about Leo's offer of a job was awe-inspiring.

'Leo? He refuses to help us but he'll make you a slave for a pittance. And Hockley! That's a slum. You can't. Heaven knows what would happen to you – lice, bugs, diseases, and dreadful men.' She shuddered, and then took a deep breath. 'We'll have to see what we can do at once. I'll organize a few genteel tea- parties for the mothers of some nice young men and maybe they'll invite us back. I suppose one of the boys might take a fancy to you. Some really deplorable girls find husbands so I'm sure you can, but then one can only suppose they have plenty of money to sweeten the pill. You do have some good points – you've a perfect complexion, and the modern taste is for curves instead of looking like a boy. Don't set your sights too high, though, Josephine – you'll never have the men flocking round you as I did. I'll have to put my thinking cap on. We can surely manage something.'

Josie ignored the disparaging remarks. To Dora, marriage was the only possible life for a woman. Josie didn't want to get married but had long ago given up all attempts to convince her mother of this. Josie was conditioned by her mother's unflattering opinion of her and thought it justified. She was too tall, too big altogether, and had that unfortunate red hair. She told herself her mother would be even worse if she were pretty and men actually wanted to marry her and she refused them.

'Mother, the money Papa George left has almost gone. I have to earn some and I can't find any other job. There's less than fifty pounds left and we'll soon get through that, paying for rent and food as well as all your clothes.'

Dora bristled, and then wiped her eyes. 'I had to have mourning clothes, didn't I?'

'Not half a dozen black gowns and several tea gowns as well as evening dresses you never have the occasion to wear, or two cloth coats and a sable fur,' Josie said sharply.

It was a constant source of dispute as she attempted to control Dora's reckless extravagance. Her mother had never understood money, and for many years George had lavished on her everything she wanted. After his death, Josie had been forced into managing their financial affairs, since it had been clear from the start that Dora hadn't the slightest idea of how to economize even if she'd wished to.

'George wouldn't have wanted me to be dressed shabbily,' she replied now. 'And I'll soon be in half mourning, I shall have to have suitable clothes then.'

'You'll soon be naked if I don't earn some money.'

Dora gave a horrified shriek. 'Josephine! How can you be so — well — *shameless*? I thought you had made an effort not to be so unruly since Papa George died. How I wish you could have gone to a good Swiss school. They wouldn't permit you to talk about nakedness.'

Josie gritted her teeth. 'We don't have enough money even to live on for more than a few months. One of us has to earn money and since you refuse even to give piano lessons, which you could quite easily do —'

'I have never been expected to demean myself with manual work and can hardly begin now. Besides, my health really isn't up to it. My headaches would be permanent, they really would. Imagine having to sit and listen to horrid children crashing about on my beloved piano. It would drive me to total distraction!'

'Then I'll have to go and work for Leo.'

Dora had flown into a formidable rage, wept, had an impressive bout of hysterics during which she attempted to throw every moveable object they possessed out of the window, and was restrained only by the combined efforts of Josie and Freddy, who, together with his mother, had been drawn to the scene because of the noise. Finally Dora sank exhausted into her chair. 'George left the wretched boy his first wife's jewels. She had some magnificent pearls, and a diamond necklace the best in Birmingham,' Dora recalled, aggrieved. 'He'd never let me wear them, he always kept them at the bank and only showed me them once when he made me deposit my sapphires there. It was the one thing he denied me. Such foolish sentimentality! If he'd left them to me they'd have kept us in comfort for years.'

'If you were prepared to sell them,' Josie said. 'You refuse to sell the sapphires.'

'That's almost the only memento George did leave me. I need some reminder of him to comfort me.'

'I've not 'eard of these sapphires,' Freddy said, smiling at his aunt. 'Do yer ever wear 'em?'

'When do I have the opportunity now of going to a function where I could wear such jewellery?' Dora demanded. 'They're in the bank. I won't sell them. I have the money George left – not that it was more than a few paltry pounds after all his debts had been settled.'

'So you admit it's only a few pounds? Don't you see I must go out to work?' Josie demanded, exasperated at her mother's inconsistency.

'You keep the jewels safe. If yer sold 'em you'd just fritter the cash away on fancy clothes,' Freddy remarked, candid if unwise.

Dora turned on him angrily. 'If all you can do is insult me, you can get out!'

'Yes, let 'er be, Freddy,' Phoebe told him sharply. 'Can yer manage now, ducks?' she added to Josie. 'Doris 'as quietened down an' I'd better see ter supper. Ann's coming tonight an' I've got a nice beef roast.'

'I'll be fine, thanks, Aunty. We'll come down when Ann's here.'

'I can't,' Dora declared. 'I just can't face food. I'm going to bed, even though I won't sleep a wink, I'm too upset, thinking of all my dreams ruined. How is Josephine going to meet a nice young man when she's lowering herself working in a factory?'

'Lucky to get any job the way things are,' Phoebe said.

'Perhaps Leo will fall madly in love with 'er and wed 'er,' Freddy suggested, laughing. 'I wonder if 'e offered 'er the job as a way to snare 'er into 'is wicked coils?'

Dora began to look thoughtful. 'Well, he does have to make amends! Tell dear little Ann I'll see her next time. Oh dear, I haven't dusted the ornaments today but I'm far too exhausted to do them now.'

'Don't worry, Mother, I'll do them,' Josie soothed her, sighing inwardly. The ornaments swamped every surface, but her mother insisted on displaying every single one. 'You go to bed and rest.'

'I don't suppose I'll sleep. But if I should drop off, dear, don't wake me up when you come to bed.'

Chapter Two

DORA always had breakfast in bed. When George was alive it had been one of the housemaid's duties to prepare wafer-thin slices of the whitest bread spread with the creamiest butter available, and a pot of Earl Grey tea. This would be carefully arranged on her best Endersby porcelain and transported reverently to her bedroom within a minute of her bell announcing that she was awake and ready to start her day. It was, she plaintively and frequently said, one of the most difficult changes she had to bear, having Josephine deposit the tray on the bedside table hours before she was ready to face the day. Presented briskly with the alternative of getting her own breakfast after Josie had departed for school, she had piteously agreed that being woken early was a sacrifice she was just about able to make.

On the Monday she was to begin her job, Josie rose quietly and slid out of the big bed, careful not to disturb her mother. She pulled on the now shabby and much too small dressing-gown she'd had for three years. Then she went down to the kitchen. She dared not risk spoiling her new skirt and blouse with dabs of butter or bacon fat, and her knowledge of Aunt Phoebe's slapdash culinary skills, combined with her habit of waving whatever pan or implement she had in her hand to emphasize a point, made Josie wary of too close contact with the furniture in the kitchen.

'Here's porridge and a good 'elping of 'am and eggs to come,' Aunt Phoebe said, ladling porridge from the pan on the hob.

'I really haven't time,' Josie began, but Phoebe waved her to silence.

'You need a good breakfast; it wouldn't do to 'ave you swooning in Leo's arms,' she chortled. 'Get that down and I'll finish your ma's tray. I started it for you.'

'Thanks. You're a dear, Aunt Phoebe. Where's Lizzie? She hasn't gone already, has she?'

'Overslept. Matthew took her out in his new motor yesterday, and they had a puncture. So she said!' She laughed meaningfully. 'Wasn't back till midnight.' She busied herself at the other end of the big table, cutting bread as Lizzie appeared, rubbing the sleep out of her eyes. She groaned at the laden plate her mother dumped in front of her but knew better than to protest. By the time Josie had finished and picked up her mother's tray she still hadn't said a word.

'Walk down with me, Lizzie?' Josie asked, and her cousin nodded and gave her a faint grin.

In the bedroom Dora winced as Josie drew back the curtains and let in the bright daylight. 'Is it breakfast time already? I hardly slept a wink all night.'

'You can go back to sleep after I've gone,' Josie said cheerfully, arranging the lace-edged pillows behind her mother, then pouring a cup of tea and handing it to Dora.

She moved to the large wardrobe. In theory she and Dora each had one half of the space but Dora's clothes overflowed so much that Josie had folded away most of her garments in the old chest of drawers under the window. She had managed to find room for her new blouse and skirt, however, determined not to let them be creased.

Dora surveyed her silently as she sipped her tea. How on earth was she to find a suitable husband now? Then she sat up so quickly she almost spilt the tea. 'What are those shameless garments you're wearing?' she demanded. 'Where is the corselet I bought you last year?'

Josie, fastening the waist slip, glanced up in surprise. 'Only a brassière and a suspender belt, they're much easier to wear, more suitable for a working girl.'

'You may, to my eternal humiliation, now call yourself a worker,' Dora said tartly, 'but you are still, I hope, a lady! No lady is decently dressed without a proper foundation, a full corset,' she added. 'I should have made sure you bought respectable clothes. Only loose women wear such shocking underwear.'

Josie shrugged and continued dressing. 'I may be big, but I'm not fat and I don't need whalebone and laces.' She endured Dora's tearful recriminations and went to kiss her mother's cheek when she was ready to leave. 'Goodbye, Mother. I'll see you this evening.'

Dora sighed. 'Poor George is no doubt turning in his grave when he sees the state I'm brought to.'

George should have stayed alive to look after you himself, Josie replied silently. She was shocked at the thought. Never before had she criticized Papa George. But since his death her mother had become bitter and peevish. There were few hints of the captivating woman she'd once been. Josie thought nostalgic-ally of her early years when her mother had enchanted her and her schoolfriends with fantastic stories of magic and fairies and wonderfully exciting lands and people, and organized delightfully original parties.

Heaving a deep sigh she ran down the stairs and met Lizzie in the hall. Her mood lightened. She would escape from her mother's tedious complaints. She'd found it a great strain keeping her temper, biting back the retorts she had longed to make, telling herself her mother had been deeply shocked by George's death and their dreadful change in circumstances. It seemed to have destroyed all her former liveliness. She had some excuse for being peevish and descending into semi-invalidism but to Josie, robust and young, Dora's complaints were hard to bear, however much she tried to understand. Calling a cheerful farewell the girls went out into the summer sunshine.

Leo stood in the office window watching Josie walk up the road. What in the world had possessed him to offer her a job, he wondered for the hundredth time. It had been just the sort of mad, impulsive gesture he'd schooled himself against making in business affairs. On several occasions during the previous week he'd been tempted to write and withdraw the offer, say his plans had changed, but his sense of fairness stopped him. It was done, and although he'd seen Josie rarely he knew she was far more sensible than the foolish woman for whom his father had forsaken him. At least she seemed determined to work for her living.

He felt sorry for the girl, having to cope with the failure of George's last desperate ploy. It wasn't her fault that his father had been weak, finally unable to face the ruin his own disastrous speculations had brought down on him. In his grimmer moods Leo occasionally wondered why George, married to such a silly, demanding woman, hadn't taken that way out years before. He pushed this thought away. It would be easy enough to dismiss Josie if she couldn't do the work. Two weeks would show whether she could be useful or if he'd made an impetuous mistake. He took many risks in the other areas of his life but was very cautious in business affairs. He regarded his inheritance as a trust to be preserved, not threatened by unwise actions. He might take what his more timorous schoolfriends told him were foolish risks, climbing rocks and trees and swimming in deep lakes and rivers, and later on pushing first a motorcycle and then a car to the limits, but he never took risks with the business. Although he didn't have his uncle's brilliant flair for design, he was fascinated by machinery, encouraging innovation where it aided production. Otherwise he was solid and cautious, concentrating on selling the jewellery his craftsmen made. His knowledge of the business had been fortunate, for on his uncle's early and unexpected death so soon after his aunt died of pneumonia he had been able to take charge without fuss.

Leo stiffened. Josie was on the far side of the road, and several urchins were kicking a football around in the roadway. As she passed them the ball dribbled towards her and to his astonishment she took a small run, grinned towards the lad chasing the ball, and kicked it hard, sending it hurtling along the street, bouncing off the bonnet of a delivery van parked some distance away. The children went tearing after it, howling with glee, and Josie put her hand over her mouth. Whether it was in dismay or to hide laughter Leo couldn't tell.

Josie crossed over towards the entrance below and he saw her quick smile of thanks as one of the workmen raised his cap and stepped back to let her go first. She had a bright, radiant smile undimmed by her misfortunes. They passed from view and Leo moved across to the desk which was littered with papers. He heard her clear voice but could not distinguish the words. Someone mumbled a reply and she laughed, then he heard light steps coming up the uncovered wooden stairs. She tapped on the door and he brusquely invited her to enter. She gave him a friendly smile, cast a swift look round the long narrow office which stretched across the front of what had once been two houses, and glanced back at him.

Leo, frowning, cleared a pile of ledgers from a chair in front of a brand-new typewriting machine. 'I bought this a few weeks ago,' he said abruptly. 'Please, sit down. Bert couldn't manage it, although the salesman spent a day here showing him. Do you think you can use it?'

Josie gravely considered the machine then nodded. 'It's very similar to the one I learned on. What do you want me to do?'

Leo pushed his hand through his hair. Was she adult enough to be of any help? 'Bert's not here. He's ill, not expected back for a few days. I'd meant him to show you what to do, but I'm behind with the work. He's been a mainstay of the business for

33

years, and I'll have to consider employing a manager now for when I'm away on selling trips.' He gestured to the desk. 'I haven't had time to do more than look at the letters this past week.'

'Then shall I sort them out?' Josie asked.

'You won't know what to do,' he said dubiously.

'I can sort them out, can't I? That's only common sense. Later we could go through them and you can tell me what to do with each.'

'I doubt if you can answer specialized queries with mere common sense,' he snapped. 'And your exhibition just now does not persuade me of your maturity!'

Before Josie could respond to this there were more footsteps on the stairs and an elderly man wearing a leather apron stuck his head round the door. 'That dratted rollin' machine's stuck again, Guv. Can yer cum?'

'OK, Jed, I'll be down in a minute.' He turned to Josie. 'Sort them into bills in, invoices out, orders, queries and other letters,' Leo said briskly and departed.

Josie looked after him, amused. He'd obviously witnessed her lapse with the football, but she hadn't been able to resist the temptation. Was Leo really so stuffy? She shrugged. He seemed glad of the excuse to go. She'd just have to demonstrate that she was efficient even if she did occasionally behave with less than total decorum. Two hours later Leo returned to find several neat piles of letters sitting at one end of the desk, two ledgers open on it, and a kettle simmering on the small Primus stove in the corner. A tray with an old brown teapot, a cup and saucer, and two biscuits on a plate, waited beside it.

'Tea?' Josie asked cheerfully.

Leo noticed that she'd rolled up her sleeves and there were smudges of dust on her blouse and skirt and across her cheek. He felt absurdly guilty. 'That'd be marvellous,' he said, trying not to feel irritated at her eagerness. He sat down. The letters had been place in date order, and attached to each was a slip of paper which he realized in astonishment contained suggestions or queries for suitable replies. Where Josie had not known how to respond there was just a large question mark.

She placed the tray in front of him. 'I hope you don't mind but there wasn't any more I could do straight away,' she said briskly. 'I thought it might help, and if you tell me what you want to say I'll write the letters now. Unless you'd prefer me to deal with the ledgers first, but it seemed as though some of those letters needed answering urgently. We might lose business if we delay.'

'Have you had any tea?' he asked abruptly.

For the first time she looked disconcerted. 'No. I – I didn't know what you wanted me to do, whether I was supposed to join the others downstairs.'

'Get a cup and some more biscuits. Bert and I always have it together and we can discuss what's to be done.'

By the end of the day, despite several interruptions when something needed to be done in the workshop, and visits from a few customers, Josie had managed to type most of the letters and learn the system Leo used to make entries in the ledgers. 'I'll deal with the bills tomorrow, shall I?' she asked when he told her to stop. 'Where do you keep stamps? I'll post these letters you've signed on my way home.'

He was busy weighing the gold which was to be put back in the big iron safe. Every single scrap of the precious metal had to be accounted for. 'There's a box in the top drawer of my desk,' he replied, not turning round. 'Are there enough?'

'Only a couple spare. Shall I buy some tomorrow?'

'Yes. Get as many as you think we need. Bert usually keeps in a good supply. The money's in the petty cash box on that shelf behind you, the key's in the same drawer as the stamps.'

'Goodnight, then.'

'Goodnight, Josie. Thanks. You've been very helpful. With you and a new manager we'll cope.'

Josie thought hard about these words as she went home. So,

Leo hadn't expected her to be useful. But if he meant to have a manager she wouldn't have much to do except type letters. He'd offered her the job out of a sense of charity. Even though he'd refused Dora's outrageous suggestion that he support them, was he feeling guilty about his father's suicide which had left her and her mother in such dire straits? She clenched her fists. She didn't want his charity. She'd show him she could do the work. It was only common sense and a little bit of knowledge of the business, which she's soon acquire. She could hardly wait to see Lizzie and find out all she could about the processes in the jewellery workrooms. As soon as possible she'd make an opportunity to go down and talk to the two dozen or so men and girls Leo employed. She'd show Leo Bradley!

Ann Preece sang as she worked. She enjoyed this job, and was grateful to Aunt Dora for suggesting it. There were only two things she regretted. The first was having to live away from the home she'd known with Aunt Phoebe ever since her mother's parents had died, the second was creepy Stanley Hodges. At least the housekeeper, Mrs Blake, had believed her when she'd caught the horrid wretch trying to kiss her in the linen room. She fumed again. How dare the little runt accuse her of dropping the sheets.

'You're the on'y one that don't jump at chance of a bit of fun wi' me,'.he'd said, barring her way so that she couldn't escape.

She shuddered as she remembered. He was not much taller than she was, although she was tall for a girl. He was thin, almost skinny, but with a wiry strength that let him heave the guests' trunks about with apparent ease. She could feel that strength every time he contrived to catch her unawares and steal a hug. He wasn't handsome, his face pitted with scars from a childhood illness, but his bright blue eyes twinkled and he was always laughing. She supposed some girls might find him attractive but she felt repulsed.

It was as well Ann had not read Mrs Blake's thoughts. The

older woman wondered if it had been wise to employ such a girl. Though still young she showed signs of remarkable beauty. Her blonde fragility, the delicate bones, slender figure, and the impression she gave that the slightest breeze might waft her away, would cause havoc amongst the men. And so far she was utterly unaware of the effect she had. There could be trouble. Mrs Blake didn't want to lose her. She was a good worker and Mrs Blake had no regrets on that score about giving her a job.

Ann carried the tray upstairs.

'Gotcha!'

Startled, Ann stepped back. The tray tilted, and as she tried to save the heavy teapot from sliding off it she moved incautiously sideways, trod awkwardly on the edge of the topmost step, lost her balance and went sprawling down the long flight.

'My dear! Are you hurt?' Ann lay with her right arm bent under her. 'Stanley, fetch Mrs Blake at once.'

'Yus, Mrs Endersby, straight away!'

Twenty minutes later Ann groaned and opened her eyes. She ached all over and her head was pounding. She tried to lift her hand to it but cried out in agony at the sharp pains which shot up her whole arm.

'Lie still, my dear. You've broken your arm and have a little bump on your head, but Dr Mandeville will have you comfortable in a moment.'

'Mrs Endersby! Oh! I'm sorry! I didn't mean to be stupid. Did I break the china? I'm sorry!'

The tall, slender lady standing beside the bed shook her head gently. 'It wasn't your fault. Don't worry. Now be brave for just a minute while the doctor sets your arm.'

Ann almost swooned away again from the pain, but the large man who appeared to be the doctor was brisk and competent, and within a minute had bound her arm tightly so that instead of the sharp agony there was just a dull ache.

'Drink this now and you'll sleep,' he said. His voice was deep and somehow comforting, and as Mrs Endersby helped Ann to sit up he held the glass to her lips. She grimaced at the taste but gulped the mixture down. 'There's a good girl. It's a simple fracture, will soon mend. You'll sleep all night and I'll be in to see you tomorrow morning.'

'But I haven't finished my work —' Ann started to say, and then her eyes began to close.

'She'll do,' the doctor said. 'Have someone look in on her occasionally, but I think she'll sleep ten hours.'

'Thanks, Paul,' Mrs Endersby said as they quietly left the small room. 'I'm so relieved you were at home.'

'I'd just finished evening surgery. But Marigold, I don't understand. How did she come to fall in the first place?'

'I do!' Marigold Endersby said grimly. 'It was that fool Stanley Hodges jumping out at her just at the top of the stairs. He thinks he's irresistible to the maids and young Ann Preece is by far the prettiest I've ever employed. What's more she doesn't like him and shows it.'

'Will you sack him?'

She shook her head swiftly. 'Not yet. He has an invalid mother who depends on him and she'd suffer if he lost his job. There aren't many jobs for hotel porters. But I'll make sure he stops being such a coxcomb!'

Paul grinned. 'You know, Marigold, you looks so beautiful and delicate no one would ever believe you're the mother of five children, one just a babe in arms, and run half a dozen very successful hotels.'

She laughed. 'Flatterer! You'd best get home to Nell and your own two. Thanks for coming. I must send to let Ann's family know and then deal with Hodges.'

'The men do all the interesting work,' Lizzie complained. 'We sometimes operate the presses, but mostly do polishing. It's so tedious, people soon leave. And some of the girls can be real bitches! In some workshops girls do jobs like laying on the enamelling, but Horobin's doesn't do that sort of work. I'd love to try designing, even engraving. I don't see why I couldn't do that as well as any man. I wouldn't want to try my hand at diamond cutting though,' she added, chuckling. 'That's a really skilled job and you can't afford a mistake.'

'I don't think Leo works with diamonds,' Josie said.

'No, he does mainly metal objects, rings and bangles and cuff-links, chains and so on. Matthew's firm sets diamonds and precious stones, sometimes rings, but more often elaborate things like necklaces and earrings.'

Josie sighed. 'There's so much I don't know.'

'You can't expect to learn it in a day.'

'A day! But Lizzie, I thought I'd know everything by tomorrow, if not today.'

Lizzie giggled. 'You're a fool, Josie Shaw. But get Leo to take you round the workroom and explain what's going on. He ought to introduce you to everyone, anyway, even though the office staff don't usually mix with us inferior beings in the factory.'

'He's so busy I doubt if he'll have time.'

By Wednesday, however, Josie was feeling quite at home in her job. She had typed all the letters, brought the ledgers up to date, and, when Leo was busy elsewhere, discreetly cleaned and tidied the office. That morning he was visiting customers, and she'd be safe from interruption for a couple of hours. She was balanced precariously on the workbench which stretched across the front wall, washing the windows, when Leo burst into the office.

'What the deuce are you doing?' he demanded.

Josie, startled, stepped backwards. Her stocking-clad foot trod on a ledger which she had left balanced on top of a smaller pile of papers and it tilted, causing her to overbalance. She would have fallen to the floor had Leo not sprung forward and caught her in a close embrace.

'I – I was cleaning windows, they're filthy,' Josie gasped,

cheeks red with mortification. 'Let me go,' she added breathlessly. 'I'm OK. Thank you for catching me.'

Leo released her so abruptly she staggered, and grabbed the side of his desk, dislodging the letters awaiting his signature. Josie groaned as they cascaded over the floor, and dived to rescue two which had landed in her bucket of water. Leo bent down at the same time, his foot skidded on a sheet of paper, and he sat down with a bump, knocking over the bucket and succeeding in ruining all the other letters.

'Damnation! Look what you've made me do!' he snarled.

Josie, on her knees as she attempted to snatch up a letter which Leo was partly sitting on, glared at him. 'It wasn't my fault!' she snapped. 'I didn't know you were going to let me go before I'd got my balance!'

He seized her wrists and shook her angrily. 'Keep still, can't you! Why the blazes do you have to do housework in an office?'

'No one else does!'

Suddenly Leo saw the office through fresh eyes. He had worked in it for years, helping his uncle long before he left school. He'd been determined to learn every aspect of it as soon as he could, knowing it would one day be his. He dealt with manufacturing, the buying and selling, the employees, and every other detail meticulously, but he'd never thought about the haphazard collection of furniture or of repainting the office. 'It's just a place to work,' he said defensively.

'And it's a mess. You can afford the latest production machines and a typewriter, but you've never thought about replacing these ancient desks and cupboards.'

'What for? They do for me.'

'My chair is so old I've spent every evening this week darning the holes its made in my stockings.'

'Don't be ridiculous!' He shook her and caused her to fall forward against his chest. 'This is what comes of employing women to do men's work. They expect offices to resemble dainty drawing rooms.'

Josie struggled to put some distance between them, but she was in such an awkward position, wedged against the desk, and he was holding her so tightly she couldn't move her face more than a few inches from his. She glared angrily at him, one part of her mind noticing his hair had a slight wave in it just above his ears.

'I want an office that's as clean and efficient as the factory,' she said curtly. 'That table's propped up on a piece of wood that sticks out so that every visitor trips on it. The desk you use is so ridged you can't write on single sheets of paper, you always have to waste time searching for some sort of pad to rest them on, and the cupboard doors stick so badly it's impossible to get at one side, so you order new supplies of stationery because you can't get at what's rotting in there.'

'If you're not satisfied with the conditions, Josie,' he began furiously, then stopped suddenly and released her wrists. Rubbing them, Josie struggled to her feet, and saw that the water from the bucket had trickled sluggishly over the worn and buckling linoleum to where Leo was sitting. She giggled as he pulled himself up, and for a moment Leo glowered at her. Then his lips twitched, and he began to laugh. 'Damn you, Josie! You're right, of course. I apologize. While I go home to change my trousers, you can be deciding what we need and when I come back we'll go and buy it. You're picking it up faster than I expected. And perhaps you'll let me make amends by being my passenger in the rally on Sunday.'

Chapter Three

'DON'T worry, I'll go along an' see the poor lass this morning,' Phoebe said as she ladled out porridge.

'Will you bring her home?' Lizzie asked.

'No, she'll be better off at the hotel. Mrs Endersby wrote that we weren't to worry, she'd be well looked after.'

'I'll go to see her straight after work. It's on the Hagley Road, isn't it?' Josie offered.

'I'll come too. What about you, Freddy?'

'Poor Ann won't want too many visitors,' Freddy said hastily. 'Besides, I gotta see a man about a dog.'

'Oh no! I thought you'd given up that daft idea,' his mother said. 'You'll keep no flea-bag in my garden.'

Freddy grinned at her. 'I'll find somewhere, but one of these days, Ma, you'll regret not takin' a share in me champion greyhound! When I'm drivin' me Rolls-Royce Phantom, smokin' cigars, expensive women by my side, you'll be kickin' yerself you don't share me good fortune!'

'Cheeky devil! You'd be better off lookin' for a job to do with motorbikes or cars; yer can cope with them! Then yer might get ter drive a Rolls-Royce.'

'I'm not slavin' over cars belongin' to other blokes.'

'At least you're not wearin' out shoe-leather lookin' for a job,' she added sarcastically.

'If all on yer give me ten quid,' Freddy said earnestly, 'we could share the dog. I'll pay yer back when 'e starts winnin', or yer can share the profits.'

'I've got better things to do with my money,' Lizzie replied. 'Do you like my new jacket?' she added, twirling to show the basque. 'I bought it for the rally on Sunday.'

'Goes well with the skirt,' Phoebe commented.

'Ma! Why buy more clothes? Lizzie's already got too many. They just get older an' shabbier, but my dog'll get better an' better. It's an investment.'

'No.' Lizzie grinned at him and went out of the kitchen. Freddy glared after her then turned to Josie.

'Now you're a workin' girl, cousin Josie, yer can see the advantages of putting your money on a cert, can't yer?'

'Sorry, Freddy, I need my hard-earned wages. Besides, it would take months to save that amount even if I wanted to buy part of a dog. We need my money to live on.'

'Come off it, you've got George's money.'

'And I'm going to keep it. Bye, Aunt Phoebe.'

Freddy, hastily seizing his hat and coat, followed Josie out of the house. 'I'll walk with yer. Tell me about yer job,' he asked as they set off for Hockley.

Josie laughed. 'Surely you're not thinking of getting work in a factory?' she said mockingly.

He shrugged. 'Yer never know when it comes in useful ter know what goes on. Are yer in the office all the time?'

Puzzled at his interest, Josie described her day. He was particularly intrigued by the process of changing sheets of gold and silver into ornaments.

'Never knew it were so complicated. What 'appens to all the scraps? Is it melted down again or what?'

'Every tiniest speck has to be accounted for,' she told him. 'The men have leather aprons fixed to the pegs – those are the benches where the craftsmen work – which catch all the pieces, and it has to be weighed in every night,

43

every grain measured. The scrap's sold and smelted down again.'

'Leo Bradley could afford to buy a dog. Would yer ask 'im if 'e'd lend me a couple 'undred?'

'No! I'm tired of your wretched dog!'

'If Leo lent me 'undred, an' Lizzie's bloke the same, they'd soon get same profits they do wi' their businesses, likely more.' He continued in this vein for some minutes until, finally, Josie, grinning, suddenly left him and sprinted to jump on the back of a tram just starting off.

Freddy stared after her in disgust, then went in search of Wilf.

''Ow much cash yer got?' Freddy demanded.

'Couple of quid. Might buy 'arf a leg,' Wilf said.

'That's a fat lot of good!'

'Will Sid wait any longer?'

'A week or so, then 'e says 'e'll 'ave ter sell the beggar; it's costin' 'im too much ter feed,' Freddy said.

'So 'ow're we gonna keep it then?'

'Keep 'im in me ma's shed. There's scraps ter feed 'im, wi' what you bring. All we need's Sid's price.'

'An' where we gonna get that? Rob a bleedin' bank?'

'You can if yer likes, Wilf. I've got another plan.'

Wilf looked sceptical.

'Well, two plans,' Freddy amended, 'one ter get cash fer the dog and me bike, then the big 'un fer the trainin'. It were Mabel give me that idea.'

'Mabel? That stuck-up tart? Don't tell me you're still knockin' round with 'er. 'Er must 'ave 'idden talents, that one.'

'Mabel's all right. Lay off.'

'Did yer know 'er dad were put away last year? 'E 'eld up a jeweller's shop wi' a gun.'

'Lay off, I said. About me scheme, it needs proper plannin', Wilf me lad, and keepin' dark. By next weekend, we'll be the owners of the fastest dog in Brummagem!'

*

44

Bert, who arrived back at work on Thursday morning, whistled in amazement when he walked in. 'By 'eck, what's 'it us, Gaffer?' he demanded, not seeing Josie behind the small screen which hid a tiny sink and the Primus stove.

Leo chuckled. 'Miss Josie Shaw's hit us, and before long she'll be organizing us as well as the office.'

Josie, to her annoyance, was blushing as she emerged from her hideaway. Bert surveyed her with interest.

'I can see I'll be leavin' the gaffer in good 'ands, miss,' he said, grinning at her.

'Do you mind?' Josie asked abruptly. 'I haven't changed any of your work, just tidied up a bit, and I know things have been a bit hectic recently.'

'Some tidy up! I never thought Mr Leo would do up this office. I'm glad,' he added sincerely. 'I 'as ter leave. It's me daughter, see? She's gone ter live in Coventry — 'er man works in the Riley place, an' 'er wants me ter live wi' 'em. I was proper torn, wantin' ter goo but worried about leavin' Mr Leo. Now 'e'll be OK.'

Josie, embarrassed, glanced at Leo. He was grinning broadly and she breathed a sigh of relief. Despite his capitulation over the furniture she still had a feeling that he resented her, perhaps regretted giving her the job.

'She's done marvels, Bert,' he said now, and was surprised at how true that was. Already he'd come to rely on her, knowing that if he asked her to do something she would calmly and efficiently do it in the shortest possible time. If she hadn't done it before and was doubtful she would ask, but once it was explained to her he could depend on her doing it conscientiously and well. She never had to ask for anything to be explained twice.

'Why didn't you want to go to university?' he asked when Bert had gone down to the workshop.

'University? Me?'

'Lots of girls do now. My aunt's friend's daughter is studying in London to be a doctor.'

Josie shook her head. 'I'm not clever like that. And we don't have the money, I have to work. And I don't want to,' Josie said slowly. 'I want to get on with life and do something practical. I don't want to spend years studying some theoretical subject. Did you go to university?'

'Yes, I did,' he said, and she realized with some surprise that she hadn't ever heard his father mention this. 'So I do know what I'm talking about,' he added with a faint grin. 'Look, now Bert's back, come and meet the rest of the people who work for me. There hasn't been time yet, but you ought to know them in case you have queries.'

'Thanks. I'd like to know what I'm talking about when I write letters,' she said briskly. 'I understand hallmarks and I've worked out what carats are, but I'm not at all sure what a wire-drawing machine does and why a fly-press is different from other presses, or why you use cyanide.'

Josie and Lizzie met after work and took tram and bus to the Hagley Road where they found Endersby's hotel. The imposing façade was long and low, painted white, discreet and elegant. 'Ought we to find a staff entrance?' Lizzie asked nervously. 'There must be one round the back.'

'They'll send us to it if there is,' Josie declared.

The foyer was furnished like a drawing room with deep armchairs and small tables arranged in cosy groups. The only sign that it was not a private house was the small elegant rosewood reception desk to one side. A tall, dark-haired young man stood beside it talking to a pretty blonde girl who was flicking through a sheaf of papers. She looked up and smiled brightly. 'Can I help you?'

'Our cousin, Ann Preece, works here and had an accident yesterday. Mrs Endersby said we might come and visit her,' Josie explained.

'Oh yes, poor Ann! But she's feeling much better now. If you'll wait here I'll send for someone to take you up to her room,' the girl replied cheerfully.

The young man, who had been staring hard at Josie, held up

his hand. 'No, don't bother, Miss Jackson, I'll show the young ladies where to go.'

'Very well, Mr Endersby. I'll sort these bookings.'

Josie looked at him as he led the way through a wide doorway and along a corridor. He was several inches taller than she was, and she judged him about the same age, though his air of assurance made him seem older. He couldn't be the Mr Endersby whose wife owned the hotel, and from what Ann had told them she didn't think Mrs Endersby was old enough to have a son that age. Perhaps he was a nephew.

'I'm Dick Endersby,' he said as he guided them up a wide flight of stairs. 'Haven't I seen you before? Playing tennis, I believe, last summer at the Gough house?'

'Oh, I remember you now! But you're so much taller. Emily was my schoolfriend.'

'And her brother Alan was mine.' He turned politely to Lizzie. 'You are Miss Preece's cousins? Are you sisters?'

'I'm Josie Shaw and this is Lizzie Preece. The three of us each have different parents,' Josie explained. She was busy admiring the luxurious décor and furnishings, the thick carpets and the attractive pictures. Even when he led them through a service door into the staff quarters the change was less drastic than she'd expected. The walls were freshly painted, prints of lively country scenes decorated them, and there was still a carpet runner, though of cheaper quality, on the floor.

Dick Endersby knocked on a door at the end of the corridor. 'Mrs Blake is the housekeeper, she'll take you to Miss Preece's room,' he explained and ushered them in. With a smile he inclined his head and took his leave.

A pleasant older woman showed them into Ann's room. It was small but neatly furnished with an armchair and table as well as wardrobe and chest of drawers. Ann was propped up in the bed, her arm in a sling, a bandage round her head, a bowl of fruit on the bedside table. She was reading a magazine but dropped it when she saw her visitors.

'I feel so stupid!' she said when they had reassured themselves she was not badly injured. 'That idiot Stanley Hodges jumped out at me and frightened me into falling down the stairs! But Mrs Endersby's been so kind.'

'How does Dick Endersby fit in?' Josie asked. 'We met him in the foyer and he showed us up here.'

'That's her eldest son. He's sixteen, away at school, but he comes in during the holidays.'

'I thought you said she had young children?'

'She does. It's such a romantic story,' Ann sighed. 'They were married during the war. He – the older Mr Endersby – was a pilot and he was shot down in Germany and spent years there, hiding. They all thought he was dead and Mrs Endersby started the hotels and then he came back. He runs ballrooms and cinemas all over Birmingham and nearby.'

They talked about the family and their jobs. Ann chuckled about Freddy's increasingly agitated search for people to invest money in his wonder greyhound, and listened with envy as they described the car rally.

'There are some lovely cars belonging to the guests here,' she sighed. 'If Freddy could guarantee his greyhound would earn enough for me to buy one I might be tempted.'

'He's always been full of get-rich-quick schemes,' Lizzie said with sisterly contempt. 'Usually he abandons them when he realizes they involve just a little amount of effort. I'm surprised this one's lasted so long.'

As they left, Dick Endersby was waiting to escort them out of the hotel. 'I hope you don't feel it impertinent of me,' he said awkwardly to Josie, 'but I wondered if you – that is, may I have the pleasure – the honour – that is, will you come to the tennis club with me one day?'

Josie stared at him and gradually the meaning of what he was saying sank in. 'Mr Endersby, I – that's very kind of you. I haven't played tennis for several weeks.'

'I'm soon back at Eton. How about Saturday afternoon?'

Josie, bemused and rather touched, agreed. She loved tennis, and she didn't work on Saturday afternoons.

'Who's that?' Lizzie asked, craning to see from the tram as they rode back to Aston.

'Where?'

'There, Freddy and a girl. I haven't seen her before.'

'She looks a bit familiar. Could she live nearby?'

Lizzie shook her head. 'I don't think so. But I didn't get a really good look. He was being so attentive, helping her cross that street. Not at all like my brother. Perhaps that explains the extra brilliantine he's been using!'

'Perhaps there's hope for him yet, with the love of a good woman to reform him,' Josie suggested flippantly.

Lizzie snorted in derision. 'Talking of which, what about you? Dick Endersby on Saturday and Leo on Sunday! Did you know there's to be a party afterwards? Matthew's taking me and William's going too. But you said Leo showed you round the factory at last?'

'Yes, and it was fascinating. I couldn't take it all in but it was beginning to make sense, and I longed to try my hand at some of the machines.'

'Do machines interest you?'

Josie considered. 'I'm not sure I'm interested in why they work like they do except in a very general way, but it's exciting to see the amazing things they can do, like stamping out the metal shapes so cleanly. Though there's an awful lot of hand work and so many different tools! I'll never learn it all.'

When they reached home Josie went to bed. Lizzie discovered that she had no blouse ironed, so, as she wasn't sleepy, decided to attack the pile of her clothes waiting to be ironed. When Freddy came in an hour later she looked curiously at him. He was smarter these days.

'Had a good bet?' she asked, testing the iron.

'Bet? What yer on about now?' he snapped, flinging himself

into a chair beside the table. 'If I get a couple of me shirts will yer iron 'em fer me?'

'You've got a new jacket.'

'Eh? Oh, yes, some good bets. Do me shirts?'

'Get your new girlfriend to do them. Who is she?'

'I don't 'ave no girl,' he insisted, and almost immediately went out of the kitchen.

Lizzie heard him clattering up the stairs to his attic bedroom and soon afterwards put away the irons and went to her own room which she had previously shared with Ann. As she prepared for bed she recalled the way Dick Endersby had looked at Josie and suddenly chuckled. It hadn't struck her before, she'd been too worried about Ann and also rather overawed by their smart surroundings, but the boy – for he was no more despite his air of confidence – had seemed unable to take his eyes off Josie. Her cousin didn't know it yet, but in the few weeks since she had left school Josie had developed into a very attractive girl. She always spoke deprecatingly of her height and assumed that fragile prettiness such as that possessed by Dora and Ann was what men admired, but Lizzie could see how men regarded her. Both Matthew and William had been attentive and Leo had, to Lizzie's experienced eye, shown that he was attracted. Now young Dick Endersby had exhibited clear signs of admiration. Perhaps, she thought as she drifted off to sleep, Dora was more realistic than they thought in trying to find Josie a husband to assume responsibility for them both. After all, surely every girl wanted to marry, especially when they had a man like Matthew.

The following evening, as Josie was dusting the top of the piano, she told Dora about Freddy's efforts. 'I can't see why he should be so persistent.'

'He asked me last week,' her mother said.

'I hope you didn't let him have anything.'

Dora sighed. 'My dear, you know I wouldn't be so foolish. I

know we have to save every penny if we're ever to get away from this dreadful house. It's so noisy.'

'I thought it was a nice quiet neighbourhood. It isn't a main road, and it isn't a slum with dozens of poor folk living in cramped houses.'

Dora shuddered. 'I am thankful for small mercies, believe me! I meant the noise Phoebe makes when she has her cronies in to gossip. They positively shriek with laughter. Really, you'd never believe we were sisters with the same upbringing. I'm so refined and Phoebe, I have to say it, is getting coarser every year.'

Josie shrugged. 'She's very generous. We'd have to pay twice the rent anywhere else for rooms like these.'

'They're too small. I wasn't able to bring a quarter of the furniture I wanted to keep.'

'You know we had to sell it. But you brought enough bits and pieces,' she added, gesturing to the Staffordshire figurines and silver photograph frames and a mass of other ornaments which filled every horizontal surface. 'Why can't we pack some of these away? It would make dusting easier.'

'I couldn't, my dear. I love every single thing. They all have such happy memories for me, they remind me of special occasions or places we went to or they're presents dear George gave me. Surely you don't begrudge me the comfort of having them about me? Do you really mind the time it takes to dust them? I will try to manage it myself if that's the case, though these days I'm afraid the least little exertion brings on palpitations.'

Josie shook her head. 'No, of course I don't begrudge the time,' she said untruthfully. Privately she thought the ornaments so hideous that the back of a dark cupboard was the only place for them. 'I want to save you the trouble, but there are so many I'm afraid of knocking some off the edges.'

'Josephine, I know you understand,' she sniffed, taking the handkerchief silently proffered, 'I have to keep these treasures to convince me that one day we'll be able to afford some of the elegancies of life again. I don't ask for much. If we could afford to rent a little house, just the two of us, I'd be content, I really would.'

The rally was a long one to the Malverns, where they were to use the famous Shelsley Walsh hill climb track. Josie's initial shyness with Leo evaporated when they had a puncture.

'Hop out!' he ordered briskly. 'Can you tell the difference between a tyre lever and a spanner?' he asked as he jacked up the car.

'Enough to hit you on the head with either!' Josie retorted as she delved into the tool box.

Leo laughed. 'I suppose you think you can change the tyre by yourself?'

'Is that a challenge?'

'Good grief, no! I want to get there today.'

She aimed a playful kick at him as he bent down to unscrew the nuts and he grabbed her foot and pushed her to the ground. 'Behave, or I'll roll you in the mud and leave you here!' he threatened.

Josie laughed. 'Better not, William's just coming and he'll rescue me.'

'Want a hand?' William called out as he pulled up in front of them.

'Swap passengers?' Leo suggested, wresting off the wheel.

'No fear. But you know that straight bit of road through Guarlford? Race you along it when we get there.'

'Done! And the loser pays for lunch.'

As they resumed the drive Josie demanded information on every aspect of driving and rallying. 'Why do you use private land for the hill climbs?' she wanted to know.

'We used to use public roads, but there was a dreadful accident at Kop Hill, near Princes Risborough. Now the clubs are forced to have much stricter safety precautions.'

When they reached the place for the private race William was waiting for them. Leo drew up alongside. 'To the church?' he suggested, and then they were off. William's car had greater acceleration and he drew ahead, but Leo was hot on his tail, and soon began to draw level. Josie urged him on, shouting friendly insults across at William who was only a couple of feet away from her. Then Leo drew slightly ahead, and as soon as he was a yard clear edged over so William either had to give way or ram into him. Josie turned to gloat at William, and tried to distract him by waving her arms about. Making a sign of surrender as they reached the church, William slowed down and Leo, his horn tooting derisively, shot ahead.

Lunch had been booked for them all at a hotel in Great Malvern, and Josie felt very conscious of the curious looks she attracted from male diners.

She decided that the women, despite having their own partners, were similarly interested in Leo, and the way in which some of them approached him and tried to keep his attention confirmed her view. She was scornful. Hadn't they any other ideas in their empty heads than flirtation? She was thankful when it was time to move on to Shelsley Walsh.

'That was fabulous!' Josie breathed at the end of the first hill climb. 'But you didn't tell me to hang out over the side like that man in front did.'

Leo laughed. 'A dangerous occupation for a woman.'

'I'll bet William will tell me to. He asked me to go with him one day.'

'But you're with me now.'

'You're just like your father, terribly protective of his women. But darling Papa George did teach me to drive. Leo, will you let me drive the Midget? It's private land. Please, just round the paddock?'

'Not if I value my friendships. Look how many cars there are you could crash into.'

'One day, Leo Bradley, I'll make you eat those words. Oh,

look, they're going to announce the results. Do you think we won?'

'We? I was driving!'

Josie chuckled. 'If you haven't won, Leo, it'll be your own fault. You wouldn't let me help even by hanging out to distribute the weight – of which I've got plenty!'

'Rubbish, you're as light as a feather. I should know, the number of times I have to carry you around and catch you when you fall off tables.'

Josie blushed, but fortunately, at that moment, the results were announced and her embarrassment was covered. Leo had won his class. William, in a bigger-engined car, had also won his, and Matthew once more came third. Leo gave Josie a friendly hug as they went back to the car, but firmly resisted her renewed blandishments to let her drive just a few yards.

'No. I intend to get to the party in one piece. Get in, or I'll leave you here!'

The party was in a private room at a roadhouse on the outskirts of Birmingham. There were about fifty people there, mostly young couples, though there was a sprinkling of older men. Tables for two had been set around the perimeter, and in the centre was a small dance floor. During the meal a trio of musicians played popular songs from musical shows, while the guests danced between courses.

Josie had never before been held in a man's embrace and at first found it embarrassing and odd. But she was athletic, had always enjoyed dancing, and the music soon absorbed her attention. She tried to forget it was Leo holding her so closely. She'd learned to dance at school, but with girls as partners, and, being tall, had always taken the man's part. After their first foray Leo regarded her quizzically.

'Do you always want to be the boss?' he asked.

'What do you mean?' she demanded suspiciously.

'The man is supposed to lead,' he said gently.

Josie's cheeks flamed. 'I – I did try. But I'm not used to

being the woman. I mean – Oh, it's always the same! I wish I'd been born a man. Men always have the best of it, in work and now even in dancing!'

'You'd have been a great loss,' Leo said jokingly. 'You're formidable enough now, and you're only sixteen! I dread what you'd have been like as a man – probably become prime minister!'

'Don't scoff! One day a woman will be prime minister, and one day I'll have my own business.'

But she tried harder to dance in the way he so clearly expected, and found she enjoyed herself as she relaxed. When the musicians finished, few of the party guests, most of whom were friends of long standing, were ready to go home.

'Let's play charades!' someone suggested, and after some friendly wrangling over what the clues should be about, twenty or so of them began to devise scenes to represent book and play titles. Josie found herself in a team with Leo and two other couples.

'What shall we do?' asked a very pretty dark girl, whom Josie had noticed was a marvellous dancer. 'How about *The Riviera Girl*?'

'Too easy,' her partner objected. 'You've only to go on as yourself, Kitty, and they'd know.'

Kitty giggled. 'They don't all know I live there.'

'We could do *Romeo and Juliet*,' the other girl suggested, casting a glance at Leo.

'Oh, Betty, don't make it so obvious!' Kitty said scornfully. 'Can you see Leo as a love-lorn youth?'

'Then make it *Taming of the Shrew*!' Betty snapped.

Eventually they decided on *The Saint Meets the Tiger*. Josie swathed herself in a striped curtain which they had appropriated from another room and perched on a table, snarling and trying to hit Leo who was draped in a white tablecloth and balancing a cardboard circlet on his head. Kitty and Betty, having objected that he looked more like an angel, decided they couldn't take part and retreated, while the two men, armed with knives, pretended to hunt the tiger.

The audience, baffled, made a variety of wild suggestions. Josie, swallowing her mirth, became more determined to make them guess correctly. She crouched on the table, and when Leo came within reach stood up and pretended to scratch his face. Unfortunately the table was flimsy, and she was on the edge. She fell, arms flailing wildly, and Leo staggered backwards, coming to rest on a conveniently placed settee with Josie clasped in his arms. The audience howled, but in the midst of her confusion Josie heard Kitty's tart comment.

'I suppose that's the only way such a lump of a girl can get a man.'

Josie struggled to her feet and turned to face Kitty, impetuous words on her lips. Leo swiftly threw his sheet over her head and smothered her angry rejoinder. He lifted her on to his shoulder and bore her into the small anteroom where they had made their preparations, and collapsed into a chair, laughing helplessly while Josie wriggled to free herself.

'Tiger is right,' he gasped. 'What is it about you and tables?' Josie discarded the restraining cloth and tried to stand up but he held her firmly. 'No, you'll stay here until you promise me not to say anything to Kitty.'

'But did you hear what she said?'

'Kitty's always like that, but sometimes she can be great fun.'

'How do you know so much about her, anyway?'

'She was married to a wealthy Italian prince who was a good customer of mine. She spends most of her time at her villa in the South of France. Don't let her see she can offend you, or she'll try again.'

Josie knew he was right and suddenly laughed. 'I'm not mad now,' she told him. 'You can let me get up. It's late, I'm sure we ought to be going home.'

'You're right,' Leo said, finally releasing her. 'We have to work tomorrow.'

*

'Josephine, dear, have you been tidying my ornaments away?' Dora asked a few days later.

'No, you said you wanted them all left out, Mother,' Josie said impatiently. If only she could get rid of them.

'Odd, I could have sworn all George's silver bottle-labels were together on the piano. And that lovely set of spoons seems to have been moved.'

'Not by me. I might have put them somewhere else but I certainly haven't packed them away. They'll turn up.'

'I suppose so. When I feel better I'll try and sort them out. I must go to bed now, my headache is worse.'

'You shouldn't give in to 'er,' Phoebe chided the next morning, when Josie was considering calling a doctor. 'Doris was always complaining of something, she's queasy, or cold, or hot and breathless. It's her blessed imagination, another of her stories when she's acting the heroine.'

'I know, but she really does seem ill,' Josie defended her mother. 'She has so many headaches and talks of palpitations. I wonder if her heart is weak?'

'Not physically,' Phoebe snorted.

'Well, it doesn't hurt to cosset her a little,' Josie said. She was feeling guilty. She'd often snapped impatiently at Dora lately, and had to remind herself that her mother had become so irritating because her life was so boring. And she had suffered through no fault of her own when George had lost their money. Dora was being less extravagant now, and Josie resolved to be more understanding. 'I was wondering whether to ask that nice doctor who looked after Ann to call,' she went on. 'Ann said he was so kind and she's feeling much better now.'

'Fancy Edgbaston doctor'd cost too much,' Phoebe declared. 'There's nothin' serious wrong with 'er.'

Josie sighed. 'Perhaps you're right. We can't really afford private doctors, anyway. I must go, I'll be late for work.'

*

57

Leo let himself out of the office. It was almost midnight and he was exhausted. Josie had offered to stay late but he had refused, saying rather curtly that he would be perfectly capable of finishing off the paperwork by himself. Now he regretted both his sharp reply and his rejection of help. Josie had momentarily looked hurt and unusually vulnerable, though she had swiftly covered it up with a grave inclination of the head. Her help would have been welcome and he couldn't understand the instinctive way in which he had responded. It was unfair to blame the daughter for her mother's failings, but if anyone was to blame it was poor, dead, gullible George. He must have been more tired than he'd thought. He most certainly needed a manager.

As he drove home he went through the list of the various people he might approach. He wanted someone young. Matthew Horobin knew the jewellery business almost as well as he did, and from various remarks he had heard around the jewellery quarter he suspected Horobin's was not doing particularly well. Old Mr Horobin was stubborn and reluctant to change his firm's established repertoire of heavy ornate jewellery which was now out of fashion. Matthew was reportedly chafing at his father's refusal to accept new ideas. He was talking of setting up his own business, but the money he'd inherited might not be sufficient. It could be a propitious time to approach him. Leo reached home in a far better mood than he had left the factory.

The following Sunday, Matthew collected both girls and drove them out to the Lickey Hills where the rally would begin and end. William had gone ahead in his new car, an Alvis, in order to make a few test runs on the uphill timed section.

When they arrived Josie looked round at the much bigger crowd of participants than there had been last week. She was rather surprised to see Leo with Kitty, but told herself sternly that he had the freedom to go out with whomever he wished. It was none of her business. She concentrated on the map she'd been given. Most of the rally was a simple circuit on public roads, at a moderate speed, for it wasn't meant to be a race. Only the final section of hill climb was a speed test and would decide the winner.

'I hope I don't let William down,' she muttered.

'He doesn't expect to win every time, you know,' Lizzie said with a laugh. 'In any case these modifications he's trying to the springs may not work and he's prepared for that. Besides, everyone has to start somewhere – it's my first time too.'

'I'd forgotten that,' Josie admitted, trying to laugh. 'You must think I'm an utter fool to worry.'

'Don't be daft! But you're not to run away. Look, there's William over there, let's go and say hello.'

The first section, a drive of four hours through the Worcestershire countryside, was like an ordinary outing. Josie enjoyed William's company, and was soon absorbed as she asked questions about the cars and the modifications he had made. To her surprise she found she understood his replies, and a great deal of what she had heard from George now began to slip into place with William's explanations.

She also indulged in her curiosity about Leo, asking William where they'd met.

'We've belonged to the same club for years; we've driven on loads of rallies together. Neither of us has any family, or at least –'

'You mean Leo and his father – or my mother – didn't get on.'

William looked apologetic. 'Sorry. I really meant after his uncle and aunt died. We've spent a lot of time together, except when Leo was making a play for a new woman. Not that he needed to make much effort,' William laughed.

'I know. They fall for him in droves.'

'He's dangerous. He once told me he'd fallen in love when he was young, and somehow it went wrong, so he made up his mind never to be serious about a woman again. You aren't – well, hoping for anything, are you?' he added quietly.

'Of course not!' she replied, a little too emphatically. No one would fall in love with plain old Josie Shaw, she added to herself.

William raised his eyebrows and grinned. 'I'm a romantic. I believe there's a right woman somewhere for me, and no doubt the ideal man for you is out there too.'

They reached the hill climb site and Josie felt her excitement rising. Soon it was their turn. Then, the engine roaring, cheers of encouragement all around, there wasn't time to think. As William shouted instructions to her Josie did her best to comply, leaning out to balance the weight on sharp bends, at one point scrambling up on to the seat to sit on the back of it. It was totally absorbing, exhilarating, and when they reached the finishing line she felt they had only just started. She uttered a protest when William braked and cut the engine, then realized where they were and began to laugh.

'We made fabulous time!' William exclaimed, and caught her into a warm embrace. Then they were surrounded and someone was excitedly telling William that he had made the best time so far.

They didn't win. Two more drivers completed the course a few seconds faster, but William declared himself extremely satisfied. As they set off back to Birmingham he was preoccupied, then he turned to Josie.

'I feel guilty about your stepfather,' he said abruptly. 'Your mother blames me for his death.'

'That's nonsense!' Josie declared. 'Papa George wanted the money he'd invested in your business back, and you paid him. It wasn't your fault you began to make profits soon afterwards when you hadn't before. My mother simply doesn't understand the first thing about business.'

'I'm glad you do. Did you enjoy today?'

'More than I thought possible.'

'Good.' He slowed and turned off the main road into a quiet lane, then into the driveway of what looked like a private estate. 'It's time you drove up a hill. You told me you could drive.'

'Not on the road! I haven't a licence, I'm not seventeen for weeks yet. And where is this place anyway?'

William drew to a halt and climbed out of the driving seat. 'Move over. And stop objecting. You don't need a licence for here. It's private land, belongs to one of my customers who lets me come here to practise on his own private hill climb course. That's where we're going now. One day, young Josie, you're going to be driving in trials yourself.'

Chapter Four

On the following Sunday, instead of taking the road home to Aston, Matthew drove into a select road in Harborne.

'Where are we going?' Lizzie asked, surprised.

'A small private celebration,' Matthew replied. 'It's easier to talk that way, and I'll be glad to get out of this weather.'

'But where?'

'A friend's lent me a room. I've arranged for a delicious meal and we can talk. We must make decisions.'

Lizzie tried to suppress her excitement. Matthew often said he wanted to be with her always. His autocratic father, though, would hate the idea of his son marrying a girl who worked in their own factory, especially one whose mother hadn't bothered to marry her father. Much as Lizzie loved Phoebe she sometimes wished her mother had not given her the stigma of her illegitimate birth. It mattered to so many people. It could matter to an ambitious businessman. Indeed, some long-established jewellery firms thought as much about marriages which would benefit their businesses as the aristocracy did. Perhaps Matthew had talked his father round and wanted to provide a suitably discreet setting for the most romantic occasion of their lives.

Matthew drove into a semi-circular gravelled carriage drive set before a large secluded house. 'Quickly, before you get wet!' he said, and they ran towards the back of the house. 'There's a way in here, we won't disturb anyone,' he explained, and let them in to a short passage ending in a door covered with green baize.

Lizzie had heard of such doors. 'The servants' quarters?' she asked, amused.

'No longer. My friend's made the house into four separate apartments and lets me use this one. This way.'

He opened the door into what had probably been the servants' hall. It was large, pleasantly proportioned, but had a low ceiling and two rather narrow windows which looked out to an overgrown shrubbery. A small table was beside the windows, and the gleam of silver and polished glass made Lizzie sigh with pleasure. It looked so luxurious. Bottles of wine were waiting in a wine cooler, and several plates covered with domed lids sat on a side table. She was hungry and felt an unromantic desire to sample the fare, but allowed Matthew to lead her to a leather settee. 'Take off your wet coat and we'll have a cocktail,' he suggested, opening a glass-fronted cupboard to reveal an amazing display of bottles. 'A sidecar would be appropriate.'

Lizzie had heard of cocktails, and envied the sophisticated people in the films who seemed to drink them all the time, but had never tasted one. 'That sounds fun,' she said slowly, watching as Matthew busied himself with bottles and a cocktail shaker. She couldn't tell Matthew she had no idea what a sidecar consisted of – if he meant to propose, her life would change and she would become used to a great many new things including cocktails. As she sipped, she lost herself in a dream of living in her own house, casually mixing cocktails for Matthew when he came home from work, and for his friends when they entertained. She dragged her mind back from such glorious imagining and listened as Matthew talked about the day. William's new Alvis had again done well, but Matthew was disappointed at his own more modest performance.

'You haven't been competing long.'

'One day we'll have a much better car and perhaps enter the

Monte Carlo Rally,' Matthew predicted. 'Have another drink. Here's to our success, my darling.'

The food, when they eventually ate, was delicious. Matthew had drawn the thick brown velvet curtains against the howling gale outside and switched on several lights which made the silver and glassware gleam even more brightly. Lizzie lost count of the different wines and wondered if she would ever remember that red wine went with some foods and white with others and champagne had its own rules.

'I feel dizzy,' she said when they had finished.

'This is a celebration. Come and try some port.' He led her to the settee and raised the small glass. 'To us, my darling, to many long and happy years together!' He pulled Lizzie into his arms and she curled up confidingly. When he began to caress her, slipping his hand under her skirt, she protested and tried to sit up. 'Darling, it's all right, I won't hurt you. We're going to live together, aren't we? Oh, Lizzie, I adore you so very much.'

She subdued faint feelings of alarm. Matthew loved her, he'd said so repeatedly. And what he was doing was so delicious she had no power to stop him. Her body had taken on a life quite independent of her will, responding to ever more daring invasions, making her breathless with anticipation, shuddering each time he touched her, longing for some unknown but urgently essential climax. When he picked her up and carried her through a small doorway into a bedroom she made no protest and helped him tear off the last remnants of her clothes. She stretched luxuriously on the comfortable feather mattress and turned eagerly to Matthew as he, having discarded his own clothes, joined her on the bed.

'Darling Lizzie, at last, at last,' he whispered, pulling her close. 'You don't know how impatiently I've waited for this moment.'

Josie had taken up Dick Endersby's offer of a visit to the tennis club and their games had become a regular feature of her

Saturday afternoons. They entered the mixed doubles competition and reached the final. Dick said they had a good chance of winning. She'd cajoled Freddy into lending her his motorcycle so that she could get to the club quickly after her morning's work, but she hadn't seen Leo's look of astonishment when he'd seen her riding away on it. She wove between the crowds rushing towards the buses which would take them to Villa Park for Aston Villa's first match of the season. Josie liked Dick. He was younger than she was, but far less callow than most of the boys she knew, neither shy nor boastful and with excellent manners. He had interesting things to say but he didn't monopolize the conversation. She had little experience of boys apart from the brothers of her schoolfriends, and most of them seemed boorish and immature. With Dick, however, she could be natural and have a sensible discussion.

While they waited for the other matches to be played they talked about their ambitions. Josie was now certain she wanted her own business, although she didn't know what. Dick was torn between several opportunities. 'There are the hotels and the cinemas, but my parents will be running those for ages. It isn't that I don't get on with them, I do, but I'd want to be the boss!' he said, laughing at himself. 'My grandfather has a pottery in North Staffordshire and he wants me to take over from him, but I'm not sure.'

'Endersby china? I never connected it with the hotel. We have some at home, it's my mother's favourite pattern.'

'I want to go to Oxford but Grandfather wants to know what I mean to do and I can't decide. He's seventy, so I suppose he thinks it won't wait.'

'Have you spent any time working with him?'

'Only a week or two. I'll spend next summer holidays there. I lived with my grandparents for years while my father was missing during the war, so I already know something about it.'

'Your grandfather must have a manager,' Josie said reassuringly. 'It isn't your responsibility.'

They went on to compare schools and then it was time for their match. It was a hard one, and they were one set all, five games all, and deuce, with their opponents to serve. It was a fast ball right out to the line, and Dick fell as he stretched for it but just managed to lift it back over the net. Josie raced in and smashed the return out of reach, and they won the point. Then she had to face the serve, and as Dick was hobbling slightly she had to cover most of the court, only just managing to keep the ball in play until, with a deceptive spin, she tempted their opponent into sending the ball out of court. Game to them. Dick was serving for the match, and Josie knew his injured ankle wouldn't hold up for long. As it was, his movement around the court was severely restricted. She had to keep the game brief, so she went to the net and with her height was able to cut off and place well out of reach most of their opponents' returns of service. The match was theirs, and Dick was generous in his praise.

'It's all due to you,' he said. 'I've not seen a girl play like that before.'

'How is your ankle?' Josie demanded.

'Just a very slight sprain, I think.'

When Josie set off on the motorcycle they found another mutual interest.

'I shall have a car next summer,' Dick said eagerly. 'I want to take part in rallies. It's my ambition to enter the Monte Carlo Rally one day.'

'Mine too! Though I've only just started being a passenger in one-day events.'

'One day we must drive together.'

Freddy led his new acquisition along the Walsall Road. He was hot, perspiring freely, becoming angrier by the minute and starting to have doubts about the wisdom of his bright idea. He hadn't been prepared for the way the young dog would leap nervously aside from the traffic, bark at all the horses and carts, and strain at the lead in an attempt to chase every cat they encountered. Would he become the champion greyhound his former owner had promised? For the first time Freddy began to think of the practicalities of training a dog. Until now he had dwelt on the glories of owning a race-winner. He had, in his imagination, already spent the proceeds – the prize money, the stud fees, and sundry other, less legal, perquisites. He had assumed the animal would be content to sleep in the garden shed and eat kitchen scraps. Now he began dimly to perceive that he would have to find somewhere to exercise the dog, and given its propensity to chase cats, letting him off the piece of string which currently restrained him would present problems. Also, given his apparent inability to understand even a single word of command, Freddy comprehended, if only inexactly, the enormity of the task he had so lightly undertaken.

His mother's reception of his new money-making machine did not improve his temper. 'You're not bringin' that blasted animal in 'ere,' Phoebe declared when he appeared at the kitchen door. 'I told you I wouldn't 'ave it. An' can't yer stop the brute barkin' like that? The neighbours will all be deafened!'

'Give over, Ma! 'E's goin' straight in the shed. I need a strong cuppa.'

'You can make it yerself. I'm goin' down ter shops.'

'Is Aunt Dora in?'

'She's in bed. Took on because Josie wouldn't buy fancy clothes to suit the new feller.'

'What new feller?'

'Someone she met when she went ter see Ann.'

Freddy shrugged. 'I'll tek the Streak to shed.'

'The what?'

'Streak o' Lightnin'. They all 'ave fancy names.'

'Oughta be Thunder an' Lightnin' by the noise 'e's makin'. If yer don't shut 'im up 'e'll 'ave ter go.'

*

'I love you so much,' Lizzie whispered as Matthew was driving her home. 'I can't wait to tell everyone we're getting married.'

'Lizzie, darling, you mustn't breathe a word. I can't tell my father yet. He's having business problems, and he just wouldn't understand. He wants me to invest my money in it. Promise you won't tell anyone, even Josie? If any word got back to him he'd turn me off without a penny. Then how could I support you in the style to which I want you to become accustomed? My own money isn't enough for that.'

'You'd manage,' she said confidently. 'I'd love to show Josie my ring, but if you say not, of course I won't.'

'It's just our secret. Later I'll buy you a better ring, my darling.'

'This one has our initials entwined. That's romantic.'

'And in the meantime we can use the apartment whenever we want to be alone. Tomorrow, for example?'

Lizzie hesitated. 'It's difficult,' she said slowly. 'My mother is beginning to ask awkward questions.'

'About my wicked intentions?' They laughed.

'She's dropped hints, saying I'm always with you and ought to go out with other men too.'

'Tell her I'm teaching you to drive. We can spend the whole day together on Sundays, and on Saturdays after work.'

'Would you really teach me?' Lizzie demanded.

'So long as it doesn't take too much time away from our other activities.'

'I'd be very, very grateful.' Lizzie said demurely. 'And you know I learn fast.'

Dora took the tram to the city centre. How fortunate that it was Ann's afternoon off. She'd replied very prettily to the note Dora had sent round that morning, with a neighbour's young son who had been demonstrating to his friends his skill on his new bicycle and had been eager to earn a few coppers. When she'd discovered Josie's new friendship with Dick Endersby she'd allowed her hopes to rise. It was trade, of course, but better than that dreadful man Scott who asked Josie out. She couldn't be allowed to marry him after the way he'd treated George. Besides, the Endersbys were probably wealthier.

Dora was at the tea rooms first, seated at a corner table with a pot of tea and plate of cream cakes, when Ann appeared, looking rather apprehensive.

'I'm sorry, Aunt Dora, Mrs Endersby wanted to see me.'

'Don't worry, child. I see you so rarely. You still have your arm in a sling. Is it mending properly?'

'Oh, yes, Dr Mandeville is quite pleased with me, and Mrs Endersby won't let me even try to do any work.'

'How are you enjoying your job?'

'Very much, thank you,' Ann replied, a delightful smile illuminating her enchanting face. Dora snatched back the impulse to tell her that she was as beautiful as the film stars whose pictures were displayed everywhere. It didn't do to spoil the young.

'It's not what dear Arthur would have wanted for his only child, for you to be a chambermaid,' she said instead. 'Poor Arthur, he had to forget Oxford when our dear parents died the year before the war broke out. I was soon married, of course, no longer a burden on him, and Phoebe had run away years before, but there wasn't any money. Vicars are unworldly and Papa never saved. Then Arthur joined the army, met your mother, and she died when you were born. I don't suppose you remember him at all?'

'I wasn't two when he was killed, Aunt Dora,' Ann reminded her gently. 'I know he came to see me when I was being looked after by my mother's parents, but I don't remember it. I have a photograph of him in uniform, though.'

'And then your grandparents died when you were no more than a child and Phoebe took you in.'

Ann smiled and nodded. 'She's always so jolly and she was so kind to me. I'd never left the village before, I had no idea what a big city was like. She made it such fun, and Lizzie and Freddy were kind, too, though they were older.'

'If I'd been informed about your grandparents' deaths I would have fetched you, but Phoebe is so impulsive. Perhaps after the state George left me in, it was as well. Tell me about your job. Is it very tedious?'

'No, it's wonderful seeing how a good hotel is run. I'm so grateful to you for suggesting it. In fact, Mrs Endersby asked me if I'd like to be receptionist. Hers is leaving to be married and she thought it might suit me. I can learn what to do while my arm is getting better.'

'She must be pleased with you. Josephine met young Mr Endersby when she came to see you. Do you know him?'

'He's been in the hotel during these school holidays. He often visits his grandparents in the Potteries. Their house was turned into a hospital during the war; it must be huge.'

'Endersby pottery is, of course, a very good and well-respected firm. Is Dick's father the heir, their only son?'

'Yes, though a brother was killed during the war.'

'Do they live in the hotel?'

'No, they have a house in Edgbaston.'

'I see. Well, Ann, it's been lovely seeing you. Do come home to visit us on your next day off.'

Dora bit into a cream cake and savoured its sinful richness.

'I'm not 'avin' it!'

'But Mabel, it dain't mean nothing,' Freddy protested, following an outraged Mabel towards the ladies' cloakroom.

'I don't go with fellers that spend more time lookin' at other girls than dancin' wi' me!' she declared, and with a final toss of the head swept through the doorway.

With a deep sigh Freddy prepared for a long wait, leaning up against a dingy wall from which dark green paint had been flaking for years. From the ballroom came the strains of the last waltz, the volume swelling every time someone opened the big double doors. Moodily, he surveyed the people who emerged. Some couples were clearly anxious to catch the buses, for these girls whisked out of the cloakroom within seconds, clutching coats and hats, barely giving their escorts time to light up cigarettes. Most early leavers, however, were girls on their own, anxious to be gone before the lights went up and their more successful friends would see they had no partners to walk them home. Some gave him inviting smiles but Freddy studiously looked away. Mabel might emerge at any time. The last thing he wanted was for her to catch him ogling another girl.

'Car' think why yer puts up wi' it,' Wilf had said once, when Mabel had insisted on going to the variety theatre instead of the cinema Freddy had proposed. 'Yer always 'as ter buy 'er drinks, an' fish an' chips after, too.'

'You're jealous,' Freddy automatically replied.

'Jealous? Of them airs an' graces? It must be summat special when yer does get 'er skirts off!'

'Wouldn't yer like ter know?' Freddy taunted.

Wilf remained unconvinced and Freddy was thankful he wasn't here tonight. If Wilf saw him abasing himself to Mabel, Freddy would never be able to hold up his head again. But he needed Mabel. His schemes depended on her. Future delights that Wilf never dreamed of would come through Mabel, and not in the way that Wilf, with his limited imagination, suspected. The cloakroom door swung open just as the last waltz ended, and Mabel emerged. Freddy pinned on an ingratiating smile and advanced.

Josie went to another rally with William in the new Alvis he'd bought, and found Leo also competing. He was with yet another new girl, remarkably beautiful. Every time Josie saw him socially he had a new, always lovely, companion. William gave her more driving lessons and said she showed a natural aptitude. He complimented her willingness to help change the wheel when they had a puncture, and her ability to understand what went on under the bonnet of the car. She was beginning to long for the day when she could take part herself. Life suddenly seemed full of excitement, and, best of all, Dora seemed reconciled to Josie's job, was more cheerful, and began to visit her friends again. Josie half suspected this was to do with her frequently repeated assertion that she must contrive to introduce Josie to suitable young men, but Josie was just thankful that her mother seemed happier, and hoped she was recovering from the shock of George's death and the loss of all their money.

She had been particularly busy at work. Bert was ill again and Josie had everything to do. She'd also taken advantage of having the office to herself to reorganize the filing system, which she'd found difficult and illogical.

When she reached the office on Monday, Leo was already there, several files on the desk, and his hair in disarray. Her smile froze when she saw the grim look on his face.

'What is it, Leo?'

'You might ask! What the devil have you been doing, messing about with all the files? I can't find a thing!'

'Then you know how I've felt since I came to work here,' Josie flared. 'It's taken me far too long to find things, wasting my time and yours. I made it simpler.'

'And I suppose you now consider yourself an expert?'

'No, but I am capable of seeing where improvements can be made. The old system was a total muddle.'

'It suited my uncle and it suits me. How dare you come in here and upset everything without asking? Your mother thinks she's entitled to everything I inherited, and now you behave as if you own my business!'

Josie, white-faced, stared in astonishment. 'I don't!' she protested. 'How can you say that? I was trying to help.'

'Then don't! You know nothing about the jewellery industry. Your job is to type my letters and keep the books, that's all. Nothing else, do you understand?'

She took a deep breath. 'If that's all you want, Leo Bradley, you can find someone else. I won't be so insulted by a pompous, opinionated, arrogant boor. Your office was antiquated, so are your methods, and so are you. You can keep your precious job – you only gave it to me out of charity, and I don't want charity from anyone!'

She swung away but Leo caught her arm. Furious, he shook her hard, then became aware that two of the girls working in the factory were staring up at them, able to see but not hear through the window which ran along the rear wall of the office. Cursing under his breath he dragged Josie away from their curious gaze. She fought hard, but he was too strong.

'Will you stop struggling and listen?' he demanded, breathless, and when Josie took no notice he folded his arms about her, imprisoning her arms at her sides. Then to her fury he laughed. 'Oh, Josie, this is ridiculous. Those girls will be imagining all sorts of scandal.'

'What girls?' she asked, startled. 'Leo, let me go!'

'Only if you'll stay and talk this over calmly.'

'What girls?'

'Just a couple of the polishers. They were getting a glorious peepshow.' Josie went scarlet, and Leo hugged her before releasing her. 'I'll make a pot of tea, we'll sit and discuss this, then if you want to go you may. Agreed?'

She nodded, and when she saw Leo fumbling with the gas, laughed shakily and pushed him aside. 'Let me, at least I can light the thing!'

A few minutes later she tried to explain. 'You had the files in separate drawers, not in one alphabetical sequence. I sometimes had to look in three places to find the one I wanted.'

'But you've mixed the suppliers with the customers, and the foreign customers were kept separately.'

'Yes, but I don't know who is what! It's all right for you. I often didn't know where to start looking, but this way we can all find files straight away.'

He grinned, rather shamefaced. 'It's the system we've always used. Oh, hell, Josie, I'm sorry. Please don't go. I may have offered you the job out of pity for the mess my father left, but if you couldn't do it I wouldn't have kept you on from charity, I promise. I'd be very sorry to lose you. Will you stay?'

'So long as I can keep my new system,' she said, laughing, and stood up to collect the teacups.

Leo caught her hand in his. 'Josie, come with me next Sunday? I've bought a new car, the C-type Midget that's being developed mainly for racing.'

Josie hesitated. She'd thought far too much about Leo's lovely companions and knew she wasn't half so beautiful. Were his invitations another form of charity? She couldn't afford to become involved with him outside work, 'I'm sorry, Leo. I can't.'

Leo turned away. 'Never mind, perhaps another time.' Josie busied herself washing up while he opened the safe to get out the day's supply of gold sheets and wire, then carefully weighed and divided it into the various amounts the different craftsmen needed. Leo was puzzled at his intense disappointment. He'd enjoyed their first rally together, and the party afterwards, but he rarely asked a girl out twice in such a short space of time. They too soon became possessive. While he measured the gold he tried to analyse his reactions. Josie wasn't as beautiful as some girls he knew, but she was extraordinarily attractive with her cheerful smile and unusual-coloured hair. William Scott clearly thought so. He'd seen them together at more than one rally. Had her mother perhaps objected? He frowned. From the moment Dora and his father had met, his relationship with his father had changed, been spoilt, and he was still angry whenever he thought about it. Because of Dora, his father had largely ignored him while he was growing up. He blamed his father's suicide on her complete refusal to understand or sympathize with George's problems, common to thousands of people following the Wall Street crash.

It would complicate their life in the office, Leo decided, if he and Josie met socially. He wouldn't ask her again. It had been a mistake he would not repeat. They would remain strictly business colleagues.

Wilf sat on a fallen tree trunk and ate his chips. He watched Freddy tug the greyhound across the open expanse of grass. The dog was frisking wildly, delighted to be out of the garden shed. Freddy had decided it was high time he began the training programme if he wanted his pot of gold to begin disgorging the fortune tied up in it, and had decreed they spent the afternoon in Aston Park.

'You stay there an' call 'im, an' when 'e gets to you grab 'old. Then I'll call 'im back,' Freddy instructed.

'I feel bloody silly yellin' "Come 'ere, Streak!"' Wilf objected, but Freddy ignored his complaints.

'I put up the cash, the least yer can do is 'elp wi' the trainin'.'

'Let's gerron wi' it then we can get back 'ome.'

He didn't need to call. No sooner had Freddy slipped the piece of string from his collar than the greyhound, relishing freedom, took off and within seconds launched himself at Wilf, who fell with flailing arms off the tree trunk. With a yelp of excitement the dog gobbled up the scattered chips, then began to lick Wilf's face enthusiastically.

'Gerroff!' Wilf shouted, struggling to sit up.

Freddy, shouting indiscriminately at Wilf and his prize possession, approached. Maybe it was his furious tone, which was Wilf's theory, or the sight of some children kicking a football about, which was Freddy's, but the dog didn't stay for the threatened chastisement. He demonstrated his fleetness of foot as he sped across the grass.

Much later, Freddy was still trying to placate Wilf. 'I know 'ow we can get some money,' he said. 'The Streak needs better food. An' I might 'ave ter pay Sid ter use the track fer trainin'.'

'That weren't what yer said ter begin with.'

'I know it weren't!' Freddy ground his teeth. 'I dain't know

75

the bleedin' dog would chase every blasted thing that moved! The daft beggar even chases birds!'

'Well, what do we 'ave ter do?'

'We mek bets at the Tote fer a forecast on each race. Them's the best odds. Then we go pickin' up the tickets thrown away, an' after ev'ry race we cut out the winnin' numbers an' sticks 'em on the other tickets. We cashes 'em at diff'rent winders to where we bought 'em, when it's busy between the races.'

'They'll see the numbers stuck on,' Wilf objected.

'No they won't. The tickets is thin card, not paper, an' if we pulls off the top layer with the wrong numbers on, an' sticks the right number back in its place, it'll stay put long enough ter fool 'em.'

Wilf was dubious. ''Ow d' yer mek it stick?'

'Wet it. That'll do, I've tried. It'll be OK if we do it careful. Then we can change the race numbers on bottom. They're often smudgy, that's easier. I was talkin' ter this feller in a pub up Nechells, 'e does it every week. Meks a fortune, 'e said.'

'Then why's 'e livin in Nechells?' Wilf demanded with one of his rare but disconcerting attacks of perspicuity.

'I don't know!' Freddy snapped. 'Mebee 'e don't want ter give 'isself away, movin' somewhere posh.'

'Give 'isself away talkin' ter yow, dain't 'e?'

'Look, do yer want a share in the Streak or not? Yer've on'y put in a coupla quid so far, an' if yer wants ter get out I won't stop yer!'

Wilf shrugged. 'If yer says it's that easy, why not try? Though if it's such a good 'un why ain't ev'ryone doin' it? That's what I car' understand. Yer'd think ev'ryone 'ud be mekin' their fortunes.'

Dora was waiting for Josie. 'I've been puzzling about that missing silver again,' she announced, the moment Josie entered the room. 'I know it's not here. Are you absolutely sure you haven't put it away somewhere strange?'

'No, I told you I hadn't,' Josie said, looking in dismay at the chaos Dora had created. Every drawer and cupboard seemed to have been emptied and their possessions littered the piano, the table, and all the chairs except the one Dora sat in. Josie transferred a pile of photograph frames from another chair and sat down. 'I haven't touched them.'

'Then it's as I suspected. We've been robbed.'

'But how?' Josie demanded. 'You don't often go out and Aunt Phoebe's in the house most of the time. If anyone had broken in surely one of you would have heard.'

'It's the only explanation. If you haven't put them away they've been stolen. And I can guess who did it.'

Josie looked in dismay. 'What do you mean?'

Dora pursed her lips. 'There hasn't been a burglar from outside. Who's been pestering us for money lately?'

'Freddy? Surely he wouldn't steal, and not from us. If he were criminally inclined he'd already have money.'

Dora shook her head impatiently. 'He hasn't the guts to steal from strangers,' she asserted. 'He's been desperate for money to buy this silly dog. He was in here just before he bought the wretched animal, snooping round. And he's got some flashy new clothes which cost a pound or two. He could easily have come in when I'm out or lying down. Phoebe refused to give me keys to our rooms and look what's come of it. I'm going to call the police.'

'Mother, wait at least until we've spoken to Freddy.' Dora set her chin stubbornly. 'He'd just deny it and we'd give him warning so that he could get rid of them.'

None of Josie's arguments could sway her, she insisted on going straight to the police station and began to put on her new lilac summer coat and hat, the half mourning she had adopted soon after the anniversary of George's death. Josie slipped away and found Phoebe in the kitchen.

'Where's Freddy?' she asked urgently. 'Mother thinks he's stolen some of her silver bits and pieces.'

The subsequent row made Josie shudder. Phoebe added her demands to Josie's that Dora ask Freddy before going to the police. Dora, prostrate, retreated to bed, and a belligerent Phoebe waited impatiently for Freddy's return.

'It's not that I don't think 'e might 'ave taken 'em,' she explained to Josie. 'I know 'e's got neither sense nor morals, but I won't 'ave 'is name dragged through the police station unless there's more in it than she's shown so far.'

'Could a burglar have got in?' Josie asked tentatively.

'No, 'cause someone's always 'ere. I expect she's mislaid 'em, unless she sold them an' now she's forgot.'

Reluctantly Josie shook her head. 'I dusted them only a few weeks ago. And I don't see how they could be hidden after she turned every single thing upside down.'

'We'll see when 'is lordship deigns to come 'ome.'

It was midnight when Freddy stumbled noisily through the door, reeking of whisky. Lizzie had come in half an hour earlier, saying she was exhausted, and had gone straight to bed without appearing to notice the tension or wonder at her mother sitting in the kitchen so late, for once not busy. Despite Freddy's protests Phoebe led him to the scullery and forced him to plunge his head under the tap. When he understood what he was accused of he was fiercely indignant.

'Silly cow's lost 'em somewhere! A fine thing when yer own aunt accuses yer of thievin' from 'er!'

'Never mind that. You could be in trouble, deep trouble,' Phoebe told him. 'If you didn't steal 'em I'll persuade Doris to wait a bit, make 'er consider. Tell me the truth now. Did you steal anything from Doris's room?'

'I 'aven't stole nothin' from nobody!' Freddy insisted. 'I don't expect me fine posh relatives ter believe me but it's the truth, an' no doubt soon enough you'll all be grovellin' ter me, apologizin'. Now gerroff me, will yer? I'm goin' ter bed.'

Chapter Five

DORA was still prostrate the following morning. Freddy had left the house by the time Josie came downstairs, pale from lack of sleep. Aunt Phoebe was preoccupied but she gave Josie a bleak smile. 'It isn't your fault, love. How is she?' Inwardly Josie sighed as she explained that her mother intended to remain in bed; she had a crippling headache. She couldn't blame Aunt Phoebe. Normally easy-going and always generous, it was natural she should be hurt to have her son accused of theft, even though she might accuse him of worse herself. She never meant it, whereas Dora did.

Lizzie had overslept again and Josie escaped thankfully before she came downstairs. She couldn't bear to discuss it. Thank goodness she could submerge herself in work.

'Have you so little to do you can read fashion magazines?' Leo asked an hour later, coming into the office.

For once he was late and Josie had opened all the post and dealt with some of it before deciding he wasn't coming in and making herself a cup of tea. She grinned. 'Bert's delivering some rush orders. The tea's still hot. Would you like a cup?'

'Please. Sorry I'm late, I spent half the night trying to do some repairs on the motor for the rally this weekend.'

'Nothing serious?'

'Just a bent pipe, but everything that could go wrong did; it took hours to do. Anything urgent?'

'No, but that's not why I'm looking at these magazines. See, the new fashions are for plain, simple shapes. And heavy-looking coats and suits designed for businesswomen. The elaborate jewellery which is fashionable now is not really suitable with these clothes.'

'You're not suggesting I go for the ornate pieces the Horobin factory specializes in? I'm not equipped for inlaid precious-stone work. Anyway, he's on the verge of bankruptcy. Do you want that for me?'

Josie grinned. 'Don't be so touchy, I'm not trying to take over the rest of the business too. But you could just admit that a woman might have some fashion sense. No, I don't think ornate settings are suitable. But it's no good being stuck in the mud, producing the same designs year after year. You have to dictate fashion, not follow it.'

'Do you ever give up?' Leo laughed reluctantly.

'Not if I'm right,' she retorted, her eyes twinkling.

He groaned. 'My designs sell well enough with the changes I make. That's why I do new catalogues,' he added, pointing to a folder of drawings on his desk.

'They aren't adventurous,' Josie persisted, 'just small adaptations from the original designs.'

'I can't afford to be adventurous. I'll stick to what's safe. I grant that you can run this office better than I can, but leave me something to do to support my claim to run the business!'

Josie laughed. 'Leo, don't be pompous. You have very profitable lines in the gold rings and bracelets, and the sort of things people buy as presents for men when they can't think of anything more original – cigarette boxes or cases and paper knives and watch cases. You're talking of enlarging the factory. What will you make if you do?'

'More of the things I know I can sell.'

'Won't you experiment even a little?' she coaxed.

Leo snorted. 'I don't take risks in business, even if you'd take them for me!' He saw her crestfallen expression and softened his voice. 'All right, then, what do you suggest?'

Josie perked up immediately. 'Are you worried about risks because of the pound's devaluation? Will that affect the price of gold?'

'It may. On the other hand I'll be able to sell more abroad. But what about these ideas for new designs?'

'The trouble is, I know we need changes, but I don't know to what. I'd like to go and see the students at the Jewellery School,' Josie said slowly. 'That's the way to find new talent, spot someone with flair before anyone else snaps him up.'

Josie knew she had offended him with her criticism of his lack of initiative, despite his attempt to show an interest in her ideas. No more was said and Leo was distant and preoccupied all day. As she was about to leave he looked up. 'Is that the time? I hadn't realized it was so late. I've had enough too. Josie, let's get something to eat and talk about your idea for new designs.'

Josie hesitated. Her mother would worry if she were late. Recalling the row the previous evening, Josie shrank from a renewal. Still, she didn't want the role of eternal peacekeeper; she was tired of Dora's tantrums, of pandering to her demands. It couldn't hurt to go out with Leo, could it?

Leo took Josie to a small restaurant in New Street. Over the soup, they talked about her suggestion, as yet very vague, of finding different designs for the jewellery Leo's factory made. Leo listened, but made no promises. He still seemed sceptical about taking risks. 'You're not at all like you were as a boy!' she told him, exasperated. 'From what my mother says you were a real devil-may-care then.'

He grinned. 'I thought you were too small to know.'

'I was, but Mother is still complaining about you sliding down the banister, and down the stairs on a tin tray, and that time you fell through the conservatory roof. She never forgave you for breaking the apple-tree branch with your climbing rope, she swore that branch always had the juiciest apples. Even your father was furious when you stole his motorcycle, and you were only fourteen.'

Leo chuckled. 'Younger than you were when you stole that poor chap's! It was a marvellous day of freedom I couldn't resist.'

'It would have been fun having you as a brother,' Josie said impulsively.

Leo looked at her and for a second Josie saw the bleakness in his eyes. 'My aunt and uncle were very good to me,' he said levelly.

Josie bit her lip. 'But you must have wanted to be with your own father, surely? I often wonder what mine was like, how different things would have been if he hadn't been killed.'

'You can't undo the past,' Leo said curtly. 'My father knew my living with him wouldn't have been possible. He needed a woman – a wife – more than a son.'

There was an uncomfortable silence. 'I'm sorry,' Josie said at last.

Leo forced a smile. 'But I'm grown up now. Taking risks with my business is different. That's serious.'

'You take risks when you're driving,' Josie said.

'Only calculated ones. Risking myself is different from risking my uncle's business.'

'It's your business.'

'I still think of it as his. Don't you behave differently now you're no longer a child?'

Slowly, Josie nodded. 'I suppose so. I used to do mad things, but I daren't any more.' She didn't elaborate. Josie suddenly saw how staid and responsible she was now forced to be. She sighed. She missed those wild days at school when she'd been ready for any mischief, usually the ringleader, uncaring of possible danger or retribution.

Over the main course they shared other childhood reminiscences and Josie enthused about his father's kindness to her. 'He'd have loved to have seen more of you,' she said quietly.

'As I would of him. Sometimes I felt I didn't know him at all.'

'He was so fond of children. He should have had a big family.'

'But I'm glad he had you, Josie, really I am.'

When the sweet arrived Leo asked her to go to the rally with him that weekend, and when she said — regretfully, he thought — that she'd already promised to go with William, he promptly demanded that she keep the following weekend free.

'I know William's teaching you to drive and I want to see how good a teacher he is,' he said as they sipped excellent coffee.

'I could already drive, even though you won't trust me with your car,' Josie reminded him swiftly. 'He's teaching me special techniques. Next year I want to drive in one of the novice classes.'

'William's usually very critical of people he teaches to drive. He's such a perfectionist, and many people just don't care about the workings of the car so long as it gets them where they want to go.'

Josie looked thoughtful. 'Leo, would it be possible for you to make some of the metal car parts? William tells me he sometimes has problems finding just what he wants and has to make them himself. But that can't be efficient.'

Leo looked at her in amused exasperation. 'First new jewellery designs, now car parts! No, I don't want to listen,' he added hastily. 'I work with precious metals. Each workshop specializes, they're too small for great variety. Doing car parts, especially just a few, wouldn't be economic. Introduce me to your plans for my business slowly, if you want to win me over.'

She bit her lip. 'Stick-in-the-mud! But I don't understand enough about cars yet. I changed a wheel by myself last weekend, though. I was very proud of that.'

'I'll ask your help next time I have a problem,' he said with a laugh. 'But as William is to have your company on Sunday, will you come dancing with me on Saturday?'

83

Josie, recalling their last devastating row, had been stiff and shy with him outside the office. She'd relaxed over the meal and the interest in talking with him, but she wasn't sure she wanted to go out with him again. She wouldn't be just one of his girls. 'You didn't approve of the way I danced last time.'

'I can endure it.'

Josie's resolve faltered, and when he added, 'We'll go to the Palais,' she didn't demur.

Josie slid out of the bed, praying her mother would not wake. Dora had been furious when she'd arrived home last night and Josie, uncharacteristically obstructive, responded by refusing to reveal where she had been. 'I have a right to some time on my own,' she said angrily when Dora paused for breath. 'I'm sorry if you were worried but you shouldn't expect me to tell you everything. Lizzie doesn't tell Aunt Phoebe if she wants to go out straight from work and her mother doesn't fuss!'

That had been adding fuel to Dora's wrath. 'I do not conduct myself as my sister does,' she said with a sniff. 'She never had any sense and look what happened to her! Lizzie will end up the same, out till all hours with men who want one thing only. My daughter isn't going to end up in a brothel behind New Street.'

Josie laughed. 'Mother, how do you know where the brothels are?' she asked, but Dora had not been amused.

'I must go to bed,' she sobbed. 'I can't deal with you now but don't think I'll forget your ingratitude, your lack of consideration, your wanton behaviour.'

As she dressed, Josie wondered why she hadn't told Dora she'd been out with Leo, either on the rally, when Dora had assumed she and Lizzie were going with William and Matthew, or this time. Was it because she thought Dora would object, recalling all her grievances about George's son? Josie decided it was more complicated. Her relationship with Leo had undergone a subtle change over their meal last night. Instead of him being her employer, ten years older than she was and far more knowledgeable about the world, or a man driving with a pleasant companion, they had talked as equals. Leo listened to Josie's ideas, even though he didn't agree with her entirely about the best designs for modern fashion.

By the time she reached work she was trying to suppress rather uncomfortable thoughts. Leo was very attractive and could be attentive and charming. Was she in danger of falling in love with him? Did he know this was a risk if they met outside work? Surely he couldn't want that. She had no illusions about her own lack of attraction for men. It didn't need Dora's constant reminders for her to know she had none of the special appeal which drew men irresistibly to some women. William liked her, she knew, but as a companion in the same way that Dick Endersby liked to talk with her. They were just friends who happened to be male and she wasn't in any danger of falling in love with them. Leo was different. As well as being her employer he was now paying her the sort of attention men paid to girls they were attracted to. But it didn't mean anything to him, and Josie knew she must be careful not to read too much into it. Learning to accept the compliments of attentive men was part of the growing up process her mother was always talking about, as was learning to know when they meant more than mere politeness. Leo couldn't possibly mean more than that, and she'd be very foolish to imagine he did. He had an endless supply of attractive girls and a reputation for never being serious, of dropping them if they began to fall in love with him. Josie feared that, if she saw too much of Leo outside work, she might very easily fall hopelessly and disastrously in love with him. That, she decided as she climbed the stairs to the office, was something which would never do and she must guard against it at all costs.

'Josephine, I found my silver,' Dora announced triumphantly. She seemed to have forgotten Josie's recalcitrance the previous night and Josie breathed a sigh of relief.

'The pieces that were missing? Where were they?'

'In the piano. Isn't that odd? They were wrapped up in a sheet of old newspaper, weeks old.'

Josie looked at the crowded display of objects on the piano top. 'How on earth did you find them? Surely you never moved everything off it?'

'I suddenly needed the solace of my music,' Dora said mournfully. 'I had the urge to play some of dear George's favourite tunes. He used to love hearing me play and sing. And it didn't sound right.'

'It hasn't been tuned since we came to live here.'

'Really, Josephine dear, I know you're not at all musical but you might allow that I know the difference between a lack of tuning and something else wrong with my beloved piano. After all, I've had it since I was a girl.'

'And the silver was inside? How did it get there?'

'Are you sure you didn't store it there, absent-mindedly of course?'

'Mother, I would never open the piano, it takes too long to move everything from on top. It's unlikely that I'd slip a parcel of silver in without noticing!'

Josie was feeling slightly hysterical. First she was afraid of falling in love with Leo, then accused of hiding some of her mother's silver in a quite unbelievable place. When a sudden clamour of barking erupted on the landing outside their sitting room it didn't seem at all improbable.

Dora pressed her hands over her ears and groaned. 'That wretched animal! It's been barking all day. What is it doing in the house?'

Phoebe could be heard shouting up the stairs.

'But if I leave 'im outside 'e barks all the time,' Freddy replied, 'an' yer tells me off fer that too! 'E's got a cold an' 'e needs somewhere warmer.'

'I said no dog an' you still brought the brute 'ere! You'll 'ave ter find somewhere else, tomorrow. An' no excuses! If you've found the money to buy the blasted thing yer can pay ter keep 'im somewhere proper!'

Their voices receded, still arguing. Dora groaned. 'He won't do it. I know my sister, I doubt she'll have the strength of mind to insist he takes it away. That boy's always been able to twist her round his little finger.'

'Where did he get the money?' Josie pondered. At one point Dora had been convinced Freddy had taken her silver. Josie thought it highly probable, but the silver having reappeared meant that Freddy couldn't have sold it.

'Some dubious scheme. He says he wins it on the dog-racing but I don't believe him. I shall be so thankful to leave this house, Josephine. It hasn't been at all what I've been used to, but then, with Phoebe shaming the family by letting that man persuade her into a life of sin, you can hardly expect her children to be what one would like.'

'Lizzie is perfectly respectable and Aunt Phoebe is very generous!' Josie protested. 'If she hadn't been left this house by Lizzie's father we'd have been much worse off with nowhere at all to go.'

Dora sniffed. 'We have to endure it. But how could my silver have been put back if you didn't put it there? I certainly didn't hide it in such a stupid place.'

Josie knew this was true. Her mother liked everything on show. 'Freddy might have pawned it, and when he won some money, or because you missed it, tried to put it back secretly. Could he have been in here long enough to move all those things and put them back afterwards?'

'Perhaps, when I've been shopping,' Dora admitted. 'It takes so long to get to town on these wretched trams.'

'Well, they're back now and undamaged, that's the main thing,' Josie said bracingly, and gave silent thanks that this mysterious return of her treasures seemed to have made Dora forget to resume her interrogation of the previous evening.

*

87

'Will you consider the job, Matthew?' Leo asked. They had met in the Jewellers' Club at lunchtime and Leo had taken the opportunity of broaching his idea of a manager.

'I'd half intended to buy shares in something to do with the motor trade,' Matthew said slowly, 'but the money I have really isn't enough for anything worthwhile.'

Leo seized on his indecision. 'I could sell more than I do, especially if I have someone who knows the trade in charge while I'm away on selling trips. I have to go early in the new year if I'm to get good orders for next Christmas. I mean to expand. The place two doors away is on the market. It's already a workshop and I have an option to buy it and the machinery. I would hesitate to go ahead without you, overseeing two factories just when I plan to be away. But I'm sure that the old man who rents the workshop in between will want to move out soon. He's very old and can't manage the work for much longer, and the owner will be glad to let me buy. Then I can rebuild to make one big factory on the site.'

'It sounds exciting.'

'We can separate the work so that the new place is almost self-contained, and I'm sure you can manage if I put you in charge there. Josie is a great help in the office, she'd be able to tell you how I do things. When could you leave your father?'

'He won't like it. I'll stay till Christmas, that's only fair. He has lots of orders to complete, it's his busiest season.'

'Good. Let's toast our future success in business and in rallies!' Leo said as they grinned and raised their glasses to seal the bargain.

Josie had spent two days wondering what to wear to go dancing. She didn't have anything remotely suitable. She didn't want to confide in Lizzie. Her cousin would be full of speculation and Josie didn't feel ready to deal with it. If she could have borrowed a suitable dress from Lizzie she might have brought herself to face it, but she was much larger than Lizzie, so borrowing her clothes was out of the question. She had only the frilly dresses Dora had bought her, which she detested. She contemplated buying a new dress, telling herself that it was almost her birthday, then decided it would be a wanton extravagance.

With a deep sigh, Josie mentally selected the least dreadful of the party dresses Dora had chosen. It was a green silk and went well with her hair, although she hated frills and flounces, but it would have to do. And what did it matter how she looked? She wasn't attempting to ensnare Leo with her charms.

By immense good fortune her mother had been invited to visit a neighbour on Saturday evening. She'd been asked by the local church to help run the Christmas Fayre and the two had met at one of the committee meetings. Mrs Frossdyke was a most refined woman and Dora approved.

'Kowtows to 'er,' Phoebe opined knowledgeably.

Josie didn't care. She'd be able to get ready without her mother demanding to be told all about it.

'I like your dress, the colour suits you,' Leo said.

Josie peered up suspiciously. 'Are you joking?' she demanded? 'It's a terrible dress, I hate all these flounces and bitty pieces.'

He grinned. 'I take it Dora chose it?'

'Of course she did. It's her sort of dress.'

'But now you'll be able to buy your own and be as serious and businesslike as you choose. Next time, perhaps you'll wear one of these very severe suits women put on when they're pretending to be men.'

Josie chuckled. 'To a dance? Give me credit for some sense of occasion.'

She firmly suppressed her instinct to lead when they danced, and her natural sense of balance and rhythm helped.

'I told you it would be easy,' Leo said triumphantly as they completed a daring spin at the end of one waltz. 'Just let me lead.'

Josie laughed up at him. 'I don't offend your sense of male superiority tonight, then?' she retorted.

For a moment Leo's arm tightened about her waist, then he released her. 'Shall we have a drink?' he suggested. Josie's face was hot and she knew her cheeks were flushed. She nodded and Leo tucked her arm into his. 'You'd best stay close to me, I'd lose you in this crush,' he said.

Afterwards as they walked to Leo's car, Josie, who had decided that her old school coat was impossible and she had to do without a wrap, shivered and Leo put his arm round her and pulled her close. 'We'll go somewhere less crowded next time, but you'll have to bring a coat or you'll freeze. I've a couple of rugs in the car.'

By the time he pulled into Freer Road Josie was warm again, snuggled into the two rugs Leo had wrapped tightly round her. They smelt of wool and leather, and the same sort of heathery spiciness Leo himself smelt of. Josie breathed it in, indulging herself. She was reluctant to unwrap herself when the car came to a halt, but knew the enchantment had to end. 'Thank you for a lovely evening,' she said shyly.

'My pleasure. I hope you're not too tired to help William tomorrow. I'll see you there.'

Freddy soon abandoned keeping the Streak in his room. Cold or not, the dog could stay in the shed and he'd get fed up with barking. That was better than constantly shoving the animal off the bed, rescuing shoes and discarded clothes from destructive jaws, and getting up in the middle of the night when the dog's insistent whining made it imperative to let him out into the garden. He was late getting up on Sunday, coming downstairs in time for dinner. Phoebe was taking the roasting tin from the oven and she glanced at Freddy before heaving the leg of mutton on to the carving dish and pouring some fat into a dish standing on the hob.

'Carve this,' she said brusquely. 'Your Aunt Doris isn't well, I'll take hers up when I've fed yer pesky dog.'

Freddy looked up, still bleary-eyed. 'Fed the Streak? What with? I dain't know yer fed 'im.'

'You don't care either if the poor devil starves! I don't want 'im 'ere, but I won't see any creature with ribs sticking through 'is skin! Wicked, I calls it, keepin' a dog so skinny there's no flesh on 'im!'

By the time Freddy had absorbed this she was outside, and when he followed her he was just in time to see the Streak wolfing down the bowlful of bread and bacon rinds, flavoured with mutton fat. 'But 'e's not supposed ter get flesh!' he protested. 'All greyhounds are skinny. They 'as ter be ter race properly. Oh, blimey! Bread's bad fer 'em. Now I'll 'av ter tek 'im out more ter run off the weight.'

Phoebe shrugged. 'Sounds daft ter me. If the poor devil's starvin' 'e won't 'ave the strength ter run. Come in and 'ave yer own dinner before it gets cold.'

Freddy sulkily complied, and even more sulkily went upstairs to fetch his aunt's tray after they'd eaten. When he returned some time later, however, he was smiling, and quite cheerfully went out to exercise the dog. Phoebe, her feet up on a stool in front of the parlour fire and a cup of tea beside her, dozed. She was thankful to be left in peace for a couple of hours. With the girls off at a rally, Doris in bed and Freddy out, she could enjoy her nap in peace.

She was laying the table for tea when Lizzie and Josie returned several hours later. Freddy had come and gone again while she'd been asleep, as the dog's plaintive barking told her. 'Did you win?' she asked the girls.

'Lizzie and Matthew did and we came second,' Josie said cheerfully. 'We'd have won if the car in front hadn't stuck and churned up the mud and made us skid.'

'Excuses!' Lizzie grinned at her. 'Matthew's the better driver, that's all. Who was the girl with Leo?'

'I've never seen her before. Another new one.'

'Take your ma's tea up,' Phoebe said to Josie. 'She's been in bed all day after gallivantin' last night.'

Josie took the tray, expecting to find her mother in bed, but

91

Dora was dressed and sitting by the window. 'Good, you're better,' Josie said. 'I've brought your tea.'

'You're a good daughter,' Dora purred and Josie looked at her in astonishment. 'I wonder if you had this in mind all the time? You're a sly puss!'

'What do you mean?' Josie demanded suspiciously. It was most unlike her mother to praise her.

Dora laughed. 'You needn't pretend to be so innocent with me, my love! I know who took you out last night. And was so attentive he didn't look at any other girl. It's probably not as good as Dick Endersby, but he's so young, his parents might object. This way we don't have those problems and you needn't wait. I think a spring wedding, or Easter perhaps, would be perfect.'

'I don't know what you're talking about,' Josie insisted, by turns flushing and going quite pale.

'Oh, my dear, you needn't be coy. Freddy was at the Palais last night and he told me all about you and Leo Bradley. It's not the ideal match, not the son-in-law I'd have chosen, but we don't have much choice. Anyway, it's rather neat, don't you think?'

Chapter Six

Dora looked guiltily at the bags and hatboxes piled inside the taxi. She hadn't meant to buy so much, but she was so tired of black and grey and violet. She craved the delicate pastels which suited her so well and she knew George wouldn't have minded. He had no right to object, she remembered, not after the way he'd left them practically destitute. It was almost Christmas, and now dear Josephine was about to make such a good match she needed to dress well. She'd give her a lovely engagement party. It was time they had some enjoyment. They'd meet important people from her world again. Her father's family had been landowners. Phoebe had once said they were yeoman farmers but that didn't sound right, they could not have been less than gentry. She had missed her best chances when her parents died before being able to bring her out, but Joseph Shaw had been respectable, the son of a solicitor from Warwick, and he'd been so handsome, so much in love with her. In retrospect it was perhaps a pity she had quarrelled with his parents when she married George. She had no idea whether they were still alive. Arthur, though, had married beneath him, taken in by the daughter of a tenant farmer from the very village where her father had been rector. And Phoebe had disgraced them all when she ran off to live openly with that married man from Small Heath.

She slipped into a happy dream about the advantages of

Josephine's marriage. Would she prefer to live with them, or would it be better to have her own little house with a house-keeper and perhaps a companion? She might buy a car. George would never teach her, saying she was too precious for him to risk her having an accident, but it looked quite easy and everyone had them nowadays.

The reception must be at the Grand hotel, and the wedding in St Philip's Cathedral. The guests could walk to the hotel in procession, rather as she remembered village weddings when the daughters of the squire had been married and everyone had crossed the village green to the big Queen Anne house. She must write to the bishop straight away and ask him, for her dear papa's sake, to perform the ceremony.

Josephine must purchase a proper trousseau. As Leo already had a house there presumably wouldn't be any necessity to buy bed linen and tablecloths, but Josephine's clothes were a disgrace. She would enjoy the challenge of kitting out her awkward daughter. Josephine would never be as pretty and dainty as her mother – the Dresden shepherdess, George had called her – but she must have clothes suitable to her standing as the daughter of one rich man and the wife of another. Fashions were for plain garments now and although Dora disliked them, finding them ugly and unappealing, she had to admit they would suit Josephine better than feminine gowns.

By the time she had carried all her new clothes up to her rooms Dora was weary. She threw out most of her mourning clothes to make room in the wardrobe. The ghastly blacks and grey could go to the church, Mrs Frossdyke said they always needed them for the poor. She was too tired even to go and make herself a cup of tea. With a sigh of contentment Dora loosened her corsets and lay down to rest.

'The poor brute's ill!' Phoebe declared. 'It was just lyin' there when I came 'ome, not even interested in a bone.'

'Yer've probably bin givin' it bread again.'

'It's lack of food, not the wrong sort.'

She stalked away and Freddy glanced worriedly after her, then back at the dog which lay panting shallowly. As Freddy crouched down the animal made a feeble attempt to lick his hand. Was it hot? Freddy had a vague notion that you could tell what was wrong with a dog by the temperature of its nose, but he couldn't remember whether it should be hot or cold, wet or dry, and what to do if it wasn't normal.

He mooched down the path, hands in his trouser pockets. For two pins he'd give up the idea of owning a champion greyhound. Freddy was stubborn, however, he wasn't going to be beaten. He'd get the Streak better somehow and prove to all the scoffers that the dog was as he claimed. Sid would know what to do.

Sid was pessimistic. 'Grey'ounds is like thoroughbred 'orses – temp'ramental. They don't like bein' in 'orrible sheds all day. Feelin's they've got.'

'Come an' see 'im, Sid,' Freddy asked urgently. 'You'll know what's wrong an' what ter do.'

'OK, on me way ter the boozer. Yer'll be there?'

Freddy nodded. The bargain was clear and he heaved a deep sigh. Sid had a huge capacity for doubles whiskies. He'd have to unearth the rest of his hoard from behind the loose panel of the wardrobe, and he hoped it would be sufficient. He'd stick to beer, make a pint last, and trust none of his cronies wanted him to stand a round.

Sid was even gloomier after examining the dog. 'Needs a vet,' he pronounced. 'Summat's stuck in 'is guts. Seen 'em like that afore, an' more often than not they're gone within days. Shame, 'e was a good 'un.'

'Could a vet do anythin'?' Freddy asked urgently.

'Mebee, mebee not. 'Ave ter ask one.'

'Who? Ain't there one near the stadium?'

'Get yersen an 'andcart an' wheel the poor beggar down to 'is place fust thing termorrer. Cost yer, though.'

Freddy shuddered as he anticipated the vet's fees. He would

need to keep the dog under observation, and possibly operate if medication didn't cure the problem.

'Some dogs keep having the same thing,' the vet informed Freddy cheerfully the following morning. 'No good for racing if they do. I'll send my bill weekly.'

Freddy regretted not giving a false name and address but he'd been too concerned at the lack of interest the Streak showed towards cats and horses and other normal stimulants. The dog hadn't even objected to being lifted into a wheelbarrow Wilf had borrowed from somebody's garden shed and being wheeled ignominiously along the streets. Freddy didn't know where he'd get more cash. He didn't want to try the same again but he might have to. He'd go to Hall Green stadium this time. He couldn't face Birchfield; he knew too many people there, both behind and in front of the Tote windows.

Josie spent her free time reading about jewellery and looking at designs in the shops. She visited the Jewellery School and talked to the teachers, asking to see the best work. She began to despair of finding the right designs.

'The trouble is I don't know what I'm looking for,' she said to Leo. 'I only know I'll recognize it when I see it.'

He smiled but was too preoccupied with the Christmas business, his plans for expansion and his selling trip to the continent in the new year to worry about an unnecessary quest. He wasn't too busy to ask Josie out again, and took her to dine and dance at the Grand.

Dora blandly ignored Josie's protests that Leo had not proposed and would not, that these outings were to discuss business matters away from the distractions of the office. Knowing how impossible it was to convince her mother of unpalatable facts, Josie did her best to ignore Dora's hints and questions about when the engagement was to be announced, and utterly refused to go on shopping expeditions.

'We can't afford new clothes,' she insisted. 'I know you needed that new blue dress and hat now you're out of mourning, but I don't need anything and we have only my wages to manage on.'

Dora shrugged this aside. They would be wealthy soon, but she did wish Josephine wouldn't keep her in suspense. She'd had some impertinent letters from tradespeople demanding payment of their bills. George had dealt with all that. She was reluctant to tell her daughter quite how many new clothes she'd bought. It was fortunate the child no longer used the wardrobe but had put hooks on the door for her own clothes. The bills must wait.

Josie visited the Jewellery School again during her lunch break. One of the teachers met her by the door. 'Miss Shaw! I hoped to see you soon. Come and meet one of my students. He's been ill, poor fellow, and away for more than a month, but he might have the sort of designs you want. I'd forgotten the new projects he'd been working on.'

Tobias Mackenzie was a tall, emaciated man older than Josie expected. In his mid-thirties, he had a pale face, sunken brown eyes, and receding hair already largely grey. He had a pronounced stoop, and as they talked he seemed unable to control an irritating cough. 'Sorry,' he wheezed. 'I was gassed on the Somme. I'm like this after every bout. In and out of hospitals for years. Sometimes I think I'll never finish my training.'

As he produced drawings and samples of his jewellery Josie's eyes gleamed. This was exactly what she'd dreamed of, known existed somewhere. So absorbed did she become that she was an hour late getting back to the office.

Dora was sure Leo would propose before Christmas. It would be so suitable. She tried on her new clothes, trying to decide what to wear for the engagement party. The deep pink, the colour George liked so much, which she'd been wearing when he gave her the sapphires. She frowned. She couldn't possibly go to parties without her jewels. With sudden energy she removed the pink dress and found a soft woollen one in dark blue. She must go into town.

'Are you quite sure?' the bank manager asked. 'It's an extremely valuable set to keep at home.'

'I'll look after them,' Dora reassured him cheerfully. 'I need them for my daughter's engagement party.'

'Miss Josephine getting married? I am pleased. She's a sensible girl, a credit to you. Who's the lucky man?'

Dora looked coy. 'Oh, dear, I shouldn't have said, it's not official yet. But he's not short of a few pounds.'

'Give her my best wishes, and buy a lockable box to keep the sapphires in.'

Dora nodded impatiently, but when she left the bank she turned towards Corporation Street. She would just look round Rackham's to see if they had any pretty jewellery boxes. There was a very tempting array of carved boxes, beautifully lined with silk and velvet, with so many partitions that for a moment Dora was cast into a wave of despondency by recalling how few she would need.

'I have this sort,' she told the saleslady haughtily. 'I wanted a special box to keep one set separately. No, these are too small, too flat. Look, I have the jewels with me. Show me something suitable for these.' Eventually she was satisfied with a rosewood box. The lid was inlaid with a delicate abstract pattern of ivory and onyx, ebony and mother-of-pearl, and the box lined with black velvet which showed the sapphires to perfection. There was a mirror inside the lid surrounded by beautifully matched seed pearls, and a tiny gold key which came complete with a gold chain so that she could keep it safely on her all the time if she wished. 'I'll carry the set inside the box,' Dora said. 'How much is it? No I don't want to see something less expensive, thank you. Put it on my account.'

'I hate having to take you home,' Matthew said sleepily, pulling Lizzie back on to the bed.

'You don't think I enjoy it either, do you?' she retorted,

tickling him remorselessly in the spot she'd discovered was most sensitive.

'Stop it, woman!' He grabbed her hands and another tussle ended with them breathless, limbs entwined, once more aroused to passion.

'I must go or Ma will be asking too many questions. And I'll be late for work again if I don't get to bed soon.'

'You've been in bed for the past two hours.'

Lizzie giggled. 'Not a restful two hours.' At first it had been embarrassing to dress and undress in front of Matthew's appreciative gaze, but she had soon lost her shyness when she saw how gradual revelation of her body excited him. He'd persuaded her to disrobe slowly, watching and occasionally coming to help, though Lizzie protested he was a hindrance if his sole objective was to undress her. It wasn't, he'd said, and she'd begun to find an equal delight in tantalizing him by deliberate procrastination. Tonight he seemed preoccupied, and when she was dressed she asked what was bothering him.

He shrugged on his jacket. 'I hate this,' he said.

'Soon we'll be married,' Lizzie said softly.

'Lizzie.'

She looked at him, her eyebrows raised. 'What, my darling?'

'We can't go on like this. I want to stay with you all night, wake up in the morning with you beside me.'

'We will soon,' she tried to reassure him.

'Lizzie, it could be ages. I don't want to bother my father, he's having a difficult time, and besides, Leo's asked me to be his manager. It's the wrong time for a wedding. I need you, Lizzie. Darling, move into this flat, then I could stay with you every night.'

Lizzie went white. 'What did you say?' she demanded.

'Come and live here. I already pay the rent. You can keep yourself ready for me in our own little hideaway.'

'And when do we get married?' she demanded harshly. She read the answer in his embarrassed, guilty look and berated herself for a fool. She should have known Matthew would never marry the bastard daughter of a woman who'd lived openly with her lover. 'You never did intend that, did you?' she added furiously. He'd expected her to behave like her mother, equally shamelessly. Suddenly, Lizzie discovered that whatever she'd felt for Matthew it wasn't what her mother and father must have felt for each other.

'Lizzie, be reasonable. I never said we would.'

'You implied it. You let me think that was what you meant,' she said with a cold anger. 'You gave me a ring and promised me a better one later. Wasn't that saying it?'

'No, I said I wanted us to be together. I'd love to marry you if things were different but it just isn't possible now. We could be together, though.'

'You want to turn me into a whore!'

'I wouldn't have thought a girl from your background would be so particular!' he snapped. 'Why isn't what was good enough for your mother good enough for you?'

'Leave my mother out of this. At least she could trust my father. I'll never again believe you, Matthew Horobin!'

'Hoity toity! If you walk out of here, Lizzie Preece, you'll find yourself out of a job too.'

'I won't,' Lizzie retorted. 'Try to sack me, Matthew, and your father will know all about your love nest. How many other girls have you deceived with hints of weddings?'

She stalked from the room, seized her hat and gloves, grabbed her jacket and ran from the house. She was too angry to cry, too shattered by the end of her dreams. One day, she vowed, Matthew would regret his treatment of her, his deception, his assumption that, because her mother hadn't married, she was a woman who didn't deserve respect.

'He's brilliant, Leo, so original. We ought to have him before he's well known,' Josie insisted.

'But you say he's still suffering from the gassing in the war. He'd be a liability.'

'He might have to take time off, but don't we all owe something to men who lost their health fighting for us? When I see the poor devils without legs, I sometimes feel that men like my father who died were fortunate. And even if he only spends a quarter of his time working, what he does is so marvellous his designs will be instant successes.'

Leo smiled at her vehemence. He wasn't eager to experiment, but it would not cost a great deal to employ this man. Some of his designs might be suitable if they were not too outrageously modern. 'If you think he's worth it you can have him. But isn't he still a student?'

'I want you to appreciate him, not give way to me as a favour,' Josie said swiftly. That attitude was too like George's way of humouring Dora. 'He's done most of the course and he can go back and do anything he's missed. The staff at the Jewellery School suggested that. And he has money of his own, his father was wealthy, made a fortune in steel or shipbuilding or something during the war. That's how Tobias became interested in metals, seeing them used for lots of different things. Will you see him, see his designs? They're plain metal, not set with stones, so your workshops could make them without any need for new machines or extra skills that might involve employing diamond cutters or whatever.'

'Tell him to come here tomorrow, after the factory closes. Afterwards, will you have dinner with me?'

It was a week to Christmas and Dora was becoming increasingly concerned. Josephine was being so irritating! She was out a good deal in the evenings as well as going to those ridiculous motoring events, coming home soaked to the skin and covered in horrid dirty mud. Dora knew that she went with Leo, but twice she'd gone with William Scott.

'You musn't play fast and loose,' she warned. 'Men like to think they come first. You could lose him.'

'I haven't got Leo to lose,' Josie insisted. 'You're reading far too much into a simple friendship. We work together, have business to discuss, we enjoy rallying and Leo often needs a passenger. That's all.'

Occasionally Dora wondered whether it was true, and the fear of it sent her to bed. She couldn't bear it if her dreams came to nothing. Not that Leo was the ideal son-in-law, but he had wealth that should by rights have been hers, and no other man seemed remotely interested in Josephine. She didn't count William Scott, he'd never asked Josephine out for dinner, and Dick Endersby was really too young.

She was huddled in the armchair when Freddy, being unusually helpful in the hope of persuading his mother to lend him the money for the vet's account, carried up his aunt's dinner. As he opened the door Dora gave a gasp of alarm and hastily concealed something behind the cushion.

'I didn't hear you knock,' she said breathlessly.

'Dain't yer?' he asked casually. 'Must 'ave bin deep in thought. 'Ere's yer dinner. I'll put it on the table. Let me 'elp yer get up, Aunty.' Before she could protest he was assisting her out of the chair. To her dismay the cushion slipped forward and the rosewood box lay revealed, partially open and with one of the earrings protruding.

'Sit 'ere,' Freddy said cheerfully. Then he picked up the armchair cushion and threw it back without even looking.

Perhaps he hadn't seen the box. Surely he couldn't have refrained from commenting if he had. Not Freddy. She knew him too well, and if he suspected she had such valuable jewels he would be trying to borrow money. She knew all about the dog and the vet's charges for treating it. The silence without its barking had been welcome, and if Freddy did ask her for money she wouldn't help restore that noise.

''Ope yer feels better soon,' Freddy said, and was gone. He couldn't have seen the box, or hadn't appreciated its significance. But to make sure, Dora locked it and hid it in the bottom of the wardrobe, under several shoeboxes. As she grimaced at the cold mutton and the gravy congealing on the plate she began to fret once more. In Josephine's place she would have made quite certain by now that a man like Leo was firmly and irrevocably attached. They wouldn't be engaged before Christmas, and would be missing a great many parties. It really was too bad of Josephine.

Leo sat back and watched in amusement. He was impressed with the man's knowledge of jewellery, but had given up trying to keep Tobias to the subject. Once started, his fierce enthusiasm took over and he talked rapidly, despite his intermittent cough, widely and discursively, but always with something interesting to say. At the moment he was happily instructing Josie, who had admitted her total ignorance of fashion history, illustrating his lecture with rapid sketches to demonstrate his points.

'Jewels follow fashion, and fashion is dictated by the leaders of society as much as by designers. In Victoria's time everything was solemn and serious, jewels were heavy and ornate, but when King Edward and Queen Alexandra reigned, society began looking for pleasure. Everything was rich and extravagant, delicate and pretty too. Combined with new techniques and new materials like platinum people could have intricate, flexible designs and so-called invisible mounts. That made different settings very popular, especially for diamonds. But most jewellery contained precious stones. After the war things changed again, people wanted bright colours, something obviously cheerful, decoration everywhere for the sake of it, not because it was needed.'

'The art deco,' Josie managed to interpolate.

'Exactly. All those bright primary colours which you can get with enamels and semi-precious stones. And people were wary of demonstrating too much wealth with real precious stones when so many men were out of work.'

'The shapes were different, too,' Josie suggested.

Tobias was getting really carried away, his speech so rapid

the words tumbled over one another. 'That's the influence of painting, the cubists, and Egyptian motifs, after they found the treasures of Tutankhamun's tomb. They'd used enamels, too. And both Liberty and the Arts and Crafts people encouraged enamel; it's cheap and more people can afford it. At first it was overdone — you got all kinds of garish designs both with enamel and quite unsuitable combinations of stones and materials all jumbled together. I want to simplify and soften the lines, to suggest movement instead of it being static. Movement, speed, is in tune with life today. Look at the attempts to drive cars and aeroplanes faster and faster, and breed dogs and horses that will break previous records. Everybody, men and machines and animals, wants to go faster. The sort of jewellery I have in mind can be done best with simple shapes in metals and some of the newer materials like plastics and paste. And it can be cheap so that ordinary people can afford it. They can have real pieces, not imitations, and be fashionable.'

He looked up from where, with a few pencil strokes, he had produced the outline of a galloping horse. It was stylistic, but so vital Leo almost expected it to race across the table. Tobias grinned disarmingly. 'I'm sorry, when I start to talk I never seem able to stop.'

'Could the machines I have and the people who work here adapt to producing your designs?' Leo asked quietly.

'Some of them. The metal ones. You don't do enamelling and you haven't the facilities for plastic, which I want to try soon. But I could design plenty to keep a much bigger workshop busy. These designs will sell too.'

'Josie says you have your own money. Why don't you set up a workshop yourself?' Leo challenged him.

'I might, one day, but I can't be bothered with the business detail. I have to become known first, and I've lost so many years through illness. When I'm well known and people want to work for me I'll employ a manager and then I'll be able to experiment.'

'When can you start here? Though I warn you I'm not turning over all my capacity to new designs. I have to keep the standard products available, but I'm buying another building and we could use some of that space for making your designs. What salary do you expect?'

Tobias shrugged. 'Whatever you think proper. I want the chance to get known commercially. If you'll give me a start I'll be grateful, not greedy. I'll start after Christmas if that's convenient for you.'

Two days later, Josie was walking home when a small motorcycle drew up alongside. The rider leapt off and grinned delightedly at her. 'I came to show you my Christmas present, the parents thought I'd better have it early to make the most use of it during the holidays.'

'Dick! I hadn't realized you'd be home yet. Time's flown, I'm so busy I haven't thought how soon Christmas is.'

'This term's seemed endless. I won't ask you to ride with me yet, I'm still learning, but will you come to a cocktail party with me on Wednesday? It's at home, mainly for the relatives who are here for Christmas and friends my parents are entertaining, but they want me to ask a few young people too. I've asked Alan and Emily Gough.'

Josie was touched. She'd like to see her schoolfriends again too. 'I'd love to come.'

'I'll call for you in a taxi. Gosh, it'll be good to talk to you again. I must go, more invitations to deliver. Dad knows how to get the most out of his investments. He only gave me the bike so that I could do his errands.'

With a flourish he set off, wobbling slightly on the cobbles, and Josie looked after him in amusement. Then she began to wonder what she could wear. She'd swallowed her pride and worn the green dress at the public dances Leo had taken her to, and usually they went out for dinner straight from work. She had, feeling guilty, bought another blouse which was less severe and of better-quality material than her others, and wore it when she knew she and Leo would be going out, but none of these would do for Dick's cocktail party.

Dora was at Mrs Frossdyke's, Phoebe told her with a grunt of disapproval. 'Gettin' close as Siamese twins,' Phoebe sniffed. 'It'll last so long as she's willin' ter listen ter Doris boastin' about when she was rich!'

Josie was thankful her mother had found companionship. She began to look at the rest of her hated unworn clothes and see whether anything was suitable for the Endersby house. She opened the wardrobe. Her party dresses were right at the back, but the wardrobe was full of clothes she'd never seen before. Dresses, frilly and impractical, brightly coloured and lavishly adorned, jostled for space. A few at the front were in the dark colours Dora had worn for mourning. Hatboxes teetered on the shelf above and the floor was covered in piles of shoeboxes.

Aghast, Josie investigated. The first boxes she opened contained frivolous coloured sandals, presumably to match the dresses, a pair of silver evening shoes and another of gold, and then, as her anger at Dora's unbridled extravagance grew, she pulled out a box stuffed with bills from, it seemed, every expensive dressmaker and fashionable milliner in Birmingham. A glance confirmed Josie's fear that none of these bills had been paid, and the letters screwed up on the top showed that her mother was being threatened with legal action.

Another box caught her eye, a wooden box pushed behind the others. Slowly Josie turned the key and the gleaming necklace and earrings spilled out on top of the pile of bills. Josie put her head on her arms and tried to still the furious trembling in her entire body, but couldn't suppress the sobs that threatened to overwhelm her.

Chapter Seven

'WE have to sell the sapphires!' Josie faced her mother across the table. She had regained her composure before Dora returned home, but she was still coldly angry.

'I can't! There must be some money somewhere. You look after it all now.' Dora's tone was accusing.

'There isn't! Mother, how could you spend so much money on quite unnecessary clothes? You've already frittered away a small fortune that Papa George meant you to save for an emergency.'

'Savings?' Dora asked. 'What savings?'

Josie looked at her tiredly. 'The account he opened, he put money into it every month, he told me it was money his creditors couldn't get, and enough for you to live on. He wasn't expecting to lose his money, but he knew some scheme might tempt him. He wanted a nest egg for you.'

'That was my allowance,' Dora said indignantly.

'He gave you a very generous allowance, Mother.'

'Not after he lost his money.' Dora was resentful. 'He never understood how much good clothes cost. I had to dip into it. And I had so many other expenses.'

'You must sell the sapphires. Or I'll sell them. If I trusted you you'd see some diamonds you preferred and forget we need to pay these debts!'

'Don't be so angry with me, darling. Frowning makes you so ugly. When you marry Leo we can pay all the bills and be comfortable,' Dora said placatingly.

'I am not going to marry Leo! How often do I have to tell you?' Josie demanded furiously. 'Why don't you ever listen to me? Apart from the fact that he hasn't asked me, I won't marry to get you out of unnecessary debts!'

'I bought the clothes so that I'd do justice to your engagement,' Dora said with a sob. 'I did it for you!'

Josie ground her teeth together. 'It would serve you right if I left you to find your own way out of the mess,' she threatened. 'I can pay for a room and keep myself, and I'd be much better off without you creating problems.'

'Josephine, you can't!' Dora was appalled. 'Darling, you can't leave me. What would I do? You're all I have left.' She began to cry in real earnest. 'I couldn't possibly live on my own, you know I couldn't!'

'Don't worry, Mother,' Josie said wearily. It was an empty threat. She could not desert so helpless a creature and condemn her own mother, however irritating, to life alone. 'But we can't pay these bills except by selling the sapphires. Maybe when I've added up what you owe, we can keep some of the pieces. If we do they must go straight in the bank, and you must let me close all these accounts and promise not to open any more.'

Dora, frightened at the thought of Josie leaving her, nodded eagerly. 'I'm sorry, darling,' she said humbly. 'I never was any good with money; George always looked after me and said I wasn't to bother my head with it.'

'George could afford it, and when he couldn't any more he escaped the problem,' Josie retorted.

'I'll give piano lessons, I'll earn money. I will try to be sensible,' Dora promised meekly, and began to plan the advertisements she would insert in the local papers.

For the rest of the evening Josie sorted bills and added up the total. It was worse than she'd feared and her nerves were fretted to breaking point as Dora kept up a continuous commentary alternating between the ruin of all her hopes because of what she described as Leo's perfidy, and her plans to solve all their difficulties by giving piano lessons. 'I might even find a really talented pupil,' Dora said, the familiar dreamy smile on her face.

'Oh, Mother, let me concentrate!' Josie pleaded at last. 'Leo has behaved perfectly properly, it was you reading too much into a few innocent invitations. And you won't earn much yet, not enough to pay these bills.'

'If he meant nothing it was a great waste of time your going out with him so often when you could have been keeping me company!' Dora snapped. 'And I'm doing my best to help. I'm going to talk to Phoebe.'

As Dora never willingly sought Phoebe's society this was an indication of how deeply she felt, but whether it was remorse or indignation Josie neither knew nor cared. She was thankful to be left alone with the bills. She would have been less sanguine had she known Dora was pouring out her grievances to the interested Phoebe and Freddy.

'I think it's a shame,' Freddy said. 'Why shouldn't yer 'ave pretty things? Still, if yer 'as ter sell 'em yer could come in with me an' share me winnin's on the dog.'

'If the dog's ever fit enough to race,' Phoebe scoffed.

'I won't help you get that wretched animal back!' Dora retorted. 'How can you plague me when I'm in such trouble?'

'If yer wants ter keep the jewels, sell some of yer silver an' such,' Freddy suggested.

Dora looked at him in surprise. 'I never thought of that! Josephine insisted it must be the sapphires. But I still mean to earn money! I'll teach every waking hour, truly I will. I prefer children, I never liked them when they got bigger, but I'll have to take older pupils, even adults, since children will be at school all day.'

'Sellin' summat's easier,' Freddy said. 'Would yer like ter see what price I can get fer yer?'

About to refuse the offer indignantly, Dora paused. She did mean to earn money, but beneath the bravado she was far from confident. If her plans failed, and her unnatural daughter closed all her accounts and gave her a mere few shillings a week for her own spending, how on earth would she manage? She'd soon be dressed in rags. But Josephine would never miss the occasional piece of silver or one of the ornaments she complained about dusting. She didn't know whether she could trust Freddy, but she'd keep it in mind if things got too unbearably grim in the future.

By January, Josie was feeling more optimistic. She'd discovered to her relief that the sapphires were so valuable the sale of just one brooch covered her mother's debts. She'd taken Dora to the bank to put the rest of them back, but had remained outside when her mother had complained at the indignity of being shepherded in by her own daughter as though Josie didn't trust her. At Dick's party she had met several of his relations, and they had all been friendly, especially his Uncle Johnny, who owned a motor factory in Coventry and to whom she'd promised an introduction to William Scott when they visited Coventry during a forthcoming rally.

Christmas had been quiet, as they were all subdued and Lizzie had been feeling ill. Dora, making a big effort, had organized a party for New Year's Eve and invited one or two of her old friends, saying that it was a year and a half since George had died, and 1932 must be a better year for them all. Best of all, so far as Josie was concerned, Tobias was proving invaluable.

He was producing designs faster than Leo, busy organizing his enlarged factory, could look at them. 'Not yet,' he said abruptly whenever Tobias, drawings in hand, appeared in the office or beside him in the workshops. He had to show Matthew everything, make sure he and Josie could cope while he was away, and finalize the arrangements with the buyers he was visiting in France and Germany and Italy.

'You'll have to let him get a few designs made,' Josie protested after Tobias had complained to her. 'If you don't, he'll go to someone more appreciative.'

'Very well, choose a dozen you like best, but keep the numbers produced to a low level until we see how they sell.'

'Why must I choose them?'

'It was your idea.'

'Don't you like them?' Josie demanded.

'Yes, more than I expected, but I'm too busy to spend time selecting from designs which all look equally good. I depend on you to know which will be popular with women.'

When she looked dubious he capitulated. 'Let's have dinner tonight. Bring the drawings and we'll choose some together.'

'Have you time to eat?' she asked with a grin.

He hadn't yet found the time or the courage to give her the locket he'd chosen so carefully as a Christmas present. Christmas had been lonely without her. For a time he'd even wondered whether he was falling in love with Josie, then dismissed the idea. At twenty he'd thought himself in love with the sister of a varsity friend, but after swearing eternal devotion she'd married a baronet many years older. Since then he'd never considered marriage, and his amorous adventures were conducted with women who expected no more from him but a good time. If any of his female acquaintances showed signs of wanting more than this he gently dismissed them. Perhaps his obsession with Josie was because she was the opposite of possessive, and he felt piqued.

He'd give her the locket, nevertheless. When he did so, just before they left the factory, to his immense astonishment Josie couldn't hold back her tears. 'Here, I meant to please you,' he said, and as she raised tear-drenched eyes to his he stepped forwards and drew her into a comforting embrace. 'What is it?' he asked gently.

Josie's momentary weakness was over and she pulled herself free of his arms. 'I'm sorry, it's stupid of me. Mother's been rather difficult lately. When she's trying to be good and earn money it's almost as painful as when she squanders it. And her pupils play excruciatingly!'

'Things can't be that bad, surely? You can't have very high expenses living with your aunt.'

Josie wondered ruefully whether he ever noticed that she still had only the one skirt, and her shoes were patched.

'We manage,' she said stiffly. 'It's just that it was so kind and unexpected of you to give me such a lovely present. Where are the drawings?' She busied herself, looking through the papers on his desk. 'Here they are, in this folder. Hadn't we better go?'

'Are you coming to the Coventry rally next Sunday? I'm going to introduce William to Dick's Uncle Johnny. It's been ages since you and Matthew have been to a rally. Or are you still not feeling well?' Josie asked Lizzie the following Monday morning. Phoebe was outside feeding the Streak, retrieved from the vet just before Christmas. Freddy was still in bed.

Lizzie shook her head miserably. 'I suppose I ought to tell you. We're finished,' she admitted.

'Lizzie? Why on earth . . .? Oh, I'm so sorry!'

'Don't be. He was a snake, a cheat, wanting to set me up in a flat and visit me when he chose. He never intended to marry me, though he made me think he did. Just because my parents never married he thought I'd have no morals. Oh Josie, I wish I was dead!'

Josie gathered the sobbing girl into her arms and rocked her gently. At least her own troubles didn't include faithless lovers, she thought grimly, wishing she had Matthew there and could tell him what she thought of him. Then she paused. He was her manager now and she dared not risk losing her job. He would be able to sack her while Leo was away if she offended him. Girls like Lizzie were so vulnerable when they attracted men who had power over them. 'Hush, your mother's coming back. Does she know?'

Lizzie shook her head. 'No, and I don't want her to. Not yet. I must go. She musn't know I've been crying.'

Dora, shocked by the sale of her precious brooch, had been thinking hard. Leo was procrastinating. In her day, if a man had shown the same attentions to a girl as Leo had to Josephine, they would have been betrothed long ago. Her male relatives would have seen to that! George would not have permitted his son to play fast and loose with a respectable girl. Who might show Leo what was due from him? Freddy was her only male relative now, but Dora instantly dismissed the idea of enlisting his aid. She sighed. There was nothing for it but to approach Leo herself.

Deciding not to warn him of her visit, she set off half an hour before Josephine normally reached home. She wore one of her new dresses, but after much deliberation decided against wearing the sapphires, apart from one tasteful ring. She didn't want Josie to discover that she hadn't been able to bear parting with them, and had not deposited them in the bank. Her fur coat was impressive enough, and although she could not afford a taxi, Leo would surely drive her back home. By the time she reached Leo's house she was throughly out of temper. After two short rides on tram and bus, where the conductor had been abusive because she proffered a ten-shilling note for a twopenny fare, and then an exhausting walk down a wide road lined with the sort of affluent houses Dora longed for, she was in no mood for Leo's excuses. She pulled the bell viciously and hammered with the knocker. She would insist he did his duty!

Leo opened the door before Dora's temper could cool. He'd just arrived home and had been standing in the hall reading his letters when her assault on the door had startled him. 'This is a surprise. What brings you here?'

'If you invite me inside I will tell you,' Dora snapped, and without waiting swept past him.

Leo ushered her into his drawing room, was solicitous in

taking her coat and settling her in a comfortable chair, then offering sherry. Dora grew calmer. He was a gentleman, he would see her point of view.

'How can I help you?' Leo asked, sitting facing her.

'Josephine,' Dora pronounced.

'Josie? Is she ill? She was at work. What is it?'

'She is not ill, though it's surprising she hasn't gone into a decline with the worry.'

'I don't understand.'

Dora sighed. He was being obtuse, like most men. She would need to explain carefully. 'Leo, this is very embarrassing for me. If Josephine's dear father had been spared, or George, the task would not have fallen to me. I have to ask you what your intentions are.'

'My intentions?' Leo sounded amused.

'Towards my daughter! When a young man pays a girl such particular attentions, inviting her to restaurants and balls, and taking her driving alone in his car, it normally signifies that he has a special interest in her. I came to ask when you intend to do the honourable thing towards Josephine and announce your betrothal.'

'But we are not betrothed,' he said, suppressing his amusement.

'Then you should be!' Dora snapped. 'You have singled her out so that other young men, honourable ones at any rate, do not approach her, and raised expectations which anyone with integrity would fulfil.'

Leo began to get angry. 'Now look, Josie works for me, we have had the occasional meal together to discuss business matters, and she has been a delightful companion on a few drives. That does not commit us to any closer relationship.'

'When I was a girl it did,' Dora sniffed. 'We knew the proper way to behave.'

'As you behaved properly to me when you married my father.'

'You were jealous.'

'I was an inconvenience to you, and you made sure my father saw very little of me. He was so besotted with you he virtually disowned me.'

'You always were a horrid, rude boy.'

'I didn't pander to you like my father did. And now, if you will excuse me, I have work to do. I leave in two days. Good night!'

Dora, finding herself once more outside the front door, rang the bell and plied the knocker unavailingly, and eventually turned away. She would never permit Josephine to marry anyone so rude, so lost to all sense of propriety.

William won in Coventry, and afterwards Josie introduced him to Johnny Smith, Dick's uncle.

'That was a great climb!' Johnny enthused. 'I've seen you a few times before. You're pretty good.'

'Do you drive in events?' William asked.

'No, my interest's in building cars,' Johnny said. 'If you've time, would you like to come and see my workshop?'

William agreed enthusiastically.

'It's really too small,' Johnny said deprecatingly when they'd driven to the area just out of the city centre where Johnny lived with his wife and two children. 'I've expanded as far as I can into the back here, I'll have to find new premises soon.'

He showed them round, and he and William were soon deep in technical discussion. Josie found that, listening hard, she could understand about a tenth of the conversation, but she was intrigued to see how many different parts Johnny was producing.

'I'm doing mainly the short runs, for when they do limited numbers of special models,' Johnny explained. 'I haven't the capital or the space for doing the numbers they want on the popular marques.'

'It's probably more profitable this way,' William said.

'I buy in, too, things like this,' Johnny said. 'It's new, I'm trying it out, but I'm often able to sell on with my contacts.'

He was pointing to a radiator grille, and William gave a start and stepped hastily forward. 'Can I have a closer look?' he asked sharply.

Johnny drew out the grille. It was slightly curved, and had a second grille, of very thin metal and slightly offset, behind the main part.

'Where did you get this?' William asked.

'I'm not too sure. My foreman found it, somewhere in Birmingham, I think he said.'

'Would you mind asking him where?'

'I can look up the invoice.'

'What's the matter?' Josie asked when Johnny had vanished into his small office at the end of the workshop.

'It's identical to one I'm developing,' William said curtly. 'Don't tell him yet.'

Johnny came back. 'I haven't heard of them before, it must be some new firm he discovered. In Hockley. Place called Bradley's.'

'Bradley's!' Josie exclaimed.

'Do you know them?'

'We know them,' William intervened. 'But Leo. It's unthinkable. He wouldn't steal my designs.'

'Of course he wouldn't!' Josie insisted.

'But he must be making them if Mr Smith's buying from him.'

'If he is it's surely a coincidence about the design.' Josie was thinking hard.

William turned to the older man. 'Mr Smith, I'll have to tell you and trust you'll keep this quiet for the moment. I'm making a grille exactly the same as this one in my factory. And Miss Shaw here works for Leo Bradley. Josie, is he making these?'

Josie was flabbergasted. 'He must be — what other explanation is there? When I suggested he made car parts he said he wasn't equipped to do them, it was a different business. But he seems to have allowed Matthew to persuade him!' she added angrily. 'Just because a man suggests it!'

'But you must have seen invoices.'

'No. I expect they're being made in the new part of the factory. Matthew is in control there, and they're doing different things. His secretary does invoices for them and I don't see them.'

Johnny and William agreed they would both investigate how Matthew could have duplicated William's design, and meet in a week's time to compare notes.

Josie silently determined that if the opportunity arose she would search Matthew's office for some evidence. If the design had been stolen it must be Matthew's doing. 'Matthew's a slimy snake!' she said angrily. 'First he's tricking Lizzie, now you.'

'Lizzie?' William asked, diverted from his own problem. 'How do you mean?'

'Don't tell anyone, please,' Josie begged. 'I shouldn't have said anything, but I know I can trust you. He wanted her to move into a flat and live with him. He implied they'd get married, but then said he couldn't offend his father. He told her it was all she could expect, being who she is. He's rotten all through!'

'Poor Lizzie. She's well out of it. I've always had some doubts about Matthew. But how can he be doing these grilles the same as mine? He must be getting the designs from my factory, but how? I wonder if Leo knows where they come from?'

'Surely not,' Josie said swiftly, then paused. Perhaps she didn't know Leo as well as she thought she did.

Freddy was once more without his motorbike. It wasn't fair, he grumbled to Mabel, that he should always be unlucky and buy dud parts that lasted a week then fell to bits.

'If yer didn't buy 'em from crooks maybe they wouldn't,' she retorted, and Freddy, disillusioned by this lack of sympathy, stalked off in a huff. Just because she'd lost her job she didn't have to be mad at him. Something had to be done.

He was in Hockley, moodily surveying the Bradley factory, when his attention was caught by the sound of giggling behind him. Suspicious, he swung round and spotted a pair of urchins dodge down into the well of a small two-seater car parked on the opposite side of the road.

'What you lot doin' in there?' he demanded.

'Jus' playin',' the bigger one, all of seven years old, said sulkily.

'Motors ain't the place fer that,' Freddy said sternly. A moment later the car began to roll forward. Freddy leapt towards it and flung himself over the side of the driver's door. He collided with two terrified children struggling to escape, but he managed to haul on the handbrake and at the same time catch firm hold of the smallest boy's flapping shirt-tail. Righting himself he came face to face with Matthew Horobin, who had seen the children playing in his car and run out from the factory to stop them. By the time Matthew had vented his rage on them they were in floods of tears, and even Freddy felt sorry for them.

'They dain't do no damage,' he said placatingly.

Matthew grinned, rather shamefaced at his loss of temper. 'I suppose not, but only because you grabbed the brake. I'm very grateful. Let me buy you a drink.'

By the time they had imbibed a couple of whiskies each at the Rose Villa, overlooking the Chamberlain Clock at the heart of the jewellery quarter, Freddy had agreed to work for Matthew for a couple of hours each week, washing and polishing his car and making sure the tyre pressures and fluid levels were maintained. Matthew had also suggested that when he went horseracing Freddy might accompany him to keep an eye on the car. Freddy began to ponder on the opportunities this would give him to repair his fortune. He needed to keep in with Matthew, and for the time being his only chance of gaining some cash was through honest toil, and maybe he could put this to practical use, since Matthew worked at the Bradley factory. He'd even be able to put in a word for Mabel.

If Leo had not already departed on his selling trip, Josie would have confronted him with William's allegations. As it was, she was thankful to find she rarely saw Matthew. He came into the office each morning to weigh out the gold and silver needed that day and deal with any queries she had, and in the evening to sign the letters she'd typed and weigh in the worked gold and silver and make sure the safe was locked. Otherwise, he seemed to spend all his time in the workshop, talking to the employees or helping mend machines that went wrong, or out of the factory on some business he didn't specify.

His frequent absences gave Josie the opportunity to search his office one day, when his secretary was also away. She'd hoped to have at least an hour, but after ten minutes Matthew returned and Josie, hearing his voice on the stairs, slammed shut the drawer she'd been looking in and moved swiftly away from the desk.

'What are you doing here?' Matthew demanded suspiciously.

'I wanted to check the figure in this letter,' she said breathlessly, handing him the letter she'd armed herself with, 'but your secretary isn't here. I'd forgotten.'

Josie tried to push her suspicions away. Leo must prove his innocence when he returned. At other times Matthew's absences caused complications. Josie received a telephone call from an irate supplier of the boxes they packed gift items in. 'Which of them do you want?' the man demanded. 'If you don't give an order today I'll have to let the supply I'm holding go to others.'

'I'll let you know in half an hour,' Josie promised. Matthew was nowhere in the factory, so she took the samples from his desk and selected one. It was a new design, more expensive than the previous one, but would show their goods to greater advantage. They would need more than before to pack Tobias's designs too, so Josie made the decision and telephoned an order.

On another occasion, he forgot an appointment with an official from the Assay Office. Luckily, Josie had talked about hallmarks with Leo and was able to keep the official happy.

The worst was when two girls came saying Matthew had promised them jobs as polishers. 'Today, it was, 'e said ter be 'ere,' they insisted.

'But that job was filled last week. We do have one for a press operator, though, if one of you is interested,' Josie explained.

'I can do that,' the older girl claimed.

'Me too.'

Josie sympathized with their disappointment. She knew how difficult she'd found it looking for a job. 'Look, I'll talk to you both, separately, take details of your experience, and perhaps Mr Horobin will be back by then.'

He wasn't, but Josie had decided that if she had the choice, she'd take the younger, though less-experienced, girl. The other was too pert, inclined to be cheeky, and would eventually cause trouble. When she demanded to know if she'd got the job Josie said that regretfully she hadn't. Then she called back the younger one and told her to come on the following morning, so long as she understood that Mr Horobin would have to confirm the decision.

Matthew was angry when she told him what she'd done, but, in the face of her undeniable accusation that he was hardly ever there, had no choice other than to allow the girl to start. Josie felt he was deliberately avoiding her, and when she thought how he'd treated Lizzie she didn't blame him. He must know Lizzie would have confided in her. She began to feel lonely in the office where she and Leo and Bert had worked harmoniously together, and when Tobias asked her if she minded him setting up his drawing board there she welcomed him.

'I thought you had an office in the new building?'

'I do, but Mr Horobin's never there, he's always in the

workshop. Besides, I wanted someone to keep me supplied with tea, I'm hopeless at making it myself.'

She laughed, but enjoyed his company and the chance to talk over problems with him. She found his comments sensible and his suggestions wise, better than Matthew's in many cases. She also learned a great deal about the design and manufacture of jewellery, for Tobias knew all the processes from having worked in numerous factories before concentrating on design and becoming a student.

'You have to move round to learn,' he explained one day. 'One firm will employ you to do one process – wire drawing, or milling, or chasing, or engraving – but they won't train you on others so you have to move on to learn them.'

The designs she and Leo had selected were being made and Josie suggested that Tobias, who was fretting at not being allowed to introduce others, ought to be the person to show them to the retail jewellers in the city.

'Why don't you spend the day taking them round, then if the orders are good, and they'll be better with your enthusiasm than if any salesman takes them round, Leo will authorize making up more designs when he gets back.'

'I'm not a salesman!' Tobias protested. 'If I'd wanted to traipse round the pavements all the time I wouldn't have spent years learning this business.'

'You won't have to do it often,' Josie told him. 'Once they've seen your designs they'll be clamouring for more.'

Tobias was not modest. 'That makes sense,' he agreed, and Josie awaited the results of his first foray with some trepidation. It was a great success. The orders had been lavish, for Josie had provided him with photographs of the latest fashions to show alongside the jewels. The retailers had been swift to see the way in which the bold but light shapes enhanced the plain lines of the clothes, and orders flowed in so that some of the workers had to be switched to the production of the new lines. Tobias was waiting with scant patience for Leo's return so that he could start production of new designs. Josie was also awaiting his return with impatience, though she wouldn't admit to herself quite how much she missed him.

Long before Leo was due home, though, Josie had other worries. She arrived home one day to find Dora in floods of tears. Seriously alarmed at her mother's hysterical state, Josie tried to persuade her to let her call a doctor.

'Doctor? It isn't a doctor I want. I want the police!' Dora wept.

'Police? What on earth for?'

'The sapphires! My necklace! Freddy's stolen them!'

'But they're in the bank,' Josie said, bewildered. 'You put them there yourself, I went with you.'

As Dora burst into even wilder sobs Josie went cold. She'd let Dora go into the bank alone. Could her mother have been so stupid as to keep the sapphires in their rooms? Eventually Dora calmed down enough to tell her she had indeed only pretended to deposit the jewellery in the bank.

'I'd had them with me so little, worn them so few times,' she sobbed. 'I used to wear the pieces when you were at work to remind me of happier days. They were mine! And if you'd been cleverer about Leo Bradley we'd have had plenty of money. It must have been Freddy, he knew I had them, he saw them before I took them to the bank and he must have known I didn't,' she finished obscurely.

'I can't believe Freddy would steal something so valuable from you,' Josie said. 'Have you asked him?'

'He'd just laugh at me. But it's got to be Freddy, he found the money to pay the vet's fees for that wretched dog and build that new kennel in the garden.'

'That was before Christmas. I expect he had a lucky bet, and from what you say you've been wearing them since.'

'Well, maybe he pawned them and then put them back,' Dora attempted. 'Like he did the silver.'

'That doesn't make sense,' Josie told her, but this opposition made Dora more determined.

'I know it was Freddy and I'm fetching the police to search his room!'

Chapter Eight

SHORT of physically barring Dora's way, Josie could not prevent her mother's angry progress to the police station. All the time Josie argued vigorously that her mother ought to speak to Freddy first.

'Why should I let him hide them? It would give him warning and he'd sneak them out of the house – if he hasn't already sold them.'

'He might not have taken them. You have no proof. Ask Aunt Phoebe to search his room,' Josie said desperately, shuddering at the thought of her aunt's reaction to such a request. But it would be better than calling in the police for what she was convinced was a mistake. 'Have you really searched everywhere in our rooms?' she tried.

'Of course not! I know where they were!'

'But is it possible that you hid them for safety and forgot? Remember the silver turned up in a very odd place.'

'So now you're accusing me of hiding that, are you?'

'Of course not, Mother. But we never found out how it got into the piano. Come home and sleep on it, and decide what to do in the morning.'

'And Freddy will have sold my sapphires and they'll be gone for ever. George's present, I've had to see most of them sold, and now you'd let the others go just for the want of a little courage to face unpleasant facts.'

Josie sighed. 'We only sold a brooch. The necklace, clips, hair ornaments, earrings and rings are still there.'

'But they're not!' Dora said triumphantly.

'No, they're not, but I expect they'll turn up like the silver did,' Josie said wearily.

When they were in the police station Josie stood back, determined that her mother should conduct these proceedings. In less than two minutes, however, the sergeant on the desk was giving her pleading looks. 'Can you explain, miss?' he asked eventually. 'What is it the lady's complaining about? Is it jewels or silver or a dog that's been stolen?'

Josie wanted to get this over with as quickly as possible. She was horribly embarrassed, certain that Dora's accusations would prove to be wrong. 'My mother believes my cousin, who lives in the same house, has stolen her jewels. Once some silver was lost, but it was found again. My cousin doesn't have a job and he's often needing money for a greyhound pup he owns.'

'Do you think he stole these sapphires?'

'I don't think he would have,' Josie said quietly and shut her eyes as Dora, growing shriller as she became more agitated, furiously demanded to be told what had happened to her treasures if Freddy hadn't taken them.

'He's a nasty, untrustworthy boy and so I've always told Phoebe, but then what can you expect with a mother no better than she should be and a father who was mixed up with guns all the time!' Dora cried, breaking into loud sobs.

'Guns?' the sergeant asked, puzzled, but with a stirring of greater interest.

'His father was a gunsmith,' Josie intervened, seeing the policeman's imagination flying out of control.

'Oh, I see. At least, I think I do.'

'What's this to do with getting my jewellery back?' Dora demanded, hiccuping and sobbing so that her words were almost indistinguishable. 'I insist the police come and search Freddy's room! I shall write to Mr Chamberlain! I shall write to the Home Secretary!'

'Mr Chamberlain's the Chancellor of the Exchequer, ma'am,' the sergeant unwisely interposed.

Dora seemed not to have heard him. 'I shall write to the Prime Minister. Oh no, not that common Ramsay MacDonald! Why did we have to have a National government? Josephine, what shall I do?' she wailed, suddenly turning to cling to her daughter.

'I suggest you go home, ma'am, and I'll come myself and see this young man, and perhaps we'll find it's all – perhaps we'll sort it out,' the sergeant said soothingly.

Freddy was with Sid in a pub in Birchfield. 'The Streak's better,' he reported, 'but 'e don't do a thing I tells 'im.'

Sid guffawed. 'P'raps 'e's a French dog and can't understand English,' he said.

'But yer said 'e were born 'ere in Brum,' Freddy protested. ''Ow come 'e don't foller what I says?'

When Sid had recovered from his bout of laughing and a rather huffy Freddy been pacified with another pint of beer, Sid explained. 'Yer can't race 'im till next year, when 'e's two. There's nothin' ter do till 'e's at least a year old 'cept feed 'im an' give 'im lotsa walkin'.'

'An' all the time 'e's costin' a mint of money!'

'Well, yer knew 'e would,' Sid was unsympathetic. 'If yow ay' got no cash I might be able ter get yer a few hours walkin' some of the dogs at the stadium. Yer could tek the Streak wi' them, an' earn a few bob as well.'

The thought of walking for miles with half a dozen greyhounds all striving to chase different cats or horses or bicycles or children was not pleasant, but it was better than the terror which attacked him when he was working his ruse at the Tote. He wasn't going to try that again. And his more profitable schemes needed time and care to mature. The few hours he worked for Matthew didn't bring much cash, although he had plenty of opportunities to drive the car. Freddy shrugged. 'It all 'elps. Ta, Sid. You'm a pal.'

'Talkin' of pals, where's Wilf?'

Freddy gulped. He was trying to forget Wilf and his activities. 'The silly twerp's gone ter track at 'All Green,' he said reluctantly. Wilf had found a sure way of making his fortune despite Freddy's warnings that he couldn't play the same trick too often in the same place. He'd been scornful, saying Freddy was yellow when Freddy refused to go with him. Freddy had borne these strictures on his manhood only by the greatest effort of self-control, but they rankled.

'Cheer up,' Sid encouraged him. 'Yer'll mek yer fortune one day, lettin' the Streak do all the work!' He chortled. 'Wonder what it'd be like if they 'ad the same sort of breedin' system fer women? Fancy givin' it ter whatever gal they shoved in a pen with yer?'

Fortunately, Aunt Phoebe was visiting a friend and Lizzie had gone to see Ann, so the house was empty when they returned. Josie led the way up to their sitting room and persuaded a still-distraught Dora to sit down.

'Why don't you search his room?' she demanded petulantly of the sergeant.

'I can't do that until I've seen the young man,' he replied placatingly. 'Now, tell me again, now I've seen the house perhaps I can understand it better. You rent this room and another from your sister?'

'Yes, but what's that to do with it?' Dora fumed.

'Do you have keys and lock the rooms?'

'Phoebe won't give me any though I've asked her over and over again. It's her fault we've been robbed. If I'd been able to lock the rooms everything would have been safe. My silver wouldn't have been stolen either.'

'You said the silver was found. Where was it?'

'Inside the piano,' Josie told him.

He blinked at the array of ornaments. 'By gum, anyone

shiftin' that lot had a job and a half! Why should you think this young man Freddy would take your jewels?'

'He's always desperate for money for his wretched dog, and he stole the silver to sell.'

'Yes, but he didn't,' Josie pointed out.

'It's more than that,' Dora went on, ignoring this problem. 'After he stole the silver, Freddy had a lot of new clothes. Where did he get the money for them?'

'He goes to the dog-racing,' the sergeant mused. 'Could he have won money there?'

Dora sniffed. 'That's what he always says. It's a good excuse.'

'Who else knew you had the jewels?'

'No one.'

'Did you, miss?'

Josie looked embarrassed. 'I thought my mother had taken them back to the bank,' she said.

The sergeant didn't press for details. 'Where did you keep them?' he asked Dora. 'I'd like to see.' After some reluctance she was persuaded to show him where she had hidden the jewellery box in the bottom of the wardrobe.

'I don't like a strange man in my bedroom,' she said, in a loud aside to Josie, then addressed the sergeant. 'He was too cunning to take the box even though that's valuable too. He thought I might not miss the sapphires if the box was still there. I bought it specially to fit them, and such a task I had choosing one just the right size, where they could be laid out properly, not all jumbled up.'

'When did you buy the box? It looks quite new.'

'When I fetched them out of the bank the bank manager said I ought to lock them away.'

The policeman looked at the key in the lock. 'Where did you keep the key?'

'Well, with the box in case I lost it. There was a chain to wear round my neck but it was uncomfortable.'

'Even without the key the box wouldn't have hindered a burglar. Where did you buy it?'

'In Rackham's. What has that to do with it?'

'And you had the jewels with you? You tried them in the box there, to see if they fitted?'

'Of course. It wouldn't have been worth paying that much for a box which was too small,' Dora said indignantly.

'So anyone could have seen the sapphires?'

'But it wasn't someone there who stole my silver and my sapphires,' Dora was almost weeping with frustration.

'I'm afraid it might have been. Now, ma'am, don't take on so! There isn't any proof your nephew stole the jewels, and if he's at the dogs he won't be home for some time. I'll have a chat with him tomorrow. Then we'll see.'

'Won't you search his room?' Dora was aghast.

'I can't do that without a warrant, or his permission. We'll see how it is tomorrow.'

He escaped before Dora fully recovered from her stupefaction, and it was Josie who had to try and calm her as she fell into one of her worst bouts of hysterics. Josie was thoroughly alarmed, but unable to leave Dora for long enough to summon a doctor. Gradually Dora's sobs subsided, and to Josie's guilty relief her mother soon began to complain she had one of her headaches and retreated to bed.

Josie, who'd had no lunch, was hungry. She felt that after such an excess of drama she ought not to be, but she was. She went to forage for bread and cheese and afterwards sat in the big armchair in front of the kitchen range. She'd wait for her aunt and tell her what had happened. Perhaps Aunt Phoebe could suggest something. The policeman hadn't believed Dora's suspicions, but could someone from outside, who might have seen Dora displaying the jewels in the store and followed her home, have burgled the house without anyone knowing? It wasn't likely, but Josie, worn out from dealing with Dora's tantrums, soon gave up puzzling about it and fell fast asleep. She didn't hear Aunt Phoebe come home, and seeing how weary she looked Phoebe crept out again. When she heard Dora calling feebly from her bedroom she went upstairs to see what her sister wanted.

Leo had little time for relaxation as he did the rounds of his customers in Paris, Berlin, Geneva and the Riviera. The orders he achieved were gratifying, proving that the Bradley products were maintaining their reputation, even increasing it. He found several new customers and had to extend his stay in order to see them. It was only during the nights, when despite his tiredness he couldn't sleep, or on train journeys, when the work he tried to do failed to hold his attention, that his thoughts drifted back to Birmingham.

He wondered how Matthew was coping with the new work-shop being fitted out for extra production. Josie would help him, and by now she was so efficient she could almost run that side of the business by herself. He was selling so much of the old designs he worried whether branching out into Tobias's new and innovative ones was, after all, a good idea. Josie was enthusiastic and would be disappointed if he didn't go ahead. He missed having her to talk to, to discuss problems with. For instance, one customer had suggested he ought to try selling to South America.

'They are wealthy and they're flamboyant, they like lots of gold ornamentation,' Monsieur Marchand said.

'You think it worth my going there? I have no contacts and little idea of where to find any.' Leo was dubious.

'We see many of them in Nice, they have plenty of money for gambling at Monte Carlo. By the way, will you be here for the Rally next week? I could introduce you to a few of the wealthy Brazilians and Argentinians then, if you are.'

It was tempting. Leo had been eager to get home, but this was an opportunity to extend his business contacts and see something of the most famous rally in the world. 'I'm going to Italy next, but I could come back,' he said.

He was back in Monte Carlo in time to witness the competitors, weary and muddy, drive down the hill and beneath the triumphal arch.

'This is the first time all the Athens competitors have got through,' Emile Marchand commented as they dined at the Metropole. 'The smaller cars had a slower average, but I wonder how they will fare in the final competition?'

'What sort of test is it?' Leo asked.

'It is a slow first hundred metres in top gear, then as fast as possible for another hundred, then stop within forty. Only one year and they abandon the acceleration and braking tests!'

'I wonder if Donald Healey will win again?'

'The man's a marvel, did you know he drove all the way from Norway, after hitting a telegraph pole there, with the back axle out of alignment? It must have been like a crab!'

'His Invicta is a wonderful car.'

As they left the hotel and walked down the long driveway Leo saw one of the rally teams busy changing the wheels on their car. On the following day he heard that other teams had changed their axle ratios, in order to improve their performance in the final test.

'Donald Healey has borrowed some wheels,' Emile told him.

Healey didn't win, however. He was beaten by Vasselle in a Hotchkiss, who covered the first hundred yards at a speed of one and a half miles an hour.

'It is crazy!' Emile commented.

Leo began to think how much he would like to watch the Rally in Josie's company. He missed her, he discovered, not just as a colleague with whom he worked successfully and harmoniously, but as a companion. She was fun to be with, undemanding, unlike so many girls he took out, and yet despite her calm efficiency she was, in an odd indefinable way, exciting too. He couldn't decide why this should be. She was beautiful, but in an uncommon way, and she certainly didn't give any impression she was aware of it. Frustrated, he tried to sleep, but the images of Josie, quietly competent in the office, vivid when angry, worried about her steps when he'd taken her dancing, eager and insistent when talking about her protégé, windblown and laughing in the open air when they were on rallies, kept him from sleep for a long time.

'Oh, it's you. Where's Josephine?' Dora asked fretfully, lying back on her pillows.

'Poor lass is asleep in the kitchen. She's worn out, doin' a job and lookin' after you,' Phoebe said bluntly. 'You could do a sight more to 'elp, our Doris, if yer stirred yourself a bit.'

'I do what I can when I'm well. I'm giving piano lessons even when I'm feeling ill. No one knows how much I suffer. Where's Freddy?' she asked suddenly, remembering what had happened and sitting up in bed.

Phoebe shrugged. ''Ow should I know?'

'Spending my money!' Dora began to cry helplessly. 'I always knew he was a villain. First the silver then my sapphires. But the police will discover the truth.'

Phoebe's loud demands to be told what the blazes this was all about woke Josie. Startled out of an uncomfortable doze she stretched her cramped legs and eased her neck. Hearing Aunt Phoebe, clearly in a furious temper, she grimaced ruefully. So much for telling the story first. She went wearily upstairs. Dora was sitting upright in bed, more colour in her cheeks than Josie had seen for a long time. Phoebe was standing at the foot of it, arms akimbo, facing Dora. In between her aunt's exclamations of fury and disbelief she tried to explain what had happened.

Phoebe was incandescent with rage. ''Ow the devil can 'e 'ave robbed yer? My Freddy's no thief! 'E might do a favour for a friend, like 'e does with the bets for old Dan Todd, but 'e'd never do anything criminal! You want ter watch your tongue, our Doris, or it'll get you into trouble one of these days.'

As Phoebe grew angrier Dora, calm and secure in her self-righteousness, looked at her sister pityingly, a superior smile on her face. 'It's what comes of immoral living,' she said smugly. 'When you went off with Alfred Warley we all said no good would come of it.'

'You leave my Alfred alone!' Phoebe said furiously. 'At least 'e treated me decent, even though 'e couldn't marry me. Left me a good 'ouse an' means ter keep it, which is more than either of your precious husbands did fer you! I'll not put up with you insulting 'im. Or Freddy.'

'You have to face facts,' Dora said mildly. 'You wouldn't have it that Freddy had stolen my silver but I expect he pawned it. He probably stole the cash from someone else to get it out of pawn.'

Phoebe turned to Josie. 'She's lost 'er marbles, and so 'ave you, my girl, to let 'er be accusin' poor Freddy of stealing. I won't 'ave it, see? I know my Freddy's far from perfect but 'e's not a thief. I'll not forget! The two of you've slandered 'im, that's what you've done, and there's punishments fer wicked folk like you!'

'It's no slander if it's true,' Dora put in excitedly.

'It's not true, but I can tell you one thing, our Doris, neither of you will stay in my 'ouse if you believe my son's a thief,' Phoebe declared, her eyes flashing. 'You'll be out of 'ere by this time tomorrow, lock, stock and barrel, and I don't want ter see either of you again until Freddy and me gets an apology!'

She almost pushed Josie out of the way as she stormed out of the bedroom. Dora, her cheeks flushed even more hotly, sank back against the pillows and Josie sat down suddenly on the chair by the door.

'I've never been so insulted,' Dora gasped. 'My own sister, too. It just shows what sort of a woman she is.'

Josie took a deep breath. She should have anticipated this new calamity. It was almost more than she could bear. Despondently, she tried to plan what would be necessary. 'I'll soon find somewhere for us tomorrow,' she said slowly.

'I won't stay another day in this house!' Dora declared heatedly. 'I shall be quite pleased to leave. I wish it wasn't too late to go tonight, but it's rather a difficult time to go to an hotel, even if I weren't feeling so exhausted. We'll go first thing in the morning!'

'I'll look tomorrow. Perhaps we can rent rooms in Hockley. It would be closer to work for me.'

'Hockley? Are you mad? I wouldn't live in such an area if you paid me,' Dora said, wrinkling up her nose in disgust. 'You'll have to find somewhere better than that.'

'We can't afford anywhere better, Mother. There's no money left, only a pound or so I've managed to save.'

'Don't be such a pessimist, my dear. Of course we will find somewhere far better than these two miserable rooms.'

Josie left the house early. Dora, exhausted, was still asleep. Tobias was already in the office and Josie explained briefly she couldn't come to work for a few days, and asked him to tell Matthew. He agreed, and to her relief showed no curiosity. She set out to find somewhere to live.

It was a bitterly cold day and Josie hugged her inadequate coat round her. The fog, thick and filthy, filled the streets, and several times Josie lost her way as she tried to follow directions along unfamiliar roads. Once she became marooned in the middle of a crossroads, and the faint sounds of a horse and cart came to her, disembodied and echoing from the invisible buildings. Fortunately she found tramlines beneath her feet and was able to follow them until a yellow gleam of light from a shop window enabled her to regain the pavement and discover where she was.

She lost count of the number of doors she knocked on. As she'd thought, the rent Phoebe charged them was far lower than for similar rooms elsewhere. They had only her wages now, and the few shillings Dora earned, and nothing at all to spare. Should she try to make do with one room only or try in a less-respectable district? One room, with her and her mother unable to have any privacy, would be impossible. She'd look elsewhere, to save as much as she possibly could.

The rents were still high, and as she had little hope of curtailing Dora's extravagance for long, they would soon be in trouble without some savings. Gradually she worked her way from the neat little houses of Aston and Lozells, through Hockley where people preferred to rent their spare rooms to workmen in the jewellery trade, into the far less salubrious areas of Duddeston and Nechells, where she eventually found two upstairs rooms available at a modest rent in a tiny, far from clean, back-to-back house close to the gasworks.

The landlady, a widow crippled with arthritis, apologized that the rooms hadn't been cleaned properly since her previous tenants left a month earlier. 'I can't climb stairs wi' me legs the way they are,' she wheezed. 'Can yow goo up an' see 'em by yerself?'

Josie went cautiously up the steep, narrow stairs, with no natural light apart from a glimmer escaping through the ill-fitting door at the top. The rooms were much smaller than those they occupied now, the walls whitewashed a long time ago, the bare floorboards warped and shrunken, and two of the panes in the grimy windows badly cracked. No doubt in winter the wind would howl through the badly fitting frames, but there was one reasonable-sized fireplace in the larger room, and the smaller room which led out of it also had a tiny fireplace, so they could at least keep warm.

She wouldn't stay there long, Josie determined as she went downstairs. It was the only place available that she could afford, but when she could find somewhere better they'd move. It was dreadful, she'd never been inside such an appalling house. It was poorly built, filthy, contained a miasma of unpleasant smells, amongst which she detected soot, gas, stale cabbage, onions, unwashed bodies and worse. The single stinking privy across the yard was shared by half a dozen families, as was a broken-down wash-house. Both had sagging roofs which Josie suspected leaked copiously in wet weather. All water for washing and cooking must be carried in from a pump in the court and heated on the fire, for which, of course, coal would also have to be carried upstairs. The entire house was, she was certain, the home of countless vermin. She shuddered when she thought of Dora's reaction. Then she hardened her heart. Dora had brought this on them by her silliness and her intemperate outbursts against Freddy which had antagonized his mother. Phoebe normally had little good to say of her son, but Josie understood that mother love might well triumph over an accusation that her offspring was a thief.

'I'll take the rooms, Mrs Sheehan,' she said abruptly. 'May I come in and do some cleaning tomorrow? I'm not sure when we'll be able to move in, probably the following day.'

Mrs Sheehan's rheumy eyes gleamed. 'A month's rent down, an' I can sell yer some coal, got some in me cellar. Yer'll 'av ter get it up, mind.'

Josie had no idea what was a fair price for a bucket of coal, but after a little haggling they agreed a sum which Josie insisted she would pay when she fetched each bucket. She wanted no arguments about how much they had had. Mrs Sheehan also seemed about to take offence at Josie's request for a rent book. When the landlady saw that her redoubtable new lodger would not be fobbed off she reluctantly promised to obtain one. Josie, however, produced paper and a pencil and proceeded to draw up a list detailing the amounts agreed.

After she had been persuaded to make her mark (plaintively explaining that she hadn't had the good fortune to be sent to fancy schools, like some she could name, and had never had the time to learn to read or write, she'd always had to work hard to scratch a living), Mrs Sheehan sought to detain Josie with offers of a cup of tea. Knowing that their comfort would to some extent depend on her goodwill, Josie reluctantly agreed. She was pleasantly surprised to be served in cups which, although slightly chipped, were real china. The tea was fragrant, the milk fresh, and the slice of home-made fruit cake delicious. She complimented Mrs Sheehan on her cooking.

'Got a good oven in this range,' she said, nodding with satisfaction. 'I were trainin' ter be cook at a real posh place when I met Mr Sheehan, God bless 'is soul. 'Ead coachman, 'e were. You can use it, if yer likes. I believe in eatin' well, whatever else I goos without. Not like the pair 'ere before. Fish an' chips was all they 'ad, an' pies an' faggots. 'Er never even boiled a kettle, they was allus down at public. Went ter prison, 'e did,' she explained lugubriously. 'Fightin' over 'is woman. Not that it did 'im any good, 'er soon scarpered, leavin' ev'rythin'. Not that it were much, mind. Just a mattress an' a coupla chairs. I think 'er found another feller. Tried ter bring one back 'ere once, the dirty slut, but I told 'er I wasn't 'avin' none of that 'ere. Yow looks a decent young party, no trouble like that wi' yow!'

'Why are you working in here instead of your own office? And where's Josie?' Matthew demanded curtly as he came in and began to weigh out the gold.

Tobias looked up at him. 'She called in, she can't come for a few days,' he replied, ignoring the first query.

'A few days!' Matthew exploded. 'I suppose she thinks that when Leo's not here she can do as she likes.'

'She looked very worried,' Tobias said mildly.

'She's worried! What about me? I have to run this place with all the problems involved and I've got enough problems – I can't manage here too when some snooty little secretary takes the day off without a word to me.'

'She did want to see you but you weren't here,' Tobias replied, his own anger showing. 'Josie isn't the sort to leave us in the lurch without very good cause.'

'You know her well?' Matthew sneered. 'Is that why you've moved all your stuff into here? It gives you opportunities for a little bit on the side?'

Contemptuously, Tobias glanced at the glass screen through which the factory floor could be seen. 'I don't think that remark was called for. I suggest you apologize – to Josie if not to me.'

Matthew looked astounded. 'Come on, it was a joke! Wouldn't all men try, closeted with a pretty girl all day?'

'Some men without scruples might,' Tobias said, his distaste and his implication obvious.

For a moment Matthew glared at him, then he swung back to replace the spare gold in the safe. 'Send her to me as soon as she deigns to show her face again. In the meantime, Mackenzie, I wanted a word with you about those new drawings. They're impossible. Won't do at all.'

'Do you mean the ones Leo approved?' Tobias asked softly. 'He gave me authority to set up production.'

'I meant those you're working on,' Matthew snapped, gesturing to the drawing board and the litter of sketches on the desk. 'I wasn't consulted about the designs Leo accepted, though I'll have a say in future, if we must have newfangled designs at all – and I'm not convinced about that! There are more profitable things we could be producing.'

'These are just ideas. I never offer Leo unfinished designs. And I believe Leo owns this business and controls all aspects of it, including my work.'

'We'll see about that!' Matthew snapped, his face flushed, and stalked out of the room. Tobias sighed. Leo seemed to have made a mistake appointing Matthew as manager. After a few minutes of staring into space he smiled, tore off the sheet he'd been working on, and began to draw rapidly. Within seconds the outlines of two snarling cats emerged, and forgetting Matthew's bad temper he spent the morning calculating how the two clips could be joined together to produce a brooch.

In Freer Road, Josie was met by a tearful Dora lingering on the stairs and a smirking Freddy lounging in the hall.

'I thought you'd left me!' Dora exclaimed, and burst into wild sobbing.

'Afraid after what she said about me,' Freddy said.

'Of course I wouldn't leave you, Mother.'

'I wouldn't blame you if you did,' Dora sobbed. 'I'm just a poor sick woman and I depend on you, and you're only a child! I wanted such a lot for you! Oh, George, why did you leave me!'

Josie, patting her back, turned to Aunt Phoebe who was standing looking on scornfully. 'Please, can we stay just another few days?' she asked. 'I've found some rooms but it's far too late to go there today, and I have to clean them and find someone to move our furniture.'

'Me pal Wilf's dad's got an 'orse and cart,' Freddy offered with a grin.

Josie almost broke her vow not to be provoked into anger. She bit her lip so hard it began to bleed. 'Aunt Phoebe?' she asked quietly.

'OK, till end of week, so long as yer doesn't say another word against Freddy,' Phoebe said at last, and with a flounce went back into the kitchen and shut the door. Freddy bowed ironically and ran up the stairs.

'When Streak o' Lightnin's made me fortune you'll regret this,' he called back to them, and Josie, her arms round her mother, felt Dora shiver.

'Let's go to bed,' she said gently. She assisted Dora into bed, then undressed and lay down herself. She hadn't eaten all day but she would not descend into the kitchen in search of food. She was bone weary and would face the rest of her problems in the morning.

Before she could start cleaning the rooms, she had a message asking her to go to the police station and give them a fuller description of the stolen jewellery. 'Then if anyone tries to sell or pawn it we'll have a lead.'

Maybe one day they'd get the jewellery back, but Josie thought there was little chance of that. The thief would break up the pieces and sell the stones separately. In an area where jewellery was made this would be easy.

It took several days of unremitting hard work to make the new rooms habitable, but by Thursday evening Josie had scrubbed every surface, including the stairs, and laid down copious quantities of popular pest-killers. They didn't banish the lingering smells but they overlaid some of them, and the vigorous application of carbolic soap disguised others. Josie had done all she could. She had set her mother to work packing the ornaments, and, rather to her surprise, Dora made no complaint.

'Doesn't trust anyone else not to break them,' Lizzie said as she and Josie left the house on Thursday morning – Lizzie to her job, Josie to her scrubbing. Lizzie had been horrified to find her cousin and aunt effectively homeless. She had pleaded with her mother but Phoebe had been adamant. No one should report her Freddy to the police and get away with it. Lizzie had then attacked Freddy, demanding to know the truth. Freddy, at first defensive but then bolstered by his mother's unexpected and unwavering support, denied any knowledge of Dora's silver or her jewels. 'Then where did you get the cash you've been splashing about?' Lizzie asked.

'I told yer, a coupla bets.'

Josie was so tense all she wanted was to escape and forget. There was no hope of proving he had taken the sapphires unless they were found, which was unlikely.

'I'm having the day off tomorrow,' Lizzie said now. 'I can help you. Have you arranged for a cart?'

'Yes, for eight. But not Wilf's dad!'

Lizzie laughed. 'You have to admire Freddy's cheek, offering it. How will you do it?'

'There are two men. Your mother has agreed to keep the piano until I can find somewhere bigger.'

'Then Aunt Dora won't be able to give piano lessons. That will annoy her.'

'Perhaps. She doesn't enjoy it. It's not the same as telling stories like she used to do, and making up songs to go with them. Besides, her pupils wouldn't go to Nechells, and few people there have money for lessons.'

'Poor Aunt Dora.'

Josie nodded. 'I'll go with the men and get things sorted out and then go to fetch Mother. She's planning to spend the day with her friend in Harborne.'

'What can I do?'

'You're a real friend, Lizzie. If you stay here for the loading up, I can go and hang the curtains and shop for food. Then you can help me get organized. I'm not sure how our furniture will all fit in, but Mother's lost so much I haven't the heart to force her to sell any.'

'Has she seen the rooms?'

'No, I haven't dared suggest it. She'll only agree to stay if there's no option. Oh, Lizzie, they're dreadful!'

'Never mind, it's only for a short while, and then you'll be able to move somewhere better.'

Josie shook her head. 'I couldn't afford anywhere better and still have enough for food and clothes.'

Lizzie was silent. There was nothing she could say. She couldn't even hope that her mother might relent. Phoebe was easy-going and generous but she had a very stubborn streak, and Lizzie suspected this was one occasion when, having made up her mind, she would refuse to change it.

'Something will happen,' she said at last. 'And we mustn't lose touch.'

'I'm so sorry for Mother, having to put up with those awful rooms all the time.'

'She has friends she can go and see, and if it were too awful she could try and get a job.'

'It's difficult to find one. Unemployment seems to be getting worse, though it's not so bad in Birmingham as elsewhere, from what people say.'

'William's very worried,' Lizzie said. 'I went as his passenger last week, and I don't understand half of what he's talking about, but he says lots of German banks are collapsing and that's caused problems in England, and we can't pay our debts. Nineteen thirty-two isn't going to be a very good year.'

'Is that why the Labour government collapsed last August?' Josie asked, anxious to subdue her own worries in contemplation of wider problems.

'Partly, I think. But it's also to do with the budget and coming off the gold standard and the huge number of men unemployed. I don't understand much of it. But it's because of all these problems they're paying less dole.'

'Thank goodness I have a job, at least,' Josie said, trying to be cheerful. 'I've had one increase and may get another one next year. Leo's a good employer.'

Chapter Nine

THE first hitch arose when Dora understood her beloved piano was not to be taken. She'd said that perhaps she would not go to spend the day with her friend as arranged but would stay to help Josephine, and instructed the men to load the piano first. Josie came out of the kitchen to find them struggling with it at the top of the stairs.

'Yow dain't say there were a bleedin' joanna,' one complained. 'We needs more'n two on us ter shift it.'

'It isn't going,' Josie replied. 'Mother, there isn't room and it would be impossible to get it up the stairs.'

Dora wept and pleaded, and finally went to lie down on the bare mattress. Josie pacified the men, left Lizzie to deal with them, and spent the next half-hour calming Dora, eventually accompanying her to the city centre to make sure she boarded the right bus to take her to her friend's.

'I'll come as soon as I possibly can,' she reassured her mother, and turned thankfully away as the bus departed.

She bought bread and cheese and tea and hurried to Nechells. She had just finished hanging the curtains from Freer Road on the canes which served as curtain poles in their new home when she heard the uproar. She looked out of the window and saw the cart, surrounded by a crowd of vociferous urchins who ought, Josie felt sure, to have been at school, turning into the malodorous court.

Lizzie, stepping cautiously through the drifts of rotting garbage which littered the cobbles, saw Josie at the window and waved thankfully. 'I really thought they'd come to the wrong place. Josie, this is terrible, it's a slum, you can't possibly live here.'

'Other people do,' Josie pointed out. 'Don't condemn it too much, Lizzie, or I shall lose what heart I have and then what will become of us?'

Lizzie hugged her impulsively. 'Aunt Dora is the luckiest woman alive to have you for a daughter.'

Josie laughed a little unsteadily. 'I do love her, Lizzie, but sometimes I could murder her too!'

'She'll have a fit when she sees it,' Lizzie warned.

'I know, but it will be dark, and once she's inside I'll threaten to run away and leave her alone if she complains. That ought to make her accept it.'

Lizzie chuckled. 'Come on, then, let's get started. We can take up the small bundles.'

Unloading the cart took far longer than anyone had expected. A few of the pieces of furniture, made for a more spacious house, simply could not be squeezed through the narrow doors and round the sharp turns of the stairs. The men had to go in search of extra help and a ladder, and remove the rickety sash windows before they could heave the large wardrobe and chest of drawers in. Once there, they took up so much space in the small bedroom that only one side of the bed was accessible as the other had to be jammed hard against one wall. Even then, the wardrobe doors and the lower drawers of both it and the chest could only be opened a few inches, and restoring the clothes in them was a frustrating and difficult job which had Lizzie flustered and hot long before it was completed. In the living room, Josie had been forced to put all but two of the dining chairs on top of the sideboard, and the rest of the furniture was crammed tight against the walls, leaving barely enough room to move. To sit comfortably at the table one of the armchairs would have to be pushed aside, and the ornaments, still packed in boxes, were stacked high on every flat surface, since there was no room for them to be displayed.

When Josie had paid the men extra for the unforeseen problems, she and Lizzie collapsed into chairs and stared disbelievingly about them. 'I hadn't realized the rooms were quite so small,' Josie said at last.

'They certainly wouldn't hold the piano as well,' Lizzie said, beginning to giggle.

Josie laughed, then hiccuped, the laughter turned to sobs as she sat holding herself rigidly, tears streaming down her cheeks. Lizzie, appalled, ran to cradle her in a comforting embrace.

'Josie, I've never seen you cry before, never! Hush, love, it won't be for long, you'll soon get away from here.'

'And go through all this again?' Josie asked unsteadily. 'I couldn't, I really couldn't bear it. Lizzie, we're stuck here until the house falls down, and by the looks of it that won't be long. What have I done?'

'You haven't done anything. It was Freddy's fault, really, wasn't it? I'm sure he had something to do with it however much he denies it. Josie, I don't like men.'

Dora wept pitifully when she saw the rooms. 'Josephine, oh my dear, how shall we bear it?' she asked between her sobs.

'It won't be for long, Mother,' Josie reassured her. 'As soon as I can find somewhere better we can move.' She knew they must be careful with money. After the move she had only a few shillings left, and anywhere else would be too expensive. She did look on her way from work, but there was so much to do at home that after a week of unremitting toil she had little time and energy for looking elsewhere.

Dora refused point blank to use the communal privy. It was, she maintained tearfully, full of unpleasant diseases waiting to leap out at her. Besides, she said with a sniff, it was so undignified and embarrassing to pick one's way publicly across the filth in the court, clutching sheets of newspaper, everyone knowing where one was going. Josie, weary of complaints, sharply told her she would empty the rose-patterned chamber pot.

'I'd tip it over her,' Lizzie said one evening, when she had arrived a few minutes after Josie had returned home and met her on her way back inside. She wrinkled up her nose. 'The other smells around here are far worse.'

'She's gone to bed, says she feels very cold.'

Lizzie watched in disbelief as Josie, in one of Dora's discarded black dresses which was far too short and tight for her, went down into Mrs Sheehan's cellar to fill their coal bucket, made up the almost-dead fire, refilled the bucket and then took the other one to fill it from the pump in the yard.

'I came to see if you'd come to the pictures with me,' she said when Josie had dumped the water bucket down, filled an ancient tin kettle and balanced it on the coal.

Josie pushed her hair out of her eyes. 'I'd love to but I can't afford it, and anyway I have to get dinner for Mother and prepare some food to leave her tomorrow.'

'Doesn't she do anything at all to help you?' Lizzie asked indignantly. 'She's here all day doing nothing while you're working hard to keep the pair of you.'

'She isn't well,' Josie excused her mother. 'Her hands have become very stiff and painful. I'm afraid it's the damp here. Besides, she's never had to look after herself, she doesn't know where to start.'

'You didn't either! Surely she could do the cooking, and if she did the shopping she'd get out for a while.'

Josie laughed. 'She tried cooking, and ruined our best saucepan. The stew was uneatable even where it wasn't burnt to charcoal. She makes a good pot of tea,' she added, grinning. 'I'm not always here to do it. And I buy in the markets, it's too far for her to walk, and too rough.'

146

Lizzie fumed, but saw that Josie was trapped by a mixture of pride and a feeling of responsibility for her mother, who had no one else. 'At least come with us to the rally on Sunday,' she insisted. 'William needs a passenger for one of his customers and he asked if you'd come. Do say yes, it's weeks since you came.'

'Does Matthew come on them now?' Josie asked.

'I neither know nor care. I don't see him, but whether he goes on different ones or not I don't know. William's teaching me to drive and he's a much better teacher than Matthew was — far more patient, and he explains things so clearly even I can understand them. Do come.'

'But how can I leave Mother?'

'You have to leave her when you go to work, and you used to leave her on Sundays before.'

'Yes, but that was different, she had Aunt Phoebe.'

'She hardly ever came out of her rooms,' Lizzie said. 'Josie, if you're not careful she'll make you a slave. Remember what she was like when you were at school, demanding you went with her whenever she chose? If you refuse every invitation for her sake what sort of life will you have? Besides,' she went on as Josie tried to speak, 'if you leave her alone she might make some effort to meet her own friends. And if she thinks you're out with rich young men who might marry you and remove her from here she'd encourage you,' she giggled.

The temptation was too much. Josie longed to escape, if only for a few hours, from the dreary grinding struggle to exist. She agreed to go but insisted that she would meet them away from the house. 'I couldn't bear them to know what I'm reduced to,' she confessed a little shamefacedly.

'What did they want you for this time?' Phoebe demanded as Freddy stalked into the kitchen.

'Bloody Wilf!' Freddy was shaking with anger.

'What's Wilf got to do with it? Why did the police ask you to go down to the station?'

It took her some time but eventually Freddy was goaded into retort. 'Daft idiot's bin cheatin' the Tote down at the stadiums an' 'e got caught. I told 'im −' he paused. It wouldn't do to admit knowledge of Wilf's activities.

'Told 'im what?'

'That I couldn't afford ter go so much. So 'e gets inter bad comp'ny an' starts that lark.'

'Then why did the police want ter see you?'

'Wilf told 'em I'd suggested it to 'im!' Freddy waxed indignant. 'I never! Wouldn't know 'ow ter do it,' he added virtuously. Phoebe eyed him keenly for a moment but he returned her gaze with a bland stare and she shrugged.

'Did they believe yer?'

'They 'ad ter, in the end. They couldn't prove any diff'rent, it was me against Wilf an' 'e'd bin caught red 'anded. Not that they'd 'a' minded chargin' me if they thought they could get away with it! All the same, bloody police! They was mad when I let 'em search me room an' they dain't find no sapphires! And then Mabel's dad's in Winson Green, as if that's owt ter do wi' me. Now they'll be on me back all the time, suspectin' me of every single thing.'

'Well, you'd best not give 'em cause ter prove it,' his mother said unsympathetically.

Freddy glared. 'Don't you start. I've 'ad enough false accusations. First me aunt, then me pal. Some pal! Well, I know one thing, I'm never again goin' ter buy Wilf so much as a bag o' chips. An' 'e can whistle fer the coupla quid 'e put towards buyin' the Streak!'

'It were Doris's fault,' Phoebe said suddenly.

'What? 'Ow d'yer reckon that? 'Er never knew which way a dog ran, let alone 'ow ter bilk the Tote.'

'She accused you, didn't she? If the police 'adn't been told yer name they wouldn't 'ave believed Wilf.'

Freddy worked this out and became even more indignant. It was bad enough being shopped by a pal, but to think the police

148

were interested in him just because his Aunt Doris had been so hasty was galling. It also made life much more difficult if the police watched his every move, as he had no doubt they would. He'd have to be exceptionally careful for weeks, and depend on his legitimate earnings from Matthew and walking the dogs for Sid rather than the other perks he'd become accustomed to. Why, they might even nab him for taking bets, and if he got in Dan Todd's bad books life would be grim. Without money he'd lose the slender bond that held Mabel to him, and he couldn't afford to lose her.

Leo was back that Friday. He was pleased by the success of his sales trip, full of the excitement of seeing the finish of the Monte Carlo Rally, had several promising new contacts in South America, but above all was eager to be with Josie again. He didn't know why, just that being with her lifted his mood and gave a spice to his days which they had lacked before. She looked tired, though, and he was concerned.

'How have things been?' he greeted her on his first day back in the office.

'No major calamities,' she replied. The loss of their rooms did not concern him, and she felt such a rush of relief to see him even though she was furious that he'd permitted Matthew to expand into the production of car parts when he'd rejected her suggestion. Now she'd be able to sort out the problems of the radiator grilles, and William would no longer be suspicious of Leo's honesty. And he could take charge of the factory again. It had been difficult while he'd been away, apart from Matthew's unexplained absences. The atmosphere in the factory had changed. The men were quieter, joked with one another less frequently, and there had been several loud arguments amongst the girls, culminating in two of them, girls Matthew had taken on as polishers, resorting to violence and pulling each other's hair. This had never happened when Leo had been there to sort out minor disputes before they escalated into open warfare.

Matthew hadn't even dismissed the girls. Josie suspected he was taking one of them out. He seemed incapable of taking decisions on his own. And Tobias was subdued, despite the success of his designs. But Leo was back, and Josie knew everything would return to normal, at the factory anyway. 'The things we're making from Tobias's designs are selling exceptionally well, and he's –'

'Leo, thank goodness you're back!' Matthew came bursting through the door. 'Had a good trip? I need your authority for knocking down the wall in between those two tiny rooms in the new building, but the fool bricklayer won't do it, keeps muttering about the wall supporting upstairs and the expense of shoring it up.'

'Hello, Matthew. I'll come and see as soon as I can, and there'll be other matters to discuss, but there are some urgent letters and questions I must deal with here first.'

Matthew hesitated, pursed his lips angrily, then shrugged. Josie thought he gave her an inimical glance as he went, but soon forgot it in getting down to the details of the report she'd prepared for Leo on his return.

'How did the trip go?' she asked as she made tea.

'Very well; I sold more than last year. And I was in Monte Carlo when the competitors came in. Doing business, as well. The final test was weird, and such a pity Donald Healey only came second. But I ought to concentrate on business now. Have dinner with me tonight?'

Josie longed to accept. Suddenly her situation didn't seem so dreadful. With the worry of moving she hadn't had time to fret about Leo, but saw with shocking clarity how much she had missed him, and not simply as her employer. This was crazy, she told herself, it didn't make sense. She thrust away the implications to think about later, and was about to nod when she remembered it was impossible. Dora needed her even more now, confined in dreadful lodgings. Much as she longed to go, she didn't feel justified in leaving her alone in the evenings, especially without warning, when Dora found it impossible to cook for herself and wouldn't know how to get coal or water. 'I can't, I'm afraid,' she told him.

'Tomorrow then?' Leo was more disappointed than he cared to admit to himself.

Josie suddenly recalled her grievance. 'When you treat my suggestions as seriously as you do Matthew's, I might!' she snapped.

'What do you mean?'

'The radiator grilles he's making. When I suggested making car parts you turned me down flat, but when a man makes the same suggestion he's allowed to do it — and with a design stolen from William!'

'Stolen?'

'Yes.'

'It couldn't be.'

'It's the same design as one of William's.'

Josie knew William still had doubts, but she couldn't believe that Leo was a thief. There had to be another explanation.

'I haven't the slightest idea what you're talking about. Matthew isn't making car parts.'

'I suggest you go and see him. And ask him where he got the design.'

'I will, even though you seem to be talking nonsense.'

It served as an excuse, but Josie was totally confused. Why, when she wanted to be with him, was she relieved to have a reason not to be?

Leo was more hurt than offended, and decidedly puzzled. He could sort out the misapprehension about Matthew, but why was Josie refusing his invitations? He'd thought she liked him, enjoyed his company out of the office as well as working with him, so why had she appeared to change? Had Dora, angered by his rejection of her demand that he declare his intentions, laid down some prohibition? Yet he didn't think Josie was so lacking in spirit as to obey her mother's unreasonable orders. He thrust away the suspicion that he might have given Josie expectations, and went to see Matthew.

Josie was left wondering how she could deter him from asking her out again or make it plain she couldn't accept. She couldn't leave Dora in the evenings, and she ought not to leave her on Sundays either, despite Lizzie's arguments. She wouldn't go on any more rallies after this next one. It would be too painful a reminder of happier days. That life was ended now, at least until she could save money and establish herself somewhere that wasn't a slum. And if she didn't go at all, perhaps pretended she had lost interest, she could avoid Leo's invitations. She was surprised to find that the ending of their occasional social outings devastated her so much, though, concluding that it was her tiredness and the searing depression of living in such bleak surroundings which were affecting her unduly.

Leo went into the new workshop and searched it. There were piles of radiator grilles in one corner, covered by a tarpaulin, and on close examination he could see where machines to cut out the shapes and bend the metal had been placed in the far end of the room. Grim-faced, he went up to the office, carrying one of the grilles.

'Perhaps you'd explain how this comes to be made in my workshop?' he demanded without preliminaries.

'Who told you? That red-haired secretary of yours?'

'Answer my question! I gave no authorization for this to be produced, so why have you brought in machines and wasted my workmen's time on making them?'

Matthew laughed. 'Oh, come on, Leo, are you saying I mustn't use any initiative at all? We had space to spare, and the men were idle. I've rented the machines, just to fill in time until you came back.'

'I'll inspect your accounts now. Are these items entered in my books or do they represent a private venture of yours?'

'Damn you, Leo! Are you accusing me of cheating you?'

'Not until I've seen the books. Now, if you please.'

With a shrug, Matthew found the sales ledger, opened it and pointed in some triumph to a few entries. Leo counted the number of grilles sold, and wondered whether Matthew had simply been clever and entered some of the transactions. There were remarkably few, judging by the capacity of the machines.

'Satisfied?' Matthew asked with a sneer.

'Yes, if you can explain where you found this design. I doubt if you thought it up yourself.'

'I bought it,' Matthew said. 'A man came to see me, and it looked good, so I bought it outright.'

'And where did he get it from?'

'How should I know? He said he was an inventor in his spare time.'

'The payment book?'

Again Matthew riffled through a ledger and pointed to an entry. 'Hugh Jones, ten pounds.'

'Not much for a revolutionary design.'

'It was a bargain, yes. It was what he asked.'

'And you didn't suspect it might have been stolen, when he was willing to sell it outright instead of asking for a share of any profits?'

'I don't have your suspicious nature. It might not have worked. I had to take that chance. But it does work, Leo, very well.'

'Perhaps, but I'm not in the business of making car parts. Send the machines back, and when you have any more such ideas you'll ask me first!'

Leo strode from the office. He was deeply suspicious, but without a great deal of time spent questioning the workmen, which he was reluctant to do behind anyone's back, and which he hadn't got time for, he couldn't disprove Matthew's story. For now he'd have to let it go, but he'd see William, ask if he'd employed a Hugh Jones, try to explain and hope their friendship would survive William's suspicions. He'd also keep a much closer eye on his manager.

The rally took them northwards into the Peak District. Josie went with William and Lizzie accompanied his customer, a man from Solihull. 'She'll explain my adaptations,' William said. 'I could employ her as a saleslady.'

'What adaptations?' Josie asked as she wrapped a rug round her legs. 'What's this?' she added, pointing to a box in the well of the car in front of the passenger seat.

'My hot-water bottle,' William replied, grinning. He leant over and adjusted it. 'See, it separates into three sections and you put your feet between them to keep warm.'

'Won't the water cool down?'

'I hope not. That's something I'm doing now. We lose an awful lot of heat through the exhaust, and I'm directing it back to heat the water. People are trying to use it in different ways, such as heating the windscreen. Tell me if the level of heat goes up or down.'

'What else is new?' Josie demanded, intrigued.

'Mainly ideas to improve comfort, especially when it's cold weather. People won't be content for ever to drive in freezing cold cars, draining their radiators every night, or heating their garages. It's a nuisance having to push up the windscreen when it gets frosted over, just to see to drive! So far they haven't managed to get efficient heating systems, just electrical wires to fix on the windscreens, and I'm working on some new ideas. When I have some really successful ones I shall enter the Monte Carlo Rally.'

'Leo was there this year for the end of it. But isn't it a race? How will having warm feet help you win it?'

'There's a separate competition, the Concours de confort, where marks are given for accessories, comfort, convenience, and so on. Humphrey Symons won it this year in a Sunbeam, but that's what I aim at, not the race itself. It would be marvellous publicity for the business.'

'It sounds intriguing. Will you enter next January?'

He grinned at her enthusiasm. 'In 1933? Perhaps. It depends on whether I have enough successful ideas before the end of this year when the entries have to be in. You can help by judging the foot-warmer.'

Josie laughed, and gave herself up to enjoying the day. The scenery, though bleak wintry moorland, was interesting, and she felt no discomfort at the frosty air surrounding them. It blew away the smells and the fog of the city, and lifted her mood.

This time William wasn't even placed, but Lizzie's driver came third. As they were congratulating him, Matthew came up behind them.

'Well, Lizzie, you've soon found a sugar daddy to console yourself, haven't you?' he said softly, but William heard and swung round swiftly.

'Take that back!' he ordered. 'I won't have you insult Lizzie or my customer!'

'If your customer's offended, then of course I'm sorry, but I think he's entitled to know what a slut he's with. All Lizzie's after is a wealthy husband, and she'll do anything to get one.'

Before anyone could move, William swung his fist and Matthew crashed to the ground, clutching his eye. William glanced round and beckoned to a couple of men who'd been near enough to hear the exchange. 'I think the duckpond's the right place for scum,' he said quietly, and the three of them lifted Matthew and carried him across to where there was a very dirty pond full of slimy weed. They tossed a struggling Matthew into the middle, and stood laughing as he scrambled to his feet, weed-bedecked, mud-plastered.

'I'll pay you for that!' Matthew spluttered, but William turned away.

'Time to go, I think.'

*

155

Although Josie was more cheerful the mood couldn't last. The very next day she and Leo had barely worked through the outstanding post when Matthew, sporting a livid, puffy eye, strode in. 'Have you time to listen to me today?' he demanded of Leo, ignoring Josie. 'You kept putting me off last week.'

Leo sighed. 'There was a lot to deal with,' he said mildly. 'Josie, can you make us a pot of tea, please?'

Josie retreated behind the screen. She was embarrassed, but unless Leo asked her to go there was little she could do but listen to Matthew's petulant complaints.

'This is important, too,' he was saying. 'I don't like that fellow Mackenzie's designs.'

'They are selling well from what I see in the books.'

'They're a fad, a flash in the pan, a fashion that will soon vanish, and he can't do anything else. I think you made a mistake employing him. Besides, he's insubordinate, does just what he chooses without any reference to me.'

'He isn't answerable to you,' Leo said curtly. 'He's employed as a designer, with his own job to do. I'll judge by results whether his designs are successful or not.'

'They may have caught the fancy of a couple of shops, but it won't last. We can't afford to take risks, Leo. This is an established firm, noted for good quality, solid and dependable products. You'll lose that by foolish experimentation.'

'Neither can we stand still. I thought that was why you decided to leave your father.'

'There's a difference between being hidebound and sensible modernization. Besides, I left him so as not to have to defer to him all the time, yet I'm in no different a position here, it seems.'

'You accepted a job as manager, Matthew. You're not a partner. I still control the firm.'

'I won't permit a damned upstart to defy me! You must sack Mackenzie.'

Josie brought the tray to set on Leo's desk. She cast Leo an appealing glance and he smiled briefly at her.

'No, Matthew. Tobias stays and that's the end of it. I'd have thought it more appropriate to sack those two girls who got into a fight. Why didn't you?'

Matthew went red and began to bluster, and to Josie's relief Leo asked her to take a message downstairs. When she returned, Matthew had left. Leo was preoccupied, and Josie silently set about her own work, worried about Tobias. It would be too bad if Matthew caused trouble.

'It's so difficult, working there and being reminded of Matthew every single day,' Lizzie sighed.

'Do you still love him?' Ann asked sympathetically. She'd grown closer to Lizzie during the past few weeks. Unwilling to confide in Josie as she had in the past, for poor Josie had enough problems of her own, Lizzie had turned to her younger cousin. They often went out on Ann's evening off, as now when they were on their way to the pictures, having a meal first in a small café nearby where they'd been lucky enough to find a window table.

'I don't know,' Lizzie said, sounding puzzled. 'What is love?'

'It's obvious when it's there,' Ann said softly. 'Mr and Mrs Endersby, for example. And a few days ago Dr Mandeville came in to the restaurant with his wife, and they were so much in love they both radiated happiness.' She sighed. 'I've never been asked out by anyone except that horrible Stanley Hodges. Shall I ever find out?'

Lizzie chuckled. 'Of course you will, one day. You're so beautiful, Ann, I expect you frighten men away. But after Matthew I'm afraid to trust anyone. I despise Matthew for the way he treated me but I do miss him. The trouble is, I can see him everywhere. Every part of the factory reminds me of some incident when we'd snatch a few words together or make arrangements to meet. Even though he's not working there any more, I can't get away from him to see whether that would cure me.'

'Move to another job,' Ann suggested. 'It ought not to be difficult, you're experienced, you know the trade.'

'I'm bored with it! Factory work is so tedious and I don't earn much. I only stayed there so long because of Matthew, and after we split up I was far too miserable to make any effort to move. I'd like to try something else, but what? I'm not domesticated, I couldn't work in a hotel, and I'd hate a shop, and I can't type like Josie.'

'There is one possibility,' Ann said, and then caught sight of a clock on the building opposite. 'We'd better go or we won't be in time.'

'What possibility?' Lizzie asked as they hurried out.

Ann shook her head. 'I don't want to say until I'm sure. It was a rumour I heard. I'll know next week.'

Despite Lizzie's urgings she refused to say any more, but when they met the following week at the same café she handed Lizzie a piece of paper. 'That's the name and address of a lady who's staying at the hotel. She wants a young girl to be a chauffeuse and companion, and I asked her if you could apply. She wants you to go and see her tomorrow.'

Lizzie was staring at her in amazement. 'Chauffeuse? You mean me drive a car for someone?'

'Why not? You keep telling me how this William Scott has been teaching you to drive, and you learned a lot from Matthew. You'd be able to do it. She doesn't have a big car, it's only a medium Austin – I forget just how big, but I think she said a Twelve.'

'If she wants a companion I'd have to live with her.' She glanced at the paper. 'Ann, she lives in Warwick!'

'Would that be a problem?' Ann asked anxiously. 'Wouldn't Aunt Phoebe like you to go? She didn't object when I had to live-in at Endersby's.'

Lizzie laughed nervously. 'Ma's in a bad temper more often

than not these days,' she confessed. 'I think she regrets throwing Josie and Aunt Dora out but won't admit it. Then she worries about Freddy and what bad company he might be getting into. Did I tell you his girl's dad's in prison? On top of all that she's got friendly with Mrs Frossdyke and started helping in some of her charity work. Ma, helping at soup kitchens and jumble sales! I'd be glad of a chance to get away,' she finished abruptly. 'What's her name? Mrs Thackeray-Walsh. Sounds posh.'

'She's lovely, Lizzie. She's not old, though she's a widow, and both her daughters are married. That's why she wants company, I believe, the second daughter only left just before Christmas.'

Lizzie had severe doubts about whether Mrs Thackeray-Walsh would consider her suitable, but to her amazed delight the lady approved. After Lizzie had, rather nervously but without incident, driven her along the Hagley Road and through the intimidating centre of Birmingham, she declared she would give her a month's trial.

'I'll have to leave Horobin's,' she said, when she told her mother, 'but that will be a relief.'

'What if she doesn't want you after the month?'

Lizzie shrugged. 'I have to take the risk. But she was really nice, I'm sure we'll get on. Are you sure you don't mind? I'll be able to come and see you quite often. Mrs Thackeray-Walsh comes to Birmingham nearly every week to see her daughters, they both live here, and she says she won't want me while she's with them.'

Phoebe smiled as cheerfully as she could. 'If only Freddy would move out I'd 'ave the 'ouse to meself! You take the job, love, and good luck ter yer. It's time someone in the family 'ad some good luck for a change.'

Lizzie's departure for her new job made Josie feel even more isolated. She hadn't seen Lizzie very often in the past few weeks, it was true, for she didn't like to invite her to their rooms when

Dora complained bitterly about Phoebe's lack of compassion and Christian tolerance. Josie wouldn't leave her mother alone in the evenings, and neither she nor Lizzie now took part in rallies. She might see her cousin when Lizzie came to Birmingham with her employer, but that was unpredictable and Lizzie's first obligation was to her mother. She saw Ann more often because Ann made a point of visiting them on her fortnightly Sundays off. Ann listened uncomplainingly to Dora's diatribes against Phoebe, just saying softly that she was sure Aunt Phoebe hadn't meant all those horrid things, and by now was regretting them. Dora seemed to enjoy listening to Ann's stories about Endersby's hotel, and after the girl's visits often fell to reminiscing about old times when George had taken her there.

Josie perceived a danger and when she walked with Ann to catch her bus she implored her not to tell Dick Endersby where she was living. 'I can't bear people to know.'

'He wouldn't care, but Mrs Endersby said he'd be here only for a couple of days, he's spending the Easter holiday with his grandparents. Don't you want to see him again?'

Josie laughed rather bitterly. 'Not while we live in such a slum. Oh, Ann, it's not a romance. We only played tennis and went for a couple of rides on his motorcycle.'

Her best friend now, she thought ruefully, was Tobias. When Leo had returned, Tobias had quietly removed himself and his drawing board back to the other building, but he and Josie had fallen into the habit of having lunch together. At first, Tobias had invited her to cafés nearby, but Josie explained that she couldn't afford to buy food there.

'That's not a problem. If I invite you I wouldn't dream of letting you pay. And you know I can afford it, I don't have to depend on the salary I get from Leo.'

'I can't let you, even if you can afford it.'

'Not even once a week? Once a fortnight then? Occasionally, to celebrate a good design?'

She brought food from home, mainly sandwiches, and he

began to do the same, joining Josie in her office where they shared a pot of tea and talked as they ate. Leo, after Josie had firmly declined several invitations from him, saying her mother was unwell and needed her company at home, had stopped asking her.

He was puzzled, but managed to hide how hurt he felt, especially when he saw how much at ease she was with Tobias.

Matthew, to Josie's relief, rarely came into the main office. He no longer urged Leo to sack Tobias, or spoke unnecessarily to Josie. He had equipped himself with a small office and employed a typist, a girl a few years older than Josie who did not mingle with the rest of the employees if she could avoid it. It was only when it was necessary to pass on a message or ask a question that she deigned to notice Josie's existence. Josie wondered whether she had taken Lizzie's place in Matthew's life, even whether she had moved into the flat with Matthew, but she didn't know Miss Gwendoline Ames well enough to speculate.

It was a gusty, wet day in March and the rain and hail were lashing at the office window when Matthew came into her office late in the afternoon. Leo was out seeing a customer, promising that Matthew would lock up. 'Miss Shaw, will you type a few letters?' he asked abruptly. 'They must go tonight and Miss Ames is ill. I'm driving her home right away, I can't permit her to be out in this weather with a temperature. She oughtn't to have come in this morning, but she's very conscientious.'

'I'll do them,' Josie said briefly and held out her hand for the sheaf of papers Matthew thrust towards her.

'They're perfectly straightforward, I've written notes of what to say and I'm sure you can manage. I'll come back to sign them after I've taken Miss Ames home.'

'The gold will be ready for locking in the safe within a couple of minutes. You'll have to do that, since Leo isn't here,' she reminded him. He frowned but waited and weighed out the gold, entering the amount carefully into the ledger before locking that away too. Then he was gone. Josie finished a letter she'd been typing and turned to Matthew's pile.

She flicked through in dismay. There were far more than he'd implied and she saw that many of them should have been answered days ago. Grimly, Josie set to work, and it was an hour after her usual time to finish before they were done, waiting on her desk for Matthew's signature.

Everyone else had gone and the workshop was dark and silent. Josie had never before been there alone and it was eerie now the clacking of the typewriter had ceased, and noisy outside where the storm had grown ever fiercer. Where on earth was Matthew? It couldn't have taken him this long to drive Miss Ames home. Josie grew impatient. Dora would be worried and fretful when she finally reached home. It really was too bad of Matthew to give her this extra work and then delay for so long coming back. If there had been a key to the main door she'd have locked up and gone, but she could scarcely leave the factory open to whoever might choose to enter it. If it had been Matthew's factory she would have done, she told herself angrily, but it wouldn't be fair to Leo to risk his property.

When she heard the street door open and footsteps on the stairs she reached for her coat. She still wore her old school coat, threadbare now, but there was no money for a better one. In this weather it wouldn't keep her dry, and she sighed at the thought of the extra work and expense of fetching more coal in order to dry it out by morning. She was glaring at the office door when Leo walked in.

'Josie! What are you doing here so late, alone?'

Tersely she explained. 'I must go, Mother worries.'

'I'll drive you, you can't walk in this weather. I'll sign the letters and then we can go. No, I'll do them at home. I came in just to leave something.'

It wasn't until they were in the car and Leo turned north towards Aston that Josie remembered she hadn't been able to tell him she had been forced to leave her aunt's house. Should she tell him now, or pretend they still lived in Freer Road and be even later and wetter having to walk back from Aston? She was so weary she couldn't face such a walk.

'I live in Nechells now,' she said abruptly.

Leo glanced at her in surprise, seeing by the light from the street lamps how grim she looked. 'Tell me the way,' he said briefly, turning eastwards into the meaner streets and silently following Josie's curt directions. When he drew up at the entrance to the court he looked from it to Josie in blank astonishment. 'How in the world do you come to be living here?'

'I can't explain now,' she protested. 'Mother will be worried and it will take too long.'

'Very well, but I want to know all about it first thing in the morning.'

Josie tried to avoid an explanation the following day, but Leo was adamant. He sent Matthew away with a sharp demand to be left alone and then, frowning, locked the office door. 'We won't be interrupted,' he said. 'Now sit down and tell me why you are living in a slum.'

'Because I have my mother to support and only my wages to do it on. It was the only place I could afford when Aunt Phoebe turned us out. And then the sapphires were stolen.' Fighting to restrain her trembling Josie related what had happened. 'She was stupid, I've called her far worse, but how can I desert her? I love her. I keep remembering how wonderful she was when I was little, the marvellous stories she used to tell me. The trouble is she still believes in fairies. She's no more able to look after herself than a fledgling bird. And has no more sense either.'

'My poor darling!' Suddenly, not knowing how she got there, Josie was in his arms. 'This is ridiculous. If only I'd known. But now I do and you won't live there a day longer. You'll both come to live at my house.'

She struggled to free herself from his stifling embrace. 'But

Leo, you don't owe us anything, you aren't responsible for us just because George married my mother.'

'Don't be such a little idiot! That's got nothing to do with it. Well, maybe it has. She ought to be my responsibility now, since my father made such a mess of things. It's not all her fault, and it's certainly not yours. But that's not what I mean. I can't bear the thought of your struggling in such a slum. God, Josie, don't you understand? I want you to marry me!'

Chapter Ten

'MARRY?' Josie stared at Leo in astonishment. 'But why? Just because you're sorry for me? Or because you think you're responsible in some way to my mother?'

Leo looked harassed. 'No, of course not! Why do people usually get married?'

'Because they're in love, I suppose,' Josie said slowly. 'But you don't love me.'

'How do you know?'

Josie considered it carefully. 'I'm not sure. You've never said so. You don't behave as if you're in love.'

'Do you know how people in love behave?' Leo demanded, thinking back to his own youthful passion. It was true he'd not felt the same overwhelming desire for Josie as he had then, but perhaps as one got older one's reactions changed.

'Only from watching Lizzie,' Josie admitted. 'I know that's perhaps a poor example, but surely one ought to feel something more than mere affection and friendship?'

'Is that how you feel towards me? Merely affectionate?'

Josie shook her head. 'Not just that,' she said, forcing herself to laugh. She dared not admit quite how much she felt for him. 'I like you a lot, Leo, but I don't know what love is, and I don't think I love you. This is an utterly ridiculous situation! You can't offer to marry me because you feel sorry for me. We'd both of us regret that, and I won't let myself be dependent on a man just because he feels sorry for me. I'm managing, I'm even saving a little every week. I'm very careful with what I spend, I have a nest egg for emergencies, and my mother isn't allowed to open accounts and buy useless clothes. Soon, perhaps, we'll be able to move to somewhere better. I'm sure I could find somewhere now but I haven't had the energy to look. When the weather's better I'll feel more like going out in the evenings and trying to find somewhere. I know it looks dreadful from outside, and it's not a pleasant neighbourhood, but we've made it cosy and our landlady is very kind to us. We're much better off than many people.'

'Then you won't marry me? I did mean it, Josie.'

'Thank you. You're very kind, Leo, but I couldn't. You'll be grateful to me within the day,' she told him, forcing herself to grin.

'Then at least I'll increase your wages by a pound.'

'That's charity!' she protested hastily.

'Not at all. I'd meant to anyway; we've done so well with Tobias's designs and that's mostly due to you. You've learned fast, you coped so well while I was away, you're a better manager than . . . Anyway, I'm increasing Tobias's salary too so you've no cause to be offended.'

'I can't afford to refuse if that's the case,' she said slowly. 'Thank you, Leo.'

'But you can afford to refuse to marry me.'

'That's quite different. I earn my wages.'

When he left her Josie was unable to do any work. Leo's proposal had been utterly unexpected and she had a strong suspicion it had astonished him too. For some time she wondered what she would feel like if she were in love, but was quite incapable of imagining she ever could be. It would be pleasant, she thought wistfully, if she could love Leo, for he was a very attractive man and it would certainly solve all her immediate problems. But it would never do. He'd regret it, and she couldn't accept such an offer just to gain security for herself and her mother.

When Leo came back into the office he was in a black mood, and told Josie he had informed Matthew that she was not again to do any work for his manager. 'If his own secretary can't cope with far less work than you have to do he must find someone else,' he said brusquely. He then departed to deal with some problems in the new building and she didn't see him again all morning. Josie surmised there had been another blazing row, and when Tobias begged her to take pity and have lunch out she gladly agreed.

'What was all the fuss about?' Tobias asked when they were installed in one of the more expensive cafés in the jewellery quarter. 'Leo came storming in and raked Matthew down as though he were a schoolboy up to his tricks. I could hear the raised voices but not the words.'

Josie explained. She knew Tobias didn't gossip and it wouldn't hurt for him to know. He'd laughed off Matthew's attempts to have him dismissed, but he was furiously indignant on her behalf. 'He left you here all alone, doing that useless Ames woman's work? No wonder Leo was mad. He would have been even if he weren't nutty about you.'

Josie looked startled. 'Leo? Of course he isn't!'

Tobias grinned at her. 'You may not know it and he may not know it yet, but to a man of experience – and remember I've had years of watching pretty nurses and wounded soldiers falling for one another – it's quite obvious.'

'Don't!' Josie said, distressed. 'It's not true.'

'If you say so. Let's talk business. I've had some ideas for new designs, clips which individually make one image and separately make two quite different ones.'

Josie forced herself to concentrate, but for the rest of that day, whenever she wasn't busy, she wondered about Leo's astonishing proposal and Tobias's even more astounding remarks. Leo couldn't possibly love her. Neither did she love him. Then Josie paused and frowned. Was it possible she did? No, of course not. She liked him, that was all. She liked Tobias and William and Dick, too. They were all friends. So was Leo, she'd begun to think, although he was her boss and she knew he still resented her mother and his father's devotion to Dora. But deep within she knew she was always happier when with Leo and missed him when he wasn't there. Was that love? Even if it were, she told herself angrily, Leo had proposed out of pity, remorse perhaps, a belated feeling of obligation towards his father's wife. He didn't love her. He hadn't said so and he'd been quick enough to change his offer to a higher wage, hadn't he? Suddenly she giggled. He'd much prefer that when he came back to his senses. And so would she, Josie told herself firmly. An extra pound a week was far better than a marriage they both might soon have regretted. She forced herself to work, but insidious little thoughts about what it would be like to be married to Leo kept intruding until she was, for once, thankful to return to her dreadful new home.

Leo went home in a state bordering on frenzy. Why on earth had he made such an ass of himself? He hadn't wanted to marry anyone since he was twenty, and even then he'd made a far better hand at his proposal. This time he hadn't meant to propose, it had just slipped out. Why on earth should that happen? He didn't love the girl. Of course he didn't. Surely he didn't? And yet − was he sure what love was? He sat over the solitary meal his daily housekeeper had left in the oven but he let it go cold. He spread Tobias's new designs over the table in his library but didn't see them. He collected together some letters and invitations he really must send replies to, but didn't get as far as unscrewing the cap of his fountain pen. He didn't even think about the devastating row with Matthew and Matthew's threat to leave.

The clock struck midnight and Leo wearily dragged himself

to bed, but spent the night imagining the discomforts Josie was reduced to. Was she warm enough? Had she enough to eat? Did her mother fret her to distraction? For the twentieth time he turned restlessly in bed, and thumped the pillow until he burst a hole in it and feathers drifted aimlessly around him. He felt equally rudderless. By morning he was ready to damn all women. Thank goodness Josie hadn't accepted him, if this was the state just thinking about her reduced him to. He went to work feeling desolate and caring little about anything.

The extra salary made a tremendous difference. Josie forced herself not to speculate whether Leo had meant it as charity. They had resumed an outwardly serene working relationship, and neither mentioned the proposal.

Dora seemed more reconciled and even talked about finding a job. She began to visit her friends again, but Josie half suspected this was to do with her often-repeated assertion that their only possible way out of this degrading poverty was for her to contrive to introduce Josie to some suitable young men. Josie was thankful that her mother was more cheerful, and hoped she was recovering from the shocks of George's death and the loss of their home and money.

Josie, giving way to the desire to enjoy herself, succumbed to William's blandishments when she met him in Vyse Street, where he was visiting a manufacturer who supplied some of his car parts, and went on a few short rallies with him. Leo had stopped asking her, for which she thought she was grateful. She didn't want to be alone with him, although she didn't know why. But he was often competing, accompanied as before by a string of beautiful girls. At work he never mentioned these occasions, although he was pleasant enough when they met during the rallies. She had several more driving lessons from William, and was longing for the day when she could take part in a novice event. But she did not think that was very likely: she had neither the time nor the money for what was really a rich man's sport.

'I'm competing in the London to Edinburgh,' William said one day as he drove her back to Birmingham. 'Will you come with me?'

'But that's a whole weekend!'

'Yes, I need to enter more of the longer rallies to prepare for Monte Carlo. Oh, are you thinking people would talk? It's quite normal, lots of unmarried couples drive together, but we all stay in the same hotels, so there are plenty of chaperones.'

'It's not that, William. I can't,' she said regretfully.

'Don't worry about the hotel bill or other expenses, naturally I'll pay,' William said bluntly.

Josie shook her head. 'It wouldn't be right to accept money from you, but in any case, I can't leave Mother for a whole weekend. It's bad enough she's alone most of the time. I can only come when I do because she's sometimes invited to visit an old friend in Harborne on Sundays.'

'Well, if ever you get the chance of freedom for a weekend, tell me. There are usually rallies somewhere and it would be good experience. And I'm not suggesting anything improper; I'd pay your expenses as a matter of course as I would any man's I invited to co-drive. I'll give you my new address.'

'You're moving?'

'I'm leaving my manager in charge in Birmingham while I spend a few months setting up a larger factory in Coventry.'

'What will you produce there?'

'All sorts of components. Remember my radiator grille that Dick Endersby's Uncle Johnny got from Matthew, when we suspected Leo had somehow stolen the design?'

'Leo didn't know anything about it,' Josie said swiftly. 'It was Matthew's idea. Leo still doesn't know how Matthew obtained the design, he said he'd bought it.'

'He may have done. I discovered that one of my clerks was stealing them. I've dismissed him now. Coventry's going to be a major car-building area and I want to be near it. Anyway, Johnny Smith and I are opening the factory together.'

'I shall miss you, William.'

'And I'll miss you. But it won't be for long, and I'll keep in touch, of course.'

'Thanks, William. You're a good friend.'

'I like you, Josie. You had a raw deal when George died. I wish you'd change your mind about Edinburgh, though. Still, there are plenty of short rallies. See you next Sunday.'

Leo's latest quarrel with Matthew had been patched up, but Matthew was aloof with Josie. She was sure he thought she'd complained about him deliberately. He made one stilted attempt to apologize for apparently deserting her, saying his car had broken down, but ignored her otherwise.

The new catalogue was ready, and they were frantically busy for days sending copies out. When Josie arrived for work one morning she found Leo had been there for several hours already. He looked tired, but he had seemed tired for some time now, since the quarrel. He looked up with a smile.

'Good, you're early. We should be able to clear most of these today, and then tomorrow we can catch up with normal work,' he commented with a sigh. 'Let's have some tea. I need something to keep me awake.'

'You look tired.'

'So do you. I'm not overworking you, am I?'

She shook her head and tried to smile. Dora had been more than usually irritating the previous evening, complaining about the monotony of the stews that were all Josie could afford. Josie had finally lost her patience and stormed out of the house, telling her mother that if she wanted better food she'd have to earn money to pay for it. She had recklessly spent sixpence at the cinema, and gone home remorseful and anxious to make her peace. Dora had been in floods of tears, endlessly apologizing and promising never again to complain, and Josie finished up wondering whether this was preferable to her endless complaints.

She handed Leo his tea.

'Josie, I've been meaning to ask you again, how about being my passenger this Sunday? I'm entering a rally.'

She stared at him in dismay. It seemed ages since he'd asked her out and she had a sudden reckless urge to accept. 'I'm sorry, Leo, but I can't. William Scott's already asked me.'

He frowned. 'You're always with Scott. Why?'

'Well, because he asks me,' she said, surprised. She didn't need to say that wasn't the reason she'd refused this time.

'Josie, is he the reason you refused my proposal? Are you in love with him?'

She stared, astonished. Surely Leo couldn't be jealous of William! It wasn't possible. More likely Leo's pride was suffering, when any girl refused his invitation.

'Well?' Leo demanded. 'Do you love him?'

'Of course not! He's just a friend. We enjoy one another's company and he's teaching me to drive.'

'Then why did you turn me down? Josie, I meant it when I proposed. I still do. Won't you consider it?'

'But – but you don't love me!' she burst out.

Leo blinked. 'Why on earth should you think that?'

'You've never said so,' Josie muttered, embarrassed.

'Doesn't the fact that I've asked you to marry me – twice – tell you that I love you?'

If only she could believe him. Josie's thoughts were in a whirl, and not helped when Leo stepped towards her and pulled her gently into his arms.

She concentrated hard on the knot in his tie, but then he took her chin in his hand and inexorably forced her head back. As she glanced up, unwilling to meet his gaze but impelled by a wild, crazy hope, his fingers caressed her cheek and gently pushed back her hair.

'Josie?' he asked softly, and his lips came down on hers. Her first coherent thought was how soft they were, how warm and comforting, and then as her own lips parted instinctively Leo's became harder, more demanding, and he crushed her against his chest until her entire body tingled and she found it impossible to breathe. At long last he released her. 'Doesn't that say anything?' he asked breathlessly.

Josie turned away to look out of the window. He sounded as though he meant it, and while the kiss lasted she'd wanted to let go, to abandon all her problems and let Leo sort them out. Then sanity returned. If she accepted him it would be for Dora's sake, and she couldn't do that to him. He couldn't possibly mean it. She was afraid to believe it. Leo had dozens of girls to choose from, all of them beautiful. He had a reputation for breaking hearts, and he wasn't going to break hers. Besides, Dora would drive him utterly distracted within a week. Even to escape their present plight she couldn't inflict her mother on him. A stifled giggle escaped her, and turned into a sob.

'No, Leo, I can't! Don't touch me!' she added swiftly as she felt him close to her. 'Please don't!'

Leo turned away. 'I'm sorry. I'll be out for the rest of the day. Please forget I said anything.'

Easy to say, Josie thought during the remainder of that interminable day. What had she lost? The trouble was, she didn't know; she had no notion what love was, or whether the liking she felt for Leo was love. She clung to the thought that it was better for them all this way. Soon she might be able to find better lodgings, then the temptation to believe him would not be so strong. Not that he would ask her again, she thought, unaccountably bleak. She'd refused him twice, and no man would endure such rejection often. That was far too much to expect.

On the surface, Leo and Josie seemed to be back in their former friendly relationship. Neither referred to his proposal, and when

Josie arrived at work on the following day Leo had behaved very much as normal. There had been a slight tension at first, but as the work absorbed them they resumed their normal friendliness. One morning, a week later, Josie was making tea while Leo opened the safe to get out the day's supply of gold sheet and wire. He carefully weighed the material out, and was about to divide it up among the different craftsmen when there was a piercing scream from the factory floor below.

Normally in the office the noises of the machinery could be heard only as a low hum. Leo looked up, startled, and peered through the window which overlooked the factory. 'One of the polishing belts has broken and someone's hurt. Telephone for an ambulance!' he snapped, and leapt for the metal spiral stairs on one corner. Though seldom used, they gave quicker, more direct access to the factory than the other staircase, which had doors top and bottom and a short passage with two more doors to negotiate.

Josie grabbed the telephone and begged the operator to hurry. Behind her someone came into the office.

'Mr Leo sent me ter say try an' get a doctor too,' one of the girls said. 'The kettle's boilin' over. D'yer want me ter look to it?'

'Please. Make some tea, the girl might be glad of it,' Josie flung back as she tried again to get the operator.

When she had finished and was sure both a doctor and an ambulance were on their way, she went to look at the scene below. Leo was kneeling beside one of the girls, who had blood all over her face. The rest of the workers were crowding round, some of the girls crying, all of them looking worried. Josie could see the broken belt. The machines made the thick belts spin so fast it was impossible to see more than a blur as they revolved. It was a constant fear that they might snap. Now, she understood why. There was nothing she could do down there, however. The other girl had gone without making the tea, though she had turned off the gas. Josie busied herself with the teapot and found that her own hands were trembling slightly. She made a full pot. It might be needed.

Ten minutes later, the doctor had departed with the injured girl, saying he hoped her eyesight could be saved, and Leo came back into the office. He gratefully accepted the cup of tea Josie handed him and slumped into the chair.

'Thanks. Josie, I can't leave the factory today. Would you be an angel and go to tell that poor girl's mother? Take her to the hospital.' He handed Josie a ten-shilling note. 'Get a taxi-cab, and stay with her as long as she needs you. Do you mind?'

'Of course I don't.'

He was looking in a small ledger. 'Here's her address, I'll write it down, it's not far away. Tell her not to worry about the money, I'll pay Lilian's wages while she's off sick and keep the job open for her. If she wants to come back,' he added under his breath.

Josie was away for most of the day. She tried to comfort Lilian's mother while an emergency operation was performed on the girl's eye. After she'd seen her daughter put to bed in a ward, heavily bandaged and still anaesthetized, Josie took her home. When she got back to work, Leo sent her home too, as soon as she had told him what had happened at the hospital.

'You look dreadful,' he said bluntly. 'Go and have an early night, and if you don't feel well enough don't come in tomorrow. I can manage.'

Josie smiled wanly. 'Thanks, I'll be OK by the morning. There are still all the invoices to finish. I'll just leave them here till tomorrow.'

The following morning, Leo looked even more haggard than he had the day before. Surely he couldn't have spent a second night working here? He was sitting behind his desk and Josie saw with some astonishment that it was clear of all papers. She glanced at the pile of invoices on a side table but it seemed the same as yesterday. He couldn't have been doing them. She looked enquiringly at him, her eyebrows raised.

'Why did you do it?' he asked. His voice was level but Josie detected a deeply suppressed anger. 'I didn't expect to see you today.'

'I don't need time off and there's so much to do. How is Lilian? Have you heard?'

'Much you care!'

'Leo, what have I done? Why are you being like this?'

He stood up and began to pace the room, throwing words over his shoulders. 'You pretend to be so innocent and so efficient and I was taken in by it. I told myself I should never trust anyone connected to your greedy, selfish mother, but I did. You seemed different, but it was all a pose, wasn't it? You were determined to make me pay for my father's mistakes. What an opportunity it must have seemed.'

'Leo, stop it! I haven't the slightest idea what you're talking about. You'll have to explain.'

'It's you who need to explain!' he said furiously, turning and grasping her shoulders bruisingly. 'I trusted you, I liked you, I even thought I was beginning to love you . . .' he paused, and turned away. 'I thought you were an excellent worker,' he said tonelessly. 'And you rob me!'

'What?' Josie gasped, taking a step backwards. 'Rob you? For heaven's sake, what of? I haven't taken anything of yours!'

He swung round to face her again. 'Then where is the gold you took when I was dealing with the accident yesterday?'

Josie, white-faced, stepped back as far as she could go. Leo turned away and spoke towards the window. He seemed to be having some difficulty enunciating the words, but Josie heard and understood despite her feeling of total unreality.

'Yesterday, when the accident happened, I was weighing out the gold to be used. I left it out and you were here alone with it for several minutes. When you'd gone to the hospital I thought some sheets were missing. Hundreds of pounds' worth. I spent hours last night weighing and calculating, checking the last deliveries and every scrap we've used. I went through all the records a dozen times, because I thought it had to be a mistake. But it isn't.'

'And you believe I took it? You actually think I'm a thief, that I'd steal some of the gold from you? Leo Bradley, how dare you!'

He laughed grimly. 'Oh, yes, I expected a display of outraged virtue. You've learned a lot from your mother, she always had the perfect air of innocence.'

'Leave my mother out of this!'

He laughed harshly. 'Look at the facts, Josie. You're living in a slum. You obviously need the money, though you can't bring yourself to marry me. You can't stomach my person, but you're happy enough to steal what's mine.'

'I haven't stolen anything!' she raged.

'I'm sure both you and your mother blame me for my father's financial failures. And you were the only person to have the opportunity.'

Josie was recovering from the shock. She took a deep breath to calm herself. 'I wasn't,' she said, trying keep her anger under control. 'I wasn't alone here all the time. There was that girl you sent up to ask me to call the doctor.'

'What girl? Why should I need a doctor? You were calling for an ambulance.'

'He came just after the ambulance.'

'He came with it. I didn't send any girl up here asking for a doctor. That's nonsense!'

'It's the truth! She came up here while I was telephoning and said you'd sent her. I looked up the doctor's number and telephoned for him.'

'Then we can sort this out. Who are you accusing? Which of the girls was it? We'll ask her at once.'

'I didn't see who it was,' Josie suddenly remembered. 'Just one of the girls. Several wear turbans to keep their hair out of the way. It makes them look alike. It must have been one of the new ones, or I'd have known her.'

'So you cannot in the least prove what you say!' he replied scornfully.

'I was busy with the telephone,' Josie, furious, tried to explain, knowing how unlikely it sounded. 'All I had was a general impression. She said I was to phone for the doctor, that you'd asked me to.'

Leo turned to stare at her, then he shook his head. 'All the girls were downstairs.'

'I suppose you were watching all of them all the time while you were trying to help Lilian? Don't be so ridiculous! That's just as unlikely as one of them coming up here. And I tell you one did. She said something about the kettle boiling and asked if she should make some tea. But she didn't. She only turned off the gas. I remember thinking that was odd after she'd offered. She must have taken the gold while my back was turned. It would have been easy enough to hide it in her pockets.'

'If you could say who it was I might believe you,' he said heavily. 'At least we could ask her. But I find it incredible that you cannot even describe her.'

'I didn't do more than glance at her! If you can't manage to believe me won't you at least ask everyone else if they saw someone coming up here?'

He stared intently at her for a moment, then shrugged. 'It would be pointless. There was such confusion.'

'So you prefer to believe I'm a thief and a liar without even considering other possibilities. I'm amazed you could ever have brought yourself to imagine I was a fit wife for the high and mighty Leo Bradley!'

'You're certainly showing yourself unfit now, as well as remarkably unintelligent. There is no alternative. Don't you think I've been searching for one all night? I don't want to think you're a thief,' he said, trying to make his voice calmer. 'It's so ridiculous. I don't want to be proved wrong about you, Josie. I depend on you. You do more to run this business than Matthew, and he's my manager. You're worth two of him. But there is no other explanation. I don't enjoy making such accusations. I was hoping –'

Josie interrupted, furiously angry. 'If that were true, you'd do as I ask and question the girls! You don't want to be proved wrong. Is that why you're so pig-headed? But you prefer to think I'm dishonest. Well, I prefer not to work for someone who doesn't trust me. I hope you can find yourself a more satisfactory secretary to take my place,' she flung at him, turning and rushing headlong down the stairs and out into the street.

She was shaking with rage, scarcely able to see where she was going for the angry tears which blinded her. It was some time before she realized that, instead of walking towards Nechells, she was heading towards the city centre. She paused, brushing away the tears and turning away from a young man who looked curiously at her. She couldn't face her mother yet. She needed to calm down, to think. Eventually, finding nowhere quiet enough to give her the peace she craved, she entered St Philip's Cathedral and chose a seat in a secluded corner. Here she wouldn't be disturbed. She could consider calmly the monstrous accusation Leo had flung at her, and the lesser worry that she no longer had a job.

Leo sat with his head in his hands. Had he made a dreadful mistake? Josie had sounded truly astonished, but if she were guilty, she must have been prepared for suspicion to fall on her, and been confident she could bluff her way through. Otherwise she would not have come to work. But if she'd stayed away that would have been as good as a confession. Her story of one of the girls coming up was unlikely, though not impossible, yet it was odd she couldn't identify the girl. She'd worked with him for long enough to know most of them. But if it were a fabrication she dared not name anyone.

Should he call in the police? Should he turn it all over to

them? He couldn't decide. If Josie were guilty she might face prison, and he couldn't be responsible for that. If she had stolen the gold it must be because of the intolerable pressures her dreadful mother put on her. Although Josie never grumbled, he had gathered from occasional comments that Dora was often difficult to live with, complaining about the changes in her circumstances and blaming them jointly on his father and himself. He hadn't forgotten Dora's assumption that he would provide for them both when his father died, or her attempt to coerce him into marrying Josie. Had Josie regretted not accepting his proposal, or not been able to bring herself to accept it, but thought it a mad sort of justice to steal from him what Dora felt he owed them, to force him to provide in this way? She'd virtually demanded that he give her a job, after all. Perhaps that was now insufficient.

He shook his head wearily and went slowly down to the workroom. He spoke to each girl in turn, asking them if they knew who had called the doctor. None of them admitted anything, some assuming he had come with the ambulance, others thinking he or Miss Shaw had summoned someone. No one knew if anyone else had left the workshop, though two girls, rather shamefaced, said they'd had to go outside to be sick. As no one else had noticed their absence it was possible one of them or someone else had gone upstairs without it being seen. There was no proof, and he could see no way of obtaining any. The only certainty was that a large quantity of gold had disappeared while he had been downstairs and Josie was still in the office.

He toyed with the idea of trying to see Josie and discuss it again, but what would it achieve? She was unlikely to confess or be able to prove her innocence. And by now Dora would know of it and be even more antagonistic towards him. She would not permit Josie to return to work for him, and unless her innocence were proved he certainly could not employ her again. There was no other explanation.

He would miss her cheerfulness and efficiency. He would miss Josie herself, he knew with painful clarity. Without his being fully aware of it he had come to value the time they spent together. He had looked forward to each morning simply because he would be with her. He'd been disturbed seeing her out with William Scott, witnessing the growing friendship between them, seeing the way in which they worked companionably together during the rallies. He suddenly realized that he had wanted to marry her all the time. He didn't know what love was, but if it meant wanting to spend your life with someone, then he loved Josie. He'd discovered it too late. And yet, if she were a thief, how could he contemplate loving her? With a heavy heart, he knew it could never come right. He might never see her again. That was a far greater loss than the theft of the gold. It was a wound that could never be healed.

Josie forced herself to think back to the previous day. She went through every detail of the frantic minutes immediately after the accident, but it was of no avail. She simply hadn't seen the girl, not even to know the colour of the dress she'd worn. Then she heard again the girl's voice. It was so clear she looked round, startled, thinking it was coming from somewhere in the Cathedral, but it was in her head. She concentrated and thought that if she ever heard that voice and those words again, she would recognize the speaker. But that was of little use. By now the gold would have been spirited away and there would be no proof. She would have to live with the suspicion.

She straightened her shoulders. She knew she was innocent and she would not behave as though she were guilty. Why had Leo accused her? He must believe it, but somehow she would disprove it, though how this might be possible she couldn't yet discern. First she must find another job. She began to feel a slight panic. What had she done, throwing away a safe, well-paid job when she was in a temper? It made her look guilty. She ought to have stood firm, insisted on searching for proof of her innocence, but she'd been so shocked Leo could suspect her she hadn't been thinking properly. She'd soon find another job, she told herself bracingly. There were many offices in the city which employed girls with her qualifications. She would have preferred to stay in the jewellery business, for she was getting to know it and finding it fascinating, seeing the plain ordinary metal transformed into objects of beauty and mastering the many aspects of the administrative work, but Leo's accusation might be known. The jewellery quarter in Hockley was close-knit, gossip soon spread, and Leo would doubtless seek to prevent any other jeweller from employing her. She would begin looking in the city centre straight away.

It proved a thankless task. She found advertisements in the *Birmingham Post*, and she visited two agencies, but when she revealed that she could not produce a reference from her previous employer, she was told there were no suitable openings. She visited two firms advertising, to find both positions already filled. She telephoned others to discover that there were too many girls looking for work. If she said she had no experience there were others who had: if she claimed experience they wanted references.

By the end of the afternoon she was despondently setting off homewards when Dick Endersby drew up beside her on his motorcycle. 'Josie! What luck to find you in the middle of town! I was coming to visit you. I'm home for just two days before I go to The Place for Easter. My grandparents' house,' he explained. 'Let's go to the pictures. *City Lights* is showing. Will you come? And we've time for something to eat first.'

Josie hesitated. It would delay the almost certain hysterical recriminations of her mother. Dora might not like her job with Leo Bradley, but she would most certainly be deeply offended by hearing that Josie had lost it. And perhaps, after an evening watching Charlie Chaplin, when she might forget the problems which had been absorbing her all day, she could think more clearly. She smiled at Dick and said she'd enjoy that very much.

'But I ought to go home and make sure my mother has all she wants first, so may we miss the meal? I'll meet you at the cinema.'

Chapter Eleven

Josie didn't tell her mother about losing her job. Dora, though gratified she was going out with Dick Endersby, forgot her resolutions and complained about her headache. When Josie got back after the cinema she was in bed fast asleep. Josie lay awake all night wondering how best to make the confession, and persuaded herself Dora might accept it more readily if she could present it as a change for the better. She would spend the day searching and surely ought to be able to find a job soon. It was cowardly, she freely admitted, but she couldn't face recriminations about losing her job as well as Dora's tearful pleadings to be allowed to buy just one new dress.

'I simply can't face my friends again in these old rags,' Dora said unhappily after one visit to Harborne.

'They're only a few months old and you've hardly worn them,' Josie pointed out.

'But these are winter clothes and it will soon be April. Oh, dear, I suppose you're right. I don't mean to be difficult, darling, but could you ask Leo to give you a little more? I'm sure you deserve it and he has a very profitable business. If only the police would search Freddy's room properly and find my sapphires!'

It would be grimmer now, for Leo's salary had been generous and she'd be unlikely to find anything as well paid.

She set off as if for work, but walked instead to the city centre. It was the same story as yesterday, and by the end of the afternoon Josie was thankful to be offered a job in a small, rather sleazy café near Snow Hill station. It was far less money than she'd been getting, but she'd begun to think it was impossible to find any sort of job which didn't have a dozen people applying for it, all with more experience or qualifications than she had. She would be looking for something else, but this would do for now, and she could start tomorrow.

Leo went wearily back to the office. The new building was presenting unexpected problems and Matthew had insisted on taking the day off, so he'd had to be over there most of the day. He was dismayed at the confusion of papers on his desk and wondered when he would have the time to deal with them. He hadn't appreciated how much of his work Josie had been doing. He must find another secretary. He glanced at his watch. There was no time to draft an advertisement for the paper now, he was late for an appointment with the buyer from a large jewellery shop. He sighed. Had he wronged Josie? He'd gone over the events of that dreadful day hundreds of times, but unless Josie's unlikely story was true she had been the only one with the opportunity of stealing the gold. He could not imagine any of the girls he employed being clever enough to take advantage of such an opportunity and make the excuse to visit the office, or cool enough to remove the gold and not give herself away afterwards by her behaviour. If it had been true, surely Josie would have had some idea of which girl it was. She could have made more effort to remember. He wished he hadn't been so reluctant to investigate her claims. He'd been exhausted, frantic with worry after a sleepless night trying to imagine some other solution, and had accused her too readily. If only he'd been more temperate.

He must make more effort to find another secretary, he told himself again as he made sure everything was locked up. Or perhaps he would employ a male clerk. He could not envisage any other girl in Josie's place. He would be forever comparing another girl to Josie, and to her disadvantage. This would, he told himself, be unfair to any girl he employed. He resolutely thrust aside the suspicion that it was more than Josie's competence he missed. He preferred not to analyse his feelings for Josie, it was too painful.

When Josie got home from her first exhausting day at the café she found Dora in bed, shivering, and with a high temperature. 'Mother, what's wrong? You're ill!'

'I feel dreadful,' Dora confessed. 'I'm sure it's typhoid from this dreadful place. Or cholera.'

'It's probably just influenza,' Josie said calmly, 'but perhaps you'd like to see a doctor?'

'It's not just influenza, Josephine!' Dora said with something of her normal spirit. 'You're never ill, you can't imagine how dreadful it is to be delicate like I am, and you have no sympathy for me.'

Fretfully, Dora refused to eat, but Josie made a cup of tea and then went down to consult Mrs Sheehan. 'My mother needs a doctor,' she said, thinking in some trepidation of how she'd afford to pay one.

'Try Dr Mandeville's clinic, that's free,' Mrs Sheehan suggested, and Josie could have hugged her. 'Opened it last year, 'e did. Fashionable doctor from Edgbaston, started one clinic in Ladywood years ago, now 'e's got another.'

'Where is it, and will anyone be there in the evening?'

'What day is it? Yes, 'e'll be there if yer 'urries.'

Dr Mandeville was just locking up when Josie, breathless, reached the small building which had been erected on derelict land. 'Am I too late?' she gasped.

'Not if it's urgent. Are you ill?'

'No, my mother. I think it's only influenza but she worries so.'

'Influenza can be serious, but let's go and see if we can reassure her. Come in my car, it will be faster.'

Josie looked in awe at the expensive open-topped Alvis. 'Aren't you afraid to leave such a car in the streets round here?' she asked impulsively.

'No, everyone knows it's mine and no one would damage it,' he said, holding open the door for her. 'I've seen you somewhere. Have you been to my clinic before?'

Josie had recognized him too, but could hardly reveal they'd met as guests at Mrs Endersby's Christmas party. She just hoped his memory wasn't good enough to recall her.

'I expect you've seen me around,' she said hurriedly.

Dr Mandeville's quiet, sympathetic manner did Dora as much good as the medicine he prescribed. Josie, to her relief, was able to leave her mother and go to work the following day, for she knew she would lose the job at once if she had time off. When she got home Dora was sitting up, much better, full of praise for such a gentlemanly doctor.

'He's the doctor who set poor little Ann's arm when she broke it,' she informed Josie. 'He has a huge practice in Edgbaston, the wealthiest people in the city. He has an independent fortune too, so he runs clinics for the dreadful people who live in the slums who can't afford to pay.'

In some amusement, Josie wondered whether her mother counted herself in this class now, but she knew Dora too well. She blandly ignored what she didn't want to face.

Within a week Dora was back to normal and Josie had a little more leisure for trying to find another, better job. Because of Dora's illness, Josie hadn't told her about the new job, feeling cowardly but telling herself the news would cause Dora a setback. It would be preferable if she could find another job before she had to reveal the truth.

Josie was learning ever-more ingenious ways of economizing. With what she earned they could just pay the rent and eat, if they were careful and if she shopped late on Saturday in the Bull Ring, where the market traders sold off meat and poultry really cheaply. Then, to her amazement, Dora said that one of her friends had recommended her for a position as saleslady in a small gown shop in Corporation Street.

'But Mother, you'll have to travel in by tram, and you'll be so tired!' Josie protested.

'I must make the sacrifice, Josephine. I realize I've been selfish, and I can't permit you to do everything. With this dreadful new fourpenny tax on tea we need extra money.'

Josie laughed. 'I know every penny counts, but we don't drink all that much tea.'

Dora gave her a conspiratorial smile. 'But we can't be reduced to steeping the tea leaves twice. Besides, it's only for three days a week, so I can rest on the other days. And I can buy clothes at a discount.'

Josie grinned and promptly bade farewell to her mother's wages. They would be spent on clothes, but that would be better than Dora's discontent at not being able to afford any luxuries. And she'd be able to get away from the awful rooms, which were becoming unbearable as the weather grew warmer. The stenches from the court intensified, the insistent flies sometimes seemed to fill the rooms, however many flypapers they hung up. Mice roamed fearlessly, breeding faster than they could be caught, and worst of all was the pervasive smell from the gasworks.

The first intimation of trouble came a few weeks later in the form of a brief note from Phoebe, enclosing a bill from an expensive gown shop.

If you want to buy on tick that's your affair. Pay on the nail's my motto, and I'd think it ought to be yours. But I will not have you claiming you still live here, Doris. There will be big trouble if any bailiffs turn up in Freer Road! Your sister, Phoebe.

Josie suspected that if Mrs Sheehan had not kept the note to give to her Dora might have torn it up. When Josie taxed her with spending money they didn't have on expensive gowns she didn't need, Dora collapsed into tears.

'But I'm earning money. I can pay for it. It was a mistake, I forgot we weren't living with Phoebe when I gave her address. Josephine, I'm sorry!'

'You were going to buy clothes from where you work.'

'I have. But the wretched woman won't allow me to have any more, she says I've already spent my wages, and this was such a bargain, I can pay for it with next week's wages.'

'I hope so,' was all Josie said.

Then a tearful Dora confessed the following day that she had been given the sack. 'It wasn't my fault. I only told that dreadful woman that if she thought she could speak to me in such a tone she'd better go elsewhere. I think that's perfectly reasonable.'

Josie couldn't help laughing. 'We'll have to sell one of the ornaments,' she said, but Dora was aghast.

'No! Josephine, I can't sell my treasures! Ask Leo to increase your salary.'

'I don't work for Leo any more,' Josie sighed, and the whole story came out. Dora was shocked, indignant with Leo for daring to accuse Josie of theft, reluctant to accept that Josie couldn't find a better job, but still unwilling to sell her treasures.

'They're packed in boxes and always getting in the way, I'm sure you wouldn't miss a few pieces.'

In the end, Dora reluctantly agreed that Josie might sell some of her least-favoured ornaments. The prices were far lower than either of them had expected, for the market was saturated with goods sold by the unemployed. More had to be sacrificed to raise the necessary amount, and Dora suggested that Josie had not haggled enough. When the second note came from Phoebe, with another bill and also demanding that, as well as ceasing to use her address, they arrange to remove the piano immediately, Josie lost her temper and threatened to leave Dora unless she agreed to sell the piano and promised not to run up any more bills.

Tearfully, Dora explained that she'd forgotten she'd bought a pair of shoes to go with the dress. She promised that was her final debt and the bill was settled, but only after more of their possessions were sold.

Dora became withdrawn, sitting with a lost expression in her eyes or clinging tearfully to Josie and pleading that she would never leave her. Josie could see no way out of her difficulties. Without a better job, her position was hopeless.

'Sometimes, Leo, you're a damned fool!' Tobias said. 'What the devil made you think Josie could ever steal from you?'

'It all pointed to her,' Leo said wearily. 'And I'd be grateful if you didn't speak to me like that. You're still my employee,' he said with a brief display of spirit. He couldn't bring himself to admit to Tobias that he'd begun to have doubts, let alone regrets.

'I don't have to be your employee,' Tobias pointed out. 'I could get another job tomorrow if I chose.'

'Then why do you stay?' Leo demanded.

Tobias shrugged. 'Sometimes I wonder, when that fool Horobin's making a tidy mess of his side of the factory, and you don't even notice. That's apart from how you treated Josie. Have you no judgement at all? I suppose it suits me to stay for the time being. But don't rely on me. I'll go when I choose, but that'll be soon if things get any worse.'

'You might go earlier than you think,' Leo snapped. 'No man's indispensable!'

'In that case,' Tobias said mildly, 'I'll hand in my notice right now.'

At the café Josie had to work all day on Saturday. After the mid-day rush, she was wiping down the oilcloth-covered tables in the window when she glanced up and stared in surprise. Freddy and the girl she had seen him with once before were walking arm in arm along the street, heading towards Snow Hill station. Both carried small cases. Then she looked at the girl again and knew she had seen her somewhere else.

Josie moved towards the door and waited. As the pair came closer a certain way the girl tossed her head as she laughed gave Josie the answer. She worked in Leo Bradley's factory. She was one of the polishers Matthew had taken on. Josie stepped behind the door and when they had passed walked out and followed them, heedless of the indignant protests of her boss. They were so absorbed in one another she didn't think they would be likely to notice her, and she risked drawing close enough to hear the occasional few sentences.

'There's a house we could afford near me brother, Freddy,' the girl was saying eagerly. 'When we get back, d'yer want me ter look to it?'

Josie almost called out in surprise. Then she knew it would be useless and turned away. As she recollected where she was and walked slowly back to the café, she was trying to puzzle it out. The furious tirade which greeted her return flowed over her head, and she scarcely heard or understood the instructions to take herself off, for he wouldn't have no truck with girls who thought they was better than them as employed them, and could walk in and out of their place of work without so much as a by your leave when there was plenty of others that would be glad of a good, clean, easy job, thank you very much. As she walked home she began to laugh. Twice now she had been given the sack by irate employers, and twice she had walked out, too furious to demand the wages she was due. It wasn't funny, but somehow the laughter bubbled up inside her. She would have to start the depressing process of looking for yet another job. And before that she would have to face her mother.

'I knew how it would be if you demeaned yourself by working in a factory,' Dora exclaimed. 'It all comes down to that. None of this would have happened if I'd been firmer. Leo was never to be trusted, and now I'm better so I will tell him! Get my best coat, my dear, and I will go straight away. He shall not treat my darling only child in such an abominable fashion, and he'll give you compensation.'

'Mother, he won't be there, it's Saturday evening.'

'Then I'll go to his house.'

'He may be out, or have visitors. In any case, I think I know who stole the gold. It would be better to tell him when he can confront the one who's really guilty.'

'You know who did it? But why didn't you tell him?'

'I've only just found out, and it's only a suspicion, but it fits all the facts. I think it was Freddy.'

'Freddy? But how on earth could he? He doesn't work there. I am prepared to believe anything of that terrible boy, but I think you must be wrong in this case.'

'I don't mean he was there, but I believe he organized it. He was desperate for money, wasn't he, and we thought he'd stolen the silver to sell.'

'Yes, but you keep telling me he didn't,' Dora said.

'It came back, but he might have pawned it.'

'That was what I said and no one would believe me.'

'I do now. It's lots of little things. He was suddenly interested in my job, especially how the gold was controlled, the careful measuring and so on. Almost immediately after we missed the silver, Freddy had a lot of new clothes. And Lizzie and I saw him with this girl. She looked familiar but I didn't recognize her properly or I might have been suspicious then. She works for Leo; she's a polisher. Her name is Mabel Jopling. Freddy could have pawned the silver so that he could make an impression with her. Then, somehow, when we missed it, he got hold of enough money to get it back and he put it in the piano.'

'I said this all along, but I don't know what it's got to do with the gold that was stolen.'

'Let me think. Freddy's been doing jobs for Matthew, I've seen him cleaning the car outside the factory. And Mabel got the job through Matthew. I don't know whether Freddy planned to steal anything, but the accident was a heaven-sent opportunity. Oh, no!'

'Now what?'

'I wonder if she could possibly have done something to the belt which broke, so that it wasn't pure bad luck Lilian was hurt? It would have been very difficult to get Leo out of the office away from the gold any other way. But surely she couldn't have been so wicked as to deliberately injure another girl and possibly blind her?'

'I'd believe anything of some of these girls Freddy associates with.'

'Well, whatever the truth of that, today I heard her say exactly the same words she said to me when she told me about the kettle boiling over — "D'yer want me ter look to it?" she said. I recognized her voice, it had the same inflection on the words. Now Freddy and Mabel have the money to go away, apparently for the weekend, but more than anything else they were talking of affording a house. How could they possibly do that when Freddy doesn't have a proper job, even if she does?'

Dora's fury was awe-inspiring. She wanted to rush to Freer Road and confront Phoebe immediately, but Josie eventually persuaded her this would solve nothing.

'We have to wait until Freddy's back,' she insisted. 'I don't know if we'll be able to prove anything then, but I intend to have a jolly good try. In the meantime we mustn't risk him finding out and getting another story ready.'

To her guilty relief, Dora succumbed to one of her headaches and retreated to bed. By Sunday morning she had a fever and Josie became seriously worried, but, just as she was on the point of calling Dr Mandeville, Dora, who had been tossing restlessly, woke and demanded some tea and thin bread and butter. Josie heaved a sigh of relief and went to prepare it. Now, once more, she had to find herself a job.

*

Leo hadn't fully appreciated how much of the business had depended on Tobias's constant flow of ideas. When he lost several orders because he couldn't promise new designs soon, he determined to employ another designer. Surely, he told himself, there were others as talented as Tobias. Once that was done he could prepare the next catalogue, and go abroad early.

Matthew, having apparently forgotten their earlier row on the subject, again urged him to produce small items needed by car manufacturers.

Leo raised his eyebrows. 'I don't think either of us is inventive enough to design anything new,' he commented acidly, 'and I won't contemplate buying any more stolen designs.'

Matthew sighed. 'You'll never believe me, will you? I admit I was taken in, but that was all. You saw William, and he said he'd never employed a Hugh Jones.'

'So we still don't know where that grille design came from. Fortunately William accepted your explanation.'

'Even if you still don't! But the other thing, what are you going to do about a clerk? It's getting desperate since Miss Ames left, she couldn't manage your work as well as mine.'

Leo's need for a clerk had become urgent, but he had put off advertising for one. 'I'll see about it today,' he promised.

'I've an idea. One of my father's former employees has had to leave his present job because his employer's cutting back, he'd be ideal. Henry's an old pal of mine,' Matthew explained. 'He used to take me to see the Villa play on Saturday afternoons, when I was no more than six or seven.'

Leo was thankful to agree. He must dismiss his worries about Matthew's honesty. The man had made a genuine mistake, first in buying the design then in starting production without consulting him. They still had to work together. If nothing else, his employment of Matthew's man eased the tension between him and his manager. That made life in the office rather more harmonious than it had been of late, and Leo had to be thankful. Besides, Henry Manders uncomplainingly dealt with Matthew's work as well as Leo's. He proved quiet, efficient, and self-effacing. He soon restored order to Leo's office, but Leo had to tell himself not to feel resentful that he wasn't Josie.

Josie could find no regular jobs. When Dora suggested she put an advertisement in the paper, Josie shook her head. 'There are far more advertisements of people looking for work than there are of jobs available,' she said. 'Besides, we can't spare one and sixpence for an advertisement.'

Dora wanted to pursue her plan to confront Freddy, but Lizzie told Josie that he'd moved out of Freer Road and even his mother didn't know where he was living. Reluctantly Dora had to postpone action.

To Josie's surprise and immense gratitude, she came home one evening to discover Dora effervescent with triumph. 'I've got another job, Josephine!' she cried. 'It's only for a few hours, but the money will help, won't it?'

'Mother! What is it? It won't be too much for you, will it? You're not strong.'

'It's the little shop further up the street. The owner is rather a coarse man, but he's an elderly widower, and he's made it very plain he admires me. I suggested he needed help for a couple of hours in the middle of the day, so that he could have his dinner in peace and put his feet up afterwards. He's getting on, and I can deal with the few people who come into the shop then, it's not busy.'

She was so pleased with herself that life became far more pleasant. Dora usually came home with funny stories to tell about the owner of the shop and his gallantries, which made her preen even while she mocked them, or the customers who did or said odd things. It was, Josie felt, almost as though they'd slipped back ten years to the time when Dora had delighted in telling stories. Josie herself got three evenings a week working as a barmaid and several cleaning jobs. The money was barely enough to pay the rent and buy food, and before long Dora was complaining of a bewildering variety of symptoms. She insisted on keeping her job, but most of her money was spend on patent medicines.

'You must see the doctor,' Josie said, worried, when she found Dora huddled in bed, shivering and feverish.

'No, my dear, I know we can't afford it,' Dora said with unusual firmness.

'Dr Mandeville doesn't charge,' Josie said patiently.

'It's charity, and I never thought I'd descend to that. The syrup you bought me yesterday seems to be doing my cough good, and the little blue pills help my indigestion. Don't worry about me. I won't let myself be a burden any more.'

Josie heard of a job in another pub, and she was able to get two more evenings, then three, and a few hours during the day, too. She was earning almost as much as she had at Leo's, though working much longer hours, but she refused to compromise by buying food locally, insisting on getting it as cheaply as possible in the Bull Ring markets. She could even begin to save a few pennies each week, and by their unaided efforts she and her mother might get out of this slum. It might take years, but they would do it.

Then, in the height of summer, Dora became really ill.

Chapter Twelve

THE next few months were the worst of Josie's life. Dora was so ill she needed constant attention. Dr Mandeville came almost daily. At first, nothing he could do seemed to relieve the pain Dora felt, though eventually it receded. Dora was so weak she couldn't get out of bed, and so restless she couldn't bear Josie sleeping beside her. Josie had to sleep on cushions on the living-room floor. There was a spell of hot weather which made the smells rising from the small enclosed court more pungent than ever. Freddy, the sapphires, and the gold stolen from Leo were all forgotten in the worry about Dora's health.

Josie had to abandon all her jobs, and was desperate for money. At first she pawned some of Dora's ornaments. They had to have money to live and Dora was too ill to notice. Soon, though, Josie realized she would never be able to save enough to retrieve them, even if Dora got better straight away and she could get another job, so she sold items, and became adept at haggling with traders, ruthless in obtaining the best possible price.

It was six weeks before Josie could leave Dora for any length of time. She began once more the weary search for work. Since she needed to be at home to give Dora regular food and medicine, a full-time job was impossible, but she could, she hoped, obtain bar work once more. Her previous jobs had all been filled, but gradually she began to find an evening at one pub, an afternoon elsewhere, and as her former employers discovered she was able to fill in for occasional absences she was often offered odd evenings. It was not enough to live on. The ornaments still had to be sold, but Dora was so listless Josie didn't think she'd have the energy to object even if she knew.

After another month, however, Dora improved enough to be left all day, and Josie began to think about a secretarial job. Although she hadn't minded the hard work of the cleaning jobs, she found it difficult to restrain her caustic comments when some of the pub customers made offensive suggestions. She couldn't think how she had kept silent when one large man, florid of face and paunchy, told her she was wasted here and ought to let him look after her.

'Nice classy-speakin' gal loike yow, could earn quids ev'ry night wi' the right customers. Plenty of nobs want a bit on side, an' I've gorra very select 'ouse where they know they'll find what they want, an' no questions asked. I'd want ten per cent, but there'd be plenty left fer yer ter save fer retirement.'

Josie had stared indignantly at him until, as he later explained to a friend, he didn't know what had come over him, but somehow he'd had to turn away.

She could earn more as a secretary than with all her part-time jobs, and now she had several previous employers to provide her with references. She began to look for clerical or secretarial work, spending more than she felt she ought on good notepaper and stamps replying to all the suitable jobs advertised in the *Post*.

It took several weeks before she even had an interview. Until now she had shied away from the Hockley area, too hurt to want to tread its streets again, but this had been the only hope of a job. She had to abandon one of her bar jobs, being told that if she did not turn up for work she need not come back, but she had to take the chance. If she didn't secure this job at the pen factory she would have less money than before.

The manager was sleek, plump, and oozing with self-satisfaction. He had a smooth, almost babyish face, but his eyes were hard and Josie immediately felt his gaze hostile as he waved her to an uncomfortable chair in front of his own spacious desk. He went through a list of questions, probing the reasons why Josie was working in what he called menial jobs when she had good qualifications.

'There are not many secretarial posts available,' Josie said mildly.

'You had one once, I believe, although you have not mentioned it. Why is that?'

Josie looked swiftly at him. There was a triumphant little smile playing round his thick lips, and his eyes challenged her to deny it. 'I worked at Bradley's,' she said quietly. 'I left when there was a dispute about the truthfulness of what I said. I refused to work for someone who disbelieves me.'

'There was also a dispute,' he mocked her, 'about your honesty? Are you truthful and honest, Miss Shaw?'

Josie stood up angrily. 'I see you've been told one side of the story! It's perfectly plain that you don't even want to hear the other. I don't know why you've wasted my time. Vulgar curiosity? I withdraw my application for your job. I won't work for you any more than for Leo Bradley!'

Furiously angry, determined not to be beaten by Leo's malicious gossip, Josie applied for more secretarial jobs, some in Hockley, and had two more interviews. Although no one else openly referred to her time working for Leo, the odd looks she received convinced her that the men who turned her down had heard the story and believed she had stolen the gold. A burning resentment towards Leo simmered within her, and she stormed as far as the door of his factory before she acknowledged that it would serve no good purpose to accuse him of spreading lies about her.

'Mr Matthew! Come quick, it's yer pa!'

Matthew, who was reading a recent issue of *Autocar* magazine, looked up angrily as Henry Manders burst into his office without knocking. He was about to deliver a blistering reproof when the sense of the words penetrated his thoughts about new developments in car instrumentation.

'What do you mean?' he demanded, casting down the magazine and rising to his feet.

'Yer pa, 'e's 'ad a turn. They telephoned. Mr Leo sent me ter tell yer.'

Matthew strode out of the office, and drove as fast as he could to his father's factory. As he entered the workshop he saw that none of the machines was being tended, and several men were crouched over the prone figure of his father in the centre of the factory floor. The other workers huddled in anxious groups, silently watching.

'Have you sent for a doctor?' Matthew demanded.

'Yes,' the foreman said, 'but I think it's too late.'

One of the older women who'd been kneeling on the floor, cradling Mr Horobin's head on her lap, looked up and explained. 'It were sudden, like, Mr Matthew. One minute yer pa were talkin' ter Bob, then 'e sort of staggered, an' fell before anyone could catch 'im.'

Matthew knelt beside his father and lifted his hand. It was limp, and Matthew imagined it was already cold. It seemed hours to him, and he was stiff from kneeling, before the doctor bustled in.

'I'm sorry, he's gone,' the doctor said after a swift examination. 'Heart attack.' He looked at Matthew standing silently beside his father's body. 'You're his son?'

'Mr Matthew,' the foreman volunteered when Matthew didn't reply.

'Can you deal with things here?' the doctor asked, ignoring Matthew, and the foreman nodded.

'I'll send everyone home,' he said quietly. 'I'll send Mr Matthew home too. He's no doubt had a shock.'

'Send someone with him. Is his mother alive? Who'll break it to her?'

'Poor lady! I'd better go, it doesn't look as though Mr Matthew could do it.'

'Good man. I'll send my bill here.'

Mrs Horobin, taking the news stoically, retreated to her room, asking not to be disturbed. Matthew, aware of the sympathetic glances of the cook and the housemaid, and becoming increasingly irritable at their frequent whispered requests to know if he wanted some tea, seized the whisky decanter and a glass and locked himself in his room.

He needed peace to think, to sort out his tangled emotions. Bewildered, half-horrified, he recognized behind the shock and the sorrow the beginning of a sense of jubilation. His more pressing debts to his tailor and bookmaker could be cleared. More importantly, he could afford to leave Leo. He need no longer swallow the insults and the contempt he was sure Leo displayed. He could make something to do with cars, and his recent reading had inspired him with a desire to make clocks and other instruments for the benefit of the motoring public. He could sell the old place and start afresh in more convenient premises. He'd get a good price for this house too. Fortunately, he still had the apartment, and his mother could go and live with her sister. First, however, there was the funeral to get through. Composing his features into an appropriately solemn mask, he went downstairs to telephone his father's solicitor and banker, and then an undertaker.

Mrs Thackeray-Walsh was entertaining her family to lunch at Endersby's one Sunday and Lizzie had a couple of hours free. She'd pay a surprise visit to her mother. When she reached Freer Road she was intrigued to find a large Humber saloon outside the house. Had her mother a visitor? Lizzie hadn't been aware she knew anyone with such an expensive car. She decided she ought not to walk in on whoever the visitors were, so knocked and waited on the doorstep.

'Lizzie! The door's on the latch, yer don't need ter knock,'

Phoebe exclaimed. 'Come on in, love. 'Ow long can yer stay for? I've got a lovely piece of beef in oven, plenty for all three of us.'

'Three? Is Freddy here? Surely that's not his car!' Lizzie exclaimed, jerking her head towards the Humber.

Phoebe roared with laughter. 'Bless yer, ducks, course it ain't! Freddy 'asn't been near me for weeks. Anyway, e's livin' with that Mabel. It belongs ter me friend. Come in parlour an' meet 'im.'

Lizzie had seen some of the changes her mother had made after Aunt Dora and Josie had left, mainly moving her furniture into the two rooms they'd occupied and taking over the big front room for her own bedroom, but until now the parlour had remained untouched. Rarely used, it had been full of heavy Victorian furniture, the chairs overstuffed and covered in dark brown plush, the huge sideboard almost filling one wall and dominating the room. A piano, never played, but ornate with gilt chandeliers, had faced it from the opposite wall, and the windows had been swathed in copiously pleated net and heavy, dark wine-coloured velvet curtains. All this had gone, to be replaced with smaller, moquette-covered settee and armchairs, a large glass-fronted cabinet with bulbous legs in a bright yellow veneered wood, crammed with china figures, and a solid draw-leaf table with similarly bulbous legs in front of the window, which was draped with fine net curtains and flowered chinz.

She had little time to take this in, however, for an elderly man, portly, red-faced, and completely bald, was struggling to his feet from one of the armchairs.

'Lizzie, pet, this is Mr Stokes. He was a colleague of your dad's, 'e made guns too. Clem, last time yer saw Lizzie she was no more'n five or six.'

Mr Stokes beamed. 'Well, now, fancy meetin' you today. That's great! Yer ma's been tellin' me all about yer smart job. I'll perhaps let yer drive me own car later on.'

'If that's your car outside, it's bigger than I've ever driven,' Lizzie said with a grin. 'So you're here for lunch? Are you sure I'm not in the way?'

Phoebe and Mr Stokes both laughed. 'We're old friends, yer ma and me. Used ter meet a lot when old Alfred was alive. And my Margaret. Then we lost touch, but we met up again a few months ago when I went to a church bazaar because I dain't have nothin' better ter do, an' Phoebe were servin' teas and some of 'er scones. I 'ad ter keep in touch then – never 'ad scones as good as Phoebe's!'

By the time she left, Lizzie decided she liked Mr Stokes. He was kind, amusing, told funny stories that often provided a laugh against himself, and tucked into Phoebe's delicious food with simple enjoyment. He had, he said without either pride or apology, made a fortune during the war, and bought himself a house out at Solihull. His only regrets were that his Margaret hadn't lived more than a few years to enjoy it, and he had just one daughter who'd married and gone to live in Australia, so he only saw her and her children once every two years, either when he visited her or she came home to England.

'Next time you've a day off you and yer ma should come and see me,' he said when Lizzie was saying goodbye. 'Just let me know and I'll come and fetch yer.'

Lizzie was thoughtful as she went back on the bus. Where was Freddy? And what was her mother up to?

Leo glanced up as Matthew strode into the office. 'How is your mother? She looked very ill at the funeral.'

'She'll recover. She's going to live with her sister in Bournemouth. They'll have plenty to gossip about,' Matthew said carelessly as he threw himself down in a chair.

'That's rather a sudden decision, isn't it?'

Matthew glared. 'I want the money from the house as soon as possible. There was no call to delay.'

'But your father's only been dead two weeks.'

'That's my affair! I'll ask you not to concern yourself with what isn't your business.'

'Very well. But this factory is my business, and since you can make up your mind to sell the house so quickly, perhaps you'll tell me what you mean to do about your job equally fast.'

'You can't wait to get rid of me, can you?' Matthew sneered.

Leo considered him calmly. 'Since you put it that way, Matthew, I think we will both be happier when we don't work together. I'm perfectly willing to forego your period of notice –'

Matthew leapt to his feet and began to stride about the small office, waving his arms and occasionally banging his fist on the desk for emphasis. 'If you think I'd stay a moment longer now I'm not dependent on you for a job, you're daft! You've never liked me, you won't trust me, you undermine my authority and you damage everything I try to do and –'

'Out,' Leo said, icy cool. 'I will not tolerate such behaviour in my office. It was a disaster employing you as manager. Josie could have done the job as well – better.'

'A girl? Rubbish. That would have been a disaster all right. Don't I wish I'd never come anywhere near you.'

'You can't manage yourself, so how do you expect to earn the respect of anyone else?' Leo continued. 'You may collect any personal belongings but I want you out of here within ten minutes.'

'I'll go when it damn well pleases me. Just because you had money, which you didn't work for, you think you're too superior for the rest of us. Well, you'll see, Bradley, one day you'll regret you didn't listen to me. You'd have made a fortune, but you're afraid to take a few risks –'

'A fortune made from stealing ideas?' Leo laughed. 'Either you were gulled, or I've been, for trusting you. Now get out before I throw you out.'

Matthew stared defiantly at him, but when Leo stood up and took a step towards him he only hesitated briefly.

'I'm going, but you'll regret it one day! You've put too many spokes in my wheel, and I don't forget. I'll get you. I'll make you wish you'd believed me ... ' he shouted as he clattered down the stairs.

Leo felt a sense of freedom. He'd have to work hard to do Matthew's job as well as his own, but he might have fewer worries.

Josie worked longer and longer hours. She managed to get two evenings a week as barmaid in the Grand hotel in the city centre, and several cleaning jobs.

She was working at the Grand one evening when Dora had seemed especially low. In her worried state, Josie barely noticed the customers until she heard a familiar voice. Startled, she glanced up. One of her colleagues was serving Leo, who didn't appear to have noticed her. She busied herself wiping glasses as she watched him through the mirror behind the bar. He carried his drinks across to a table in the corner and sat down beside a slender, exceedingly fashionably dressed woman. She was slim and lovely, wearing elegant clothes and a diamond necklace that was discreet but undeniably very expensive. Her dark hair was beautifully waved, and she smiled intimately up at Leo from vividly painted lips as he handed her the glass. She touched his hand briefly then leaned forward talking quietly to him. Josie breathed deeply. She thought the woman was faintly familiar. Maybe she had seen her with Leo at a rally. She was older than the girls he normally escorted.

'Who's that? The dark woman over in the corner,' she asked Phil, the chief barman, when there was a pause.

He glanced across and grinned. 'The delectable *principessa*. So she's back? I wonder for how long?'

'*Principessa*? Isn't that Italian? She doesn't look Italian even though she's so dark.'

'Oh no, she lived in Edgbaston, one of the nobs there. Denver, her name was then. Her mother was involved with the suffragettes, so I've heard. Then she took it into her head to go on the stage. She was at the Folies-Bergère, and you know what they are!' he added, winking. 'She married some elderly Italian. Wore him out I suppose. I expect she's back looking for another husband.'

Then Josie remembered. It was Kitty, the girl she'd seen at the party after the first rally Leo had taken her to, when they'd played charades.

When she again looked across to the corner table Leo was alone. She hadn't seen the *principessa* leave. At that moment, he glanced up and saw her and shock registered on his face. A second later he was striding to the bar.

'Josie, what the devil are you doing here?'

'Working. Can I get you a drink, sir?'

'You can't work in a bar. It's quite unsuitable.'

'I can and I am. Any job which provides me with money is suitable. It's a very superior bar,' she added curtly. 'Better than the others I work in.'

'But – it's quite wrong! A young girl like you shouldn't be in a bar. I thought – I imagined you'd have no difficulty in getting another office job.'

'With the stories you've put about? It's none of your business where I work, Leo Bradley,' she said softly. 'Please go away. Phil is looking at us and I don't want to lose another job through you.'

'That's what I want to talk about. We must talk.'

'What were you having, sir?' she repeated, willing her voice not to tremble.

'What time do you finish?'

'If you don't want a drink leave me alone,' Josie hissed, conscious of Phil's interested glances.

'Only when you agree to talk to me. I must know what – whether you're all right.'

'Why should I not be, living off the proceeds of my criminal activities? Which you didn't consider me too young to indulge in,' she added bitterly.

'Can I help you, sir?' Phil asked smoothly. He'd decided to intervene before Josie's raised voice was noticed by the other patrons.

Leo glared at him. 'Whisky,' he snapped.

Josie escaped, but she knew Leo watched her for the rest of the evening. Fortunately the Grand was so big there were several exits and she was able to leave without encountering Leo. He was back the next evening she was working there, however, and Phil told her he'd been in every night.

'Usually with the *principessa*,' he added. 'I wonder what they get up to? She's staying here and the chambermaids say she often has a man in her room all night.'

Leo had not been too preoccupied to discover the exits the bar staff used. He was waiting for Josie when she left.

'Josie, let me drive you home,' he offered quietly.

She turned and shook her head. 'I don't want to talk to you,' she said, equally quietly.

'I wanted to apologize and offer you your job back. I was far too hasty, I know that now. If I'd stopped to think I'd have known you couldn't have stolen the gold. Will you forgive me? You can't enjoy doing this sort of work.'

Josie was astonished to hear him apologize, tempted to accept, and then detected a note of pity in his voice. He probably didn't believe in her innocence at all but had a bad conscience and was trying to make amends, she thought, her mind whirling. She wouldn't accept charity. She would earn every penny and not be beholden to anyone.

'My car's round the corner. Let me drive you home.'

'Go back to Kitty! I will not accept help from someone who believes I am capable of stealing. And I'd be grateful if you would not haunt the Grand or I'll lose my job. There are plenty of other bars where you can meet your women.'

She stormed away, angry tears blinding her. She half expected Leo to follow her but he did not. Leo was watching her, a smile playing over his lips. She knew who his companion had been the other night, did she? She wasn't as uninterested as she seemed.

Suddenly he made up his mind. He swung round and went towards his car. Now he knew what he wanted. He'd give her time to cool down, then he'd make Josie listen to him.

Josie tried to subdue her anger and what she refused to recognize as regrets in even harder work.

'I'll walk to the bus with you,' Josie said, and Ann kissed Dora goodbye, promising to come next week. 'Ann, I've got two extra hours a day at the Grand! I'll be able to get some sugar. Mother has so missed it in her tea. Perhaps I won't need to sell any more of her trinkets.'

Ann smiled briefly at Josie. 'That's good, but I do wish you'd let us help you, Josie. Lizzie and I could easily spare a few shillings a week.'

'No, Ann, I won't let you do that. Though we do appreciate the food you bring from the hotel kitchen. Mother loves the occasional treat.'

'They're only things left over from functions, and Mrs Endersby lets the staff help themselves. By the way, Dick was at home last weekend and wanted your address.'

'I've been hoping he'd forget me while he was at school and with his grandfather in the summer. I can't let him know how dreadful these rooms are. I'm too ashamed.'

'It isn't your fault, except for not taking help when it's offered.'

'What did you tell him?'

'That you'd changed lodgings and I didn't have the exact address. I hate telling lies.'

Impulsively, Josie hugged her. 'I know, and I hate asking you to cover up for me. When will he be back?'

'Only just before term starts. It's his last year at school. Oh, there's my bus. 'Bye!'

Josie had hesitated about taking the extra hours at the Grand, knowing she would be likely to meet Leo there, but they paid well and she couldn't afford to turn any work down. She would know how to deal with Leo if he tried to talk with her again. For two weeks, however, she didn't see him and began to hope he wouldn't return. Kitty Denver was often in the bar with a succession of men, none of them Leo, so perhaps she'd lost interest in him. Then one evening Josie, horrified, saw the *principessa* fling herself into the outstretched arms of Dr Mandeville. Josie greeted him nervously when he came to order drinks, but though he smiled at her and asked how her mother was he didn't appear embarrassed. When another tall, slender woman appeared and the *principessa* leapt to her feet with a flurry of dropped bags and scarves, and kissed the newcomer, it was a moment before Josie understood that it was Mrs Mandeville.

'They were both dancers, the *principessa* and the doctor's wife,' Phil whispered. 'I remember seeing 'em once, here in Brum. Great legs they had. Still do, I expect. Did you think the doctor was one of her conquests?'

Josie grinned at him. 'I did wonder for a moment,' she confessed. 'I should have thought: he's too well known in Birmingham for him to risk meeting another woman here.'

After another week when Leo didn't appear she began to think she'd exaggerated the threat from him. He didn't want her, he'd regretted his attempts to talk with her, to persuade her to forgive his suspicions and take back the job. She was polishing glasses during a lull late one evening when Leo walked into the bar and came straight across to her. 'Josie, I must talk to you. I'll take you home after you've finished here.'

'No, Leo. I prefer to be left alone. Please go away.'

'Josie, just once. Then I promise I won't try to see you here again.'

'There's no point,' she insisted, but when she left work Leo was waiting for her. When he tried to lead her to his car she wrenched her arm from his grasp. 'Let me go! I've no wish to talk to you!'

Leo ignored her protests. 'Just listen for a minute. Matthew's left me. His father died and he's starting his own business, though he seems incapable of managing the finance, and I hear he has huge debts through betting on the horses. I wonder how long his father's money will last?'

'I'm not interested in Matthew, or you, Leo.'

'I think he was relieved to go, but he was so incoherent, uttering vague threats and curses, I didn't pay much attention. But that won't affect me, it's just difficult since the house in between's just become available and I must take the opportunity to acquire it and make one factory. Somehow I must manage it.'

'I'm sure you will,' Josie said stiffly.

'I'm not sorry he's gone. I'd begun not to trust him − not just over that radiator grille, other things too. I'd do far better if you came back to me, Josie. Nothing has been done so efficiently since, neither Matthew nor Manders is anywhere near so competent. No, let me finish! I was quite wrong not to believe you. Of course you would never have stolen that gold. I can't apologize enough. Will you come back to me? Please?'

Josie was tempted. It would solve all her problems, she could earn enough and have time to care for her mother, and Leo would understand if she sometimes had to take time off. Then she hardened her heart.

'I might be prepared to work for you, except that I despise people who spread malicious rumours,' she snapped. The thought of the lovely *principessa*, with whom Leo was having a blatant affair if what Phil had heard was true, fuelled her anger. He was just feeling guilty about his accusation and the dreadful life they'd been reduced to since he'd sacked her. He couldn't make amends this way. 'No, Leo, it's too late. I know now who stole the gold, but I can't prove it and you wouldn't believe me if I told you. You never listened to me before, so why should I help you now? I don't want your job. And now, please leave me alone!'

Chapter Thirteen

Leo castigated himself for his ineptitude. If he'd been more adept, Josie wouldn't have spurned his offer of her old job back. He'd hoped that once they'd regained their old friendly ease she'd have been willing to listen to a different proposal. Then he grew angry. Women didn't turn him down, and Josie had done it too often. Women like Kitty Denver were the sort he'd stick to in future. Instead of driving home, he returned to the Grand and telephoned Kitty's room. Her invitations had been clear enough. She'd welcome him.

'Wouldn't she listen to you, darling?' Kitty cooed an hour later. 'You should forget her. A woman who doesn't appreciate you properly doesn't deserve you.'

'Who?' Leo demanded, sitting up in bed. 'Who are you talking about?'

Kitty laughed and pulled him down beside her. 'Leo, my pet, I don't mind. You're not my property. The red-haired barmaid, of course. I quite accept that men have, shall I say, baser appetites that women of the lower orders can satisfy better than their wives or properly brought-up girlfriends. I'll tell you a secret. Even respectable women like to have the occasional adventure outside the normal range of society. Only when they can't find men like you, though,' she added softly, and her hands began to rove over his body.

'It's a pity I won't be staying much longer,' she whispered some time later as, replete, they lay back amongst the pillows.

'What do you mean?'

'I really can't bear to stay in Birmingham, it's tedious,' she said rather petulantly. 'My old friends are all so stuffy, even Nell Mandeville. You'd never believe Nell once danced with me at the Folies-Bergère. She used to be such fun, but now she's married to that boring Paul Mandeville, she can't think of anything but him and her wretched babies! I'll have to go back to the Riviera soon, to find some lively company.'

'Am I not lively enough?' Leo asked indignantly.

Kitty chortled. 'Of course you are, darling, but how often do I see you? And hotels become dreary after a time, and the staff become impertinent.'

'Then come and live with me,' Leo said suddenly.

'Darling, is this a proposition or a proposal?'

'Neither. We'll both be free to end it at any time. Of course, I shall enjoy your company while you're there –'

'And my body, I hope,' Kitty put in mischievously.

'And your body,' Leo agreed, laughing.

Josie had made it painfully obvious she didn't want him. Kitty wasn't possessive like other women. With her lively company he'd be able to forget Josie. And, he thought with a spurt of satisfaction, perhaps he could make Josie regret her refusal. No woman yet had scorned him.

For some reason, Josie didn't feel any happier when Leo failed to appear for a couple of weeks. She was jumpy, she told herself, worried in case he suddenly came into the bar. When she did see him again she was breathless, with fright or apprehension, she couldn't decide which. And then she saw that he was with Kitty. He seemed to spend every night Josie was working there in the bar with the luscious beauty. Phil told her quietly that he never appeared when she was off duty, though the *principessa* was frequently with other men on those nights. What was he doing?

It was Lilian, the girl who had been injured by the polishing machine belt, who enlightened her. Josie was walking towards the Grand one evening when Lilian shyly spoke to her. 'Miss Shaw? I don't know if yer remembers me? Yer took me mom ter the 'ospital when me eye was 'urt.'

'Of course,' Josie said. 'How are you now? I — I left Bradley's the next day, so I never heard what happened. Can you see properly?'

'Yes, thank yer, miss. Mr Bradley, 'e made sure I 'ad the best surgeons, an' 'e paid fer me and me mom ter goo ter Barmouth fer a month afterwards. I can see as well as ever.'

'I'm glad about that.'

'Yes, miss, but I couldn't goo back ter polishin', not after what 'appened. Mr Bradley, 'e got me a job with one of 'is neighbours that wanted a nurse fer a babby. Ever so nice, it is, in 'Andsworth. I sees 'im nearly every Sunday when I'm tekin' the babby fer an airin'.'

Josie was cynically amused at the tone of hero-worship in the girl's voice. It only needed the expenditure of a little money and influence, which Leo could well afford, to make a slave of this girl who might have been blinded while working for him. Lilian was still speaking, however.

'Mr Bradley, 'e's got ever such a pretty young lady livin' in 'is 'ouse. They say she's Italian, but she's spoken ter me an' she speaks proper posh English. Got a title, they say, summat funny like "Essa". Course, I don't believe what they're saying, that she's Mr Bradley's fancy bit. 'E's not like that! 'E's a gentleman!'

To Josie's intense relief Lilian smiled at her and said she was glad she'd seen her, but she had to rush, she was meeting a friend outside the Odeon. Josie had to lean against a wall for a moment as the fury which consumed her made her shake uncontrollably. Then she squared her shoulders. It was nothing to do with her that Leo should have installed his mistress in his house. After all, she had no claim on him. In fact, if she'd ever been tempted for a single minute to believe his protestations or accept his proposal, some instinct must have prevented her from making a fool of herself and believing a man who was capable of outraging propriety and living openly with a woman who was no better than a whore.

The *principessa* had danced at the Folies-Bergère, and everyone knew they danced without a stitch of clothing on. She experienced a niggle of doubt when she recalled that Dr Mandeville's wife, who was so respectable, had also been a dancer at the famous Paris music hall. Surely she couldn't have danced naked? That was impossible to believe. Yet Leo had enticed the *principessa* to go and live with him. All evening, and long after she was in bed, Josie found her thoughts in a whirl. She was bewildered, angry, scornful, and oddly desolate.

As winter approached, Dora became ill again. She suffered badly from the cold, and lost weight. She refused to see Dr Mandeville, saying she wasn't prepared to accept charity, and as she wasn't in pain Josie let her have her way, hoping she would improve. After her previous illness the stock of ornaments, which had seemed so enormous, had been reduced and only the cheaper items were left. They were disappearing at a frightening rate when Josie once more had to give up her jobs to take care of Dora, who was so ill she could scarcely move. Josie had to buy extra coal as well as expensive food to tempt her mother's capricious appetite.

'I'll have to sell some furniture,' Josie told Ann one week. 'I wonder if the table and some of the dining chairs would fetch much? We never use them now, Mother has her meals on a tray and I could too.'

'You'll have to let me help you,' Ann said. 'I can afford two or three shillings a week, I get good wages and I've quite a bit put by. Surely she'll be better soon, and then you can go back to work.'

'Even if I can I'm getting a reputation for being unreliable,'

Josie said, trying to smile. 'I've let so many people down by not arriving for my work.'

'That wasn't your fault when Aunt Dora's been so ill.'

'Employers won't make allowances. They aren't willing to take me on a second time and I'm running out of pubs.'

'I don't think that's likely, there seems to be one on every corner.' Ann tried to speak lightly.

'There are hundreds of men and women looking for a few hours' work. Look at how many went on the hunger marches.'

'Rioting and fighting the police won't help. If I ask for a regular day off and come to look after Aunt Dora you could work then,' Ann suggested. 'It would help. Then, with my two bob, and I know Lizzie wants to give you the same, you wouldn't have to sell so much.'

'It's my responsibility, I don't want to ask for help.'

'It wasn't your responsibility Aunt Dora spent all her money so recklessly and brought you to this state, nor that she quarrelled with Aunt Phoebe,' Ann declared.

Josie had never heard the gentle Ann speak so robustly. 'You sound quite fierce,' she commented, smiling.

'I am. Josie, I hate criticizing Aunt Dora, she was such fun when we were children. I know we didn't see her much, but when we did we all adored her stories. When I see you slaving away, doing so much for her, and her always complaining, I wonder you don't walk out and leave.'

'So do I, Ann, so do I. But how could I? I'd never rest easy if I did. She's my mother, she depends on me and she's got no one else. But she doesn't always complain. And she really does try to help when she can. If only Mrs Sheehan could climb the stairs, she might sit with Mother sometimes, but that's impossible.'

'Here's five pounds from my savings to start with. No, Josie, don't push it away. I'll see Mrs Endersby as soon as I get back and ask which regular day off I can have. I'll send a telegram, you can try and find work for that day.'

'Thanks, Ann. I'll never forget this, and it's a loan, not a gift.'

For several weeks Leo, more and more frustrated, haunted the Grand hotel's bars, but Josie was never there. Phil wondered whether the lovely *principessa* had deserted him, for she seemed to have vanished. Little did he know that Leo was feeling utterly disgusted with himself for having allowed his anger against Josie to tempt him into his brief affair with Kitty. She was fun, but since she'd gone back to Nice he'd begun to wonder what he ever saw in her. The contrast between Kitty and Josie had served to show him he was unequivocally in love with Josie, but whether she would ever believe him was something that kept him awake at night and distracted him from business during the day.

Phil was curious, wondering just how a prosperous business-man could be involved with one of his barmaids, and whether this accounted for Josie's sudden defection. A brief note had been delivered, apologizing and saying that, as her mother was ill, Josie would have to give up her job, but Phil wasn't sure whether to believe it. It was more likely she'd made this excuse to escape from what were obviously unwelcome attentions.

Leo assumed the same. For a while he hesitated to go to Josie's home, but his longing finally forced him to act. When he eventually knocked on the door and Mrs Sheehan, grumbling at having to answer it, called Ann downstairs, he didn't recognize her. Ann hadn't met Leo, but she guessed who he was from Josie's description before he introduced himself, and stepped out into the court so that the inquisitive Mrs Sheehan couldn't hear them.

'Miss Shaw, is she at home?'

'No, she's working.'

'Can you tell me where? I have to see her.'

The thought of Leo queuing for fish and chips bought a smile to Ann's lips, but Leo misunderstood.

'I don't mean her any harm,' he began, but Ann interrupted. Josie had been afraid Leo would pursue her to her home and been adamant she didn't want to see him.

'She won't talk to you,' Ann told him, 'so it's no use my telling you. She's left her job at the Grand –'

'Yes, because of me,' he said swiftly, and Ann's eyes narrowed. If this was what he thought then it might deter him from following Josie. She was clearly afraid of meeting him, from what little she'd told Ann.

'You wouldn't want to cause her to lose her this job too, would you?' she asked gently. 'It's difficult enough to find work these days.'

Leo stared at her, then frowned and turned away. Ann breathed a sigh of relief that he hadn't asked any more questions. She decided not to worry Josie by telling her about this visit, and fobbed off Mrs Sheehan by saying dismissively that Leo was one of Josie's former employers who wanted her to do a job.

It wasn't until much later that Leo, back home, began to wonder who it was that had answered the door to him. She'd been beautiful, he recalled, though at the time he hadn't registered this. She'd been far too neatly and smartly dressed to be one of the neighbours in that dreadful court. She'd clearly known who he was. Eventually he decided she must be the other cousin, and dismissed the puzzle. Had he lost Josie? That was a far more important problem. He was utterly confused. Should he humiliate himself still further by continuing to search for her when it seemed so clear she didn't want him? Would it be kinder to leave her in peace? Josie was working, so she was financially secure. Perhaps he should just try to forget her.

'So yer see, love, me an' Clem's goin' ter be married.'

Lizzie hugged her mother. 'I'm so glad,' she said, 'he's a lovely man.'

Phoebe wiped a tear from her eye. 'I never thought anyone could take the place of yer pa,' she said with a sniff. 'I know we wasn't married, and lots of snooty folk turned their noses up at us, and came over all pious, but at least we were honest about it, and Alfred would 'ave married me if 'e could, I always knew that. It was because he'd married young, to please his folks. They never did get on and she didn't 'ave any kids, so 'e were that pleased when Freddy was born, and over the moon to have a little daughter too. I do wish 'e'd lived ter see you grow up. Though on second thoughts perhaps it's as well he didn't see Freddy,' she added with her more normal acerbity.

'Where is Freddy?'

'Livin' wi' that Mabel Jopling in Lozells, as far as I know. 'Ow the blazes they can afford ter rent the house for themselves, I don't know, when Freddy ain't workin'.'

'Josie must have been right about that stolen gold,' Lizzie said thoughtfully.

'I wouldn't put it past that Mabel, but I don't believe my Freddy 'ad anythin' ter do wi' it,' Phoebe promptly said. 'Not when 'e saw it caused Josie ter lose 'er job, and come down in the world. I know our Freddy's no angel, but 'e wouldn't thieve from Josie, nor Dora, whatever she says. 'Er and 'er blasted jewels!'

'Aunt Dora's very ill and Josie's had to give up most of her jobs to look after her,' Lizzie said. 'I was going to ask whether you'd forgive her and take them back.'

Phoebe looked indecisive. 'I don't wish them ill.'

'Ann and I are lending them money, and Ann spends one day a week with Dora so's Josie can get out and earn a bit. I wish I could too, but I can never depend on having the same day off,' Lizzie went on, seeing her mother weaken.

Phoebe sighed. 'I might 'ave done, love, but I'm going ter sell up. Clem's got a lovely 'ouse in Solihull, and it'll be a nice change ter live in country again – or as near as makes no matter. I liked it in the village when I was a kid, but they wouldn't ever let me go back after I run away with Alfred. I'm sorry for

Josie,' she went on in a firmer tone, 'but she believed Freddy 'ad stole the perishin' sapphires too. They've made their beds, like Dora told me when I ran away, and they'll 'av ter lie on 'em.'

For a while, Josie was able to work every Tuesday, rushing from an early morning cleaning job in an office to another at a pub, then serving for twelve hours in a fish and chip shop. With the fifteen shillings she earned, and the few shillings Ann and Lizzie gave her, she struggled by, only selling items when she needed medicines for Dora.

'Sell her clothes, she never wears them,' Ann suggested one evening when Josie, exhausted, returned from work.

'I need the coats on the bed, she feels the cold so. I never thought I'd be glad she'd bought fur coats.'

'There are lots of dresses she wouldn't wear again because they're too out of fashion,' Ann said, and Josie, despite her tiredness and worry, grinned back at her. 'Shoes, underwear, a lot of it hardly worn.'

'I wish I was small enough to wear some of them,' Josie sighed. 'At least being kept here so much gives me the time to make clothes for myself, even if I do have to patch pieces from two of Mother's skirts to make one for me.'

'I wondered where you'd got that outfit,' Ann said, and Josie grimaced.

'I know the material's not a perfect match, but I hoped no one would notice the back of the blouse is a different pattern, and the top of the skirt's lighter than the rest.'

'You'll set a new fashion.'

'At least in the shop they provide me with overalls.'

The overalls didn't, however, prevent Josie's clothes from absorbing the smell of fried fish, and within weeks she noticed that the reek of it made Dora feel queasy. Josie asked Mrs Sheehan if she might change downstairs on Tuesdays and leave the offending clothes in the cellar. 'It doesn't matter what I wear in the house, but I can't afford to give up that job,' she explained.

'Do what yer likes so long's yer pay me rent, which, give yer yer due, yer allus 'ave,' Mrs Sheehan said. 'Tek 'er a slice of me fruit cake, cock. That'll buck 'er up.'

For a few more weeks the ruse succeeded. Josie told Dora she'd found alternative work. Then, one Tuesday morning, Ann arrived and found Josie slumped on the stairs with a raging temperature, soaking wet from the water which had spilled from the bucket she'd been carrying.

'So please, Mrs Endersby, could I have a week's holiday now, to look after my cousin? I know it's a busy time, just before Christmas, and I'm so sorry, but there's no one else and her mother's ill too.'

'We'll manage, Ann, of course you must go. You're entitled to some holiday – you haven't taken any since you worked here, and that's more than eighteen months now.'

'I had such a lot of time off when I fell down the stairs and broke my arm,' Ann explained. 'I didn't like to ask for a holiday, and I have nowhere to go, anyway.'

'Then you must take as much time as your cousin needs you, a week for last year, another for this, and, if necessary, extra days to make up for all the times we've asked you to fill in when anyone else has been ill or away.'

'But you already pay me extra for that. Thank you, Mrs Endersby. I'll be back as soon as I possibly can.'

Marigold Endersby smiled at her. 'If it isn't inappropriate, let me wish you a happy Christmas. And before you leave, come to my office, I'll give you your Christmas box, and wages due. You might need them.'

Ann had helped Josie into bed, then rushed back to the hotel. When she came back she looked pleased.

'There was an extra ten pounds,' Ann told Josie. 'I'm sure she doesn't give all the staff that much.'

Josie was in the living room on the cushions which she had used as her bed since Dora's first major illness. She was flushed with fever, and though the fire was built up as high as was safe she was shivering violently.

'It's just a cold,' she croaked. 'I don't know what happened, I must have fainted for a moment on the stairs.'

'It's a wonder you haven't got pneumonia,' Ann scolded.

'I'll get the sack,' Josie fretted.

'You aren't fit to work, anyway.'

'Mother keeps calling and I can't find the strength to go to her.'

'I'll see what she wants and persuade her to stay in bed away from you, then you can perhaps get some sleep. How long have you been ill?'

'I can't remember. I felt terrible last Tuesday when I got home. Ann, I don't think I've been to the shops, and without my wages today I'll have to sell something else. We haven't any food in.'

'Don't worry! As soon as I've seen to Aunt Dora I'll go shopping. I have plenty of money, so we needn't bother about what to sell just yet.'

By the time Ann had convinced her aunt that it would be better for her to remain in bed away from possible infection instead of spending the day huddled in one of the armchairs, and made a small fire in the bedroom grate, Josie was fast asleep. Ann went to the shops and also left a message for Dr Mandeville at the clinic, asking him to call when he could. Josie was still asleep when Ann returned, but the fire was low, so she changed into her oldest clothes and went to investigate the cellar to refill the coal bucket.

'There ain't no light down there, but there's a shovel,' Mrs Sheehan told her, and proffered the stub of a candle set on a saucer. Carefully, Ann felt her way down the gloomy, uneven steps, holding the bucket and candle in one hand and with the other clutching a rough handrail that creaked and moved ominously if she put any pressure on it. Something brushed against her face and she gave a shriek of fright, swinging the candle wildly to try and see what it was. At first she thought it was a body. Then, telling herself not to be silly, she forced herself to look more closely. Swathed inadequately in a torn sheet, hanging from a hook in the ceiling, Ann recognized Josie's working clothes. She wiped the sweat from her forehead, then put out a hand to push the clothes out of her way. They felt gritty with coal dust and clammy to the touch. Ann sighed. No wonder Josie had caught a cold, having to wear these damp clothes.

She filled the bucket and heaved it up the stairs. How had Josie endured doing this several times a day for months? She prayed she might be able to do it for a week or two.

Dick went to find his mother. 'Where's Ann?' he asked.

'Ann Preece? My receptionist? On holiday. Why?'

Dick flushed slightly. He felt shy of telling his mother he needed to ask Ann where Josie worked now. He'd enjoyed her company, but had seen so little of her during the past year, not at all since Easter, and he'd rather expected to forget her. After all, they'd only played tennis occasionally. She was just a pal.

He set out once more on his motorcycle for Freer Road. He'd been there twice already during his two days at home, but the house had been empty and unwelcoming. If there was no one there this time he'd conquer his reluctance and ask the neighbours. Perhaps Josie had moved and they'd know where. Once again the house was empty, and he had to knock on three doors before an old man shuffled down the hall to answer. 'I'm looking for Miss Shaw, she used to live opposite,' Dick said. 'Do you know if she's still there?'

'Nah, moved out, year cum January,' the old man said.

Dick was startled. Josie hadn't told him at Easter, but now he remembered she'd been very insistent he didn't see her home. 'Do you know where she lives?' he asked.

'No idea, lad. All t'others seem ter 'ave gone, too, though I sees the old woman sometimes.'

'Mrs Preece?'

'Mrs if yer likes!' The old man cackled. 'I remembers when 'er fust cum 'ere. Dain't speak ter nobody, turned up 'er nose, an' we all know 'er feller were married.'

'When is she likely to be back?'

He shrugged and prepared to close the door. 'Can't say. 'Er went off in big posh car wi' another feller, an' that many cases an' boxes you'd 'ave thought 'er was gooin' fer good. Don't expect 'er'll be back afore Christmas. Now it's parky wi' this wind, I gorra shut the door.'

Dick stood facing the glass panels. How was he ever to find Josie if she'd left this area? At length common sense returned. Ann would be back to work one day, and unless Mrs Preece had sold the house she'd be back, too. Perhaps in the meantime he ought to write to Josie through her aunt, and hope the letter would be forwarded. He wasn't likely to see Josie these holidays, though. He would just have to wait until Easter.

Lizzie arrived at the Nechells house, her arms full of Christmas shopping, and exclaimed in horror when she heard about Josie's illness.

'Ann, why didn't you let me know!'

'You couldn't have done anything and I could get time off. Dr Mandeville came and said it was only a heavy cold, fortunately. As you can see, Josie's much better already.'

'You don't look it,' Lizzie said bluntly, looking at Josie curled up in one armchair and Dora in the other. 'You're much too pale. How on earth have you managed?

'Ann insisted on sleeping on the floor since I had the chair cushions and Mother the bed,' Josie said ruefully. 'I wasn't in a state to object.'

'Mrs Sheehan offered me some pillows and an old bolster,' Ann said quickly. She suppressed the fact they had been so full of bugs and fleas she'd returned them with a specious excuse that she could now share Dora's bed.

'I've brought your Christmas presents,' Lizzie said with an attempt at brightness. 'Look, some of Aunt Dora's favourite tea, a big tin of biscuits, and some Cadbury's chocolates. And since you won't be able to do a roast joint I bought a ham for Christmas Day.'

There was more, enough food to feed them for a week, and Josie had to blink hard to keep back the tears. She was fortunate in her cousins.

By the beginning of the new year Josie was well enough to look after Dora again and Ann returned to work. It was too late for Dick, however. He, frustrated that his letter had not been answered, had left Birmingham to pay a long-promised visit to his Uncle Johnny and Aunt Lucy, and was going straight back to school from Coventry.

Josie was once more out of work, and before she could resume the weary search Dora became worse.

'I'm sorry, there's nothing I can do except relieve the pain,' Dr Mandeville told her after he'd examined Dora and they'd moved back into the other room.

'She doesn't complain of pain,' Josie said, 'just being tired all the time, too tired to eat. What's wrong?'

'I'm afraid it's cancer – a tumour on the brain. She could last for several months, but it's more likely she'll die in a matter of weeks. Is there anyone who can share the nursing with you?'

'My cousins,' Josie said, stunned. 'You mean she's going to die?'

'One can never be totally sure in such cases, there have been some miraculous recoveries. But it would be wrong of me to hold out hope.'

'I never believed her when she kept saying she was ill,' Josie whispered. 'I thought she was putting it on to get sympathy and attention. And I made her come and live in this dreadful hovel. But it was all I could afford.'

'Conditions are not ideal, but many live in even worse, and it's nothing to do with this place, the disease must have been present for a long time.' Josie nodded. The headaches . . . 'You mustn't blame yourself,' continued the physician kindly. 'You'll have to stay strong to look after her. She needs you.'

Josie gulped, trying to force down her terror and dismay. 'I'll be all right, it's just been rather a shock,' she said through her tears.

'Good girl. I'll call in whenever I can, but send to the clinic if you need me.'

'I'm 'aving all the trappings,' Phoebe declared.

'A white dress and bridesmaids?' Lizzie teased.

Phoebe laughed. 'I'd look a sight, wouldn't I? I wish it was you, love, in white and with lots of confetti. I don't suppose . . .?'

Lizzie shook her head firmly. 'Matthew was enough, I'm never going to let any man hurt me again.'

Phoebe eyed her shrewdly. The child still hadn't got over it, and for two pins she'd go and tell Matthew Horobin what she thought of him. It wouldn't do her Lizzie any good though, and she was better off without him, so she started to talk about the matching silk dress and coat she'd bought, the hat and shoes, and how, although the church would be decorated for Easter, they were adding lots more flowers.

'Clem wants to 'ave the reception at the Grand, but I think it'd be nicer at his place – homelier, like, and less fuss,' she added with an embarrassed laugh. 'Then we're going to London, and afterwards ter visit 'is daughter in Australia! Fancy – me, off to the other side of the world!'

'You deserve it, Ma, you've always worked hard for us,' Lizzie declared. 'Clem's a lucky man.'

'Oh, Lizzie, there's so much ter do! I never knew we 'ad such a lot of stuff. It took me all day just clearing out the spare bedrooms. But I'm selling every last stick of furniture. The man as is buying the 'ouse wants it, and Clem's got some really nice stuff, better than this rubbish. Most of his comes from Maples or Waring and Gillow.'

'I know, I saw it when he asked me there at Christmas. What does Freddy say?'

'Our dear Freddy ain't even bothered ter answer me letter, so if 'e comes 'ere after Easter 'e'll find the bird flown! I told 'im 'e's welcome ter come ter wedding, but not that Mabel.'

Lizzie didn't think it was the right moment to ask if Josie and Dora had been asked to the wedding. She was going to see them on her way back to the station, the first time she'd been able to since Christmas. She knew from Ann that Josie was better, but had her cousin been able to find any work?'

Josie was standing beside the pump in the court, an empty bucket at her feet, staring unseeingly at the privies, when Lizzie walked in.

'Josie, glad to see you better.'

Josie turned towards her and Lizzie was shocked at the blank look in her eyes. 'Lizzie? Is it you?'

'Josie, love, what on earth's the matter?' Lizzie demanded in alarm.

Josie held out her hands as if in supplication. 'I've only just heard,' she said, sounding surprised.

'Heard what? What is it?'

'These houses have been condemned. They're going to pull them down. They call it slum clearance. We're to be evicted. And Mother's dying.'

Chapter Fourteen

'MA, how can you be so hard?' Lizzie stormed. 'Josie's at the end of her tether and Aunt Dora's really ill. She's dying. You have to do something. I've missed my train to come back and ask you to help, and Mrs Thackeray-Walsh won't be pleased – I'm supposed to be driving her to Leamington.'

Phoebe sighed, and looked up from where she was packing summer clothes into a trunk. 'Lizzie, I'm movin', they can't come back even if they wanted to and if I'd 'ave 'em.'

'Josie can't go out to work because her mother needs her all the time, and they haven't a lot left to sell.'

'Has she explained that ter the Public Assistance? What about them perishin' sapphires?' Phoebe demanded. 'Aren't they counted in the means test or 'ave they told 'er ter sell 'em first?'

'Don't you think if they had them they'd be better off now?' Lizzie demanded but Phoebe remained unconvinced.

'Either Doris 'as lost 'em and won't admit it, or hid 'em where Josie can't get at 'em, or they were paste all along.'

'Ma, she wouldn't do that!' Lizzie was incredulous.

'Lizzie, I know my sister,' Phoebe went on angrily. 'She doesn't know fact from fiction. She lives in a dream world, always did. Even when she was a kid she'd say black was white and twist facts to get 'er own way. Do you wonder I don't believe 'er when she accuses Freddy of stealin' the silver –

which it was proved 'e didn't do — and then says 'e's stole valuable jewels?'

'Couldn't you help for Josie's sake? On top of everything else, they're condemning the house and they'll have nowhere to live.'

'It's this scheme the City Council's got ter build 'ouses more local,' Phoebe explained. 'People don't want ter move out to these great big estates miles away. They're goin' ter build where Cavalry Barracks used ter be. Josie and Dora'll be able ter goo on the Council list.'

'But that won't help if Josie can't afford the rent,' Lizzie pleaded. 'She's asked, and they're charging at least eight bob in Bordesley, in those new mansions the Council built in Garrison Lane. She's only got a few bob a week from Ann and me, and what she gets from selling clothes and such. As it is she doesn't even have a proper bed.'

'I'm sorry fer Josie, but best thing fer 'er to do would be ter put Dora in workhouse.'

'It would kill Aunt Dora to have to live with tramps!' Lizzie protested, shocked.

'Well, she's dyin' anyway or so she says,' Phoebe said cynically. 'It'll p'raps bring 'er to 'er senses, mek 'er do somethin' fer 'erself instead of dependin' on poor Josie. She 'as ter be one up on anyone else even when she's sick!'

'Ma! She hasn't been complaining lately, I promise. And it's the doctor who says she's dying, not Aunt Dora.'

Phoebe looked discomfited for a moment, then she pursed her lips. 'Doctors can be wrong.'

'Josie wants her to have some comfort, to be looked after properly by people she knows.'

'I 'elped Dora after George died, an' look at the thanks I got! I charged 'er practically no rent, and fed 'er, while she 'angs on ter jewels and silver and buys more clothes than I could wear in ten years. No, Lizzie, and that's me last word.'

*

'What are those noises?' Dora demanded feebly.

Josie, harassed, came in from the living room where she had been instructing a couple of men who were carrying the sideboard down the narrow stairs.

'I've sold the sideboard,' she said wearily.

'There'll be nothing left soon. I'm not complaining, but all my precious bits and pieces have gone, and no doubt I shall have to lie on the floor.'

'We have to eat,' Josie almost snapped. She was finding it more and more difficult to remain patient. After her illness she had so little energy, but couldn't sleep.

'I'm so cold,' Dora said now. 'Make the fire up a little more, please, Josephine.'

Josie looked at the fire, already built perilously high in the small grate. 'In a little while, Mother. Let me pull the coat back over you, that'll help.'

'It's too heavy,' Dora protested fretfully. 'Surely the men have finished by now? I'm so tired, and I can't sleep with all this banging and shouting.'

Josie soothed her, persuading her to take some of Dr Mandeville's medicine, and Dora fell into a restless doze. Josie went back into the living room and looked despondently about her. It still looked very small, and she wondered how they had managed to fit in all that furniture which had now been sold. The room still looked crowded, even with the one remaining armchair (which she couldn't sell because Dora was sometimes well enough to sit out of bed), the makeshift bed of cushions she used, a rickety backless chair, and an old pine table she had bought in place of the mahogany dining set, on which stood their remaining few pieces of crockery and single cooking pot.

She put the marrow bone she'd bought into the pot with a few onions and carrots she'd scavenged from the gutter after one of the local market stalls had been overturned by a runaway delivery van, then sat down to calculate how much longer they could manage. There was still one box packed with Dora's favourite ornaments, trinkets George had given her during the early days of their marriage, which Josie had tried to hold on to. Some clothes her mother would never again wear still hung in the big wardrobe. She could struggle on for a while with the money her cousins gave her and the food Ann brought regularly from the kitchens of Endersby's hotel, but soon she'd have to join the line of ragged, dispirited men and women waiting at the relief office for the meagre help provided there. And they would tell her she was young and strong, she must get a job and not depend on them. Josie almost wept at the hopelessness of it. She'd welcome a job, any job, however hard or dirty, but Dora needed her constantly. It wasn't possible.

Despite her anxiety, Josie grinned faintly as she recalled the scene a few days ago. Dora had asked for one of the patent medicines she swore helped her more than Dr Mandeville's prescriptions. 'I can't leave you alone while I fetch it, Mother,' Josie explained, but Dora seemed unable to comprehend this, dissolving into weak tears and accusations that Josie meant to desert her when Josie, exasperated, tried to leave the house.

'Get Ma Prentice ter sit wi' 'er,' Mrs Sheehan suggested. 'Old woman wot lives at number fower. Gi' 'er a copper or two, 'er's on relief an' needs it.'

Mrs Prentice had been only too willing, but by the time Josie had helped to push her considerable bulk up the stairs, encouraged by Mrs Prentice's cheerful if somewhat breathless instructions to 'shove harder, put yer shoulder under me bum, ducks, or I'll never mek it!' Josie was regretting asking her. Half an hour later when Josie returned, having run the mile there and back to the only shop where that particular medicine could be obtained, Dora was rigid with offence. She barely waited for Mrs Prentice to descend the stairs, fortunately for Josie assisted this time by the force of gravity, before bursting into loud and tearful complaints.

'Josephine, where in the world did you find that dreadful woman? She was so inquisitive, asked all sorts of impertinent questions, peered in all the drawers and the wardrobe without even asking me! And she stank! I was nauseated just by having her in the room. I don't think she'd washed for a year, and I could smell beer. I feel utterly besmirched and I must have a bath. I won't feel clean until I've scrubbed her stink off me.'

Josie groaned inwardly. It took hours to fetch enough water for a bath, heat it, and then carry it all down the stairs again. Josie made do with one small bowl of water, sponging herself down, and in the end persuaded Dora that she was far too weak to get into the old zinc bath. Dora had to be satisfied with letting Josie help her to wash.

There was nothing to do but to carry on, Josie decided wearily. The doctor had warned that Dora would probably sleep for longer and longer periods. Perhaps then she might be able to find some sort of work to earn a little money.

Leo frowned, staring in front of him. Once or twice before he'd had suspicions that Henry Manders, his new clerk, had somehow unlocked his desk and seen the private papers he kept there, papers to do with his own affairs and not the factory's. He'd shrugged off these suspicions, he hadn't any proof, apart from a vague feeling that sometimes papers were not in the precise order in which he'd left them, but he'd concluded he was mistaken. He wasn't the tidiest of men, but he was always careful to lock the desk. Now it was open, and he was certain some of his papers had been put back in the wrong order. His private bank statements, the bills for the house, papers relating to his car, and private correspondence were all here, and since Tobias had left he also kept the new designs he planned to introduce. But there was something else. He'd been trying to find a manager to replace Matthew. He'd interviewed two applicants who had seemed enthusiastic. They had exchanged letters in which he had explained further details, and then, without explanation, the enthusiasm had evaporated and with some embarrassment on their part they had declined his offers.

Manders had worked at Horobin's. He was Matthew's man. Could he be behind this? Had Matthew meant the threats he'd uttered during the final row? But why? His products didn't compete directly with Matthew's. Was it pure spite? It didn't make sense, and he knew of no connection with any other rival. Already Leo had been forced to delay his normal visits to his continental buyers until he had a manager, and he knew the business would suffer. Well, he could deal with one thing at once. He sent for Henry Manders. Ten minutes later a demoralized clerk crept thankfully out of his office. He hadn't suffered such a harangue in years, and he'd always rather despised Mr Leo for being too mild.

'Surely we haven't any more furniture to move,' Dora complained.

'No, it's a cart in the street,' Josie said. She dared not tell her mother Mrs Sheehan was departing.

'Me sister's on 'er own now. 'Er son's got wed an' moved ter Redditch, so 'er said why dain't I goo an' bide wi' 'er,' Mrs Sheehan had explained. 'Lives in a nice 'ouse out Shirley way, wi' a scullery an' kitchen as well as two parlours. 'Er man did well, but 'er feels like a pea in a pod rattlin' round in such a big 'ouse. I can 'ave me bed in front parlour, no stairs ter climb. It'll be a palace after this dump! An' 'er's sendin' a couple of friends ter fetch me an' me stuff.'

'What shall we do?' Josie asked fearfully.

'You'm not ter fret, I spoke fer yer. Landlord says yer can stay on paying 'im wot yer pays me, an' 'e's gorra coupla nice gals 'oo'll tek on my rooms, till Council boards 'em up.'

Josie tried to ignore that horror to come. She wondered who the girls were and hoped they'd be friendly.

'What about the coal that's left?' she asked instead.

'Keep it,' Mrs Sheehan said, her mood generous. 'But if I was yow I'd get it upstairs before others come.'

Josie decided it was good advice, or there could be arguments with the new tenants. When Mrs Sheehan, with much waving to her erstwhile neighbours, had been carried off perched on top of the cart in one of her armchairs, Josie lit a candle stub and went into the cellar to begin the task. She looked round in dismay. Instead of the sizeable heap that had been under the chute from the court yesterday, there were a few scattered lumps and a pile of dust and slack. Josie now knew what had been in the numerous hessian sacks piled at the bottom of the cart.

It was still bitterly cold weather and she needed plenty of coal for heating as well as cooking. She'd have to go and buy it by the sack, which would be more work carrying it home, and create problems when Dora didn't want to let her out of sight. Grimly Josie set to work salvaging what coal and slack she could, grateful at least for the two rusty buckets she found in a corner of the cellar which, though full of holes and with disintegrating bottoms, would enable her to store the slack up in their rooms.

It didn't take long, but she was covered in coal dust by the time she'd grubbed through the heap to save what was burnable. Dora shrieked in alarm at her black face, then laughed until it turned into a cough. Josie must have carried up dust which was affecting her lungs, she said weakly.

'It will settle soon, when I've been able to wash,' Josie said calmly. 'Mother, I've been thinking, wouldn't it be better if we moved your bed into the other room? The fire's bigger there and would keep you warmer, and if you want company I'll be there when I'm cooking, and won't have to leave you alone.'

Dora approved and Josie breathed a sigh of relief. She'd only have to keep one fire going, which would save work as well as money.

To Freddy's secret amazement the Streak won his first race. 'There, what did I tell yer?' he crowed to Mabel and various cronies who crowded round to congratulate him and help him drink his prize money.

'Don't forget, Sid's tekin' 'alf,' Mabel reminded him.

'Well, Sid's trained 'im, mostly,' Freddy tried to mollify her.

'We've not won a fortune, so watch 'ow much yer treats 'em all,' was Mabel's only response.

Freddy ignored her warnings, and by the time they were ready to set off for home his pockets were empty. Mabel raged at him, saying he'd promised her a new dress from his first winnings, and she was going shopping in the city centre the next day to look for a dress she liked, so Freddy had better find the money somehow.

Freddy racked his brains. He couldn't even work the Tote, the blasted courts had closed it down, saying it was illegal for dog tracks. He thought about Phoebe. Would she help? Then, with a jolt, he remembered that his mother was getting married and selling the house. He'd have to go and see her soon, but he kept putting if off. He hadn't been to see her for months, but certain salacious acquaintances had made sure he was kept informed. He'd heard that his prospective stepfather was wealthy, but Freddy realistically rated as low his chances of appealing to the charity of such a man. He didn't get enough money from Matthew. He'd have to risk doping the favourite for one of the races. Mabel's dad was out of prison now and had offered him a tenner to slip the dog a pill while he was walking it for Sid. If he would, he'd been told, he'd be given a few easy driving jobs. They knew too much for him to refuse.

The favourite duly lost, and Freddy was thrusting the tenner into his pocket when a hand descended on his shoulder. 'Just a minute, lad.'

Freddy leapt into the air then turned to run, but the hand slipped down his arm and held it in an unbreakable grip. As Freddy lifted his gaze to the solid figure of the policeman beside him he slumped in despair. He'd never get out of this.

Mrs Prentice lent her the axe. Dora's bed had been moved into the living room when Ann came for the day. Josie had emptied the wardrobe and packed the remaining clothes into the almost empty chest of drawers. She couldn't sell these pieces of furniture, it would cost too much to get men to come and take out the windows again, and besides, the upheaval would upset her mother. She could, however, chop them up and use the wood to supplement their coal. Her first attempts to chop the shelves, which she'd thought would be the easiest to start with, had brought cries of alarm and protest from Dora in the other room. Josie had begun the long process of pacifying and convincing her mother that she had no alternative. Dora wept hysterically and Josie finally lost patience.

'If you'd saved the money George gave you, you'd have had plenty to live on. If you hadn't splashed round money we didn't have and got us into debt things might have been easier now,' she told her mother angrily. 'If you'd taken the sapphires back to the bank as you'd promised we'd have had enough money to live in comfort for years. I'm tired of slaving all day, trying to stretch a penny to do the work of a shilling, and surviving only on the charity of my cousins. Do you think I want to be here listening to you complaining when I could be out working, keeping my self-respect by earning money for us? I know you're ill but you could try to help by not criticizing everything I do.'

She'd ignored her mother's tears and stalked back into the other room, venting her frustration on the wardrobe and hacking at it until it had been reduced to jagged strips of wood. Then, as she paused from sheer exhaustion, remorse hit her. Dora was dying. She couldn't help feeling ill, and no doubt that made her peevish. Josie pushed away the reflection that, even when she had been healthy and rich, Dora had still often been dissatisfied. It didn't matter. She was young and strong and able to look after herself, but her mother was ill and had no one else. She had to show more tolerance and patience. Slowly Josie went back to her mother, who looked up at her fearfully.

'Are you going?' Dora whispered, and Josie, struggling to suppress her own tears, shook her head.

'I'm sorry, I shouldn't have shouted,' she said, and bent to kiss her mother's pale cheek. Dora clung to her with surprising strength and sobbed out her own apologies.

'Please don't leave me, Josephine,' she pleaded. 'I know I've been difficult, but as soon as the winter's over I'll be better and I'll try to help you more, really I will, and I'll try not to be impatient, I promise!'

For a few days she managed to keep her promises, and then the new tenants moved in downstairs and things changed.

'Bert, I'm so grateful to you for coming back,' Leo said.

'I couldn't let yer miss yer sellin' trip,' the old man said easily. 'Where yer off to fust?'

'Germany, then Italy and back home via France. D'you think it's safe to go to Germany? It's in a right mess.'

'Germany's in a state. What d'yer think of this Hitler bein' chancellor?'

'His Nazi party lost some seats in the November election, so perhaps he's not so great a threat. And Roosevelt's now president in America, and with his New Deal the economic situation might improve.'

'Let's 'ope so. Where's Miss Josie?'

'Working somewhere else, I haven't seen her for ages,' Leo said curtly. 'She wouldn't want to come back.'

'Pity. It'll take a week ter sort out this mess. Could 'ave done with 'er.'

So could I, Leo thought. But she'd left her job at the Grand, and her cousin Ann had said she had another. He'd walked past the Nechells house the other day and most of the windows were boarded up. He'd been told the houses had been condemned. Perhaps she'd gone back to her aunt. She'd made it plain enough she'd didn't want him. While he'd been away he'd concluded he'd have to forget her.

*

'My lad in prison!' Phoebe exclaimed. 'I knew it would 'appen one day!'

'You can't 'elp 'im, luv,' Clem said.

'No, an' if I could I wouldn't! 'E's a grown man and it's up to 'im what 'e does with 'is life. But 'is pa would be 'eartbroken.'

'I'll buy the dog,' Sid offered. 'Freddy can't pay 'is share now, nor 'e ay' paid over me share of winnin's, so be rights I could claim dog. I'll give yer five quid.'

Phoebe accepted this generous offer. She'd keep it for Freddy. As she went home she determined she'd tackle Freddy's room, which until now she'd left in the hope of his doing it himself. She'd also, she decided, accept Mr Parsons' offer for the useless kennel, and put that money aside for Freddy too. She'd call in at once and tell the old man to come and collect it.

'What's that noise?' Dora groaned. It had become a constant refrain and Josie was running out of excuses which would prevent her discovering the truth.

'A party somewhere, Mother,' Josie murmured. 'Try to sleep. The church clock struck midnight some time ago.'

Dora sighed and turned over, and soon her gentle breathing showed she slept. Josie, however, remained wakeful, her mind churning as she fought to devise ways out of their dreadful situation. It had grown worse. At first, when Bella and Ruby had moved in downstairs she'd thought they were pleasant, friendly girls. They were both pretty and fair-haired, lively and full of smiles. It was only after the first few days when it became apparent they had no jobs to go to that Josie, for so long immune to the changes in fashion, suspected they were far better dressed than she might have expected. Bella and Ruby never went out until evening. Only that morning, when Josie had crept through their kitchen to reach the by-now almost deserted court, she saw that one of them, she thought Ruby, was untidily asleep on a makeshift bed in the corner, while loud snores unlikely to come from the dainty Bella's mouth reverberated from the other room.

Warily Josie had watched from her upstairs window, and half way through the morning her suspicions were heightened when a big, heavy man emerged and walked jauntily across the yard. How could she voice these suspicions to her mother?

They were confirmed a few days later when Josie, late at night and carrying the water bucket, was entering the house. Another man, standing under the light cast from the single gas lamp at the entrance to the court, young and slim, dapper in a shallow bowler hat, waisted overcoat, wide trousers with turn-ups and two-tone shoes in pale cream and chocolate brown, called out to her.

'I say, miss, are you Ruby?'

Josie shook her head. 'I think she's out.'

'The devil! Bella sent me, said her sister was here. Oh, well, no harm done if she has more than one sister. What's your name, my lovely one? I haven't met Ruby, but I doubt she's a patch on you, by Jove! I rather go for Amazons when they've good ripe figures like yours!'

Josie sidestepped as he moved purposefully towards her. She felt vulnerable, since by now theirs was the only occupied house in the court and all the others had been boarded up. There was no one who might, even had they felt willing, have come to her aid. 'You're making a mistake, sir,' she said sharply. 'I live upstairs with my mother, who is very ill, not with Ruby and Bella, so if you'll be kind enough to move I can get back to her.'

He laughed, and Josie saw with a sinking feeling that he was drunk enough to be unreasonable but not so much as to be incapable of aggression. She'd seen several fights start in bars when men had been in this state.

'It's true,' she said, trying to be calm. 'Why don't you go back and ask Bella where Ruby is?'

It didn't work, she hadn't really expected it to, and when he came closer she gripped the bucket more firmly.

'Coy, are you? Or are you expecting someone else? But first come first served, what? Two bob, and you could still satisfy him later on, or five for all night. Which?'

Josie swung the bucket. The water sloshed over them both and the bucket caught him on the side of the head. Because of the weight she hadn't been able to swing it really fast, and by the time the water had poured out it wasn't heavy enough to do much damage. As she turned to the door, hoping to get inside and bolt it against him, her foot slipped on the wet and greasy cobbles and Josie fell awkwardly. The man, made angry but not incapable from the blow, flung himself on top of her.

'You'll pay for that, you little vixen,' he threatened, and Josie, with agonizing stabs of pain shooting up from her twisted ankle, her head reeling from where she'd hit it on the door jamb, desperately tried to fight him off.

Chapter Fifteen

THE man was slight but strong, and though Josie struggled furiously she could not push him from on top of her. Her ankle was hurting, she was unable to put any pressure on it, so her efforts to heave herself out from under him were hampered. She tried to scream, but as he sprawled on top of her he clamped one hand across her face and with the other began to tear at her clothes. They were old and worn and the seams split easily. The man grunted as Josie's blouse, the one she'd bought when she first started work, ripped down the front and he was able to drag it away from one shoulder. She grabbed for it but merely entangled her arm in the ripped sleeve, trapping it. Desperation gave Josie the strength to dislodge her attacker enough for her to bite his hand, and as he gasped at the sudden pain she wriggled sideways.

Josie bumped against the bucket as she moved. She reached out and by good fortune seized the handle. She lifted the bucket, gasping as the last dregs of water dripped on to her face, but swung it round so that it connected with a satisfying clang against his head. He winced and rolled away. The moment his weight was removed, Josie struggled to her feet, hobbling, and swung the bucket repeatedly at him until with an oath he scrambled up and moved out of range.

'You vicious trollop!' he gasped.

Josie laughed harshly. 'Perhaps you'd better make sure you're with a trollop next time!' she shouted as she slipped through the door and slammed it closed. She pushed home the flimsy bolt and then leant against the door, suddenly breathless and painfully aware of her twisted ankle and a multitude of bruises.

She heard a few more curses, then silence, but she dared not go out to replenish the water. She'd have to wait until one of the girls returned; she would not draw the bolt until they were home. She felt around in the dark until she located a candle and some matches, and tried to see what damage had been done to her clothes. They were wet and filthy but that could be remedied. She thought she could mend the tear in her blouse. The difficulty was what to wear while she dealt with them. The only spare clothing she now possessed was a second set of underwear.

Josie looked round the kitchen for inspiration, and saw what looked like a man's overcoat hanging on a nail beside the door. Had one of the men who visited Bella or Ruby forgotten it, no doubt warmed by his welcome and activities while in the house? Reasoning that if they didn't ply their dubious trade here she wouldn't have been attacked, Josie appropriated it and put it on after she'd taken off her wet skirt and the tattered blouse. She found a needle and some white thread and threw some more coal on to the dying embers, then sat down to mend the rips. Dora was asleep and she could occupy her time usefully while she waited for the girls to return. Her skirt, though muddy, was dry and her blouse mended by the time Ruby came home an hour later, with a middle-aged man who looked embarrassed when he saw Josie. Briefly, Josie explained and then wearily climbed the stairs. Her ankle was swollen, but if she took care she could walk on it. It was more painful the following day when she hobbled down for water.

Ruby was awake, drinking a cup of tea. 'Yer should join us,' she commented. 'I know yer's short of the ready, but with just one customer a night yer could mek a good livin', yer know.'

She misunderstood Josie's look of dismay. 'Yer could use one of our beds, no need to disturb yer ma. An' ter start with me an' Bella'd bring men in. We knows where ter find 'em, see. Yer'd soon get a reg'lar set of fellers, bonny lass like yow.'

'If you make so much why do you go on living here?'

'No point payin' fancy rents,' Ruby said with a shrug. 'We'm savin', see, ter buy 'ouse. Then we can charge double, get quality customers, an' no bloody pimp ter tek a cut! It were lucky we 'eard of these rooms, landlord lets us 'ave 'em fer nowt 'cept 'is turn once a week. 'E car' rent 'em out like they are. If 'e charges yer rent, suggest summat different. Car' get enuff on it, 'e car'!'

'I'm afraid it's a matter of days,' Dr Mandeville said to Josie a week later. 'She doesn't seem to be in pain, so just keep her as comfortable as possible. Would you like me to see if I can find anyone to help you?'

Josie shook her head. 'Thank you, no.'

'You're looking ill yourself,' he said bluntly. 'Are you sure?'

'I don't need anyone.' Josie said. 'My cousin comes today so I can have a rest. I'll manage, truly I will.'

The following day, Bella and Ruby departed. 'Landlord's bin told 'e can't let 'ouse no longer,' Ruby explained. 'We've all gorra get out.'

'But — I've nowhere to go!' Josie exclaimed.

Ruby shrugged. 'Well, we've bought our own place, an' if yer wanted, we could use another gal. Told yer it'd solve all yer problems. Yer ma could come, 'ave 'er own room, yer could pay us rent an' 'er'd not be troubled.'

Josie shuddered at the thought of her mother's reaction, but Dora was too ill by now to do more than lie, half-asleep, rousing only occasionally to eat or drink what Josie fed her. 'She's too ill to move, but thank you for the offer,' Josie said. 'Surely they can't force us to leave? Not when she's dying?'

'They'll tek 'er to 'ospital, I s'pose,' Ruby said.

'It would kill her.'

'Then yer'd best get ready fer siege. Ta'ra a bit.' She waved and started off towards the entry of the court.

'Aren't you taking any furniture?' Josie asked, surprised.

'There's bugger-all worth tekin. Yer can 'elp yerself ter what yer wants an' welcome.'

Josie looked after her, then at the furniture. Most was too big for her to carry up the narrow stairs, but it might be used as firewood. She had very little coal left, and if there was a real risk they might be turned out she dared not leave Dora alone. Luckily, Ann had brought them enough food yesterday for a week so she wouldn't have to go out to the shops. By next week, probably, her mother would be past caring, but Josie vowed that for her last few days Dora should be as comfortable as she could contrive.

A sudden noise startled her. The sharp rap on the door was unexpected. Cautiously she went to open it. The landlord stood outside. He was a small, ferret-like man with ginger hair so greasy the colour had almost been obliterated. He grinned at Josie.

'Well, that's the last gone from 'ere bar you. When'll yer be out?'

'I haven't anywhere to go,' Josie explained, 'and my mother is dying. Please can't you let us stay here for a few more days?'

'Not up ter me,' he said, far too cheerfully for Josie's ears. 'I've bin told ev'ryone's ter be out by tomorrow. If not, bailiffs'll chuck yer out in 'ossroad. Yer can't say I dain't warn yer!'

Josie began to think seriously of Ruby's advice to prepare for a siege. What could she use to barricade herself in? Nothing would deter them for long, the door and window were flimsy, or they could bring ladders and enter through the upstairs window, but every hour of delay might prevent her mother from being thrown into the street to die.

Josie hurriedly filled every receptacle she could find with water, blessing Ruby and Bella for leaving their old zinc bath and a bucket and several cooking pots. She dragged in the bath from the nail where it hung outside and filled it with water, carrying bucket after bucket across from the pump, worried that she might not have time to finish. With furious energy Josie set about dragging all the furniture she could across the kitchen. A heavy sideboard barred the door, and the table heaved on top helped. From the other room Josie dragged a wardrobe and wedged it as well as she could against the window. Then she thought of the cellar and the chute for the coal. A thin man might slide through there, so she placed the chest of drawers by the cellar door. When she had finished she was exhausted and Dora was calling weakly to ask what was going on, why she had been left alone. Josie went upstairs to prepare some food and try to keep her mother calm.

'Lizzie, I haven't seen you for months!'

'Hello, William.' Lizzie turned to speak as William drew up beside her. 'How's Coventry?'

'The factory's running well. Can I give you a lift?'

'I'm going to see Ma,' Lizzie said, and William jumped out to open the passenger door. 'She's getting married at Easter and is so busy clearing everything out, I come over to help when I can.'

'How's Josie? I've been so busy I've hardly been in Birmingham.'

Lizzie sighed. 'Her mother's dying and poor Josie can't leave her to get a job. They're living in a dreadful hovel, and for everyone's sake I hope Dora dies soon. I know it's wicked of me but I can't bear to see Josie so weary, so hopeless.'

'I didn't know about this. How awful! She's no job?'

'Leo and she had a frightful row,' Lizzie told him. 'Some gold was stolen and Leo accused Josie.'

'He accused Josie of stealing?' William exclaimed. 'How dare he! Did you know about the radiator grille Leo and Matthew were producing?' Lizzie shook her head. 'The design had been stolen from me.'

'By Leo? But how?'

'I believed Leo when he said he knew nothing about it, and later I discovered it had been one of my clerks. I dismissed him, but then I find Leo's employing him. Why should he do that?'

'I used to think Leo was great, until he sacked Josie. Ever since then she's been unable to get a proper job, even when her mother wasn't ill. It's been terrible for her.'

'Does she need money?' William asked. 'You must let me help if that's a problem. I didn't know.'

Lizzie smiled but shook her head. 'Ann and I give her some, but she's so proud I don't think she'd accept anything from anyone who wasn't family. We had a dreadful job to persuade her to take anything from us, but if she gets desperate I'll remember. Thanks, William, you're a pal.'

He shrugged. 'She's a great girl, Josie. I wish I had her as my passenger again. She was never afraid of hard work. How about you? Do you go on any rallies now?'

Lizzie shook her head. 'I haven't been for ages, and even though driving's my job now I miss it.'

'Then come with me next Sunday. Are you free?'

'I'd love to. And I can change a wheel too, now,' she said, laughing. 'Look, we're home. Have you time to come in?'

'Sorry, on my way to Walsall to see someone about one of my gadgets. I think it will be better made of leather. I'll pick you up on Sunday, in Warwick, by the East Gate, nine o'clock.'

Phoebe was putting on the kettle for a cup of tea when Mr Parsons knocked on the back door.

'Ta, missus, I've got kennel loaded on barrow.'

'Come and have a cuppa,' Phoebe invited. 'I'm knackered, just finished turnin' out Freddy's room, and you wouldn't believe the rubbish 'e kept there! I suppose I'll have ter find somewhere ter keep it.'

'Silly chump. Oh, don't know if this is anythin' of Freddy's. Found it down under kennel,' he explained as he handed over a bundle of hessian. 'Thought it were just a bit of sackin' at first, nearly chucked it on yer bonfire, then I sees it were tied up like a parcel.'

'More rubbish, I suppose,' Phoebe sighed, and rather gingerly took the parcel and put it on the sink drainer. 'I'll look at it later, when I've got some strength back.'

It was the following day before Phoebe remembered the parcel again. She'd ignored it when she'd washed up the few dishes she used the previous evening, and in the morning had rushed out of the house to the Home and Colonial before washing up her breakfast dishes. On her return she was filling the kettle when she saw it and decided she could look at it after she'd taken her hat off and while the kettle boiled. She hung up her coat and hat, donned an apron and spread some clean newspaper on the table, then took the parcel across to it. It was wet and filthy, the knots in the string so tight Phoebe had to find a sharp knife to cut them. With a grimace she began to unroll the hessian, and then sat down suddenly on the chair, staring in utter amazement at the parcel's contents.

'Freddy,' she whispered eventually. 'Freddy, how could you?' she said and Lizzie, walking through the front door at that moment, came hastily into the kitchen.

'Ma? Is Freddy here?' she demanded, looking round in some bewilderment for Phoebe was alone, though the kettle was singing on the hob. To her horror her mother burst into tears, wiping her eyes on her apron, seemingly incapable of speech. She gestured towards the table and Lizzie glanced at the dirty sacking spread out there. She saw the gleam of something bright. Suddenly her attention was fully caught and she stepped close and pulled the sacking aside. 'Ma, it's Aunt Dora's sapphires!' she said, aghast. 'Where were they? How did you find them? Not Freddy?'

'Mek us a cuppa,' Phoebe said faintly, and didn't speak again until she'd taken several gulps of strong sweet tea. 'The parcel was hidden under that blasted dog's kennel,' she explained. 'I sold the kennel ter Mr Parsons, an' 'e brought it in yesterday. I didn't open it till just now. I didn't believe Freddy could have been so wicked! He told me lies, 'e swore blind 'e dain't tek 'em!'

'And he's let Josie struggle on for months when she and Aunt Dora could have been living in luxury,' Lizzie fumed. 'I could kill him for this.'

'Only if yer got to 'im fust,' Phoebe said with more of her customary fire. 'Ter think 'e let me quarrel wi' Doris and turn 'er out of my 'ouse when all the time 'e knew they were tellin' the truth! I expect 'e was behind that theft at Leo Bradley's place too, and it was the money that fetched what 'im and his slut's been livin' on since!'

'But why did he leave them here?' Lizzie asked. 'Why didn't he sell them?'

'Too 'ot! The police had a good description, any jeweller in Birmingham would have recognized 'em.' Suddenly she burst into tears. 'Lizzie, where's my 'at? I'm goin' straight to our Doris. I can't rest another minute till I've made my peace with 'er and give 'er back what's 'ers.'

They came early in the morning. Josie woke to furious knocking on the door, and leant out of the window to ask what they wanted.

'These 'ouses is condemned,' one of the two men, in bowlers and heavy overcoats, told her roughly.

'What proof have you?' Josie asked coolly, though she was feeling anything but composed.

For a moment this puzzled them, then they started to bluster that they were officials and didn't need proof.

'But I do,' Josie retorted. 'This is my home, and my mother is too ill to move. If you don't believe me, go and ask Dr Mandeville.'

The men looked at one another, tried the door again, and withdrew for a brief consultation. Then one of them turned back to Josie. 'Yer'll be sorry fer defyin' us,' he threatened. 'We'll not be beat by a slip of a gal!'

They departed, but Josie knew they wouldn't be away for long. When they returned they'd have tools for breaking in, or ladders, and she couldn't hope to hold them off. She'd do her best, she vowed. Terrible though this place was, it was Dora's home and she should remain there, if possible in peace, until she died. By immense good fortune Dora had slept through this altercation, but now she woke and seemed a little improved. Josie made tea, cut some of the fine white bread Ann had bought for them, spread it with the good butter, and persuaded her mother to eat. By the time Josie had gently washed her hands and face and tidied away, half the morning had gone. Suddenly there was another knock on the door, this time tentative. Josie, fearing the worst, looked out of the window.

'Lizzie! And Aunt Phoebe! What are you doing here?'

'And why is yer window blocked up?' Phoebe demanded.

'The bailiffs,' Josie began, and then recalled that her mother was awake. 'I'll come down,' she said. Ignoring her mother's questions she ran downstairs and tugged the furniture away from the door. She had only just finished and pulled open the door when the bailiffs returned, bringing a couple of brawny men armed with axes. Seeing the open door they gave a shout of triumph and ran across, but Phoebe interposed her bulk between them and the door.

'Quick, Lizzie, go an' telephone Clem an' tell 'im 'e's got to come straight away,' she ordered, and Lizzie sped off. Phoebe turned towards the older bailiff. 'My sister's in 'ere, dyin',' she said with unusual dignity. 'I'll ask yer to respect 'er last few days on this earth.'

'Well, we don't mean no disrespect,' the man replied in a conciliatory tone, 'but we gorra job ter do. No one's allowed ter live 'ere no more.'

'You can't think anyone would live 'ere if they could 'elp it,' Phoebe said sharply. 'But me sister's too ill ter move. Leave 'er in peace fer a coupla days. Yer don't want ter knock the place down this minute, do yer?'

To Josie's surprise they accepted this and agreed to come back the following day. 'But yer'll 'ave ter find a way of shiftin' poor woman,' they said as they left.

'Aunt Phoebe! Thank God you came!' Josie said unsteadily, clutching at her aunt and struggling to regain her composure.

'How's Doris? I should 'ave come months ago.'

'She's a little better today, but you know – the doctor says it will only be a few days.'

'Take me up.'

Phoebe stared in shuddering disgust at the flaking whitewash, the crumbling plaster, and the damp, rotting floorboards. She trod cautiously up the narrow stairs and stepped warily through the door at the top. The room, though bare, with minimal furniture, was as clean and bright as Josie could manage, and a good fire burnt in the grate. Dora lay propped on pillows, her hair neatly braided, wearing an old but clean nightdress. She gave an involuntary smile when she saw Phoebe, then recalled their last acrimonious meeting and looked apprehensive.

Phoebe moved to sit on the bed and leant forward to kiss Dora's papery cheek. 'Doris, love, I've come ter say sorry. I'm sorry I didn't believe yer,' Phoebe said quietly. 'I'd have come before if I'd had the sense ter believe you instead of that devil son of mine.' She paused and swallowed. It was more difficult than she'd expected, laying the blame on Freddy, but after a slight pause she went on steadily. 'I was clearin' out, and I sold Freddy's dog's kennel, and they found these under it.'

She delved into her large handbag and drew out something wrapped in a silk scarf. Carefully she opened it and Josie gasped

249

as the sapphires gleamed at her. 'Freddy must 'ave stolen them. It's all his fault. I'll never forgive 'im, Doris and Josie, for what 'e's done ter you.'

Dora was smiling gently. 'I always knew it was him,' she said weakly. 'Josephine, dear, put them on me please. Now I have these I shall get better, and one day I'll wear them again at your wedding.'

It was Phoebe who fastened the necklace about her neck, pinned a brooch to her thin, threadbare nightdress, and gently pushed the bracelets up her wasted arms. Dora shook her head at the earrings, but slipped the ring on her finger herself. Josie was standing by the foot of the bed fighting back her tears and the overriding fury which possessed her when she thought of all the misery they had been caused by Freddy's theft of these jewels. If they'd had them earlier her mother could have spent her last months in dignity and comfort, with all she needed to make her life bearable. If she ever saw Freddy again, she knew she would have difficulty in not taking revenge.

She moved away, for the sisters were talking softly about their childhood and her mother even laughed once or twice. When Lizzie, breathless, returned and said that Clem was on his way the girls retreated downstairs.

'Can Aunt Dora be moved?' Lizzie asked anxiously.

Josie shook her head. 'Dr Mandeville says the strain would kill her, or he'd have tried to get her to go to hospital. But she didn't want to. I don't know if she knows she's dying, but in a funny way I think she wants to stay here. Lizzie, I was so thankful to see you and your mother! I couldn't have held them out for long on my own, but I was going to have a jolly good try.'

With Clem's help, Phoebe organized the bringing in of a good meal, lots of early daffodils which Dora said had always been her favourite spring flowers, and a bottle of champagne. Lizzie and Josie brought up chairs from downstairs, and they were soon sitting round the table eating and drinking, with Dora propped up in bed and smiling fondly at them all, decked in her sapphires.

'Ought Mother to have rich food?' Josie asked anxiously. 'We haven't had a great deal to eat lately, she didn't have much appetite.'

'She won't want more than a taste,' Phoebe reassured her. Dora seemed to enjoy her mouthful of watercress soup, the sliver of chicken breast, and even a tiny portion of treacle tart. She sipped at the glass of champagne and afterwards closed her eyes and fell gently asleep.

'Lizzie, you must get back to Warwick,' Phoebe began to organize them. 'Clem, be a dear and get rid of this food and go and find some more coal and a mattress and more blankets. We'll make a fire in the other room and Josie can sleep there while I sit with Doris. You look worn to the bone, child,' she told her firmly as Josie tried to protest.

Replete with champagne and the first good meal she'd had for months, Josie found herself incapable of argument. All she wanted was to sleep, to relinquish responsibility. Now Aunt Phoebe was here all would be well. Almost before the fire was lit and the mattress which Clem had found spread before it, she was asleep. Phoebe stood looking down at her, and suddenly turned and clasped Clem's hand.

'She's still a child, too young for what she's had to do,' she whispered.

'Never mind, old girl. Let's leave 'er to sleep. What can I do next?'

'You're a darling! When – when it's all over, can I bring Josie to your 'ouse?'

'So long as you come too,' he said in some alarm.

'Of course I'm comin'! I wouldn't leave you alone with a pretty young lass like Josie,' she said with a pitiful attempt at a joke. 'But my 'ouse will be sold in a couple of weeks, an' I can't tek 'er there.'

'Bring her to Solihull. We'll feed 'er up. Now, shall I stay with you?'

Phoebe shook her head. 'You go home and have a good sleep. But please come back as early as you can, I don't think she'll last more'n a day or so, and I'll need you.'

Phoebe called Josie softly about eight the following morning. 'Yer ma wants yer,' she said gently.

Josie sat up quickly. 'Oh, I've slept so long! Aunt Phoebe? Yes, I remember. How – how is she?'

'Awake. Go and sit with 'er.'

Josie did as she was bid, and for several more hours she watched her mother, sometimes awake but mostly sleeping. As it was growing dark outside Dora woke once more, turned her head on the pillows, raised her hand to finger the jewels she still wore, smiled faintly and then stretched out her hand to Josie.

'You've been a good daughter,' she whispered as Josie took her hand. Then she fell suddenly, deeply asleep. Within an hour she was dead, her fingers still clutching the sapphires at her neck.

Chapter Sixteen

Afterwards, Josie could remember few details of the following week. At first there had been people coming and going in the living room, hushed voices, loud footsteps on the bare boards, while she lay on the mattress in the smaller room. She recalled seeing Dr Mandeville, and afterwards thought she fell asleep for a long time with only brief periods of consciousness. Aunt Phoebe had spoken to her once or twice, and a big, bald man with a gruff, kindly voice had sat and held her hand when she was awake. Then Aunt Phoebe was wrapping a warm blanket round her, and she remembered walking down the stairs and getting into a big car smelling of leather and cigars. Next she woke up in a pretty chintzy bedroom and through the window could see a garden with wide lawns and a thick belt of rhododendron bushes, beyond which were fields stretching into the distance. When she awoke again, Aunt Phoebe was there and told her she was at Clement's house in Solihull. She couldn't recall who Clement was, but it didn't matter. She did what they told her, ate, drank, washed, dressed in strange clothes which felt thick and stiflingly warm, and rode in the big car again to the church where they had arranged Dora's funeral. It was cold, bitterly cold, the wind vicious in its intensity, and no one lingered long beside the open grave. There were few people to mourn Dora.

'It was my fault,' Josie said as they drove back to Solihull. The biting wind seemed to have brought her back to life. 'I could have made it easier for her.'

'You did all you could and wore yourself out doin' it,' Phoebe said bracingly. 'If anyone's ter blame it's me fer chucking the pair of you out, believin' that devil Freddy instead of poor Doris.'

'I used to think she was pretending to be ill.'

'So did I, and I think in the beginning she was. Clem thinks people can make themselves ill if they want to.'

'No, Mother was truly ill,' Josie protested. 'But I could have been less proud, when Leo . . .'

'When Leo what? Did 'e offer you yer job back?'

'Yes,' Josie said quickly, thankful for this excuse. She didn't want to tell anyone Leo had asked her to marry him. It was too painful to recall. If only she'd accepted! Then Dora could have spent her last days in comfort instead of in a condemned slum with bailiffs trying to force their way in. But Leo surely did not really want to marry her. It had to be some perverse notion that he owed her something, after George's death and later perhaps after his own suspicions about her honesty. She was glad, despite it all, that she hadn't succumbed. She would have been a burden to him, eventually he'd have hated both her and her mother, and that she couldn't bear.

Clement drove through a wide gateway and Josie noticed the house where she'd been staying for the first time. It was huge, low and sprawling, with wide bay windows and a large pillared porch. There was a maze of bare branches clinging to the walls and suddenly Josie could imagine what a riot of colour there would be in the summer, roses and wistaria, honeysuckle and clematis, fighting for space.

'What's done can't be mended,' Clement said as he drew up by the porch, 'so there's no sense in fretting about it. What you must do, young Josie, is get on with your life as your mom and dad, and that Mr Bradley who was as good as a dad to you, would have wanted. Mek 'em proud on yer. And show the rest of the world they can't keep yer down!'

By the following day Josie had recovered her strength and was determined to take this advice. Rather shyly she asked Aunt Phoebe to show her round the house. 'If Mr Stokes won't mind,' she added quickly.

'Why should 'e? It's my 'ouse too now, or will be come Easter when we get wed,' Phoebe said. 'I still can't believe it though,' she mused as they wandered through the ground-floor rooms and Josie admired the light, airy spaciousness. 'Freer Road was good enough for me, I was lucky to have that, but this is a palace. Clem made a fortune and he can't wait to spend it on me. And he says you're to make your home here for as long as you want.'

'I couldn't,' Josie said hastily. 'I'm so grateful to you for looking after me and – and making all the arrangements. I'll have to pay you back as soon as I can, the funeral must have cost a lot.'

'Now just you look 'ere, young Josie, there's to be no talk of paying me back. I've got my own money, it's not Clem's, and I wanted to do it. I'd be real upset if you didn't want me to.'

Josie saw that she meant it and hugged her impulsively. 'You're a dear! But I can't stay here playing gooseberry. I must get a job as soon as I can and find a room nearby.'

'What sort of job?'

Josie shrugged. 'I'll try secretarial, it's what I prefer, though I became very slick at tossing fried fish on top of the chips.'

Phoebe chuckled. 'There's my girl. Don't let it get you down. But what about your own business? Clem thinks you could make a go at one.'

'I used to dream about that,' Josie admitted. 'It seems so long ago since I left school and I thought then I might one day own a shop.'

'It's eighteen months since you left school, you're only eighteen! You talk as though it was a lifetime.'

'It seems it. It is, Mother's lifetime.'

'Don't be morbid. Now, Clem said I was ter talk with you. Do you want to keep her sapphires?'

Josie shuddered. 'No. I never want to see them again! I know it's silly but I blame them for everything.'

'That's understandable. Will you let Clem sell 'em for you? He'll get a good price, you can trust 'im.'

'Of course I trust him –'

'Good, then with the money you can buy a business. And if you'll let him, Clem would help you set it up. It'll give him somethin' ter do instead of gettin' in my way while I'm organizin' the wedding,' she chuckled.

'Everything well?' Leo asked the first day he was back from his selling trip.

Bert nodded. 'But I'm glad to see yer, Guv! It's time I went back to Coventry. Did your trip go well?'

'Yes, trade seems to be picking up slightly, except in Germany. I don't think I'll go there again for a while.'

'Bad, is it?'

'The Jews are being persecuted, and many are leaving. Some of the stories I was told are incredible.'

'Mr Churchill keeps saying we're not in a position to fight.'

Leo shrugged. 'If we have to, that's all there is to it. I don't hold with standing back and letting Mosley or Hitler walk all over us for the sake of some resistance.'

'If yer'd bin in the last war you'd not be so ready,' Bert said. 'I'm not sure I'd fight again if I were young enough. It were real bad. But it won't 'appen. 'Ow did yer go on elsewhere?'

'I've several new customers.'

They settled down to discussing details and finally Bert said, 'One of the men died, heart attack. I sent a wreath from you an' told 'is widow you'd see her when you got back, but she weren't short of money. And a couple of polishers left. We took new gals on a month's trial.'

Leo nodded. 'Thanks.'

Bert departed and Leo forced himself to settle to work.

While he'd been away he'd thought more deeply than ever before about his feelings for a woman. In his youth he'd fallen in love and been badly wounded. He'd allowed it to happen again with Josie, though he knew that this time his suffering was all his own fault. Reluctantly he'd decided Josie would never accept his proposal. How could she, when he'd hurt her so unbearably, be expected to forgive him? He must forget her.

'Cor!' Freddy was for once overawed, and then his agile brain began calculating the benefits he perceived for himself when his mother was married to the moneybags who owned this pile. It wasn't a stately home but it would do for him, Freddy decided, beginning to grin. Fancy the old girl pulling this off! A slight doubt penetrated his absorption. She hadn't married him so far, had she, yet according to the neighbours in Freer Road she was living here with the old geezer. He'd have to make sure she didn't repeat her mistake with his father. Men didn't willingly shackle themselves when they could get it for nothing. Momentarily his mind boggled at the thought of his mother, an old woman by any standards, frolicking between the sheets with an equally elderly admirer. He had a sudden urge to meet this ancient Romeo.

Phoebe opened the door and Freddy felt disappointed. He'd anticipated a butler at least. He pinned a smile on his lips. 'Hello, Ma.'

'What do you want?'

His mouth fell open. 'It's me, Ma, Freddy. Don't yer want ter see me?'

'No.'

'But – but – they let me out this mornin'. I ain't got nowhere ter go. The 'ouse in Freer Road's closed up.'

'Find that fancy woman, let 'er feed an' board you.'

'But Ma, she's moved. I went there fust. Yer even sold me

257

dog,' he accused. 'I bin ter see Sid. An' yer sold me kennel. That cost money, that did.'

'And what was with the kennel.'

'What? What yer mean?' he blustered.

'You're not my son, Freddy. Yer told me lies, you thieved from yer Aunt Doris, an' you let me throw 'er out. She died a couple of weeks back, in the worst kind of slum I've ever known, an' it's your fault.'

'Ma, yer got it all wrong. I don't know what yer talkin' about!' he protested. 'Let me come in, an' yer can tell me what yer means. Don't want ter let the neighbours know all our business, do yer?' he added ingratiatingly.

'What neighbours?'

He'd forgotten the size of the house and garden. He looked at it now. The lawns in front of the house spread for what seemed acres, and any neighbouring properties were concealed from view by dense evergreen hedges. Even the road was invisible since the driveway curved round so that the gates were hidden. The only other building was a large carriage and stable block to the side of the house.

'Won't yer let me in ter discuss it?' he tried.

'No. There's nothin' to say, except this. You're a thief and a liar, a cheat and a lazy layabout. I'm sorry you were ever born, and I'm just thankful your pa never knew what a monster he'd fathered. I know yer stole Doris's silver, even though yer put it back. It was that as started you off, got you in with that drab! Then yer pinched the sapphires, and I wouldn't be at all surprised if you 'adn't 'ad somethin' ter do with that gold our Josie was accused of stealin'! I won't go so far as turnin' you in, Freddy, not yet, but just do one more thing to 'arm young Josie and I'll be right round the police station. An' don't you think I couldn't prove it! Now get off, I don't ever want to see you again. You're no son of mine!'

With which she slammed the door, leaving Freddy gaping at the impenetrable oak panels. His shoulders slumped. He'd been hoping she maybe hadn't discovered the sapphires. They could still have been with the kennel. As he turned to tramp away, he realized that if Mabel knew about this she wouldn't take him back. He clenched his fists. It was all Josie's fault! While he'd been rotting in prison, unjustly accused, she'd wormed her way into his mother's good graces. She'd seen her chance, no doubt, when his mother had taken up with a rich man. The sly little madam. By the time he reached the road he'd convinced himself Josie had been plotting to oust him from his mother's affections ever since she'd come to live with them. She wouldn't have what belonged to him, he vowed. One day his mother would own this house, and after her it ought by rights to be his. Josie had to be stopped and somehow he'd do it.

Despite her barely concealed impatience, Clem refused to be hurried in selling the sapphires for Josie.

'It don't do to accept the first offer, not when it's something as special as this set. I mean to get the best price I can,' he told her, adding privately to Phoebe that the longer Josie could stay with them to recover the better.

'But you've been offered thousands already,' Josie pointed out. 'That's far more than I need to buy a shop.'

'And with a little bit of cunning I can push up the price by a few more thousands. When yer buy your business you don't want to fail because you haven't got the cash to keep it ticking while yer get organized, do you?'

'No, but I could start with a smaller business.'

'Why, when a larger one would mek more profits? Have you found one you want yet?'

Josie sighed. 'Not yet. I've looked at all the shops for sale but none of them attracts me.'

'If you haven't settled on one there's no haste, then. But why are yer lookin' at shops?'

'It's something I can do.'

'From what your aunt tells me you practically ran Leo

Bradley's jewellery business. Why don't you set up making the same sort of things?'

'But I don't know the first thing about making bracelets and silver boxes and all that,' Josie protested.

'You do know how to manage a jewellery workshop, and you can always employ jewellers and a foreman. There's plenty of good workers lookin' for jobs in Hockley.'

'That means trade is slack, so where would I sell whatever I made?'

'Trade's pickin' up, I'm told, so get in now. There's talk of armaments.'

'Not another war!' Phoebe exclaimed.

'I know I made my pile wi' guns, but I don't like wars. We 'ave to be strong to deter folk like that Hitler.'

'Not even he'd want a war, surely?' Josie said. 'About my workshop. I could aim for the top end of the market, good quality – there's a bigger profit margin there.'

'Then there's the souvenir market,' Clem suggested. 'Once the jewellery's established you can get into that. That's where you can do cheap stuff.'

'Souvenirs of what?' Josie asked.

'Anniversaries. Soon it'll be the king's Silver Jubilee, and people will go mad buying anything with 'is head on. You can do real silver as well as coloured tin, though most of 'em won't know the difference. And though I don't wish 'im any harm, he probably can't last much longer and there'll be a new king.'

'Of course! And a coronation, probably a royal wedding and royal births to celebrate. The Prince of Wales was popular when he come to Hockley in '31.'

'Then there's local anniversaries,' Clem said. 'In 1938 it'll be a hundred years since Birmingham got a charter, and the following year it'll be fifty years since it was made a city.'

'And if I could get a reputation for producing souvenirs, local firms will come and ask me to design things for their own celebrations. How exciting!' Josie said, laughing. 'I'd like to get back into the jewellery business, but could I really employ people I could trust?'

'I'd help you find them. And I still have lots of friends in Hockley. If you'd let me help, that is. I'll put in some money too, if you want.'

'No! Oh, dear, I'm sorry, I didn't mean to sound rude. I'd be very grateful for any help, but not money. I can't risk your money.'

'Why not?'

'Papa George lost his through depending on other people to run businesses successfully. I won't be responsible for that sort of risk. I've always dreamed of making a success by my own efforts, not by speculating.'

'Fair enough,' Clem said, satisfied he'd gained his major objective. 'Shall I ask around to see whether there's a suitable factory for sale?'

When Leo met William one day during a rally he couldn't, despite his resolution to forget her, resist asking if he knew how Josie was.

William was unwelcoming. 'I haven't seen her for several months,' he said. 'Lizzie said her mother was very ill and she couldn't leave her to come on rallies. She had a bad time after you sacked her. How could you believe she stole from you?'

'I know now she didn't. I was a fool, I admit it.'

William looked sceptical. 'I believed you when you said you didn't know about Matthew's little enterprise. And now I hear you're employing the man I sacked for stealing that design.'

'What's that? Who? I thought you didn't know who'd stolen them? It wasn't anyone called Hugh Jones.'

'No, but just before Easter Henry Manders was caught carrying one of my new heated windscreen wipers out of the factory. I sacked him then.'

'Manders! And you think he'd stolen the other design?'

'I couldn't prove it, but it seemed likely.'

'So that's how Matthew got them. William, I sacked Manders myself, he was prying in my desk. But I swear I didn't know he'd worked for you when I took him on. Matthew told me he had worked at Horobin's.'

William looked hard at him, then smiled. 'I'll believe you.'

'Thanks. I wish I'd had the same faith in Josie. So you've no idea where she is?'

'Perhaps that young chap Endersby found her?'

'Who?'

'He was round here at Christmas, knew she'd driven with me, and wanted to find her.'

'But who is he?'

'Son of the hotel people, Endersby's in Edgbaston.'

'How does she know him?'

William shrugged. 'I really don't know. But he'll be back at school now, so that's not much help.'

'School?'

'Eton, I think, Leo. While you're here come and see my latest heated windscreen. I tried it out in December on the London to Gloucester run, and it was great. And I'm working on faster windscreen wipers too. I hope that'll be ready for the RAC rally to Hastings in March. Put together and I'll have cured one of the problems of winter motoring.'

William was outside Patrick Motors in John Bright Street, staring lost in thought at Aston Martin's new Le Mans model, when she hailed him.

'Surely you're not buying another car?' she asked cheerfully. 'Can't you resist the new three-letter number plates?'

He glanced up, then grinned at her. 'It gave me an idea. You look a lot better than when I last saw you,' he said noticing the smart grey coat edged with black fur, and the black wide-brimmed hat.

Josie grimaced at the recollection. 'New clothes make a difference,' she said quietly.

'It's lunch time. Will you have some with me?'

'Thanks, I'd love to.'

Later, when they were seated in a small, exclusive restaurant, she said with a sigh: 'It's ages since I had a meal in such comfort.'

'How is your mother?'

'She died,' Josie said briefly. 'It's over a month now. I'm staying with Aunt Phoebe and her fiancé — isn't it odd to think of one's elders as fiancés?'

'I'm sorry,' William said quietly. 'I know what a bad time you've had. Leo Bradley was asking where you lived. Is your aunt still in Aston?'

'No. Please, William, I don't want Leo to know where I am. Promise you won't tell him you've seen me?'

'I can't tell him where you live, I don't know,' William pointed out. 'Surely you're not afraid of him?'

'Not afraid, exactly. I just don't want to meet him for a while. I'm thinking of going into the jewellery business, and we could be in competition.'

William eyed her closely. After the way Leo had disbelieved her, he doubted this was the real reason. 'I don't think one more competitor will ruin him. But talking of competitions, can you come rallying again? With Lizzie away I'm often short of a passenger.'

Josie's eyes gleamed. 'I'd love to!'

'You might meet Leo,' he felt compelled to warn.

She hesitated, then tossed her head. 'What if I do? He won't know where I'm living, and I'm not going to hide away. When?'

'There's a short one this Sunday, to Buxton. A pity I've already got a co-driver for the thousand miles Hastings run, but how about the London to Edinburgh at the beginning of June? I'll have my new car then, an Invicta. It's like the one Donald Healey drove in the '31 and '32 Monte Carlo Rallies. It's big, four and a half litres, much bigger than I've had before, but a heavy car's better on snow and ice. Now your mother's — that is, could you get away?'

'Try and stop me!'

'I ay' got nowhere else!' Freddy complained.

'Go an' mek a fool o' yerself again, so's coppers nick yer, then yer'd 'ave a bed in Winson Green,' Mabel retorted, preparing to close the door.

'Give over! It were bad luck, that's all.'

'Yer can come in if yer's brung them sapphires,' she said, relenting. 'Yer ma's moved out an' it's safe ter try an' sell 'em now.'

'I don't carry jewels like that round wi' me,' Freddy said indignantly. 'But I know where they are. An' plenty more like 'em,' he added, thinking quickly.

Mabel opened the door a fraction wider. 'Yer not 'avin' me on?'

'Let me come in, we can't talk about it 'ere.'

It was a smaller house than the one they'd rented before, and Mabel only had the downstairs front room, but there was a double bed, and Freddy used all his arts to persuade her it would pay her to team up with him again.

'Unless yer's found another feller,' he suggested, pulling his trousers back on. 'By crikey, I missed yer, Mabel. That were real good.'

'Yer needs more practice,' she commented.

'Then gi' it me!'

'If yer can pay.'

He looked startled. 'What yer mean? Yer've never gone on the game?'

Mabel laughed. 'I mean if yer can keep me in the manner I used ter be accustomed to,' she explained. 'Now, them sapphires, where am they?'

'Safe enough,' he hedged, 'but it'll take a few days ter get 'em,' he added cautiously. He'd have to find a way into the house at Solihull.

'I'll give yer a week,' Mabel conceded.

'Come on, Mabel, the gold were my idea, weren't it? That kept us fer months.'

'An' I took all the risk! It were as much as I could do, goin' back ter Bradley's as if nowt 'ad 'appened. I could 'ardly wait ter get outta there, but I waited weeks so's they wouldn't suspect. Got meself a job at William Scott's motor factory now, machinin' leather, but I've bin there a year an' it's dead borin'.'

'Scott? Me sister knows 'im.'

Freddy fell into a reverie, but rack his brains as he might, no brilliant scheme for profiting from Mabel's new job occurred to him, and after a few days of Mabel's grumbling that she wasn't going to keep him much longer he was so despondent, and so short of cash, that he began thinking about approaching Matthew to see if he could do jobs for him again.

Josie was in the highest spirits William had ever known. She had been positively bubbling with excitement from the moment he picked her up, and when they reached the hill near Buxton where the climbing trials were to take place, she begged to try her luck.

'I've been your passenger so many times,' she urged. 'I know what to do, and it's not as though this trial's important to you, it wouldn't matter if I muffed it.'

'It would matter if you wrecked the car.'

'Spoilsport!' she accused. 'The car's insured, surely?'

'But I'm not, and I couldn't be patched together again so easily.'

She heaved a great sigh, and began to look round her at the other competitors. 'I wonder if there's anyone else?' she mused to herself. When this produced no response she laughed. 'Oh, William! Can we stay behind afterwards and I could have a go then?'

He agreed to this, rather reluctantly, but to his secret surprise Josie managed the first attempt remarkably well, only stalling at the trickiest bend where the competitors had churned up the icy mud into a dangerous, rough and slippery surface.

'Let me try again,' she demanded, and this time got to the top without incident. William had idly flicked on his stopwatch and he looked at the time disbelievingly. It was about average for that afternoon's results.

'Again?' he suggested, making sure that this time he started the watch without any chance of its being wrong. Josie bettered her time by over a second.

'How was I?' she demanded, her cheeks flushed with triumph, her green eyes sparkling.

'Good,' he told her. 'You're good enough to enter a novice event. We'll find one soon.'

'Like tomorrow?'

He insisted on driving back home, fearing that in her excitement she would make mistakes, and they stopped for dinner at a hotel on the outskirts of Birmingham.

'What's got into you today?' he asked when they'd ordered. 'I've never seen you take risks like that.'

'Did I take risks?' she asked contritely.

'Not stupid ones,' he reassured her. 'Driving in these events always carries a certain amount of risk, the cars are powerful and heavy and anyone who gets in the way or does something silly can be harmed. But to win we have to be prepared to take risks.'

'I used to do crazy things at school,' Josie admitted. 'Before Papa George died I was always getting into trouble for being unladylike, such as climbing out on to the school roof, and when I was really little I'd been to see a circus and I tried to walk the tightrope on the washing line in the garden. But after George died I had to be the sensible one, to look after my mother. I suppose that now she's — now I no longer have to worry about her, I can let my hair down again. William, I do miss her dreadfully, but at the same time I seem free suddenly, for the first time in my life, and I feel so guilty!'

'From what you've told me, and that hasn't been a tenth of

it, I'd guess, you're right to feel a sense of release. And your mother was so ill; she's at peace now. But if you have money for new clothes and to buy a business now, why didn't you before? Was it some silly sort of trust?'

Josie hesitated, then shrugged. Why should she protect Freddy? She told William about the sapphires, stressing that, although they suspected Freddy, she could prove nothing. 'If only we'd had the money for my mother,' she sighed, her lip trembling. 'It would have made such a difference to her last few months. Sometimes I think I could kill him for what he did to her.'

Freddy glanced back along the road but there was no one in sight. These wealthy suburbs were more like country lanes, he thought sourly, than roads where there were houses and people. The houses were mostly invisible behind high hedges and the inhabitants probably never walked further than their garages. They might even have chauffeurs to bring their cars to the front steps. He ground his teeth together at the thought of his own mother living in such style and refusing to lift a hand so that he could share in her sudden prosperity. He shivered. He wasn't frightened. He just didn't have a thick overcoat and it was freezing cold. He took a deep breath and congratulated himself on choosing a night when the clouds obscured the moon. Unfortunately, it had been raining steadily for several hours too. Mabel had been urging him to do something for days, but he had resisted her. He'd show her who was boss. He wouldn't be pushed around by any woman. He felt quite aggrieved, for wasn't it Mabel who'd persuaded him to dope the dog for her dad, causing him to fall into the hands of the police? She owed him for the time he'd spent in Winson Green.

With a final glance round he took another deep breath and slid silently through the gateway. The bushes rustled when he tried to find a way through them, and moisture dripped unpleasantly on to his neck. The gravel on the drive crunched under his feet, but fortunately there was a narrow strip of grass edging it and he could walk on that, balancing a little insecurely, for it was very narrow and slippery from the rain. All too soon he came to spacious lawns, and after circling the building from the precarious cover of the trees, looking in vain for a spot where the shrubs were close to the house and would cover his approach, he was forced to cross the open space.

That was nerve-racking, but he made it without raising any alarm. It was long after midnight and everyone must be asleep. At least no light showed. Striking matches with difficulty because of the rain, he worked his way round the house, hoping to find that someone had left a window open. But it was winter and all the windows were tightly shut. Freddy sighed, pulled out a penknife and began with the kitchen windows. It had seemed simple when some of the other prisoners had boasted of their exploits, but after a frustrating few minutes Freddy began to suspect they hadn't revealed everything about their tricks. He couldn't get the blade of the penknife through the cracks between the window and the frame, and when in a surge of fury he pressed harder the blade snapped off short. It was useless. The other blade wasn't much longer, but he didn't have anything else, and he couldn't bring himself to break the glass and risk rousing anyone.

He was swearing softly when he heard a faint noise immediately behind him, a cross between a wheeze and a snuffle. Freddy jumped and the ineffectual blade stabbed the fleshy part of his palm. Then he heard a voice, a deep masculine voice, some distance away but far too close for comfort. As Freddy looked over his shoulder the clouds parted and a shaft of moonlight lit up the garden. Simultaneously the unseen man called 'Rover! Here boy!' and Freddy spotted the most enormous dog he'd ever seen standing two yards away and eyeing him with hostile curiosity. At Freddy's start of alarm the dog barked, a deep, baying sound, and stepped forward. Freddy turned and fled.

'The brute would 'ave gobbled me up if I 'adn't got up that tree,' he complained to Mabel some hours later.

''E dain't leave much of yer jacket,' she commented. 'Yer'll 'ave ter get a new 'un, this is past mendin'.'

'Later,' Freddy pleaded. 'It were only when the feller called 'im away I was able ter run fer it. 'E dain't know I was there, must 'ave thought the dog was chasin' a rabbit.'

''E was,' Mabel snorted, but Freddy was too deep in his own woes to comprehend her scorn. He shuddered, recalling the desperate hours after he'd climbed down from the life-saving apple tree and struggled through a hedge which seemed to consist solely of thorns, only to find himself in a ploughed field. It had taken hours to make his way back to a civilized road, all the time wondering whether the dog was on his track. He was so muddy and dishevelled he hadn't dared try to find a bus back to the city centre and had been forced to walk, reaching home at dawn. There had to be an easier way of retrieving the sapphires.

'I've found the right business and there's living accommodation with it,' Josie announced.

Clem looked up from his newspaper and smiled across at her. 'Where?' he said calmly.

'In Albion Street. It's just one house that's been converted, but the third storey was kept as a flat: bedroom, living room, kitchen, even a bathroom!'

'Old man Bertram's place?'

'You knew about it?' Josie said accusingly. 'Why didn't you tell me?'

'There are others, but I think that's the best-equipped. You haven't done anything about it, have you?'

'Just been to see it. I don't know whether I can afford it until I know what you can get for the sapphires.'

'Oh, yes, you'll be able to get it, but Bertram's daughter is anxious to sell. If we don't look very eager she'll drop the price.'

269

Josie began to laugh. 'You're a cunning old devil,' she said affectionately.

Phoebe chuckled. 'Clem knows 'is onions. But I'm not so sure about your living there on your own, Josie. We'd hoped you might stay here with us.'

'It's very sweet of you, but I couldn't. It's too far away, I'd want to be close by all the time.'

'You could have a little car, no need to travel on buses or trams.'

'No, don't try to persuade me. You've both been so good to me but I want to prove I can do it on my own.'

Phoebe snorted. 'And what have you been doing since you were no more than sixteen?' she demanded. 'You've had far more to cope with than most people ever do, so that's a load of nonsense.'

'I'd love to come and see you often,' Josie placated her. 'And I want Clem's advice on all sorts of things, I'll be forever asking his help.'

'Right, no more argument! If that's the one you want we'll have to get a move on to get you set up before we sail for Australia.'

'So soon?' Josie gasped. 'That's only a few weeks, and I thought you said wait until she dropped the price?'

'It's the middle of March now. There's a month before the wedding. We'll change tactics,' Clem declared, grinning at her. 'Bustle, tell her what we'll offer on condition she accepts straight away. There's more than one way of persuading people, it depends what you want to achieve.'

'They ought to 'ave 'ad you directing the war instead of just making the guns,' Phoebe said.

'I've sometimes thought so meself,' Clem acknowledged, laughing. 'Josie, you and I will go into town tomorrow morning. My solicitor's already primed, and I know who'll pay the best price for the sapphires. I've got just the right man in mind for your foreman, and we'll get on to him and get an inventory, then order the rest of the things you'll want, and get all the formalities out of the way. You can be in full production before the wedding.'

'No.'

'What did yer say? No? What do you mean?'

Josie, suddenly pale, shook her head. 'I – I'm so very grateful to you, and I do appreciate your help with selling the jewels and negotiating a good price for me, but I have to do the rest myself.'

Clem looked astonished, and then hurt. Phoebe was staring at her, frowning. 'Don't yer want Clem's help?'

'Of course I do, but I want it to be my business, that I've started, and that I'm going to make successful. If Clem organizes it all it'll be his achievement, not mine. Don't you see?'

Clem nodded slowly. 'I think so. I've been a domineering, insensitive old fool. I got carried away,' he said mournfully.

'No you're not, you're a dear, and you've given me lots of ideas, inspired me, and I want you to go on doing that. I'll be immensely pleased if you'll help me until the building is mine. I haven't the slightest idea how to set about that side of it, but I practically ran Leo's office on my own. I do know the jewellery trade a little and I have ideas about what I want to do; I don't want to be rushed into starting things I may regret later on. I'll see the man you suggest, but he might not be the right man for me, he might not have the same ideas. Besides, I don't want to start full-scale production straight away, I need to take it slowly so that I'm familiar with what's happening. Please say you understand.'

'I think I do,' Clem said, and gave a rueful smile. 'My gal, if yer can manage everyone like you can manage me, you'll make a success on it! Don't let anyone boss you about, and you'll do.'

'I feel an utter fool, being bridesmaid to my own mother,' Lizzie complained.

Josie laughed. 'You've got Ann and me for company. At least Freddy's not giving her away.'

'Thank goodness! I've been terrified she'd forgive him like she always has, and he'd always be sponging off Clem.'

'Aunt Phoebe will forgive him if he hurts her, but never for hurting Josie and Aunt Dora,' Ann said quietly. 'Are you ready? We ought to go down.'

'It's odd, I thought the bridesmaids were supposed to help the bride get dressed, and calm her nerves,' Lizzie said as they filed out of the bedroom in Clem's house which he had declared was to be Lizzie's, and went down the wide, carpeted stairs. 'Ma's been up since dawn supervising the caterers, she's practically knocked in all the tent pegs for the marquee herself, and I swear she was polishing the glasses half an hour ago. When I went to offer to help her to dress she snapped my head off and said she'd be a lot quicker left on her own.'

'Nerves,' Josie said with a laugh.

'I keep forgetting it's the first time for her,' Lizzie giggled. 'But if getting married is always like this, I think I'll follow her first example!'

Ann shook her head. 'It'd be worth it for a man like Clem. He's a darling.'

'Did I hear my name?'

Ann blushed and laughed. 'Listeners never hear good of themselves,' she warned, and he twinkled up at her.

'Come on down, I have presents for the bridesmaids.'

The gifts were simple gold lockets, each inscribed with the girl's name.

'Oh, what a lovely idea!' Lizzie exclaimed, flinging her arms round Clem and kissing him.

Meanwhile, Ann had opened her locket and was staring at the two photographs inside. 'How on earth did you get these?' she whispered, staring at the photographs of her parents taken on their wedding day.

Josie was also staring at photographs of Dora and her father, and Lizzie, after a swift glance at her cousins, opened her own locket to find a much younger Phoebe and the handsome man who had been her lover smiling out at her.

'Well, Phoebe helped me, she had all the photographs, and I had someone copy them and make them the right size,' Clem was explaining, somewhat embarrassed.

'But I bet it was your idea,' Josie said, hugging him.

'Well, maybe. Now I'd better get along to the church. Don't let the bride be late.'

'No fear!' Lizzie said. 'We're not letting you get away from her, and if she chickens out I'll be along to marry you myself.'

Chapter Seventeen

'WHAT was yer doin' out in Soli'ull?' Mabel demanded.

Freddy sighed. He'd been reluctant to tell Mabel where he'd been but she was persistent and he'd let slip some information. 'Give over,' he muttered.

'What are the sapphires doin' out in Soli'ull?' she went on, disregarding his pleas.

'Me ma found 'em,' he confessed at last. 'When she sold the dog's kennel. I'd 'idden 'em under it; the coppers never thought ter look there. But it's O K, 'er's still got 'em, an' what's more,' he went on quickly, forestalling her disgusted protest, 'Ma's livin' in a great big mansion out in Solihull. The feller wot owns it, 'e's marryin' 'er. I 'ad a look through the winder an' the stuff 'e's got's worth thousands. She must 'ave the sapphires there too.'

Mabel stared at him. 'An' yer tried ter break in? Is that it? Yer bloody fool!'

'No I'm not! The sapphires must be there, an' all I've gorra do is get inside. I'll manage it some'ow. They owes me,' he justified himself.

'I thought they were yer aunt's? Won't yer ma 'ave given 'em back? Besides –'

'Me aunt died, an' me cousin's livin' in Solihull too,' Freddy broke in. 'They've gorra be there.'

Mabel gave an exasperated sigh. 'So what? 'Oo'll they blame when the blasted jewels goes missin' again? Yer wouldn't be able ter sell 'em fer years this time, even if yer got 'em, which I doubt!'

Freddy gulped. 'I dain't think of that.'

'Yer never thinks, that's yer trouble.'

'Mabel, it'll be OK. I went ter see Matthew. 'E give me some more money, an' 'e wants ter meet yer.'

'What for?'

''E said 'e'd explain then. 'E's gorra job fer yer, I think.'

'They're lovely, Ken,' Josie enthused.

'Up to standard?' the big, grey-haired man asked, smiling broadly.

Josie nodded and slipped the silver bracelets on her arm, admiring the sheen as the interlinked chains sparkled in the light above her desk. 'Let's increase production. I think it's time we started to sell what we've made. It seems a long time since we started.'

'Only two weeks since the wedding, Miss Shaw.'

It had been a frantic time. She'd acquired the factory premises only a few days before her aunt's wedding, and there had been no time then to do anything except set Ken, whom she'd employed as her foreman, to tidying up the workshop. Then, after the wedding, with the help of Ann and Lizzie, she'd moved into the rooms above and installed the minimum of essential furniture. Her cousins protested at the bareness of it, but Josie insisted she couldn't spare the time for shopping and would buy more things later on.

'I just need a desk so that I can work there in the evenings,' she said. 'I don't fancy being in the office downstairs when everyone else has gone home.'

'Aren't you scared, living on your own?' Ann asked.

Josie shook her head. 'I can lock and bolt the door, and no one can get in except through the factory. Ken made that secure.'

'He seems good,' Lizzie said. 'How did you find him?'

'Clem did. He knew Ken somehow, and that his former employer was closing down. I was able to offer him this job before anyone else could snaffle him. I've been amazingly lucky, he knows the trade inside out.'

He'd found skilled craftsmen for her, too. To attract them Josie had offered wages slightly higher than most jewellers did, and the ploy succeeded. Already half a dozen men and girls were installed in the factory.

'Do you know a good salesman?' Josie asked.

Ken nodded. 'It seems presumptuous, miss, but I'd like you to see my son. He was working for Horobin's, but now the old man's dead the son's sold out and bought a smaller factory making clocks and so on. But I don't want you to take him on if you don't think he'll suit,' he added hastily.

'Send him to me,' Josie said firmly. 'I don't see why a good workman should be disadvantaged just because he's related to you, when so many people get jobs because of their good fortune to be born the boss's son!'

Ken chuckled. 'I've known some disasters,' he said. 'Now we'll need at least one more engraver and a couple of polishers, to start with. That will just about fill the front part of the factory. Have you thought about what else we'll produce?'

'I want to stick to silver-plated stuff first, get known for that before branching out into gold or enamels. We haven't got many designs for jewellery yet, and I haven't seen any others I like, but I've been thinking about anniversaries and special occasions. Where are those designs for eggcups and stands, and napkin rings and goblets? We could perhaps start a line suitable for christening or wedding presents, with individual names or dates engraved on them to order.'

'And as well as single items, we might look at making sets and having them in boxes for the Christmas trade. My Donald says that's a good line.'

'Then send Donald to see me as soon as possible. Could he

make tomorrow morning? It sounds as though the sooner he's working with us the better.'

Leo, on his way to the Jones and Palmer printing works in Albion Street, glanced idly up at the newly painted sign and blinked. The Shaw Studio, he read. He'd been wondering who'd bought the Bertram factory. What a coincidence that it was someone called Shaw. Surely there was no connection? There couldn't be. It wasn't a particularly unusual name, it was simply that he couldn't stop thinking about Josie.

'Who's your new neighbour?' he asked casually after selecting designs for the new catalogue.

'A young lass,' he was told. 'We're doing a lot of work for her now. She's no more than a youngster, but knows just what she wants, and determined to get it just so!'

It had to be Josie, but how in the world did she have the money to set up in business? It was clearly well financed, but when he'd last heard, she was living in poverty. Was it the wealthy man her aunt had married who was backing her? His lip curled. How had she got round him, and where was her vaunted independence now? Unable to concentrate on his own concerns, he decided on impulse to lunch at the Jewellers' Club in St Paul's Square, and a few discreet questions brought forth a tide of information.

'Rumour has it that the set of sapphires old Clement Stokes sold belonged to her and the money bought the factory,' he was told. 'Stokes was certainly involved in the purchase, and he's just married the gal's aunt.'

Leo excused himself as soon as he could. His brain was seething. The jewels must be the ones his father had given to Dora. They were comparable to any of his own mother's jewels, and even as a boy he'd been furiously resentful on his mother's behalf that George was lavishing such gifts on the avaricious Dora. Josie had lied when she told him the sapphires had been stolen. She'd been living in poverty, and both she and her mother had been in considerable want, and yet she had these jewels worth a small fortune. It didn't make sense. He tried to think of excuses but it was impossible. If such a valuable set of jewels had been stolen and then recovered he must have heard of it. Such gossip flew round the district. But why had Josie not sold them to ease her own and her mother's plight? Had she deliberately kept them so that she might start her own business after Dora died? That didn't fit with what he'd seen and heard about the dreadful conditions Josie had endured, or the fact that she'd been prepared to work in bars to earn her keep. Or had Dora stubbornly refused to sell them? Yet when she'd been so ill, surely Josie could have sold them? Dora would hardly have been able to stop her. Josie was obviously not the honest, straightforward girl he'd thought. He was wasting his time thinking so much about her. She really wasn't worth it.

Josie returned from the London to Edinburgh Rally excited by the thrills of this new, longer type of event. 'It's so different,' she enthused to Lizzie the following weekend when Lizzie came to tea. 'It's much more tiring, driving so far almost without a break, but I really enjoyed the navigating over quite strange country as well as the driving. And in such a powerful car it's somehow so much easier, despite the weight. The weather was glorious, the night so short it didn't seem at all odd to be going somewhere totally new in the dark!'

Lizzie grinned. 'I can see you won't be happy with just one trip.'

Josie laughed. 'No, and William's already asked me to go on the Eastbourne Concours d'élégance next week! That's what he's really interested in, showing his new gadgets, but the rest is fun too.'

'And the London to Edinburgh – did you finish?' asked Lizzie.

'Oh yes, practically everyone did, well over a hundred and

fifty cars, and most of us got premier awards. There was a bit of mist after we'd had breakfast at Harrogate at some unearthly hour, and some horses straying on to the road, but they said a lot of the hills were much easier than in previous years. I met so many famous people, Lizzie, people who win important rallies like Donald Healey.'

'So when are you going to buy your own rally car?'

Josie grinned at her. 'I know, you think I'm going mad with new enthusiasms like at school. I can't afford any sort of car until my business begins to make a profit, then we'll see. You'd have to come with me, an all-lady team.'

'That's the first time you've ever called yourself a lady,' Lizzie teased, and Josie laughed.

'I'm not a child now, I'm a sober, respectable businesswoman. You can't imagine how difficult it is sometimes not to laugh at some of the men I have to deal with. They hate it, they really do, having to talk to a woman, and a girl, at that! But Ken's a tremendous help, and I've hired his son as my salesman. He's keen, and he's good. I know in my bones I'm going to make a success of this business,' she said. 'And I'm going to be a top rally driver, too,' she added, ignoring Lizzie's sceptically raised eyebrows.

'Josie! Where have you been all this time?'

Josie turned swiftly and saw Tobias striding towards her. He grasped her by the shoulders and looked carefully into her face. 'Tobias! Oh, it's been so long! How are you? Are you still with – with Leo?'

'Have you time for lunch? I was just going for mine.'

An hour later they were still sitting over their meal. Tobias had understood far more than Josie had said about the time she had struggled to care for her mother, but apart from wishing she had come to him for help, said little. Now he listened as Josie was explaining her future plans. 'I need some imaginative designs like yours,' she sighed. 'When I can afford to expand I want to do more jewellery, but so far I haven't found the sort of things I like.'

Tobias was silent for a while, absently stirring his coffee. Then he looked up, took a deep breath, and spoke. 'Will you take me on?'

'Take you on? What do you mean, Tobias?'

'Employ me. Or even let me come into partnership with you. We worked together well before, didn't we?'

'You'd leave Leo?'

'I left him some time ago and have been working alone, designing. But it's frustrating and a waste of time trying to get firms to produce them. I was thinking of setting up on my own, I just didn't want the fuss. If you need money to expand into my sort of jewellery let me provide it.'

'I couldn't do that!'

'Of course you could. In case you don't remember, I'm quite a rich man, Josie. I could trust you to get on with organizing the business, leaving me to do the designs.'

Josie laughed. 'I didn't want to be a partner, I wanted to do it all myself, but I can't design the sort of pieces I want to make. Tobias, do you really think it would work?'

'I wouldn't want control, or at least perhaps I'd want some control over design, but not the rest. I'd be happy for you to keep the majority share and make all the other decisions. And I wouldn't mind taking over occasionally if you have to be away,' he added.

'How soon can you start?'

'I'm terrified!' Josie admitted.

'Rubbish, you've nothing to be scared about, and I shall be in the passenger seat,' William said encouragingly.

'But it's so different doing it in front of a crowd like this. I'm quite confident on the ordinary driving –'

'And you're up with the leaders, no points lost,' William reminded her.

'— but I know I'll stall or skid or do something dreadful on the hill climb,' Josie finished.

'Well, it would be nice to win your first novice trial, but it wouldn't be a disaster if you did stall or skid or turn the car upside down with both of us inside it.'

Josie chuckled. 'I don't think I'll do that. But it's your car and I might wreck it.'

'You won't, and anyway I'm getting a new one soon.'

'Another new car? What sort? And why do you want a new one?' Josie demanded, distracted from her own worries.

'A Triumph. I can't afford a Rolls-Royce yet! I want it for next January's Monte Carlo Rally. I've decided I really do mean to enter in 1934.'

Josie was so busy asking questions she forgot her nervousness, and wasn't even properly aware of the other competitors roaring up the twisting track, the dry, rutted surface made slippery with loose stones littering it. When it was her turn she gave William a petrified look but started the car and drove smoothly forward to the start.

Seconds before the sign to go was given she happened to glance up towards the first bend, a right-hand hairpin where the adverse camber made it difficult to control the car. The banks beside the route were lined with spectators, but Josie saw only one face. What on earth was Leo doing here? She had no time for speculation. The signal was given and she needed all her concentration to coax the greatest possible speed out of the car while navigating the course. At the back of her mind lurked a thought that she would show Leo, but quite what she had to prove she couldn't say. She reached the first bend, where several of her fellow competitors had come to grief, and hung on grimly, fighting to get the car to obey her. There was a momentary sensation of slipping tyres, but somehow Josie controlled it and then she was going flat out up the short, straight section. She hung on round the curve, to the left this time, and was into the second and final bend, a less-sharp hairpin with a better camber which she could afford to take fast. She hardly saw the finishing flag, but braked when they were at the top, out in a wide open space with the cars of the earlier competitors neatly parked at the far side.

'You were marvellous!' William exclaimed. 'That's got to be the best time! You must have beaten all the earlier ones, and I doubt if anyone will better it.'

Dazed, Josie scrambled out of the car and let him lead her over to where the results would be announced. She watched the last few cars, and listened when William excitedly confirmed that they were much slower than she'd been. She was looking for Leo, but he was nowhere to be found. William shook her arm slightly when the judge climbed up to the makeshift platform to read out the results. Josie had won her class, but as the other drivers, many of whom she knew, crowded round to congratulate her, she seemed to be in a dream.

'Did I really win?' she asked William as they walked back to the car to drive home.

He laughed, put his arm round her and hugged her, and when she looked at him in a puzzled way, dropped a light kiss on her lips. 'The first of many times, I hope.'

'Miss Preece! I hoped to find you here.'

Ann turned to him and smiled. Dick Endersby had grown another inch and was already taller than his father. 'Good morning, Mr Dick. Do you want Mrs Endersby? She's in the restaurant, I think.'

He shook his head. 'No. I hoped you could give me your cousin's address. Miss Shaw, that is. I haven't been at home much, and it's over a year since I saw her. Your aunt seems to have moved and no one knows where she is.'

'Aunt Phoebe married and sold her house. She's on a visit to Australia. Josie's mother died just after Christmas. She'd been very ill and Josie was looking after her, that's probably why you haven't seen her about,' Ann explained diplomatically. Josie would hate somone like Dick to know what kind of a slum she'd been living in.

'Then where is she now?'

'She's started her own business,' Ann explained, and laughed when Dick looked astonished. 'Why not? I don't think your mother was much older when she started hers.'

'Er, no, of course not. I was surprised. What sort of business? Is it here in Birmingham?'

'In Hockley, in Albion Street. You'll find it easily, and she lives in rooms at the top, there's a bell and a speaking tube by the main door.'

'Thanks. I'll go tonight. I'm back at my grandfather's soon, I haven't much time. Thanks again.'

'These are marvellous, Tobias,' Josie said. 'They're full of strength and movement and yet so light. How many can we produce? Will we be ready for the Christmas trade?'

Tobias nodded. 'It's only the start of August; we can set up the machines and get samples out in a couple of weeks, and Donald can take them round and get orders. We'll see which are the most popular and concentrate on them.'

'Do we need more polishers? I thought they were looking a bit weary yesterday.'

'It's mainly the heat. It's been the longest drought I can remember. And they're working hard for this new bonus system. But get Ken to put a notice in the window downstairs. We'll need someone else by next week, perhaps two more. We can't afford accidents through tiredness.'

Josie shivered. She still did whenever she recalled the broken drive belt at Leo's, and not because it had led indirectly to her own dismissal. 'Those new safety guards will work, won't they, if a belt goes?' she asked.

'Ken swears by them. He's seen a belt snap without warning, the guard deflected it and no damage was done. He's talking about ways of guarding the other machinery.'

When the bell rang that evening, soon after Josie had locked up and gone up to her flat, she assumed it was someone who had seen the notice for the jobs and perhaps knew she lived on the premises. She suppressed the pang of annoyance and recalled how desperate she had once been for work, and how any chance had to be seized. Now she wasn't half-starved, and her supper could wait a while. 'Who is it?' she asked through the speaking tube.

'Josie? It's Dick, Dick Endersby. Can you come down? I wanted to ask you if you'd come out with me.'

'Dick! I'll come straight down and let you in. How lovely to see you again!'

He'd changed in the sixteen or so months since they'd met. He was older, taller, and very good looking. Josie suppressed a smile. With parents like Richard and Marigold Endersby he'd have been very unfortunate not to have inherited their handsome looks.

'Can you come out for a meal?' he asked anxiously. 'I know it's very short notice but I have only just over a week in Birmingham.'

Josie shook her head. 'I've a better idea. I was just going to eat, and there's a pie in the oven of my new gas cooker. It's plenty big enough for both of us, so come and share it with me.'

He looked delighted. 'Really? I'd like that. I'll go and get a bottle of wine. I don't suppose I can find champagne, but surely there'll be something.'

Josie shook her head. 'No, I have some wine, and I don't want to have to come down all these stairs again!'

'If you're sure. Then you must let me take you out tomorrow. Oh, Josie, I'm so pleased I've found you again.'

It was midnight before Dick left. They had so much to tell one another, though Josie said very little about Dora's illness and Dick, seeing her eyes cloud over at the mention of her mother, swiftly began to talk about something else. She explained about the factory and showed him over it, and he compared it with his grandfather's pottery where he'd been working for the past few school holidays.

'I have to go there again for several weeks, and then I'm going to Oxford,' he said as they went back upstairs to the flat. 'You will let me take you out tomorrow?'

'I'd love it,' Josie said. He was so easy to talk to, a friend her own age, unlike all the older men like Tobias and William who had so much more experience than she did. 'Are you looking forward to Oxford?'

'I'm looking forward to meeting those utter idiots who said they wouldn't fight for their country,' he said fiercely. 'And beating some sense into them.'

'You sound so belligerent! What do you mean?'

'The Union debate, last February. Surely you heard about the fuss it caused?'

'No, I was too busy to think about anything else,' Josie told him.

'Well, now Hitler's banned all opposition parties, and they've actually admitted they have concentration camps and are sending all Jews to them, I don't see how anyone can refuse to stand up to him. They said when the Reichstag building burned down it was the end of democracy.'

'But war is so awful, Dick. Surely you aren't condoning another one?'

He looked embarrassed. 'My parents suffered terribly in the last war, Josie. They were separated for years and each thought the other was probably dead. Of course I don't want another war, but I'd certainly fight for my country and for what I believe is right. It's not just a question of patriotism. Some of the things the Nazis are doing on the continent are pure evil. Somebody has to stop them.'

Chapter Eighteen

'HAVE we done everything?' Lizzie fretted. She looked round the dining room where the table gleamed with starched white napery, highly polished silver and crystal. The perfume of late roses spilling out of a huge rosebowl overlaid the resinous scent of the log fire burning in the fireplace.

'Yes, stop worrying!' Ann chided, laughing. 'It's going to be a perfect homecoming for them.'

'I hope Josie gets here before they do.'

'She's coming on the train. And she told me she'd bought a new dress. She'll be here to change.'

Lizzie bit her lip, then grinned. 'Sorry! Am I being a pain? It's just – well, I haven't seen Ma for six months, and it isn't often I welcome her home either from a trip to Australia or a honeymoon, let alone both.'

'That will be Josie now, I expect,' Ann said, and they both went to look out of the window to watch a taxi-cab approach the front door.

Josie, in a very elegant, pale grey costume with narrow skirt and belted jacket, carrying a darker grey fur-trimmed coat, was descending from the taxi. The driver was busy with a rather large suitcase, and smiled broadly at her, tipping his hat as she paid him.

'Am I in time?' Josie asked as Lizzie opened the door for her.

'Gosh, I'm glad to get rid of this hat! Wide brims are a mistake, believe me, when you're on trains and in cars, especially when I've so much else to carry!'

'It's a marvellous green, though,' Ann said as she picked up the hat from where Josie had slung it on the hall table. 'The emerald colour goes so well with your hair!'

'So do grey and black, and they're more practical. I could hardly wear this colour in the factory.' She delved into her bag. 'I've got everything, but I'll unpack later. What a job I had finding them. Meanwhile, these are for you both, and I thought Aunt Phoebe might like this, it's a new design and this is the first one we've made.'

Ann and Lizzie barely had time to exclaim over the intricately twisted necklet chains Josie thrust upon them before they had to look at the silver powder compact she was holding out. 'It's a koala bear, isn't it?' Lizzie demanded, entranced. 'It's super, Josie!'

'Yes, we've found a marvellous engraver, and he and Tobias are full of ideas for pictures to draw on compacts and cigarette cases. I had him do the same picture on a case for Clem. Where is it? Oh yes, I put it in my pocket, these bags are too small for carrying much.'

An hour later the three girls, in long dresses of silk and chiffon, with flowing lines, pleats and the occasional row of ruffles, were sitting in the drawing room. 'I feel overdressed,' Ann confessed. 'It's usually the guests I see wearing these sort of clothes. They don't feel right on me.'

'It looks perfect,' Lizzie reassured her. 'And that silver necklet goes so marvellously with the powder blue. It might have been specially made for it.'

'And Aunt Phoebe and Clem will have dressed for dinner every night on the boat, we have to keep up the tradition!' Josie said, grinning at her. Then she became serious. 'It's rather different from this time last year, isn't it?' she said soberly. 'But I didn't mean to make us all feel miserable. Is that a taxi? Yes, I'm sure it is. Come on, girls, have you got everything?'

Giggling, they stood up. When Phoebe and Clem walked into the room they were met by a trio of musicians barely able to perform for laughing. Lizzie was blowing into a small trumpet, and had cymbals strapped round her knees which she was trying to bang together in time to the drum Josie was beating with one hand while swinging a rattle in the other. Anne was the only one attempting a tune on a mouth organ, while vigorously shaking a tambourine. With a final flourish the girls ended their brief concert and Ann stooped to grab a banner which, unfurled, read *Welcome Home!* Then they went forward to kiss Phoebe and Clem.

'You crazy lot!' Phoebe said, wiping tears of laughter from her eyes. 'Josie, love, I bet this was your idea. Just the daft sort of thing you used ter do at school.'

Josie grinned at her. 'I'm a sober businesswoman now, but I need to let my hair down at times. Look, go and have a wash and brush-up, dinner will be ready in half an hour.'

It was long after midnight before they went to bed, the travellers had so much both to tell and to ask.

'Thank goodness it's Sunday tomorrow,' Josie yawned as she and Lizzie went upstairs together. 'I don't think I'll get up until lunch time!'

'A fashion show's what we need,' Josie said slowly. 'I wonder if we could team up with one of the clothing shops, a good one, expensive, and have mannequins showing our new jewellery as well as their clothes?'

Tobias nodded thoughtfully. 'At the Grand hotel, in the Grosvenor Room,' he said. 'And as well as jewellery we must exhibit the other things we make, for gifts. There's a boom in housebuildiing , and people will want table ornaments.'

'Don't get carried away!' Josie said hastily. 'That's where they hold the Jewellers' Banquet every year. I can't compete with that. Why, they have prime ministers to speak! Besides, we could never afford it, it's a huge room.'

'Before Christmas, the beginning of December,' Tobias said, grinning at her. 'All those wealthy men who can't think what to buy their pampered wives. And jewellers who are madly curious to know what we're doing. We could ask the shopkeepers, who will want to stock our pieces to be in fashion, and your motoring friends must surely have girlfriends and money to spend on them. William can tell them, and Clem will bring all his cronies. We can't fail.'

'But they'd expect a feast,' Josie objected.

'We'll provide one. And we'll charge, that'll make them come.'

'They'll only come if it's free.'

'Not so. We'll be mysterious, have it talked about as one of the main events of the year, no one will want to miss it. You'll see. We'll recover our costs a hundredfold.'

'I still can't afford to take the risk.'

'We can afford it. I'm a partner, remember. I'll finance it and if we do by any misfortune make a loss I won't ask you to repay me. Are you on?'

They argued briefly but amicably, and Josie found she was becoming more and more eager for such an event. 'We won't be able to book the room at such short notice,' she said, having accepted the main idea.

'If we can't there are others. I'll go round to the Grand straight away, and leave you to find a suitable shop to supply the clothes.'

'But what about the girls to model them?'

Tobias shrugged his shoulders. 'The shops will know girls they can use, and if all else fails you and your cousins can do it!'

'Leo Bradley, isn't it?'

Leo smiled at the older man. 'Yes, but I'm afraid I don't know your name.'

'Someone pointed you out to me. You're a jeweller, I believe?

It's likely, here in St Paul's Club. I'm Clement Stokes. I believe we're distant connections by marriage.'

Leo stiffened. Now he knew who the man was. Mr Stokes was determined to explain, however.

'My wife's sister was married to your father,' he said firmly. 'I knew your uncle a little, though we were in different businesses. Good man, your uncle. Left a neat little business. But that wasn't what I wanted to say. I want you to buy a couple of tickets for a jewellery fashion show my wife's niece is putting on at the Grand in a couple of weeks. Josie Shaw. You must know her, being her stepbrother, but she says she doesn't see you now, and couldn't sell you the tickets herself. Got a brilliant new designer, from the work I've seen, and they're showing their first collection. Well, will you come?'

Leo had been trying to break in but Clem ignored all his interruptions. Now, as Clem waited, his head on one side, Leo was able to speak. 'Of course I know Josie Shaw,' he said grimly. 'Did you finance her factory?'

Clem smiled. 'She wouldn't let me, though I offered,' he admitted. 'There aren't many young girls that would have turned down my offer, but she's independent, is Josie.'

'Then how –?' Leo began before he recollected himself. 'I'm sorry, it's none of my business.'

'How could she afford to buy a factory when she and her mother had been living in that dreadful slum, barricaded to keep out the men who wanted to pull the house down, so that her poor mother could die in peace?'

'I didn't know that.'

'It happened. Phoebe will never forgive herself for quarrelling with Doris, but she couldn't believe Freddy was wicked enough to take the jewels until she found them.'

'Jewels? You mean the sapphires my father gave Dora?'

Clem nodded. 'And very generous he was too. A magnificent set, beautifully mounted.'

'What happened to them?' Leo demanded, by now indifferent to all notions of whether this concerned him.

'Phoebe's boy, a bad lot if ever there was one, stole 'em from Doris. Josie and her ma blamed him, but Phoebe couldn't believe it and threw them out of her house. That's why they were in that hovel. Then Doris got ill and Josie had to give up work to look after her. Lived on less than a pittance at times, I don't know how the poor girl coped. She was even chopping up furniture to feed the fires, she'd sold everything else. When it was too late to help Doris the sapphires turned up, under Freddy's dog's kennel where he'd hidden them. Josie didn't want to keep them, not surprisingly, so I sold them for her and she bought the factory.'

'I see,' Leo said slowly. How he'd misjudged Josie! When he'd thought she was working in a reasonably paid job it seemed she had been striving to exist on nothing. And if he had accused her unfairly, that was his fault. He groaned and Clem looked closely at him.

'Are you ill, lad?'

Leo shook his head. 'This fashion show. I'll have two tickets. No, make it six, I'll bring a party.'

'Do you fancy some winter driving?' William asked.

'Isn't it cold enough now?' Josie laughed at him.

'It isn't snow and ice. I want to get extra practice in really bad conditions before the Monte Carlo in January,' William explained. 'Several crews are going. It will be fun. We'll drive up to John o' Groats non-stop. The problem is neither of my Monte co-drivers can fit it in, and I have to go this week.'

'I'm terribly busy, with the fashion show to organize,' Josie said, but her voice was wistful.

'That's all done, apart from selling tickets. Tobias can manage without you. Just for a couple of days. And it would do you good to get away, you've been working so hard since you set up the business.'

'We haven't solved all the problems, we still need another girl to show the jewellery, but I can't find anyone who's pretty enough. I'm determined our best pieces will be shown by someone really beautiful.'

'Aren't you afraid the audience would be looking at her instead of the jewellery?'

Josie shook her head vehemently. 'No. Jewels and clothes look ordinary on a woman who isn't pretty, but they look magnificent on a beautiful model,' she explained.

'Ask Tobias to take over, and come and slide about in snow and ice over terrible roads, and probably get stuck in snowdrifts,' William tempted.

Josie suddenly capitulated. 'When do we start?'

'Rather you than me!' Lizzie said as she went with Josie to select a warm fur coat for her trip north. 'I like the sun, though I confess I'm a bit worried about driving in France, on the wrong side of the road.'

'You'll manage perfectly well,' Josie said cheeringly. 'This one's got a nice big collar. And I'm going to buy some trousers. However efficient William's' heating system, I refuse to have cold legs just because I'm a woman and they expect me to wear skirts!'

Lizzie giggled. 'Marlene Dietrich wore a man's suit. If she can, why not us? I'm getting some beach trousers. Just fancy, me in the South of France for the rest of the winter! I never imagined even going abroad when I worked as a polisher.'

'Does Mrs Thackeray-Walsh often go to Nice?'

'I don't think she's been before, but she had some bad colds last winter and the doctor suggested it. I'm so lucky she's decided to take me too! I'll be driving her and her friend round, but she's promised me lots of free time.'

'You may be able to go to Monte Carlo to see William when he gets there. How far is it from Nice?'

'I'm not sure, I haven't looked at that map yet. Not very far, I think. I've been concentrating on the north. Luckily she doesn't want to go through Paris, that would really terrify me. Look, here's a nice fur hat which would come down right over your ears. And you're staying at the hotel, so you'd better buy an evening dress too.'

'I have one,' Josie protested.

'Get another. You can afford it now.'

Josie permitted herself to be persuaded. Lizzie made straight for a deep golden yellow gown, which Josie was doubtful about, but which, when she tried it on, suited her so well she didn't bother to look at any others.

'Good, you're settled. And take some of your new jewellery too. I'm so sorry I'll be missing your show,' Lizzie said, as they took a taxi back to Hockley with all their parcels. 'Have you found that last girl yet?'

Josie sighed. 'No, and it's getting so near I'm really worried. None of the shops know anyone who'd be suitable, and neither do I.'

'Yes you do.'

'What do you mean? Who?'

'Someone beautiful, delicate, graceful, with a long slender neck that will show off your necklaces. Use Ann.'

'Ann?'

Lizzie smiled at Josie's astonishment. 'Why not? She's one of the loveliest girls I know, especially the last year or so. We never notice what's under our noses, do we? But when she was in evening dress at Ma's I thought she could have been a princess.'

Josie was concentrating hard. 'Darling Lizzie, you're right. She would be perfect. In fact I think I've been imagining her ever since I began to have this obsession with getting someone special. Could she do it? She'd have to walk up and down in front of hundreds of people. Ann's very shy. She's never been out with a man, which is incredible when you think how lovely she is.'

'She's so beautiful she probably scares most men off,' Lizzie said. 'It would have to be a very confident man who'd ask her out.'

'I suppose so. Do you think she'd do it?'

'You can persuade her. She'll want to help. Let that be my contribution to your show, since I can't come to it.'

'Thanks, Lizzie. Now I can go off to Scotland with a clear mind.'

'I'm shattered!' Josie exclaimed. 'I don't know how I kept awake the last few miles.'

'We're here now. A good hot bath and you'll be like new,' William encouraged her. 'You were great, Josie, and your navigation is impeccable, considering how little time you had to prepare.'

'Perhaps that was as well; I didn't have time to get scared of those mountains and the gradients. As for a hot bath, I shall fall asleep in it.'

'I'll come and drag you out if you're not down in time for dinner!'

The soak revived her and Josie, wearing the new golden yellow evening dress, went down to the cocktail bar where she had arranged to meet William. He wasn't there, but across the room there was a noisy party of a dozen men and girls, and as Josie sat down to wait scraps of their excited conversation wafted across to her. As it concerned crank shafts and the merits of ice-chains against special tyres she knew they must be the crews of the other cars William had said were making the same trip, who had started out before them and presumably arrived earlier.

Then the door opened and Josie turned towards it with a smile, expecting William. The smile froze, and Leo, entering hurriedly, halted abruptly. Then he took a deep breath and crossed towards her. 'All alone?' he asked.

'I'm waiting for William. I drove up with him,' Josie explained.

'Come and join us. What will you have to drink?'

Josie tried to refuse, shaking her head, but Leo seized her hand and pulled her to her feet. 'Don't be silly! We're all having dinner together. You can't escape. Besides, it's ages since I saw you to talk to. Just a few glimpses at rallies.'

Within seconds Josie found herself part of the group, sitting on a settee beside Leo with a White Lady cocktail thrust into her hands, being bombarded with eager questions about her journey and excited comments about their own.

She was aware of one silent girl, who soon made an excuse to change her seat and perch on the arm of the settee next to Leo. As Josie glanced at her the girl, a ravishingly pretty blonde, bent down to whisper in Leo's ear. Then she giggled, and as Leo smiled up at her blew him a kiss and began to stroke his hair back from where an unruly lock had fallen across his forehead.

'Stop messing with my hair, woman,' Leo commanded, laughing.

'Darling, but it's so untamed.'

'Like Leo,' one of the men warned. 'You'd better not annoy the lion, Snooks.'

'Rubbish. I'm as harmless as a kitten,' Leo protested. 'Snooks knows that quite well.'

The blonde smiled, a secretive little simper, Josie thought, as Snooks glanced at her. 'I must buy you some hair oil,' she said, 'I know one which doesn't stain the pillow slips,' she added with a chuckle and then shrieked as Leo snatched her hand and dragged her down across his lap.

'For that you deserve six of the best,' Leo threatened, and amidst general hilarity and wild struggles from Snooks which precipitated both her and Leo on to the floor, tried to administer the punishment.

To Josie's relief William appeared at that moment, and the talk turned to technical details about the driving conditions. Dinner was served at a big table in one corner of the dining room. Josie sat beside William and was thankful that Leo and

Snooks were at the far end of the table, and she wouldn't have to speak to either of them. The food was delicious. William was in a reminiscent mood and described motoring events he'd taken part in. 'My grandfather had one of the very early Daimlers, before the war, and I used to ride in it with him. I've had a passion for motors ever since.'

'Where did you live? You're not from Birmingham, are you?' Josie asked. William had never spoken of his family.

'In Somerset, not far from Bristol. My parents were drowned in a boating accident when I was two, I can't remember them. My grandparents brought me up but they died when I was at Cambridge. When I was twenty-one I inherited some money from them and came to Birmingham.'

'You've no other family?' Josie asked. 'I never knew my real father, nor met his parents, or knew anything about his family. My mother lost touch with them and would never tell me anything. I've often wondered what he was like.'

'Have you never tried to trace his family?'

'No. Could I?'

'Do you know where they came from?'

'Warwick. My grandfather was a solicitor.'

'Then they'd be quite easy to trace, and even if they are dead they may have had other children. You could have lots of relatives.'

Josie frowned, then shook her head. 'Perhaps, one day. But I'd be so afraid they'd be a disappointment. Or I'd be one to them.'

William gave a faint smile. 'I doubt that. But you have your cousins. I've a distant cousin or two, on my mother's side, but I haven't met them since I was a child. I've grown accustomed to being alone. How are you finding living in that flat above the factory?'

'I'm not there much except to sleep, and usually there's work to be done so I don't notice being alone.'

The others, apparently tireless, planned to dance to a gramophone in the empty ballroom.

'I'm far too tired,' Josie claimed hastily and William nodded.

'Me too. Shall we have coffee in the lounge?' When they were settled on a sofa facing the roaring log fire and Josie had poured he spoke again. 'I'm beginning to think it's not good to be alone too much.'

'Do you miss having a family? Would you like children of your own?'

'I used to think I was a romantic, that one day I'd see the girl of my dreams. But I've watched people who fall in love, and after a while they don't seem so happy. The old system of arranged marriages had a lot to commend it. People had no choice, they made it work. They didn't expect undying devotion, but they developed a working partnership, friendship. That's probably more important in the end.'

'I don't know. I've never been in love,' Josie said. Leo didn't count. She didn't know if it was love she felt for him. 'It's true it didn't serve Lizzie very well.'

'Precisely. So why don't we get married?' Josie looked at him, astonished, and he laughed self-consciously. 'Don't look so aghast! We're both very much alone in the world. I like and admire you, Josie, we get on well, we could have a happy and successful marriage.'

'I – Oh, William, I couldn't! I'm fond of you, but surely there needs to be more? I don't love you, William.'

'You just said love didn't serve Lizzie.'

'But she chose the wrong man! It must work sometimes. Look at Mr and Mrs Endersby.'

'I don't know them, do I?'

'The hotel people. My cousin Ann works for them and I know their son Dick. They've been married for nearly twenty years and they're still devoted to one another. I think I'd hope for that sort of marriage, if I were ever to fall in love. And you might meet the girl of your dreams one day. It would be a disaster if you were tied to me.'

'Then it's a refusal?'

'I'm afraid so, William. But I'm honoured you asked me, I do like you.'

In bed later, Josie could not sleep, despite her weariness. William was a mature man of thirty, established, honourable, she liked him and they got on so well. They could have had a successful marriage without the sort of love people expected to feel, but she couldn't do it. She thrust away intrusive reminders of Leo. His had been her first proposal. Suddenly she laughed. Plain, big, unfortunately red-haired Josie Shaw, a hopeless case according to her dainty mother, had received two proposals before she was nineteen from very eligible men, and she had rejected them both! Dora had had reason to consider her hopeless.

Chapter Nineteen

'I couldn't possibly do it!' Ann said, horrified.

'Of course you can,' Josie said bracingly. 'You're used to dealing with lots of people at Endersby's, you aren't nearly as shy as you were.'

'But they aren't all looking at me,' Ann protested. 'I can't walk down that enormous room and have hundreds of people staring.'

'They'll be looking at the gowns and the jewels, not you,' Tobias said quietly.

Ann looked unhappily at him. 'You mean I'm thinking too much about myself?'

'No. But if you think about the jewels, concentrate on showing them to people, you can do it. Imagine you're behind the hotel reception desk. When people come in they are looking round at the hotel, and you are a part of it. The people we have invited will be looking at the jewels, they will think you are a very attractive way of displaying them, like the hotel visitors are pleased to have someone young and pretty at the reception desk, part of the general atmosphere. Won't you try? Josie's been searching for the right person, and if we can't find someone she'll call off the whole thing.'

'Of course I won't, after all the work you've put in,' Josie said indignantly. 'Don't let Tobias blackmail you, Ann,' she went on. 'If you really can't face doing it then we'll just have to share out the items I planned for you between the other girls.'

Ann sighed. 'The jewels are absolutely lovely, Josie. The evening has to be a success after all you've done. OK, I'll try. But if I'm petrified with fright and unable to walk for shaking knees don't blame me!'

'We're having a rehearsal in the afternoon so that you will all know just where to go and in which order. Can you arrange to have time off?' Having persuaded her, Tobias was brisk, giving her no time for reflection, no time to withdraw.

Later he and Josie once more went through the order in which the girls would model the jewels.

'Do you think she'll be all right? I'd hate to force her if she doesn't feel able to do it. You really should have told her that Mr and Mrs Endersby are bringing a large party. She might freeze when she sees them.'

'Josie, don't worry! She'll be marvellous.'

'Don't worry, you'll be marvellous,' Josie whispered, giving Ann a swift hug. 'It went perfectly smoothly this afternoon.'

'I'm thankful Tobias is doing the announcements, and you're back here to help me,' Ann confessed.

'Tobias can wax lyrical over his designs,' Josie said grinning. 'I love them but can't describe them like he does. I'm far more use here sorting out the changes. Now, are you ready? That's the music about to end. And Tobias is beginning his welcome speech. Good luck!'

Ann gulped, gave a tremulous smile, and prepared to follow the other two girls through the door into the huge, ornately decorated ballroom.

'We begin, ladies and gentlemen, with a selection of our daytime jewellery – pieces which are bold yet simple, suitable for wearing to the office, for shopping, or for luncheon parties. Pamela is wearing a simple yet striking necklace of linked motifs, geometric patterns, and the same motifs are repeated in the earings and brooch, each motif in a different metal, one superimposed upon the other. An optional matching bracelet completes the set.'

Josie peered round the screen which had been placed just in front of the door. The room was full, the diners seated at tables all round and on the balcony, leaving a small central space and a velvet-covered dais where the girls could stand while one of the modistes described the gowns and Tobias the jewels each wore. As Pamela reached the dais there was a spontaneous burst of applause.

'Pamela is carrying a boxed set of napkin rings. She will show you these, each one different. These are available either as sets of a single design, such as the car or the aeroplane, or a mixed set for, let us say, your family, each different in the shape of their appropriate zodiac signs, or birthday flowers. They could, alternatively, be personalized with inscribed names.'

Pamela waited, turning so that everyone could see the jewels, holding up the napkin rings in turn, and then strolled easily amongst the diners for them to get a closer look. She finally placed the napkin rings on a table covered with ruched black velvet before leaving the ballroom.

Josie pinched herself. It was really happening. She was putting on a show for the cream of Birmingham society, the men in their evening jackets acting as foils for their brilliantly bedecked women, robed in gowns of every hue and loaded with thousands of pounds' worth of precious gems. Would they like Tobias's plainer pieces? More importantly, would they buy them? The huge chandeliers gleamed, the gilt glistened, and the rich curtains drawn across the range of windows opposite the balcony gave a warm, luxurious feel to the room. The setting was magnificent and, she told herself firmly, so were the jewels.

As Tobias began to describe the second set of jewellery Josie had to step back to help Pamela change the jewels. She hadn't expected anywhere near so many people to come, but the room was filled to capacity and there had been many disappointed people. Tobias had obtained publicity in the local press, hints that the designs were new, exciting, and innovative. Everyone who wanted and was rich enough to be fashionable, or wanted their friends and acquaintances to believe they were, had bought tickets. The occasion was going to be a success as a social event in any case.

The food had been excellent, and the wine, and now everyone was eagerly watching the exhibition of the new range of jewellery. Josie snatched a moment to watch Ann's first display, and breathed a sigh of relief. Her cousin looked confident, showing none of the signs of nerves which had attacked her earlier. And she looked so elegant and so astoundingly beautiful that Josie couldn't tell whether the applause was for her or the jewels.

For the next hour Josie was busy sorting out the pieces each girl was to wear and helping to deal with the fastenings. As each set was removed she carefully arranged it in the portable display cases which were later to be placed with the other items for people to make their selections. She had no time for watching the show, and could only guess at the enthusiasm by the level of the applause. When Tobias moved on to describe the less-severe jewellery for daytime wear, and then the elaborate and frivolous pieces for evening, she had to help the girls change their clothes too.

Finally, the girls went on together wearing Josie's most spectacular exhibits. There was another burst of prolonged applause. Tobias promptly announced that orders would be taken after the show, and he and Donald were immediately surrounded by eager buyers. Ann came out into the anteroom and Josie began to remove the intricate necklace with delicately interlinked scrolls and spirals, and a brooch, bracelets and earrings which echoed the shape without reproducing it exactly. The girls took the display cases into the ballroom and put them on the table.

'They like it,' Ann whispered. 'It's been a success!'

'I knew you could do it, young Josie.' It was Clem, bearing

down on them with a beaming Aunt Phoebe following in his wake.

'I wish Lizzie could have seen it,' Phoebe said. 'I doubt there's anything better in the whole of France!'

Josie laughed, and allowed Clem to take her arm and lead her towards some of his friends who, he said, wanted to meet a girl who could run a business so successfully that within no time she was being talked of as the most promising jeweller in Birmingham.

'But I'm not the designer, that's all thanks to Tobias,' Josie protested, flattered and pleased.

'That's as may be, but he couldn't have put on this show without your flair for business,' Clem maintained.

'And your friends, who bought tickets.'

Clem had to give way then to many other people who wanted to congratulate Josie, and it was a long time before she moved further into the ballroom. When she had a quiet moment she saw William Scott sitting at a table nearby with a group of friends. He looked abstracted, and Josie hesitated to approach him. Although he had behaved completely normally for the rest of their trip to Scotland, and concentrated on instructing Josie how to control a car in ice and snow, she felt embarrassed, reluctant to speak to him after his astonishing proposal.

She spoke to the Endersbys, sitting with Dr Mandeville and his wife and some other people she did not know. Then she saw Leo. She hadn't known he was coming. Why should he be interested in her display? Was it professional interest, to see what she and Tobias had managed to produce? She lifted her chin slightly. It was more than a year since she'd spoken to him. She wondered who his latest female conquest was. Why should she care? But she looked at the other people at his table, two men she didn't know and three attractive women. From the adoring glances she was giving him Josie guessed that the slender brunette next to Leo was his latest conquest. At least it wasn't Snooks, but Josie found her lips curling at the thought of the profusion of girls Leo managed to attract.

Josie moved past Leo's table, scrupulously ignoring him, and reached the far end of the room where a doorway led into a smaller room. She paused beside Tobias, but he was so busy he could spare her no more than a distracted smile. She turned to walk back and found Leo in front of her.

'Congratulations, Josie,' he said quietly. 'I must talk to you.'

'Oh? I have nothing to say to you.'

'Don't be silly,' he said furiously. 'There have been too many times when one of us has refused to listen, and that's where all the misunderstandings have arisen. Please, just listen to me.'

Josie glanced over his shoulder. Their raised voices were attracting attention. Suddenly aware of this Leo grasped her by the wrists, and his body shielded her struggles as he forced her to step backwards until they were in the room and the doors had closed behind them.

'Let me go! Just because you can't explain why you thought I was a thief, you try to bully me with your physical strength. This won't get you anywhere, Leo,' she told him and took a deep breath.

She hadn't made up her mind to call for help. She was conscious of the uproar such a fuss would cause, and the damage to her reputation, but Leo clearly expected her to scream. He released one wrist and clamped his hand over her mouth. Josie employed the freed hand to deliver a stinging slap to his cheek, while doing her best to bite his hand. He winced, but held on and ignored Josie's frantic tugging at his hair.

'Can't we have a civilized conversation for once?'

'I've nothing to say to you,' Josie gasped.

'All I wanted was to say I was sorry.'

'It's rather late for that.'

'I know. I'm not making excuses. I was wrong to think you could have stolen the gold, wrong to refuse to help you and your mother, and I'm deeply ashamed.'

Josie breathed deeply. 'It's over now,' she said quietly, and Leo released her. Josie moved a few steps away to the window, rubbing absently at the wrists where Leo had bruised them. 'Why did you come tonight?' she asked. 'Did you want to see Tobias's new designs?'

'That, and to make my apologies. I'm very impressed with what you've achieved here, and even though we're rivals I wish you well.'

'Thank you.' She glanced at him. He hadn't changed, and her heart was still pounding from their recent struggle.

'Josie,' Leo began, stepping towards her, then swung round impatiently as the door from the ballroom opened behind him.

'Leo, darling, why on earth are you out here? I want to order some of these delicious silver bracelets, and I need you to advise me which.'

It was the brunette. She was wearing some of the largest diamond earrings Josie had ever seen, and a pendant set with diamonds and rubies. She barely glanced at Josie as she slipped her hand under Leo's arm.

Leo smiled down at her and nodded. 'I'll be right back.'

'No, now!' she pouted. 'You know I depend on you!'

Josie watched them move away. She was breathing hard and knew that her cheeks were flushed, her hair in disarray, and her carefully applied lipstick probably smeared all over her face. As the door from the ballroom began to open again she fled for the nearest cloakroom.

William sighed and firmly turned back to the maps spread out on the table. He picked up a ruler and once again began converting kilometres into miles. In the Monte Carlo Rally teams had to maintain a steady average speed between check-points. Careful preparation was vital so that drivers knew how far they had to travel. William had been warned that the official distances rarely tallied exactly with the distances marked on maps, and referred to the shortest not necessarily the fastest routes between checkpoints. But this seemed unimportant. He had a great deal to do before setting off for Norway, the starting point he and his friends had chosen. He also had a great deal to arrange with his managers while he was away. None of it seemed remotely important.

With an angry exclamation he flung down the ruler and picked up the telephone. He asked for Josie's number. He let the ringing continue for long after it became clear she wasn't there. Where was she? Ten minutes later he tried again. There was still no reply. He had no idea where Tobias lived, or he would have tried to contact him. Perhaps Josie was with her aunt in Solihull. He knew that number, but what he had to say could not be said unless Josie was alone. He would have to wait until morning.

After a sleepless night, William hesitated. In the cold December dawn it didn't seem like a good idea to ask Josie to introduce him to the girl who had modelled the jewels. It was only a very short time since he had proposed to Josie herself. He liked Josie, they got on well together. He'd have been happy to marry her and have someone to share his life with. How could he confess that he had become instantly obsessed with a girl he didn't know, had never spoken to, but a slender girl with a delicate beauty that caused him to lose all concentration?

'William!'

William looked round. He was exhausted. After almost a hundred hours of virtually non-stop motoring he'd begun to imagine things. Even two nights in a comfortable bed hadn't fully restored his vitality.

'William Scott? It is you, isn't it?' Lizzie asked, laughing at his bemused expression.

'Yes. Lizzie, what are you doing in Monaco?'

'My employer is staying on the Côte d'Azure for the winter, and she gave me the day off so that I could try to find you. How did you get on?'

'We lost a few penalty marks being late at the first checkpoint, but that was the snow. It had snowed in Stavanger for days beforehand, then there was a sudden thaw, so we were driving through mud practically above the axles.'

'From what Josie told me you wanted to try it out this year, not win anything,' Lizzie said comfortingly.

'Yes, and I've learned a lot. Did you see the cars in the Concours?'

'The beauty competition?' Lizzie asked, grinning. 'Not yet. I came down to the harbour first.'

'Let's go and look. But we'll take a taxi, they're on the Casino Terrace and I refuse to walk up that hill!'

'I never knew you could get so many ingenious devices into one car,' she said a couple of hours later when they had walked across to the Hermitage hotel for lunch. 'And it must take hours polishing all the tools as well as the car.'

'It's given me ideas for next year,' William said.

'Surely you won't have an umbrella above the fuel tank, or a big bed in the car?'

'Not like that one,' he said, grinning, 'but the third driver has to be able to snatch some sleep somewhere. I'm more interested in finding things which will make life easier or safer for the ordinary motorist.'

'Why were all the cars bright and shiny except for one? It spoiled the impression.'

William chuckled. 'Most of the starters from Athens got through this year. Normally they don't, and that fellow was so proud of it he refused to remove the mud.'

'You mean all the cars were like that and the crews cleaned them for today? It must have taken hours.'

William nodded wryly. 'It did. It's such a shame Lord de Clifford didn't make it with the new Lagonda, after he did that trial run which was so successful.'

'What happened?'

'He hit a rock too many near the Greek border and broke the

crank case. But it's a very good car. All the motoring journalists have been saying it's a winner, and I'm thinking of buying one for next year.'

'Aren't they expensive?'

'Very cheap for what they are, about eight hundred pounds.'

Lizzie gasped. 'That's not cheap to me!'

'A lot cheaper than many in its class. Will you be here tomorrow for the procession and the prize-giving?'

'I can't stay. Mrs Thackeray-Walsh needs me, she's going to visit some friends in Antibes. When are you going home?'

'On Monday. The others want to take several days and stay in Paris this time instead of rushing through.'

'Don't you want to join them?'

'I want to get home as soon as possible,' William said abruptly.

'Give my love to Josie when you see her,' Lizzie said, wondering why he suddenly sounded so tense. Was he having problems with his business? It would not be tactful to ask. 'She wrote that her fashion show was a great success, and they are still working very hard to meet the orders.'

'They certainly had to work hard to complete all the orders for Christmas. I barely saw Josie apart from once when we passed in the street. Lizzie . . .'

'What is it?'

'Oh, it doesn't matter. Something I thought to ask you, but you couldn't know, you weren't there.'

'Weren't where? William, is something bothering you?'

'No, of course not. Now, let's see some of the sights. I've been too busy to take any of it in, and it's my first visit here too. Shall we go up to see the old town and the palace? Another taxi, it's all hills here!'

'Ann will model the jewels for the catalogue photographs,' Josie told Tobias.

'Good. They look so much better being worn, instead of just

lying on the table. We'll include drawings too, they often show the intricate bits better than photographs. When can we do it?'

'Ann can have two days off next week, and the studio and the photographer are free. I've already booked them. The only question is what she is to wear, whether you want several gowns, and where to get them.'

Tobias riffled through the folio of drawings. 'These more elaborate sets will look best with a low-necked evening gown. And this one. For the brooches and clips I think a simple, high-necked black dress. Some of the plainer necklaces would go well with that.'

'And a costume, to show the pieces we hope businesswomen will like?'

'Yes, but a very plain one. Take Ann to Rackham's and buy her what's necessary.'

'Can't we borrow them from the gown shops that helped with the fashion show?' Josie asked.

'I think they're too exclusive,' Tobias said slowly. 'They were fine for the sort of invited audience we had, but in the catalogue we have to appeal to women who can't afford exclusive clothes, show that the jewellery will look good on them too.'

'It will cost more.'

'But we have to spend. What do you mean to pay Ann?'

'She says she won't take anything.'

'Then insist she has the clothes instead of a fee.'

Two days later Ann, protesting, emerged from the store clutching several boxes. 'They were so expensive, Josie.'

'Never mind, they have to be just right, and if they cost a few shillings more than the ones you'd have liked, just because they were cheaper, Tobias and I are paying through the business. Now we'll put you in a taxi back to the hotel, and you can try them on again and make sure they fit and that you feel comfortable in them.'

Ann sighed, but made no further objection. 'And I'll be at the studio tomorrow at nine o'clock.'

'Mind you take a taxi. We're paying. Goodbye.'

Josie was waving to Ann when William Scott appeared beside her. He was panting slightly.

'Josie? Hello.'

'William. I haven't seen you for ages! How did you get on in the Monte Carlo?'

'Not too badly. I was busy preparing for it after your fashion show. Wasn't that one of the girls who modelled your jewellery?'

'Ann, yes. But what do you mean, not too badly? I know you didn't win, I saw some reports and Lizzie wrote to say she'd seen you, but were you satisfied?'

'Yes, it was perfectly satisfactory.' He'd hoped to elicit the information indirectly, but that wasn't proving very successful. He'd have to ask. Embarrassed, his face a dull red, he coughed to clear his throat, tugged at his collar, and in a strangled voice asked: 'Ann who? Where does she live?'

'Ann?' Josie stared at him in astonishment. 'Why do you want to know?'

William sighed. 'Josie, come and have a cup of tea. I need to talk to you.'

When they were seated in a small tea room and Josie had poured the tea, William seemed unable to speak. He sat nibbling at a scone, gazing abstractedly into his cup.

'Why do you want to know about Ann?' Josie asked.

William glanced awkwardly up at her. 'This is difficult. Almost the last time we were together I asked you to marry me. I truly meant it, Josie, I'm sure we could have had a successful marriage.'

Josie's eyes were sparkling. 'And I refused you, William, because you don't love me any more than I love you. We're friends, that's all. I said that one day you might meet the girl of your dreams. Is Ann that girl?'

He grinned shamefacedly. 'She's so beautiful,' he said simply.

'But you don't know her. You've never even spoken to her.

She could be a dreadful person, greedy, grasping, a nagging harpy.'

William protested fiercely. 'Of course she's not! Why, she looks the gentlest, loveliest girl in the world.'

Josie chuckled. 'In Scotland you were singing the praises of arranged marriages. Love didn't seem to come into it.'

'But then I hadn't seen her!' Suddenly his eyes widened in astonishment. 'In Scotland you mentioned your cousin Ann. Is that her? You told me where she works, but I've forgotten. Josie, for the Lord's sake put me out of my misery. Where can I find her?'

Josie took pity on him. 'She *is* my cousin, Ann Preece. Her father was my Uncle Arthur, my mother's older brother, and her mother was a girl from the village where they lived. They both died and her grandparents brought her up. Then, when they died, she came to live with Aunt Phoebe.'

'But where is she now?' he demanded, uninterested in past history.

'She works as a receptionist at Endersby's hotel in the Hagley Road. Where are you going?'

'Why, to find her. Oh, sorry, I haven't paid for the tea. Here,' he dragged some coins from his pocket, 'be a dear and pay for me.'

Josie, ignoring the startled glances of two elderly matrons at the next table, grabbed William's hand. 'Oh no you don't!' she said. 'William, for pity's sake be sensible. Ann won't be there, she has a few days off. And she's very shy, almost timid. If you go charging after her in your present mood you'll scare her off completely.'

He sank back on the chair, and sighed. 'You're right. But I've been dreaming about her ever since I saw her. It was like a miracle seeing her again today.'

'You could always have asked me to introduce you,' Josie pointed out gently.

William looked rueful. 'I know, but having just proposed to

you it was too embarrassing. Seeing her with you made me act impulsively.'

'Ann's going to model all the jewellery for our new catalogue tomorrow, at a photographer's studio. She and Tobias are coming back to my flat afterwards for supper. You come too, and I'll say it's to tell us all about the Monte Carlo Rally. She knows who you are, I've mentioned you often enough, and she won't be afraid to let you take her home. Will that do? Can you do the rest yourself afterwards?'

Beaming, William once more leapt to his feet, but this time to come round the table to drop a kiss on Josie's cheek. The scandalized matrons hastily gathered up their shopping and departed, loudly commenting that they didn't know what the modern generation was coming to.

Josie watched William and Ann with considerable inner amusement. It was obvious to her observant cousin that Ann found William's stocky good looks both attractive and reassuring. He treated her with a judicious blend of admiration and protectiveness, and Josie had to applaud his tactics. He seemed to understand that fulsome praise would merely frighten Ann, so his compliments on how excellent the fashion show had been were brief and encompassed Josie's and Tobias's contributions too. He asked her to tell him about the photographic session that day, and in his turn told her of the photographs he had taken of devices he was developing. Ann showed more interest in the technical details of car heating systems and how to ensure efficient and reliable windscreen wipers than she ever had in the manufacture of jewellery. Josie, returning from her small kitchen with an apple pie, was astounded to hear Ann eagerly accepting an invitation to tour William's factory.

Then William told them some of his experiences during the Monte Carlo Rally, and Ann shuddered in dismay, paling as he described the time they'd driven into a ditch.

'How dreadful!' she exclaimed. 'You might have been dreadfully hurt!'

William bit back the description, which he'd already given to Josie, of how one competitor's car had actually turned a somersault, but this had not prevented him from reaching Oslo on time. If his plans matured he had no intention of making Ann suffer agonies worrying about the accidents that could happen. Later, when Ann said she really must go and William, with suitable humility, offered to drive her back to the hotel, Josie had to bite her lip hard to restrain her laughter. Then she rapidly had to invent a problem she needed to consult Tobias about to prevent him from leaving with them.

'We discussed that yesterday,' Tobias said, puzzled, after William and Ann had left. 'Nothing's changed, has it?'

Josie laughed. 'No, but I couldn't let you spoil William's good work. He deserves to have Ann to himself.'

'I thought he was rather taken with her. She's remarkably pretty, of course.'

'William thinks she's the most beautiful girl he's ever seen, and has been pining away ever since the fashion show because he didn't have the nerve – or the sense – to ask me who she was.'

Tobias grinned. 'So that's why he was here tonight.'

'He's just right for her. He's kind, considerate, protective, and he has an excellent business. She's lost so many people, and she's worked hard and was unselfish helping me with my mother. She deserves a man like William.'

'You speak as though you'd like him for a husband,' Tobias said quietly.

'No. I like him enormously but that isn't good enough. I don't love him, but I hope Ann can.'

Two weeks later, when Josie was visiting Phoebe and Clem in Solihull one Sunday, she found Ann and William there before her. Clem was in the act of pouring champagne.

'Hello. What are we celebrating?' Josie asked, and then glanced at Ann. 'Already?' she gasped.

'I know it's rather sudden,' Ann said with a tremulous smile, 'but we're both utterly certain. 'I – I knew as soon as I met William, and he says it was the same for him. You will be pleased, won't you?'

'Pleased? I'm delighted!'

'And we'll have another Easter wedding,' Phoebe said.

'Easter? But that's only a month away!'

'What's the matter with that? They've neither of them any family apart from us, they say they don't want a big wedding, and I'll manage what they do want, or my name's not Phoebe Stokes!'

Chapter Twenty

'ANN ought to go with you,' Josie protested.

'Tobias is quite capable of looking after your business for a few days,' said William.

'And I can't drive, Josie, and William needs a driver. Besides, I'm much too busy,' Ann put in.

'You could come as a passenger,' suggested Josie. 'It's a beautifully comfortable car. The dresses are all bought, and you've given up your job. Aunt Phoebe's in charge of the reception and thoroughly enjoying all the bustle, so why not?'

Ann shook her head vehemently. 'I'm quite happy that William goes on rallies, truly I am, but I don't fancy driving for days on end, through the night with no sleep, and no time to have a bath or a proper meal.'

William laughed. 'We are clearly not going to be a husband and wife team like some of the rally drivers. And that suits me fine, I won't even try to persuade Ann to drive if she doesn't want to, so I still need you, Josie. I have to try out my new Lagonda, over a long distance, and I must enter the RAC Rally now if I'm to show some of my new devices.'

'What have you got this time?'

'I've improved the springs and put in a new oil filter which shouldn't get clogged. The drink and food containers are placed within reach of the driver, and I've had a differently shaped tonneau fitted to give greater wind protection, to deflect the wind from the passengers.'

'They sound super.'

'I have to get publicity for them. That's an important part of my business. Besides, there isn't a great deal of time before the Monte Carlo next January, and I mean to do well there.'

'Well, if you really don't mind, Ann. It would be fun. When, and which route?'

'Leamington. I want to impress local customers and that's the nearest starting point. A thousand miles to Bournemouth! We set off on Tuesday afternoon so I'll collect you early that morning. Thanks, Josie.'

Leo nodded in approval. His business was improving. Without Tobias's designs, and allowing for not selling to Germany, he'd collected fewer orders than in the previous two years on his annual European trip. Much as he hated admitting it, Tobias was right: to prosper he had to have innovative designs. The man he now employed was too timid. He thought back to Josie's fashion show. The jewellery there had been superlative, new and interesting, yet not so outrageously modern that the older, more conservative customers had been dubious about it.

He wondered if he'd been sensible to go. He'd tried hard to forget her, and taken out many other girls, yet when they'd been alone had discovered he wanted Josie more than ever before. Resolutely he thrust thoughts of Josie aside and concentrated all his energies on organizing production so that he squeezed as much profit out of it as possible. He'd found another designer. Now he had two men, good in different ways. One devised new shapes for the jewellery, the other was also an engraver who did the most exquisite pictures on the flat surfaces of boxes and compacts and cigarette cases. Neither of them was anywhere near as good as Tobias, but their designs were selling well. Even more satisfactorily, he had found a good clerk, and instead of a manager had taken on a foreman who had been in the trade for thirty years, and who was completely reliable. Leo was confident he could leave them in charge without a qualm.

He felt he needed a break. He'd bought a new car, a Triumph, and he was eager to try it out in a long rally. Bill White, one of his schoolfriends who often drove with him was urging that he enter the RAC Rally, and Leo finally agreed. 'If you prepare the car I can take that week off, after Monday,' he offered. 'I have to see an important buyer from South America then.'

'Leave it to me. But we'll start from Leamington, we won't want a long drive on Monday evening.'

'It doesn't matter where. It'll be good to be doing something apart from business!'

They drove to Leamington on Tuesday morning and Leo spent an hour going over the car, making sure everything was in order before they checked in to have the various seals and the RAC stamps put on vital parts of the car and its engine. The first competitor was setting off at two o'clock, and Leo an hour later, so he and Bill strolled round the town and had lunch at the Regent before going back to the starting point in time to see the mayor shaking hands with Mrs Richards, a member of one of the Midland Automobile Club teams, the first to set off with her co-drivers in her two-tone Standard.

Gradually the cars were waved away, and Leo walked to where his Triumph was parked. He stopped so abruptly that Bill cannoned into him.

'What the —?' Bill began, but Leo was oblivious. A sleek, elegant dark green Lagonda M45 was parked next to his own car, and Josie stood beside it.

He forgot all his resolutions. 'Josie! I didn't know you were coming on the rally.'

Josie turned towards him. She looked pale. 'How should you?' she asked, slightly breathless, and immediately turned away.

'Are you driving? Whose car is this?'

'Hello, old chap,' William intervened, rising from where he'd been inspecting the nearside rear tyre. 'D'you like her?'

Leo looked bemusedly at Josie, and then shook his head slightly. 'Oh, yes. Very elegant. I've always liked Lagondas.'

'Me too. I met Bert Hammond some time ago on a rally and he invited me down to Staines to see this new four and a half litre model. A grand little chap. He's been with them almost from the start, their chief tester, knows every car, and has raced most of them too.'

'Yes, I saw him at Brooklands once,' Leo replied. 'I see this model doesn't have cycle guards.'

'No, they were fashionable, but threw up a lot of mud. The sloping running-board's much better. She's a beautiful car, a Meadows engine, and very quiet. Look at the arm-rest in the back, and the back seat's lower, the passengers are below the windscreen, they don't have to dodge the wind.'

Leo nodded, but he was looking at Josie. By now Bill had come up and he and William were soon deep in discussion of the merits of twin exhausts and preselector gearboxes. Leo spoke quietly to Josie. 'There isn't time now, Josie, but can we, when we get to Bournemouth perhaps, talk? I want to apologize.'

Josie was silent, and just then William suddenly realized it was time for him to start.

'Sorry, old chap, we must go,' he said, firing the engine. Josie scrambled in. 'By the way, haven't seen you for weeks,' he shouted over the roar of the engine, as Leo stepped back. 'We'll have a celebration in Bournemouth, you can wish me luck. I'm getting married at Easter.'

'Can you see the verge?' William asked.

Josie, who had been leaning out over the side of the car, in peril of overbalancing, shouted back reassuringly. 'You're right on course! I'll yell if it vanishes.'

An hour later they ran out of the fog, and Josie collapsed into her seat with a sigh of relief.

'Try to sleep,' William suggested. 'I know the road from Norwich to London quite well, I won't get lost. And I can see the lights of some of the others in front.'

Josie yawned but shook her head. 'I'm too excited to sleep.' And, she added to herself, too confused by seeing Leo and wondering what he wanted to say to her. 'How long have we been on the road? Twelve hours? We're nearly a third of the way through.'

'At least you didn't have to lie on the bonnet.'

'Lie on the bonnet? Whatever for?'

William laughed. 'In the Monte this year there was fog south of Harrogate, and Kay Petre had to lie on the bonnet and shout back to tell the driver which way to go.'

'And I thought hanging over the door upside down was difficult!' She relapsed into silence, but thoughts of Leo kept intruding, and she could still see both the lovely, elegant *principessa* and the girl at the fashion show laughing up at him so intimately. She didn't want to talk to him. He couldn't have anything to say to her. That was all finished. She wanted to be left in peace to concentrate on her business. After a few minutes of trying to banish unwelcome images from her mind she decided talking was the only way to succeed. 'Why didn't you start from John o' Groats?'

'That route is different, down the western coast and through the Pyrenees. I didn't fancy it since I wanted to try out a route that converged early on with others from several starting points. Then I'd know some of the route if I started elsewhere another year. Athens and Bucharest are virtually impossible most years anyway, but the teams which start from northern Europe, Tallinn and Umeå as well as Stavanger, do well. I shall try Umeå next time, the Swedes keep their roads clear, and there's the very devil of a steep hill out of Stavanger which can get you a bad start.'

'The only steep hills this run are at Buxton.'

'And they're nothing like Norway! If you're not sleepy, do you want to drive? You can't get lost, and I'll take a nap and change back before London.'

At the checkpoints, Leo studiously avoided William and Josie. He was thoroughly confused. He'd tried so hard to forget Josie, taking out other girls, telling himself he'd hate to be married, tied to one woman for the rest of his life. Then when he'd seen her at John o' Groats and compared her with the foolish Snooks, his doubts had been revived. If he hadn't succumbed to temptation and gone to her fashion show he might have been able to forget her again, and now the prospect that she might be marrying William had thrown him into another turmoil. William had said 'I', not 'we'. Several times Bill looked anxiously at him when Leo failed to hear his comments. Twice during a severe blizzard near Buxton which reduced visibility almost to nothing, he had to shout urgently at Leo to demand which way he was supposed to go. Bill wasn't the only one relieved to reach Westover Road in Bournemouth and drive up the ramps into the garage where the RAC officials directed them to the floor allocated to their class.

'Now where?' Bill asked when the car had been inspected and locked up to await the final tests on the following day. 'I could do with a bath and a sleep, then perhaps we can go to one of the special dinners tonight? All sorts of invitations await us, I hear.'

Leo hesitated. He wanted to find Josie straight away, but common sense told him neither he nor she was fit to talk sensibly. He could see William's Lagonda already parked, but he didn't know where they were staying, so he couldn't even ask the most urgent question of all upon which every other hope depended.

'Bath and bed, I think,' he said reluctantly.

Fending off Bill's eager attempts to discuss what they might be asked to do in the final tests, Leo gained his room. A long soak in a hot bath partly revived him, but then he found he was unable to sleep. Was Josie going to marry William? She seemed to spend a lot of time with him, and he'd heard of the rallies they'd entered together. That time when she'd won her first novice rally he'd seen William kiss her. Leo mentally berated himself as he tossed restlessly. He'd been unfair to Josie just because he'd resented her mother, and because his father had appeared to favour them over himself. Then he'd accused Josie of theft. It was no wonder she wouldn't forgive him. Owing to him she'd spent months in degrading poverty. And he'd flaunted Kitty before her, angry at her obstinacy. Josie no doubt despised him over his affair with Kitty. It had been brief and was long over, but if he'd ever hoped it might spur Josie to jealousy, that hope had faded. He'd compounded his folly by almost creating a scene at her fashion show.

Leo wrestled with plans of how he might say all this to Josie. There was no way, he concluded as, utterly worn out, he dropped into an uneasy sleep.

'What's the matter?' Josie asked as William almost ran into the hotel lobby where she was waiting for him before dinner.

'I've been looking at the other cars. One of them has an identical hot-water bottle arrangement to my new one, even the special shape I designed for fitting round shoes.'

'How could it? That one was only fitted into your car just before we started. No one could have copied it.'

'Of course not. But I've been making them, improving the design, for several weeks.'

'Someone who works for you stole one? Is that it?'

'I don't see how they could. None's missing. We kept a very careful check on every single one. They were locked up all the time apart from when we were working on them, as I do with all the new designs.'

'Can you complain? Could this man have stolen it?'

'It's unlikely. He comes from London, he'd have no chance of stealing from my factory. He said he'd bought it from a small garage in west London. It seemed quite normal, he wasn't embarrassed, he even wanted to show me just how it worked. I'm going straight back to Birmingham. Do you mind? I must ask questions there.'

'Of course I don't mind. But you'll miss the final tests and the Concours.'

'I know, but there's no help for it. Someone in my factory is stealing the design, if not the actual thing, from me. If I enter the Concours someone is bound to spot they're the same. I might not even be able to prove it's my design. Besides, if word gets out that I suspect someone at the factory there'll be no chance of finding the culprit. Do you feel rested enough to start straight away? If I can get there before the factory opens in the morning I may surprise someone into giving themselves away.'

'I'm OK, I had a good sleep this afternoon. Can you get the car out of the garage? Aren't they all locked in?'

'That's no problem, I've explained to the officials there's an emergency at home. They think it's illness and we'll leave them all to think that. Let's pack. I'll see you down here again as soon as possible.'

Josie wondered, as she changed back into her warm motoring skirt and pulled on an extra cardigan, if she was relieved to be escaping from Leo. She'd been on edge all the time since he'd spoken to her. There was nothing to say. There couldn't be anything to say, and trying to make normal conversation would be impossible. For her, if not for William, this theft had perhaps been lucky.

'Josie, don't tell Ann what I suspect,' William said as they came close to Birmingham.

'Why ever not?'

'I don't want to worry her. I don't ever mean to worry her with business problems. I love her too much.'

'You'll be doing her an injustice.'

'How do you mean? Surely you don't want her to fret, be afraid, concerned about saving money because she feels my profits might be falling? I'll deal with all that.'

'That's how George Bradley treated my mother, and she was hopeless with money, because she didn't understand.'

'Ann's not like your mother. Oh, Lord, I'm sorry, Josie, that sounded dreadful.'

'It's all right. No, she isn't like Mother was. I don't know whether my mother would have been any different whatever George had done, but Ann is certainly not anything like her. She's strong, William, despite her fragile air. Look how she helped me when we were in such a dreadful plight. She gave practical help and she never flinched at the awful conditions. She slept on the floor when she was looking after me. She'd be hurt if she thought you didn't trust her.'

'It's not that!' William exclaimed, appalled.

'You're not trusting her enough to share your problems with her. She'd rather know and perhaps be able to help, even if it's only by listening to you, than fret because she doesn't know what's worrying you.'

He was silent for a while. 'I suppose you're right. I hadn't thought of it that way. I'll tell her if I don't find out who's stealing my designs.'

'Oh, William! You'll have to tell her why we came back early, why you didn't win the Concours. Don't wriggle!'

He laughed out loud. 'Josie, why do you always have to be right?' He yawned. 'Lord, I'm tired. I'll drop you off at your flat, then I'll have to go in and try to discover what's been happening before anyone else arrives.'

'It's still the middle of the night. Couldn't you have a couple of hours' sleep first?'

'If I go to bed I'll sleep till Sunday. I must have a look first, though I'm not sure what I expect to find.'

*

When Leo discovered that Josie and William had departed precipitately from Bournemouth his first reaction was frustrated fury. When he'd calmed down he became puzzled. William was far more dedicated to rallying than he was, and it mattered to him, as someone in the trade, to do well. Josie and William hadn't lost any points during the road test, and from the glimpses Leo had had of the Lagonda he thought they would have had a good chance of a prize. So why had William abandoned this? Had Josie been so determined to avoid him that she'd persuaded William to return home early and give up this opportunity? If William had agreed he must be besotted with her. That reflection made Leo angry again, but he was thoroughly confused whether it was because he despised William's weakness, Josie's manipulation of him, or his own total failure over the past year to follow his true instincts and force Josie to listen to him, to tell her how mistaken he'd been, and if necessary beg her on bended knees to forgive him.

He watched the final competitions on Friday and played his own part with so distracted an air that Bill was seriously beginning to think he was ill. This opinion was strengthened when Leo said he didn't' want to stay for the final celebrations but wished to get home as soon as possible.

'It'll be late when we get back, but I'd prefer to start now if you don't mind.'

Bill didn't object and offered to drive first. Leo was so distracted they'd passed Oxford before he roused himself and suggested he took the wheel.

'Come in for a drink?' Leo asked abruptly as they drew up outside his house.

'No thanks, old chap. It's well after midnight and I'd better catch up on my sleep. I'll just get my car out of your garage and be on my way.'

Leo wasn't sorry. He needed time to think, to plan. He wouldn't allow Josie to marry William, she couldn't possibly love him. But how could he make her see that it would be a disaster? How could he persuade her to abandon William and marry him instead?

He put the car away and drained the radiator. It was still cold enough for a frost, and despite the trouble he preferred to do this rather than install heaters in his garage or use the under-bonnet heaters many of his friends swore by. There were several letters awaiting him but he pushed them to one side without looking. He wanted to begin telephoning his friends who might know about William's marriage plans, but a glance at his watch made him pause. They wouldn't thank him for being woken up in the middle of the night. He'd better go to bed, and he could start asking questions in the morning.

But in the morning, when he came downstairs, the letters on the doormat caught his eye and he recalled the ones he'd pushed aside last night. He'd better just glance at them while he drank some coffee. Five minutes later he let out a gleeful shout. In his hand he held an invitation to the wedding of Mr William Edward Arthur Scott and Miss Ann Margaret Preece, on Easter Monday at the church of St Alphege.

'Why did you ask Leo Bradley?' Josie said in dismay. She'd been opening the letters of acceptance.

'He's one of William's friends, he was on the list William gave me,' Phoebe said briskly. 'Look, Josie, just because of that affair of the gold when you worked for him, we can't not ask him.'

'I suppose not.' Aunt Phoebe didn't know that there were other reasons why she didn't want to see Leo, and Josie had no intention of enlightening her. Since Ann's engagement, her aunt had been dropping all sorts of heavy hints that it was time she and Lizzie found suitable men so that she could organize two more weddings.

'You won't have to sit in his pocket, he's not the best man, and there are plenty of people coming, even though it's such short notice. Now, come and try on your bridesmaid's dress and I can be getting on with doing the hem.'

'It's a liberty, not even askin' 'er cousin,' Freddy said indignantly.

Lizzie sighed impatiently. 'You don't really expect Ma to forgive you just because Ann's getting married, do you?'

Freddy had come, he said, because he thought it was time to visit her and make it up with his family. Lizzie suspected other motives.

'Mabel's proper offended,' he said plaintively.

'Mabel! She's got a cheek! Why, you and she haven't even bothered to get married, so what's she got to do with our family?'

'Well, it's 'er only chance ter see a weddin' at one of the nobs's 'ouses,' he said, trying to sound convincing. 'Besides, er does work fer William.'

Lizzie laughed in his face. 'William employs a couple of hundred people in Birmingham and Coventry. How many of them do you think he's asking?'

'Do us a favour, Sis, get Ma ter ask us ter weddin'.'

Ann and William were married in front of a good collection of their friends. Opinion was unanimous that Ann was the loveliest bride they had ever seen. In her lace-trimmed dress, with long, tight-fitting sleeves and a slim skirt which widened into delicate flounces below the knee, she was radiant. Her eyes sparkled as brightly as the specially designed silver jewellery, dozens of tiny hearts intricately woven together or joined with invisible fastenings, which was Josie's present, designed and made by Tobias. William's expression as she walked down the aisle towards him brought tears to every female eye and quite a few of the men's.

'You're the luckiest dog alive!'

William was pleased yet exasperated when at least the twentieth man used the same words to congratulate him later, as they gathered in Clem's house for the reception.

'I know,' he replied, trying to smile, and wishing it could all be over so that he could begin cherishing his darling as he had just vowed to do.

'I hope you'll both be wonderfully happy.'

William grinned in relief at the variation. 'Thanks, Leo. I'm glad you could come. I know I can't help being happy. Isn't she lovely?'

Leo had to pass on. He mingled with the other guests, but did not once come near to Josie, who was preoccupied in seeing that everyone had plenty to eat and that their champagne glasses were constantly replenished. She'd given him a cool nod on the only occasion their eyes had met, and turned smoothly away. Later he saw her in earnest conversation with William, but wasn't close enough even to guess what made them look so serious.

'You have no idea who it was that stole your design?' Josie was asking.

'I can't think how it was done, but I've seen the very same design advertised in the *Autocar* by a London dealer. It certainly wasn't Harry Manders this time. Even worse, they're advertising something that looks exactly the same as another invention of mine, a special light which can be fitted either near the front passenger seat or in the back.'

'Can't you go and see the dealer, ask him who his suppliers are? It might be easier to trace it back from there than keep watch in your factory, especially if you say none of these things have actually gone missing. Someone must be either making very exact drawings of the completed object, or somehow getting access to the plans.'

'I intend to go when we come home from our honeymoon in Paris. It must be someone copying the finished article. I'm sure I can trust the men who make the drawings for me, and those are always locked away. It's easier to get to the real objects when they're being worked on.

'You'll find out soon,' Josie tried to sound encouraging. 'Meanwhile, forget it. Just enjoy your honeymoon!'

Phoebe had hired a small group of musicians, and after William and Ann led off with the first dance in the big marquee everyone joined in. Josie managed to avoid Leo until it was time to go and help Ann change into her going-away outfit.

'Josie, I'm so incredibly happy!' Ann said wonderingly.

'You deserve to be. Now hurry up, stop dreaming, or you'll miss the train!'

Ann laughed, but obediently changed into the blue silk dress and slipped on the mink coat which had been one of Clem's presents.

'I wish you and Lizzie could find someone,' she said wistfully.

Josie gave her a shake. 'Stop it! All brides want all their friends to take the same step, but some of us are content to be businesswomen.'

'Not if you're in love.'

Josie thought of those words later when, the bridal pair having departed, Leo cornered her and insisted that she dance with him.

'No arguments today,' he insisted, as he whirled her on to the polished boards which had been laid to provide a dance floor. 'Tell me about your business. Are your sales satisfactory? They should be with Tobias's designs.'

'I'm very pleased with what we've done,' Josie said stiffly.

'Josie, will you have dinner with me one night?'

'I don't think we have anything to —'

'Won't you even let me explain?'

Josie wordlessly shook her head. He couldn't explain. And she could not undergo the pain of listening to excuses.

'Why not?'

Suddenly she lost her temper and rounded on him. 'You accused me of thieving from you, you dismissed me without even considering any other possibility! You said before then that you loved me, but what sort of love is it that prefers to jump to conclusions rather than look for the real facts? It was your fault I couldn't earn enough to give my mother even the barest comforts when she was dying. Your father left her destitute because he couldn't face a life of poverty, but it would have been riches compared with what she had to endure in the end. How can you excuse that? I'm sick to death of your family, Leo Bradley. Leave me alone. Go back to your damned mistresses! I'm sure they have a lot more to offer you than I ever could.'

She broke away from him, her eyes blinded with tears, leaving Leo, white-faced with fury, staring after her. A few of the wedding guests were staring, some amused, others shocked, and with an oath Leo strode to his car. Well, he'd tried! He wouldn't demean himself again, he'd drive what emotion he felt for Josie out of his mind, free his heart from the grip it had been held in. No woman would treat him like that and expect him to continue — what? He grabbed at his errant thoughts. Of course he didn't love her! Not now. And whatever else it might be called, their association had not been anything like a conventional courtship. He drove away, condemning all women and vowing perpetual bachelorhood. Heaven help any man caught in the toils of a capricious female!

Chapter Twenty-One

'WHAT are you doing in here?' William demanded. 'This room is supposed to be locked when no one's here.'

Mabel jumped and then turned round slowly. 'Jus' lookin', Mr Scott,' she replied, offering him an ingratiating smile.

'What's that you're hiding?' He lunged forward as Mabel tried to sidle out of the room and seized her arm. She fought ferociously but was no match for him and he soon wrested from her fingers a key which he recognized as a duplicate of the one which opened this room where all his new designs were kept.

'I found it, lyin' just outside, an' I thought it might fit that door, so I tried it – afore bringin' it ter you,' she said, widening her eyes in a parody of innocence.

William's foot skidded on something as he pulled her out of the room and he looked down. It was a pencil, broken now. As Mabel resisted William caught a glimpse of paper in her overall pocket, and before she knew what he intended he'd dragged it out.

''Ere, that's my private property!' she shrieked, trying to snatch it from him.

He held it aloft as he straightened it out. 'I don't think so,' he said quietly. 'This is a drawing of the new windscreen heater I'm developing. It's not good, but adequate for someone to copy the design. How often have you stolen these designs from me? And who is paying you for them? I can't believe you're working on your own.'

'I found it on the floor,' she muttered sullenly. 'I don't know what it is.'

'If you confess and tell me who is employing you I won't press charges. If not –' he shrugged.

Mabel glared at him. 'It's the truth,' she insisted. 'I found the key an' that paper lyin' 'ere. Yer can't prove no diff'rent.'

William left her under the guard of one of the chargehands while he questioned the women who'd worked with Mabel. None of them knew anything, or would admit it, but one of them happened to mention that Mabel didn't always eat her dinner with them, though they didn't know where she went, and she never came back with any shopping, which was the usual reason for missing their dinners.

Frustrated, he went back to his office and sent to have Mabel brought to him. He knew that if she stuck to her story and he could uncover no further evidence any charge would fail, however convinced he was of her guilt.

'Well, Mr Scott?' she demanded angrily the moment she was in the room. 'Are yer goin' ter apologize?'

'No,' William said levelly. 'I know you're guilty. I'll give you a week's wages and I want you off the premises within ten minutes. Have you any possessions you need to collect?'

She shouted, pleaded and wept, but William remained firm. At length Mabel, promising all sorts of vengeance, was escorted out of the factory, and the gateman given strict orders that if he allowed her to return his own would be the next job to go.

It remained to be seen, William thought, whether the theft of his designs continued. But first he would change the lock on the door and make certain that the only keys were held by employees he could trust.

*

'We're doing fabulously well,' Josie enthused. 'It's all your new designs, Tobias. The profits for the first half of the year are enormous.'

'Don't get carried away,' Tobias warned her, grinning. 'There are some new machines we could do with if we're to get maximum production for the Silver Jubilee souvenirs, and I want to start experimenting with both enamels and plastics for my next designs.'

'I could afford a small car,' Josie said wistfully. 'Sixpence off income tax will help. Do you think I might? Or would it be too extravagant? Ought I to put everything back into the business?'

Tobias grinned. 'If you want one of these new Lagondas William Scott's bought, then I'd say you can't afford it. What did it cost? Over five hundred pounds?'

'Well over, by the time he's done all the modifications he's planning for the Concours competitions,' Josie said, laughing. 'It's a wonderful car, so sleek and elegant with the low doors and that long, curving running-board. But he can afford it. I could get a second-hand MG for much less than two hundred.'

'Those thefts he was worried about seem to have stopped now. Did he tell you he'd found the culprit?'

'Ann said he found one of the girls in the room where he keeps the new devices, with a key to the room and a drawing of one of the new things. The girl said she'd found them on the floor and he couldn't prove otherwise, but he sacked her and there don't seem to have been any thefts since. Every rally we go on he spends his time looking at other cars for copies of his designs, but he's found no more.'

'If you drive with him why have a car of your own?'

'He needs to take the two friends who are driving in the Monte Carlo Rally with him now, to get used to the car. I know he won't tell me I can't go with him, but it wouldn't be fair on them. Lizzie and I can go together, before she goes off to the South of France for the winter again.'

'Then I suggest you start looking for your MG straight

away,' Tobias recommended. 'The season will be over before you start, else.'

'That's Freddy!' Lizzie exclaimed. 'With Matthew. What on earth is he doing driving Matthew's car?'

Josie had acquired a two-year-old J2 two-seater MG a week earlier, and they had entered a half-day reliability trial. The cars were gathering in a paddock before the final test, a hill climb up a steep incline on the far side of the paddock, winding through a copse of beech trees at the top before finishing in another open space.

Matthew had seen them and to her dismay was walking towards them. 'The jewellery business must be good if you can already afford a car,' Matthew said to Josie, a faint sneer in his voice, but she didn't reply. 'Are you planning any more fashion shows?'

'No.' She turned and walked away. It wasn't just that she resented the way he'd treated Lizzie, or herself, she told herself firmly, somehow she didn't trust him. Mingling with other jewellery manufacturers she picked up odd snippets of gossip that his business was not doing well.

Matthew had to return to his car for the next test and Josie breathed a sigh of relief. It was short-lived. As the competitors crowded round to congratulate her on winning her class Freddy approached, and before she could dodge he'd pulled her to him and planted a wet kiss on her cheek.

'Well done, coz!' he exclaimed loudly. 'Matthew only came fourth in his class. He should have let me drive.'

Josie scrubbed furiously at her cheek. 'If you ever even try to speak to me again I'll forget Aunt Phoebe's feelings and put you back in Winson Green,' she threatened in a clear, carrying voice. Some of the crowd who had been surrounding them began to murmur, puzzled, as Freddy turned away muttering darkly about jealous bitches.

*

'Leo?' William here. Can I come round and see you? I need a favour.'

'Now? Or for dinner?'

'Now, if it's possible. I'm taking Ann out tonight,' he explained. 'It's six months since our wedding.'

Leo chuckled. 'I'd forgotten for a moment, you're a sober husband now. Come straight over.'

When William came in Leo was busy looking at some new designs. With a sigh he pushed them to one side.

'Sorry, have I disturbed you?' William apologized.

'No. I'm glad of a break. Somehow they don't seem in the least attractive. I thought my designers were quite good, but they are producing the same old designs. I do wish Tobias were still here.'

'They look OK to me,' William said after a cursory glance at the drawings. 'I won't keep you long. Colin Pettigrew's had to drop out of my team for Monte, he's been posted to Egypt by the bank in rather a hurry. I was wondering if you could come instead?'

Leo's eyes gleamed. Ever since he'd watched the final tests in Monaco almost three years before it had been his ambition to take part. He couldn't afford it alone, though, not if he meant to maintain the improvement in his business fortunes. 'I'd love to,' he said eagerly. 'Thanks, William! What can I do to help?'

'John's doing all the map work, he's been on the Umeå route before. He'll prepare navigation plans. I'll be busy fitting the car with the special equipment, so perhaps if you can tune the engine? You're good at that.'

'Of course!' Leo's eyes gleamed. He'd heard glowing reports about this car. 'What else?'

'Get warm clothing, fur-lined if possible. But you know all this, I'm sure. And that there's almost no room for luggage – razor and toothbrush in your pockets, I'm afraid, and just one spare pair of socks. We're staying at the Grand this year –'

'How much? I'll contribute, of course.'

'If you wish, just accommodation, though. Autocheques are taking the main luggage ahead by van, and it's ten pounds fifteen each, including the stay. Hewlett's are taking the cars by steamer, the contingents for Norway and Sweden will travel together. It's good fun, Leo, as well as good for my business. Especially now I don't think there'll be anyone stealing my ideas.'

Ann turned round from where she was brushing her hair. 'Of course you can't pull out,' she said urgently. 'You've done so much, worked so hard, it wouldn't be fair on the others.'

William paced about the bedroom, distracted and running his hands through his hair until it stood up in spikes. 'But darling, how can I leave you, now?'

'If I'd known you were going to make this fuss I wouldn't have told you,' Ann said, but she was laughing. 'William, it's a perfectly normal condition, most women experience it, and it's nothing to worry about.'

'You'll be on your own for at least two weeks.'

'We have a housekeeper and a maid. They both live in.'

'But what do they know? Neither of them has had a child, and what if anything were to go wrong?'

'Nothing will go wrong, I've never felt better in my life, but if it will make you happier I'll go and stay with Aunt Phoebe. She'd asked me to anyway, and so long as she doesn't fret me to death I'd love to stay with her.'

William hugged her gently. 'Promise you won't take risks at all?'

'Of course I won't! I want our baby as much as you do.'

'Shall I move into another room?'

Ann giggled. 'What on earth for? If you think I'm going to spend the next eight months sleeping alone I shall begin to resent the baby. I want you more than ever, William. I want you to hold me, to make love to me, until I get so fat and ugly you can't bear to look at me.'

'You'll never be that!' he protested. 'But – won't it harm the baby?'

'Pregnant women, I'm reliably told,' Ann said rather grandly, 'have to be humoured. Their every wish has to be granted. Oh, darling, stop looking so worried and come to bed. It's less than a month before you go. I don't want to waste a minute of it.'

'Who is it?' Josie said into the speaking tube. It was late at night, and living here alone she was cautious about answering rings at her door.

'Josie? It's Dick. Dick Endersby. Can I come up?'

'Dick! How lovely! Wait and I'll come down.'

He'd grown, was her first thought. Just over a year at Oxford had matured him both physically and, she suspected, emotionally. He was hatless despite the cold night, and wore a single-breasted blazer and flannel trousers, with a wide silk tie she thought must be that of his college. He was still the outgoing, friendly person she'd known, but now he was a man, even more confident and even more attractive, better-looking than his handsome father, and with a direct look in his eyes as he regarded her.

'Josie, it's good to see you! I only got home today.'

'Come in and have a drink.'

'May I? I don't want to take up your time if you're busy, but I'd like to talk to you.'

'Wait until we get upstairs.' She led the way and hushed his attempts to speak until she'd poured them both whiskies. She sat opposite him in one of the low chairs she'd recently bought, and nodded. 'How is Oxford?'

'The studying is fine, and the social life.'

'Have you spoken in the Union yet? Remember you told me that's where the future politicians were trained?'

Dick sighed. 'It's frightening sometimes, Josie. The politics of some of them horrify me.'

'What, the conscientious objectors we've been hearing so much about?'

'That, partly. But also there's far more support than one might expect for people like Oswald Mosley and his fascists.'

'I've heard that a lot of intellectuals support Hitler.'

Dick laughed. 'Not so many of the women now he's saying he'll abolish the vote for them and put them back in the kitchen where they belong!'

He fell silent, and Josie could tell that something else was worrying him. 'What is it?' she asked quietly.

'Do you know what love is, Josie?' he asked after a while.

'No. I doubt if anyone does.' He was silent and gazed into his drink. Josie waited. 'Tell me about her,' she eventually invited, her eyes dancing with amusement.

Dick looked puzzled for a moment, then laughed. 'There isn't a "her", or at least' – he hesitated, looking embarrassed – 'there are several!'

'What, several girlfriends?' Josie asked, laughing.

Dick sighed. 'It's hard to explain. I met someone within a couple of weeks of going up, and thought she was marvellous. I once thought – well, we were such pals – but before the end of term she seemed very ordinary and I'd met someone else. It kept on like that,' he said ruefully. 'Eventually I decided that as I couldn't choose between any of them, I hadn't a clue what I was doing.'

Josie was laughing openly and after a moment Dick joined in. 'You haven't been in love,' she chuckled. 'You'll probably know when you find someone to love. At least that's what Ann tells me. Now what are your plans? Are you staying in Edgbaston this vacation?'

'If only Lizzie was here,' Phoebe lamented. 'That's two Christmasses she's missed.'

'If she's still with Mrs Thackeray-Walsh next year, and down on the Riviera again, we could go and stay there too,' Clem suggested.

'Don't you want to go to Australia this next winter? I thought you planned to go every two years.'

'We could be back in France for Christmas, and Josie could come too, unless she's married by then, and Ann and William bring the nipper. How's that sound?'

'It sounds lovely,' Ann said, smiling affectionately at him. Clem, the moment he had heard about the baby, had raided all the shops. One of the bedrooms in his house was crammed with baby carriages, a cot, two trunks full of baby clothes, a huge piebald rocking horse with real hair in its mane and tail, and numerous other toys including both a doll's house and a railway set.

'If this one's a girl, there's bound to be a boy later,' he said with deep satisfaction when he showed them proudly to Ann and William.

'Don't stop him,' Phoebe had begged when William had protested quietly to her that it was too much. 'He never has the fun of buying things for his own grandchildren, except when he's in Australia with them. Let him enjoy giving you things instead.'

It was a merry Christmas Day, but Josie had difficulty in maintaining an air of contentment. She didn't know what was the matter, just that for some reason she felt restless. Yet everything was going well for her. Her business was thriving; she had her own car and was doing well in the competitions she entered; the pain of her mother's death was diminishing, though she would never forget the horrors of those last few months, or cease to regret not having been more patient with Dora. Aunt Phoebe was blooming with all the love and attention Clem showered on her, Ann was deliriously happy, and even Lizzie maintained that her job was quite sufficient for her and she wanted for nothing.

Perhaps it was seeing Phoebe and Ann so happy that made her envious of their good fortune in being loved so devotedly. She couldn't imagine what it must be like, but she had come to understand that her solitary existence was lacking in some vital ingredient. If things had been different, if she could have accepted Leo, if there had been no complications, might she have experienced that same happiness? Wearily she shook her head. Ann and Phoebe relished being protected, adored and cherished. She had no intention of ever submitting to any man in such a fashion. She had her own business now and meant to keep it. She simply couldn't imagine being nothing more than a wife and mother, however adored. She had to be independent, and if being free to arrange her own life meant that she had to live it alone, so be it. She drove home two days after Christmas feeling cold in spirit, and with less relish than normal for tackling the problems of increasing the manufacture of the special souvenirs for the Silver Jubilee.

'Don't tell either of them,' Ann advised.

'But when they find out, if one of them won't go, I'm scuppered! Why did John have to break his leg just now?'

'Darling, Josie hasn't agreed yet. You haven't asked her. But they wouldn't let you down at the last minute.'

'They'd tolerate each other? What a prospect! Teams have to work well together to be successful,' William said distractedly. 'We're fighting the snow and ice, probably fog too, and cold, and mostly in the dark because the nights are much longer in Sweden. People get dreadfully tired after three or four nights with only the odd snatches of sleep. Tempers fray and the best of friends get snappy with one another. I suspect that's why husbands and wives often drive in different teams. The last thing we need is a team whose members are at loggerheads. Why do they dislike one another so much, anyway? I used to think Leo was sweet on Josie in the early days.'

'He was. He still is, and I think she loves him too, but neither of them will accept it.'

'Are you expecting me to play Cupid?' William asked suspiciously. 'Is that why you suggested I asked Josie? I won't! The slightest sign of a lovers' quarrel and I'll throw them over the side and do all the driving myself.'

Ann was gurgling with laughter. 'You don't have a Cupid's figure,' she gasped when she could speak again. 'No, William! Not now! You have to ask Josie, there's only a week left before you must leave. Go and ask her now, she'll have so much to arrange and if you delay any longer she'll refuse, and so will anyone else with any sense.'

William sighed, then grinned like a little boy caught raiding the larder. 'Yes, ma'am,' he said dutifully. 'And if she doesn't agree I'll send you round to persuade her.'

'I can't!' Josie said in horror.

William took a deep breath. He'd marshalled his arguments carefully before presenting himself at Josie's factory. He hoped he could remember all of them now.

'Josie, I'm absolutely desperate,' he began. 'If I can't find anyone else to co-drive I'll have to withdraw.'

'There must be lots of people wanting to drive,' Josie protested.

'But not people I know and trust. You don't think I'm going to pick a name out of the advertisements in the *Autocar*, do you, and trust my precious car to them? If I have to withdraw again after I dropped out at Bournemouth it won't do my reputation any good.'

'I can't get ready in time.'

William seized on her objection. 'The RAC will get visas and passports organized. There's still lots of time to pack the things you'll need in Monte Carlo and send them ahead by the van. Rooms are already booked at the Grand there.'

'My business. I can't be away for over two weeks.'

'Tobias is perfectly capable of running that while you're away. Shall I call him in and ask him?'

'It would be fun,' she admitted wistfully. 'But William, I'm not experienced enough to do you justice. I'd spoil things for you.'

'Everyone has to start some time. Miss Anderson is only

twenty-one, and her Riley is a birthday present. She's doing it from John o' Groats. And she's in charge, she'll have to do any repairs, but you'll have no responsibility.'

'I couldn't face that,' she admitted.

'John feels so bad about letting me down, but he's done all the preliminary work with the maps, and the refuelling points are sorted out. All you have to do is drive and navigate, and then try to get some sleep. You managed several sleepless nights on the RAC Rally, you can do that. I'll be doing the final test, the wiggle-woggle –'

'The *what*?'

William laughed. 'That's what they call it. A sort of figure of eight with complications. I've been practising at the mock-up they've done at Brooklands. And my main concern is the comfort competition, as you know. It would be nice to finish the Rally in a high position, too, but it isn't really my objective to be the fastest.'

'I suppose Colin would be disappointed too,' she said slowly. 'It's his first time too, isn't it?'

'Then you'll do it? Josie, I am terribly grateful.'

'I know I'd feel guilty if I didn't.'

'I've brought a list of what to do. I'll see to the formalities, you concentrate on sending some glamorous evening dresses ahead and buying the warmest clothes you can find. You'll have to make do with just a small bag with the barest essentials, I'm afraid, and the more you can carry in your pockets the better. And get fur-lined boots and a pair of goggles.'

William picked Josie up first. 'That looks a very fetching outfit,' he commented, and Josie aimed a playful punch at his helmeted head.

'I feel such a fool in a huge fur coat, a hat which swamps me, trousers made for a man, and fur boots. The sun's shining!' she complained.

'It won't be in Sweden. There are reports of deep snow. I'll leave the hood down until it rains, you can get acclimatized!'

341

Josie shivered. 'Don't, you're making me cold already.'

He was driving towards Handsworth, but it wasn't until he drew up in front of a large double-fronted Victorian house that Josie began to look puzzled.

'I thought Colin lived in Moseley,' she said.

'Yes. I'm sorry, Josie, Colin had to withdraw. It's Leo who's coming with us.'

'Leo? Leo Bradley? William, how could you? He detests me. We always fight when we meet. William, I won't!' she declared.

'Typical Josie Shaw, won't stop to listen, let alone think.' It was Leo, standing on the steps and looking sardonically down at her.

'I won't drive with you,' she repeated.

'Josie, do it for me,' William said gently. 'Please? Ann would be so disappointed if you let me down.'

Josie struggled with her feelings. 'How long have you known?' she demanded of William.

'Before I asked you,' William admitted. 'I didn't dare tell you in case you refused to come. Look, I don't know what it is between you and Leo, but can't you pretend he's a stranger, and forget your fight for a couple of weeks?'

'I have no option, do I?' Josie said harshly. 'Good morning, Leo,' she added coldly as Leo came down the steps. 'Did you plan this between you as some sort of joke?'

'I didn't know, or believe me, I'd have objected! I take it William didn't tell you either?'

'No, he didn't.'

'I had no choice if I wished to get a good team entered,' William said curtly. 'I am willing to apologize endlessly if only you'll try to work together until this is over. But decide now: do we go on or give up right here?'

Josie looked at Leo. Suddenly he smiled and her heart did a crazy little dance. No, she wasn't frightened of him. How could she be? He meant nothing to her apart from being an extra driver. She held out her hand and he grasped it tightly in his.

'Pax?' he asked softly. 'We'll resume the war after we get to Monte.'

She laughed and William smiled broadly. 'Get in the back, then. There's not much room but you'll have to put up with it.'

Leo stepped on to the running-board and, disdaining the rear passenger door, stepped over the low side into the back seat. '*Allons-y*', he said.

Chapter Twenty-Two

'What did they call this?' Josie asked, helping herself to more of the pickled herring and stuffed eggs laid on on the long table. 'And whatever's in that dish?' she added, pointing.

'The buffet's *smorgasbord*, and those are smoked eels. Delicious. Want some?' William asked.

Josie grinned. 'Why not? I'm committed now, I'm determined to make the most of this experience.'

She looked round at the other people on board the steamer. When they'd come aboard at Gravesend she'd been intrigued to see some of the men and women she'd met on previous rallies, and gratified when they remembered her and welcomed her as a friend. It all seemed like one big club, with no hint of the fierce competition that was before them spoiling the camaraderie. When the dulcimer had sounded for dinner, instead of the bugle which William had told her to expect, Josie felt she was entering a dreamlike state which would end only when she returned to Hockley.

During the journey, William had tried to tell them as much as possible about the rules, their fellow competitors, and the tricks he had discovered the previous year which might gain them precious seconds, even save the whole enterprise from failure. She hadn't been able to take it all in but William was patient, she knew he would tell them again when it mattered.

Leo had been cool but businesslike, and Josie's initial shock when she'd realized he'd be joining them had faded. They could work together, and she silently vowed she wouldn't permit their personal differences to damage this trip which meant so much to William.

At Gothenburg, thankful to be free of the buffeting the North Sea had given them, they set off northwards, a jolly procession of cars threading their way along roads kept clear of snow by huge ploughs. There was more snow than Josie had ever seen before, piled yards high on either side of the road. Once out in the countryside she could scarcely take her eyes off the snow-covered forests, the vast mountains and the hundreds of frozen lakes. The intense silence was broken only by the roars of finely tuned engines.

'These chains are useless,' William declared after a few miles. 'We can't go fast enough in them, they just break when we speed up. Can you drive without them, do you think?' he asked Leo.

'So long as I don't have to brake hard,' Leo said cheerfully.

Josie helped take off the chains, something she hadn't done before, and they made better speed towards Stockholm where they were to stay the night. Then came the final lap to Umeå, almost at the end of the Gulf of Bothnia, less than two hundred miles from the Arctic Circle. There they could rest in between making the final checks on the cars.

'We have a dinner-dance at the hotel tonight,' William told them as they were once more checking the spares.

'In these clothes?' Josie asked, horrified, looking down at her warm, practical but decidedly unglamorous thick tweed trousers and heavy Aran jumper.

'You brought a skirt, didn't you? I allowed space for that to preserve your modesty!'

She chuckled suddenly. 'I don't suppose anyone else is better-equipped. And I do have three blouses on under this jumper. I'll manage. I've sorted the maps into order, they're clipped under the navigation table, with the route card on top. There are spare batteries and bulbs for the light in the glove compartment, together with watch and compass and so on, and all the phrase books. I've kept the route book, the papers for Customs and the currency in my room.'

'Keep me the first dance,' Leo said suddenly.

Josie glanced at him uncertainly. He'd been checking the tool kit on the far side of the car and she hadn't known he was listening. She swallowed hard. She didn't know if she wanted to dance with Leo again. Yet she couldn't refuse to dance with a member of her own crew. They'd agreed a truce. 'OK, Leo,' she replied, grateful that her voice sounded normal and didn't waver.

'Why is Kay in such a temper?' Josie asked later in the evening, looking across the brilliantly lit room to where the beautiful Kay Petre was haranguing her co-drivers mercilessly.

Josie's current dancing partner, a large Norwegian who, Josie was thankful to find, spoke competent English, laughed. 'Sammy and Charles have been charging us a *krone* each to dance with her. I believe she has just discovered it.'

Josie laughed. 'She has that delicate air, and such a butter won't melt in her mouth look, you wouldn't think she could race at Brooklands, or do these long rallies.'

'I am told she lapped Brooklands at one hundred thirty miles an hour. But Mrs Petre has a huge temper in that small body. I would not like to anger her.'

'It vanishes as quickly as it comes.'

'And now I must give you up to your man. He does not like that I monopolize you.'

Josie turned swiftly, almost colliding with Leo. He was grinning, clearly having heard the Norwegian's last words, and she flushed. 'I'm dancing with —' she began hurriedly, then stopped, staring at the doorway in blank amazement. 'What are they doing here?'

Leo turned to look. 'Good God!' he exclaimed. 'I didn't know Matthew Horobin was driving.'

'Nor Freddy! How on earth did he contrive to come?'

'Matthew and Freddy are crewing for Bob Jenkins,' William told them as they were waiting for their turn to leave. 'He owns a garage in London. His car's the big Singer, the red one. One of his team had to drop out at the last minute.'

'They're before us,' Leo said. 'They'll be off in a few minutes.'

'They've both taken care to avoid us,' Josie said looking at the cars in front of her, the crews milling round in last-minute bustle, watched by a huge crowd. It was snowing but she was thankful the blizzard conditions which had been reported a week ago had ceased.

Then it was their turn to start. 'Good luck!' William said as he scrambled, with some difficulty, into a sleeping bag stretched out over the back seat and pulled the two extra blankets and the scuttle canvas hood over him. 'If we're not fast enough to catch the ice-breaker don't worry, we can get the next ferry. Wake me up in four hours.'

Josie was navigating for the first stretch. Apart from the icy roads, the first part of the race was relatively easy. William's various heating devices and her thick clothes kept her warm, and the only problem was manipulating the maps and the instruments while wearing gloves. She felt utterly confident in Leo's ability to control the car, and though he drove fast when the roads were straight he was cautious enough round bends and used the gears to slow down rather than the brakes. They passed one car which had slid off the road, but the crew were using the unditching gear and winching the car back. They waved away Leo's offer of help.

'That tree looked solid enough, they won't uproot it like the girls did,' Leo said with a laugh.

'At least they aren't tied to a pillar,' Josie chuckled, recalling another crew practising in Umeå who had almost demolished a building.

After Hudiksvall William drove, and Josie tried to sleep in the back seat. She discovered that there was barely room to lie down, and none to stretch out or even turn over once she had managed to tuck herself in. How on earth could she endure almost a hundred hours, four days and three nights, of this? She was too excited to sleep but she tried to force herself to relax. It was difficult, for the road was a slippery switchback with a high camber and deep snow-filled ditches to either side, and many slow-moving timber-lorries were using it. Once or twice she thought they would be blown off the road when a vicious side-wind caught them, but William rushed the gradients and held on grimly round the corners, countering the lack of adhesion in the chainless tyres.

Then came disaster. Josie, her eyes closed and a woolly scarf pulled over her face, saw nothing. She had felt the car gather speed down the slope, then Leo shouted a warning and Josie was almost thrown out as the car swerved, bucked fiercely over a series of bumps, and then spun round in a dizzying whirling of twists and turns before sliding to a halt. Cautiously she sat up.

'What happened?'

'Damned car was stopped on the bend,' William said angrily. 'I didn't have time to see who it was, but it was red and had Monte plates on. Of all the idiotic places to stop!'

'They've driven off,' Leo said. 'The fools haven't even waited to ask if we're OK, or offer help.' He was standing on the running-board looking backwards. Josie looked round, and her eyes widened as she worked out that they were sitting on the ice covering a small lake.

'Will it hold us?' she asked nervously, shivering.

'It has so far,' William replied reassuringly. 'If it can withstand the thump I gave it coming down the bank it won't break now. I might even be able to drive back up to the road, it looks like a track over there, and a boat-house.'

He proved right. They regained the road and reached Stockholm in time to rest for an hour and have a meal at the Automobile Club before the next stage to Helsingborg, where they and the crews who had started from Stavanger were able to snatch more rest on the huge, train-carrying ferry which transported them to Denmark.

Mabel, teetering on high heels and struggling to manage a huge suitcase, fought her way to the barrier which led to the boat-train platform. She'd had a job, but at last she'd persuaded Freddy it was her due, and he'd got her tickets. She'd have such a time in Monte Carlo! She was excited about this, her first trip abroad, and she'd indulged in an extravagant shopping spree to fit herself out with clothes she deemed appropriate to the French Riviera, but she was blowed if she'd pay a layabout porter to carry her luggage. She was saving every penny she had left for the Casino. She dumped her case and fished in her handbag, finally producing the wad of tickets Freddy had given her. With a smile she meant to be condescending she handed them over to the ticket-collector. 'You sort 'em out fer me,' she ordered.

He looked down at them, flipped through, then looked more carefully at each separate piece of paper.

'Sorry, love,' he said, holding them out to her, 'these ain't the right tickets.'

'What? What the bleedin' 'ell d'yer mean, not the right tickets?'

He pushed them into her hand. 'These are just useless bits of paper. Now please move so that the passengers can come past.'

'But I was giv' 'em!' Mabel protested, not properly understanding. 'Freddy, 'e said they was all there, special papers fer Customs an' so on. What d'yer mean, useless?'

'Someone's played a joke on you, love. They don't look nothing like tickets, they're just typewritten bits of paper with names and dates scribbled in. Sorry, but you've been had.'

One of the despised porters came and moved Mabel gently aside. 'Come on, luv, come an' 'ave a nice cuppa.'

'The return ticket to Birmingham's valid enough,' the ticket-collector said, intending to be kind.

Mabel suddenly came back to life and rounded on the porter. 'Yer can stuff yer bloody cuppa! 'E's cheated me, the dirty sod! After all I've done fer 'im this is 'ow 'e pays me back! When 'e gets 'ome I'll kill 'im! I'll twist 'is bollocks off, I will, an' choke 'im with 'em! Freddy Preece, yer ain't gonna do this ter me! Just you wait till I get me 'ands on yer!'

All Josie saw of Copenhagen was the Control, where Sammy Davies, the left wing of his big Railton crumpled and the light out, was explaining that some car had shot across their path from a side road without stopping and Kay had averted disaster by seconds, just clipping the carrier. 'But the wheels are out of track and we haven't time to do repairs now. We'll have to make up some time first.'

The roads in Denmark were even more slippery, and Josie had to become accustomed to driving on the right. They had no problem finding the way since boy scouts were on every corner with illuminated arrows, and every five kilometres placards showed distances to the ferries. She was thankful for the respites on the ferries, but when they ran into dense fog was relieved it was Leo's turn to drive, even though she had to hang out over the side of the car peering at the far verge as she helped him keep on the road. They knew they were following some of the other cars. At the last stop Donald Healey in his rather peculiar Triumph, on to which he had fitted specially large wheels to improve ground clearance, had been just in front of them.

Suddenly Josie jumped in alarm. A hideous, shrill scream whistled through the darkness. 'What on earth's that?' she gasped, and William in the back woke up and began to ask questions. Before anyone could reply they heard the sound of crunching metal, and then Josie was tumbling over the side of the car as Leo swung it violently round to avoid the shapes looming up out of the dense fog.

She lay for a moment, dazed and bruised, then Leo was beside her. 'Josie! My God, darling, are you all right? Don't move! You may have broken your arm! Are you able to move it?' he demanded, kneeling beside her and gently putting his arms round her shoulders as she struggled to sit up.

William had scrambled out and was also kneeling beside her. 'What the devil was that unearthly noise?'

'I'm fine, no bones broken,' Josie said, rather shaken. Had she imagined that Leo had called her 'darling'? Her fur hat had cushioned the blow to her head as she'd hit the ground and rolled, so she couldn't have concussion. 'Let me get up. I can hear shouts. Let's see what's going on.'

They went towards the noise, Leo solicitously supporting Josie, and came upon a scene of horror. The front of Healey's car was a mangled wreck, and looming over it was a long train, ghostly faces peering down from faintly lit windows. The train driver and the crew of the following car, which had stopped abruptly and caused Leo to swerve, were already there and one of them was helping Donald Healey out of the Triumph.

'You mean you're not hurt? That's a miracle! What about Pearce?'

'Supercharger's seizing! That's what we thought the noise was. Some supercharger!' came a voice from inside, and Healey's co-driver, Lewis Pearce, scrambled out of the wreck. 'I suppose it was one of these damned unmanned level crossings. I think I've lost a tooth,' he added calmly, putting a hand up to his face.

They were over the border into Germany, through Hamburg almost without stopping, and to Hanover where the officials were in full uniform, with interpreters ready to deal with every competitor's needs. Josie stared in amazement as armed men on huge motorcycles prepared to guide them through the city. It was her turn to drive and she could barely keep up with them as they swept along, all other traffic kept rigorously out of the way.

'Why are so many people saluting?' she asked William quietly, though no one could have overheard her.

'The military discipline. It's everywhere in Germany now,' he replied soberly. 'I dread their efficiency if they ever again decide to go to war.'

Josie shivered, and looked unamused at the contortions of the traffic policeman, hampered by his sabre, almost dancing through a series of manoeuvres which culminated in a *Heil Hitler* salute.

After Brussels, the weather eased, and the snow and ice of real winter weather was left behind at Mons. 'We'll have no more huge drifts through France,' William promised. 'It might snow but it won't be much.'

Josie slept through Paris, apart from a bleary-eyed appearance at the Control to sign the route book. By now she was so exhausted after her four-hour spells of driving, followed by the intense concentration of navigating over unfamiliar territory, usually in the dark, that she didn't notice the discomfort of the small back seat whenever she had a chance to crawl thankfully into it. She now appreciated William's dictum that after sleeping they had to drive, so that the navigator would be fully awake for what was the trickiest task.

'You can drive half-asleep, but you can't read a map,' Leo had said, 'or see those damned small street nameplates they have in France.'

Josie had scant leisure to ponder Leo's attitude. Over the miles his features had relaxed, his earlier self-conscious manner towards her had changed to the same friendly joking or shouting of instructions or comments he used towards William. And when she'd been thrown out of the car he'd called her 'darling'. She didn't know what to think about it. Long ago she'd decided to forget Leo, to suppress her own strong attraction to him. She wouldn't think about it. It had probably been an involuntary exclamation, or in her dazed state she'd imagined it. She certainly had no intention of thinking any more about it.

They had a couple of hours to spare at Lyons, and staggered to the hotel nearest to the Control where they found food and members of the other crews trying to snatch some sleep, rolled up in blankets on the floor or, where possible, sprawled in chairs.

'Why the devil do we do it?' Leo muttered as he and Josie found a corner in one of the lounges where there was space to stretch out.

'Because it's fun,' Josie said, then gave a gigantic yawn and promptly fell asleep.

As Leo rolled himself into a blanket and lay down beside her he looked at her, a tender smile on his lips. She was fun, her enjoyment was infectious, and just being with her made him feel more alive.

Josie woke an hour later to find William shaking her arm. 'Come on, some strong black coffee and buttered rolls, then we must be off.'

There were a number of other competitors eating in the small room where the food had been laid out, among them Matthew and Freddy, who left the moment Josie and the two men walked in. She was too weary to think about it. They and Bob Jenkins, who owned the Singer they were driving, had avoided her at every Control, and Josie had just been thankful not to have to speak to them. Now she listened to the talk flowing about her. Some crews were bad-temperedly arguing about the problems they'd encountered, blaming one another for inattention or incompetence. Josie tried to ignore them and listen to the other, friendlier snatches of conversation as the crews compared notes. The major routes converged at Lyons and people were eager to discover news of their friends.

'Ferreiras ditched his Railton. So did Norman Black in the Singer, but he had to retire.'

'Stanley Barnes dug his Singer out OK.'

'Hear about Rupert Riley? His car went over a cliff. Caught on a bush, they were damned lucky to get out. Nearly pulled the car back too, but it got dislodged and went right down a precipice.'

'I don't know why anyone bothers with Athens, they rarely get through and it doesn't carry any more marks now.'

'I hear they've had three feet of snow and ten degrees of frost near Bucharest. No one will get through from there this year.'

'Whalley's lucky. He ditched the Ford, but Cathcart-Jones and his Lagonda crew pulled them out.'

'Hear about Harry Symons? He hit a cyclist near Copenhagen and nearly got lynched. Police let him go, though.'

Many of the comments were about Donald Healey's miraculous escape, and Josie found everyone eager to hear the details.

'So that's him for this year. Pity about the Dolomite, that looks like a good model for Triumph. Still, he's had a first, second and third since '31. It gives the rest of us a chance.'

It was an easy run to Avignon, though everyone was suffering from the lack of sleep. Josie couldn't appreciate the wide Rhône valley, or the massive walls of the old papal city. She shivered in the cold mistral that was blowing, setting the lights dancing in front of the Control. One day, she sleepily promised herself, she might come back and see some of these places they'd whisked through.

'The last stretch now,' William said with unabated cheerfulness. 'Are we on the RN7?'

Josie peered out, looking for the red-topped kilometre stone. 'Yes, we're OK.'

'We have to maintain a faster average speed from now on, thirty-five miles an hour, but that shouldn't be a problem unless we have very bad weather. It's Aix-en-Provence, then the last Control at Brignoles, over the Esterels and into the sun!' Josie smiled at him and nodded. He was so calm, nothing bothered him, but he kept them under strict control. From some of the bad-tempered exchanges she'd overheard in Lyons she knew other teams didn't always get along so well, and was grateful to him. She was more tired than she'd ever been before in her life, but it was still tremendously exciting and she wouldn't have missed it for anything.

'Why did they put in this Control?' one of the old hands asked. The crews were sitting on the few seats available or standing about in the central square of Brignoles, a long, triangular space surrounded by tall thin houses, into which they'd debouched from the narrow, winding main street shortly before. The café owner was serving hot drinks, and doing a roaring trade. It was still very cold, despite the Mediterranean being so short a distance away.

'To hold us up,' someone replied. 'It stops us bunching on the final section. There used to be some fine queues going down into Monaco.'

'Are we really almost there?' Josie asked, wonder in her voice. 'I can hardly believe it!'

'We'll see dawn breaking as we come down in Cannes,' William promised. 'Come on, we'd better go and get the route book signed. Only ten minutes before we're due to leave.'

Josie was driving but William had decreed that now they took spells of an hour only, since they were all so tired. He'd filled up every vacuum flask they possessed with hot strong coffee, and, despite the cold, pushed up the windscreen so that the wind blew straight into their faces. Then it was Leo's turn, and William made them take a short, brisk walk before they resumed. Soon they came to the steep, twisty roads of the Esterel mountains, and the big cork oaks which covered the slopes threw strange shadows in the light of the headlamps. It was snowing again, and the roads were icy. They could see deep gorges to the sides, and occasionally through the trees or across the hidden valleys the lights of other cars which sometimes, because of all the hairpin bends in the road, appeared to be going the wrong way.

They saw it at the same time, and as Josie clutched the side of the car Leo stamped on the brake. The car slewed round and for a moment appeared to teeter towards the unguarded edge and the steep drop beneath, but Leo wrenched at the wheel, and by a superb exhibition of heeling and toeing managed to bring it to a halt inches from the edge.

Before he cut the engine William leapt over the side of the car. He ran to the front and bent down, then spoke, his tone a mixture of bewilderment and fury. 'It's a rope, stretched across the road, tied to these trees. It must have been rigged up in the last few minutes, or someone in front of us would have run into it.'

'They might have done and gone over the drop,' Josie said, breathing deeply as she struggled to calm her racing heart.

'We'd have heard any crash,' Leo said curtly. 'And whoever played such a damn fool trick must be still around.'

'Pull forwards, slowly, away from the edge, while I cut the rope,' William said calmly, and began to follow the rope towards the trees on the slope above them as Leo fired the engine. Josie was peering anxiously at the steep drop almost directly below her side of the car, and looked towards William only when Leo shouted a warning.

Two men had emerged from the shadows and as William, becoming aware of the danger, turned to face them, they attacked him with what looked like heavy clubs. He raised his arms to protect his head, and Josie heard the snap of a bone. Then she gasped as Leo swung the Lagonda and drove it at the attackers, forcing them to leap hurriedly aside and scuttle back into the trees.

Chapter Twenty-Three

'CANNES is the nearest place where we'll find a doctor,' Leo repeated as he helped William into the car. His broken arm was supported by branches they'd hacked off the cork trees, and bandaged by one of the crew in the next car to come along seconds after the attack.

'Monaco is only another hour's drive. We're going to finish now we've come this far!' William insisted, biting his lip.

'Your arm needs to be set properly,' Josie tried to persuade him.

'An hour will make no difference. I'm not bleeding to death. We'd be delayed for hours and I have not gone through all this to be thwarted at the last moment by either murderous thugs or over-solicitous friends. If you won't drive I'll do it myself.'

Josie would have tried further persuasions but Leo shrugged. 'OK, so we'd better get on. If I do the rest of the mountain stretch, Josie, can you do the final run along the Corniche?'

'Of course.' She was no longer tired. There was too much to think about. In the brief seconds when Leo had been aiming the car at William's attackers she had caught a glimpse of them. They'd worn hats pulled well down over their eyes and scarves covered their lower faces, but she had recognized Freddy by his general shape and the way he moved. At least she thought she had. Was she certain enough to challenge him once they were at

Monte Carlo? And if Freddy had been involved, Matthew and the owner of their car must be too. Faintly she recalled hearing the sound of another engine as they'd been running towards William. But why would any of them want to attack William, even try to murder him? And was it William they were really after? It could be Leo, or even her.

As Leo drove cautiously along the twisting road, now visible in the frosty dawn light, and later gleaming as the sun rose in front of them, Josie cast her mind back to the other accident which had befallen them. Had that been a deliberate attempt to injure them, or was it just rivalry to eliminate them from the Rally? Or had it been pure accident, quite unconnected with this deliberate ambush? She'd been asleep and caught no sight of the car which had caused it. Neither Leo nor William could say from their brief glimpse what make it was, as it had been covered with snow, but they thought it could be red. Freddy's car was red. The only other detail they had noticed was the distinctive rally plate attached above the number plate.

Their delight as they came down from the mountains into brilliant sunshine, the blue sea sparkling beyond the palm-fringed shore, hundreds of boats visible in Cannes harbour, all over-looked by luxury hotels and villas, was tempered by these worrying reflections. William was the only one to express his satisfaction at having completed the Rally proper. 'We'll stop in Nice, I've arranged it with a garage there, we can go over the car.'

'We have to get to Monaco and a doctor as fast as possible,' Josie objected.

'We have to make the car ready for the final tests,' William said sharply. 'Once in Monte Carlo it's locked away in an open park and we have no chance to touch it before the braking and acceleration test tomorrow. It's a cold start, so the engine's got to be tuned properly and the battery charged. I can't do more than watch, you'll have to check the brakes and so on, and make sure everything is working, replace lamps, do whatever we can. We'll also get rid of all the surplus spares.'

'You could see a doctor while we're doing that,' Josie suggested, but William shook his head impatiently.

'There simply isn't time. As it is, Leo's going to have to drive in the wiggle-woggle test.'

'I know,' Leo said grimly. 'You practised it on that mock-up at Brooklands, but I don't even know the shape!'

William gave a shout of laughter. 'From the colourful cursing at Brooklands I'm not sure knowing it's much of an advantage. Some of the professionals were making a dreadful hash of it so I doubt if you'll disgrace us.'

Josie had time as they drove along the Promenade des Anglais to admire the hotels overlooking the sea, the broad road lined with palms, the elegant people strolling along in the warm sunshine. Then William directed her away from the coast to a quiet street where two friendly mechanics were awaiting them in a small garage.

Josie checked the spares under William's supervision while Leo delved under the bonnet. In an amazingly short time they were ready to depart once more, and Josie took the wheel for the final few miles along the spectacular Corniche. She admired the deep bay of Villefranche, the imposing promontory of Cap Ferrat, and joined the procession of cars moving slowly down the hill towards the triumphal arch which welcomed them to the glittering, flag-bedecked, bunting-strewn principality ruled by the Grimaldis for over six hundred years.

Then it was all bustle and confusion as the officials on the Quai de Plaisance welcomed them, checked the official seals, weighed and measured the cars, and directed them to the park where the cars, the hoods of the open ones all raised, were placed in two long rows ready to be locked up under guard overnight. Leo transferred the minimal amount of personal luggage they had carried to a taxi, while Josie arranged with a friendly official that a doctor be summoned to the Grand hotel as soon as possible. They drove up the steep hill on the far side of the harbour, catching a side-on glimpse of the imposing Casino, and turned into the Place Beau Marchais where two of the large hotels used by the crews, the Hermitage facing the square and the Grand on one corner next to it, were busy welcoming them. Josie was drooping with fatigue, but still able to admire the magnificence of the marble-pillared foyer of the Grand, and the efficiency of the liveried staff who welcomed them.

'I've booked a suite, there should be champagne waiting, and then your doctor will be in attendance and you can go to bed,' William announced with an affectionate grin at Josie. 'Thanks, both of you. You've been magnificent!'

Josie thought she would sleep for a week, especially after draining the largest glass of champagne she'd ever seen, but she woke early, stiff, refreshed and eager to see more of this enchanting place. Leo and William, the latter with his arm now professionally strapped up and in a sling, were already having breakfast in their sitting room.

'William, how's your arm? I ought to have stayed with you while the doctor set it,' Josie said remorsefully.

'Leo was a competent substitute,' William said cheerfully. 'You needed a long soak in the bath.'

Josie grimaced. 'That was the worst of it, no chance for a proper wash even. And was I glad to see my other luggage and change into fresh clothes! How are you?'

'The break's a clean one, no problems. He even allowed me to have a bath. Help yourself to coffee, and the rest of breakfast is on that trolley. I was just going over the wiggle-woggle course with Leo,' he added, indicating the large sheet of paper spread out before them. 'The cars are pushed to the starting line, then on "Go" when the flag is dropped each driver has to run for the car, get in, start from cold, and go as fast as possible for the finishing line a couple of car lengths away. Then off to the Quai Albert Premier for the final test.'

'That's the central bit, facing the sea?' Josie asked.

'Yes. There's a wider crescent-shaped section where the course is laid out. The wiggle-woggle is a combination of fast acceleration, doing a tightish figure of eight, reversing round barrels, and braking. Here's a drawing.'

Josie looked at the sketch and shuddered. 'Good luck!' she said. 'Rather you than me. But this means everything is decided on this test alone?'

William nodded. 'Most of the competitors will have got here without losing any points. The six longest routes carry the maximum, a thousand, so only drivers who started from them stand any chance of winning. Other points are added with these tests, but the winner need be only a second faster than anyone else to come out top.'

'It seems rather strange, after coming two and a half thousand miles through snow and blizzards.'

'Winning would be great, but most people are happy just to have taken part,' William said.

'Yes, I do understand that, and I'll be forever grateful to you for asking me,' Josie said fervently.

'Have some more coffee and then let's go.'

As the taxi halted, a worried-looking official came up to them.

'Mr Scott? Please will you all come with me?'

'What's the matter?' William asked as he began to lead them towards the parked cars.

'Nothing, I hope. I'm afraid that despite the guard we kept last night an intruder was caught near your car. We wish you to supervise us – as you may not touch it yourself, of course – as we check that nothing has been interfered with.'

'Are you certain it was my car he was after?' William demanded.

'No, but that is the one he was near and it appeared that he was trying to reach under it.'

'Who is he?' Josie asked slowly. Was it Freddy?

'An Englishman, I'm afraid, but he refuses to give his name. We cannot believe it is another competitor, but what other explanation is there? Why should anyone take the risk of being caught here if his purpose is to damage your car, when he could do that at any time afterwards? When today's events are concluded, perhaps you will see him and tell us if you know who he is.'

William watched intently as the officials went over the Lagonda, until they were all satisfied that nothing had been touched. Several other cars nearby were also being inspected by officials, worried owners watching and speculating about the reasons for such an attempt. Finally, all were declared safe and ready for the competition. William and Josie wished Leo good luck and went to take their places in the grandstand which had been erected on the Quai, overlooking the square-shaped harbour, with a backdrop of steep, protective hills.

Wild theories about possible sabotage were flying round amongst the spectators. Apart from a muttered aside to Josie that it was probably the mysterious people who had attacked him the previous day, William was silent and Josie overheard much of the gossip.

'Humphrey Symons's Magnette had flat batteries, the switch controlling the current had been turned off. That ruined the cold start. Wonder if it was the saboteur?'

'Someone started too early from Brignoles. They'll be disqualified, surely?'

'Grant-Ferris's Bentley has a damaged wing, it's rubbing on the tyre.'

'That's unsafe, surely?'

'So he's told them, but the rules say no repairs are allowed.'

'Charles Brackenbury's taxi was in a crash on the way to his hotel yesterday, but he wasn't hurt.'

'I hear most of the warming lamps left under the bonnets went out.'

'And the rugs on top can't be moved. I hope they don't slip and foul the wheels.'

In between worrying whether Freddy had been the saboteur, and anticipating what might happen to him, Josie was looking at the complicated course laid out before her. Gradually it became clearer. First a fast straight run, then the figure of eight which included reversing round a barrel, another fast section and a second reverse, then a final straight. It tested the manoeuvrability of the cars as well as their powers of acceleration and braking, and it seemed to her that the smaller, lighter cars would fare better than the cumbersome giants.

As the first car began, Josie forgot Freddy and concentrated on willing Leo to do well.

'It doesn't look so bad after all,' William said as the second car completed the run successfully.

'It's Grant-Ferris next,' someone behind them said.

The big Bentley set off. And then on the first turn the damaged wing threw the steering out of control and Josie watched in horror as the car slid inexorably towards the far end of the grandstand. In slow motion, the car crashed heavily into the first tier, which seemed to give a weary sigh before gently collapsing. As shocked spectators cried out and officials ran to help, the second and then the third tier crumbled.

Fortunately, few people were hurt, and with only minor injuries. While they waited for the wooden grandstand section to be repaired Josie and William were able to look about them and Josie really saw Monaco for the first time. 'I don't imagine bankers and shopkeepers relish climbing these hills too often!'

The rumours had started again. 'Hear Madame Mareuse skidded and had a head-on crash. The other car caught fire.'

Someone chuckled. 'Wish I'd been at Le Mans. There was a fire there too.'

'What's so funny?'

'The driver, a girl, suddenly stopped and leapt out and started stripping. They'd been trying out underwear heated electrically from the accumulator. It had shorted and was on fire!'

'Madame Hustinx has been disqualified for leaving Brignoles fifteen minutes early.'

'So has Bob Jenkins. He left even earlier, I hear.'

'Didn't do them any good, Cathcart-Jones got here half an hour before anyone else in his Lagonda.'

'He must think he's flying in one of his air races!'

Josie didn't hear any more. The reference to Bob Jenkins had re-activated her fears that Freddy had been involved in the attempt to wreck their car. To start from a Control early was foolish if a competitor was seriously interested in winning, for it meant automatic disqualification. But maybe they'd needed time to look at the road and select a suitable spot for the ambush. Then one of them would have had to find a lookout from where they could both identify William's car and signal to their accomplices ahead that the target was approaching. Having failed, Freddy must have risked trying to do something in the overnight parking compound.

She tried once more to concentrate. Many more competitors lost marks by not understanding the course. Symons was fast but hit the sandbags at the second reverse, and an Alvis went out of control but fortunately came to rest on the sandbags instead of in the grandstand. Trevaux, one of the favourites, swerved in his Alfa as he braked at the end of the first straight, and also hit the sandbags. The big Railtons were fast but their braking was erratic.

'The Renaults are good, look at how they're sliding through the turns,' William exclaimed.

'It's Leo next,' Josie said, and clenching her fists, leant forward to urge him on.

Despite his lack of practice, Leo had remembered the complicated course. He made no errors, did not have to reverse to achieve the turns, and controlled the Lagonda superbly. He was not, however, fast enough to hope to be amongst the winners. When the final marks were counted a Renault from Stavanger was first, and Ridley, who had been with them from Umeå, won the small car class in his two-seater Triumph and was second overall. To Josie's delight a woman, Jackie Astbury, had beaten all the men to win the group prize from John o' Groats.

'You were magnificent, Leo,' William said when they were able to find him again.

'Thanks. I was relieved just to get round.'

'Well done,' Josie added.

'William, the officials have just told me the fellow they caught in the *parc fermé* has escaped. They put him in some room, not a proper cell, and he got out of the window. I imagine by now he's miles away.'

'Damn! We'll probably never know who he is now,' William said in annoyance.

Josie felt a guilty stab of relief. She had no sympathy for Freddy, indeed she'd like to strangle him with her bare hands if he had been responsible, but it would be hard for Aunt Phoebe if he were convicted and imprisoned in a French jail.

'A rest day tomorrow, thank goodness!' Leo exclaimed as they drove back to the Grand with Lizzie, who'd found them earlier.

'What do you mean, rest?' William demanded. 'I can't do much with one hand so you two will have to work doubly hard, scraping off the mud and polishing the bodywork until there isn't a speck on it! Everything's got to gleam, including the engine. No oil, every crack and crevice totally free from mud or dust or anything else.'

'Slave driver!' Josie groaned.

Leo chuckled, casually throwing an arm round her shoulders and hugging her.

'Not to mention all my devices which have to be in perfect order,' William continued. 'Every tool polished, any paint chips touched up, everything laid out and accessible, hot-water heaters filled, food boxes replenished. Perhaps you'd best not go to bed tonight, get started on it straight away.'

'How is Ann?' Lizzie demanded, cutting ruthlessly into this

catalogue of essential tasks. 'She wrote to tell me about the baby. I'm so pleased for you both.'

'I'm delighted,' William said, suddenly serious. 'I'm longing to get back to her.'

For the rest of their time together Lizzie chatted happily about her plans. She had finally decided that she wanted to see more of the world, and found herself a new position with an elderly American lady. She'd written to Phoebe, and her mother had given her blessing. William asked her if she knew Freddy had been driving with Matthew.

'No, I didn't, but my dear brother rarely tells any of us what he's up to. Usually it's something dubious,' she added caustically.

'Since they were disqualified for leaving Brignoles too early I imagine they'll be leaving here in disgrace,' Josie said quickly.

They'd explained the attack during which William's arm had been broken, but made as light of it as they could, trying to imply that it had been more accidental than deliberate. Lizzie seemed to accept this.

'Lizzie, promise me you won't say a word to Ann or your mother, or anyone at home, until I can get back and show Ann I'm relatively unharmed?' William said urgently.

'Of course not. How long will it take you to drive back?'

'We can't leave till after the prize-giving on Sunday, and we'll take it more easily this time, especially with only two drivers. We could get back by Wednesday.'

'If you can't drive anyway, why don't you go by train and leave Leo and Josie to drive home?' Lizzie suggested.

'That's an idea! And you could put your other luggage in the back seat, perhaps stay in Paris for a few days. Would you?' William asked, turning eagerly towards Leo.

'Of course they will,' Lizzie declared, refusing to meet Josie's eye.

Josie was nonplussed by the suggestion. During the Rally she and Leo had gradually recovered their old friendly relationship, working together well, knowing almost by instinct what the other was about to say or do. Any lingering antagonism had long vanished, and she had to admit she had enjoyed his company. The thought of several days alone together, though, without the stresses of the Rally or William's calming presence, unnerved her. They'd have nothing to talk about except the recent journey. All too soon the old arguments would surface. Before she could think of an appropriate reply Leo spoke.

'Of course we'll do it, old chap. You can get a sleeper leaving on Sunday and be home in no time. Josie and I will have a marvellous trip, I'm sure. Won't we, Josie?'

Josie had no time to think about the homeward journey on the following day. She was far too busy getting the Lagonda ready for the Concours de Confort to be judged on the Casino terrace. William, when he wasn't giving her and Leo more instructions, wandered round inspecting other cars, coming back at intervals to describe the various wonderful gadgets he'd seen and wished he'd thought of first.

'I must fit special pockets in the upholstery,' he said once. 'Pascoe's Talbot has them for vacuum flasks, but I can think of other things which would fit in if they were specially made. And Minshall had his route card fixed on rollers. We're not going to win, but we'll do quite well, I hope. My heating system's better-designed than most, and the windscreen wipers are much faster, and the luggage space is more conveniently arranged, without silly gimmicks that take up too much room like let-down washbasins!'

'Go away!' Leo said at one point. 'If you don't I'll down tools and catch the train home myself.'

'I'll go if you can spare Josie for half an hour. There's something I want to show her, ask her opinion on.'

He led Josie towards one of the other cars, being lovingly burnished. 'Look at that badge,' he said pointing. 'Most car badges are cheap metal with enamel colours on them. I'm sure that one's silver. I've never thought of it before, but some people might pay for a really exclusive design on their own cars. What do you think?'

'It is attractive,' she agreed. 'When you say "exclusive" do you mean unique? Or just something priced highly only a few people will be willing to pay for it?'

'I had meant priced highly, but would it cost a great deal more to have a different design for each customer?'

'Yes, a lot more, but there are ways we could alter the basic designs fairly easily, such as incorporating initials or personal motifs that could be engraved or added afterwards to specification. I'd have to talk to Tobias. And I'd like to look at this one more closely to see how it's made.'

'I'll go and make your excuses to Leo! Take all the time you need, we're almost finished.'

Josie, deep in thought, was walking slowly back towards the Grand, through the gardens which stretched past the Café de Paris in front of the Casino, when she heard her name called. 'Psst! Josie!'

'Who is it?' she asked, suddenly realizing that it was getting dark, and there were deep shadows where the lights didn't penetrate below the trees.

'Me.'

'Freddy!' she exclaimed. 'What are you doing here? If they see you it'll mean prison!'

'I know! Blasted Matthew 'Orobin! Gets me ter tek all the risks an' then disowns me. Josie, what am I goin' ter do? I ain't got no money, not even ter get back 'ome.'

Josie was thinking rapidly. Much as she blamed Freddy for her own misfortunes, he was Aunt Phoebe's son and could still hurt her. And they still had no idea why they'd been attacked. Freddy could tell her. 'It wouldn't help you, unless you could explain away why you were trying to sabotage the cars. Did you try to ditch us in Sweden?'

Freddy nodded miserably. 'But we dain't mean any 'arm! Matthew just wanted ter put Leo out of the runnin', 'e's got a grudge from the time he worked for 'im.'

'Is that the only reason?' Josie asked, incredulous. 'It was always Matthew in the wrong then.'

'Leo stopped 'im earnin' on the side, mekin' them car bits an such. An' 'e's 'ad a grudge against Scott since 'e knocked 'im down. That proper riled 'im when 'e were chucked in the pond. 'E don't like lookin' silly.'

'What about the rope? That could have killed us all!'

'I dain't wanna do that, but Matthew was so mad by then, after the car dain't sink in the lake, 'e wouldn't lissen ter reason.'

'He couldn't have done it on his own. If you and this Bob Jenkins had said no, he wouldn't have been able to.'

'They're both mad at Scott too, fer sackin' Mabel.'

'What has Mabel got to do with this?' she asked sharply.

Freddy wriggled, but had to confess. 'She worked at Scott's, an' was drawin' these new things 'e meks. Some pal of Matthew's did it before, but Scott sacked 'im too. Matthew copied 'em in 'is factory an' Bob was sellin' 'em, 'e's gorra garage down London.'

'I see,' Josie said slowly. Would they ever be free of Freddy's schemes? 'Do you want to go back to Birmingham?' she asked as a sudden idea occurred to her.

Freddy thought about Mabel, justifiably aggrieved, and her dad awaiting him in Birmingham and shivered. 'No. Thought if I could get ter Nice I could get a job on one of them posh boats. I don't wanna see Matthew or Bob again, they'll blame me fer lettin' 'em down.'

Josie smiled inwardly. This would suit her very well. 'I'll get you some money, enough to get to Marseilles. You'd be more likely to find a ship there where they wouldn't ask questions or want papers. But only on one condition.'

'What?'

'You write a confession which describes the parts Matthew

and Bob Jenkins played. If we don't have some hold over them they might try again, and that won't do.'

'Nobody'd believe it,' Freddy said gloomily. 'An' they'd kill me if they knew.'

'We'll manage, I'll see to that. Matthew won't be able to trace you, he won't know where you are. He'll believe you could appear at any time to be a witness against him. You needn't, of course,' she added quickly to forestall Freddy's objections. 'Only we'll know that, though.'

Eventually she persuaded him and they found a cheap café where Freddy painstakingly wrote out a confession largely dictated by Josie. The barman, who had been intrigued by them, willingly witnessed Freddy's signature, adding his own name and address with a flourish. Josie very much doubted whether this document was in any way legal, but she relied on Freddy not discovering this, and never having to show it to Matthew. He'd be too concerned to hear of it, he wouldn't have the guts to risk challenging it in a court.

Freddy, reluctantly, had to wait while Josie fetched some money from the hotel but, as she briskly told him, he had little alternative. She watched him as he scurried away. He hadn't even thanked her. If he never reappeared in their lives it would be too soon.

Leo was very quiet that evening at dinner, and Josie wondered whether he'd been offended she'd left the work to him when William had taken her away. He said he was tired and excused himself early, which gave her an opportunity to tell William what she'd discovered from Freddy.

'Do you think it will work?' she asked anxiously.

'How is he connected to the girl I sacked?'

'He lived with her. I don't know how much she's to blame. Freddy was into all sorts of minor villainy before he met her. But I believe she stole the gold from Leo's factory, that he accused me of.'

'If I'd been you I'd have handed him over to the police.'

'I couldn't ! Even though Aunt Phoebe says she's disowned him he's still her son, and she'd be devastated if he were accused of attempted murder. She can laugh at him cheating the Tote or running bets for a bookie, but if she thought he'd gone so much to the bad she'd never be happy again. Promise you'll never tell her?'

'I won't.'

'How will we stop Matthew and Bob Jenkins trying again?' Josie asked anxiously.

'When we get home I'll have my solicitor send them each a threatening letter saying we'll prosecute if anything else happens. That should stop them. Matthew's a coward at heart, and both their businesses would be ruined. But can you tell Leo? He has a right to know. He was nearly killed too.'

Leo was still cool the following day, and Josie began to wonder what the journey home would be like. Was he regretting the necessity, now the excitement of the Rally was over, of spending so much time in her company? She shrugged, and put off telling him about Freddy until he appeared to be in a more receptive mood.

The judges for the Concours de Confort took an inordinately long time to come to their decision, and most competitors had gone in search of lunch long before Pascoe's Talbot, as William had predicted, won the Grand Prix d'Honneur. It was almost over, and as Josie explored a few more streets of the principality she was sorry she'd soon be leaving the sun and the glamour and the excitement.

On the following day each car climbed the long slope up to the big cobbled square in front of the Palace where the prizes were distributed, and each car, after its moment of glory, was guided smoothly out of the arena and into yet another parking place. Then there came the business of seeing William off at the station, sending good wishes home, and finally Josie was back in the suite alone with Leo. She could put off the explanation about Freddy no longer.

When she had finished, Leo looked unaccountably pleased.

'So that was the man I saw you with!'

'What do you mean?'

'On Friday evening, as it grew dark, I was coming back to the hotel and I saw you with a man. It was your cousin?'

'Yes, of course.'

'I've been worried, and terribly jealous ever since. I didn't know you knew anyone apart from the competitors, and he was behaving so oddly, furtively. Josie, I thought perhaps you might be in trouble, and I had no right to intervene, to help you.'

Josie decided to ignore the admission of jealousy. It couldn't mean anything important. 'I trust that if you'd seen me being kidnapped you'd have come to the rescue,' she said lightly.

Leo laughed. 'If you'd appeared unwilling! So it was Mabel who was drawing William's designs, stealing them. And she was the girl who stole my gold too.'

'You believe me now?'

Leo strode across to the window which looked across to the side of the Hermitage. Then he turned and faced Josie. 'Josie, my dearest, I've believed you for a very long time, and so often tried to tell you. I've regretted a million times that I lost my temper and my common sense. Can you forgive me? Can you ever forgive me for placing you in such a dreadful position in that slum?'

'It was Freddy stealing the sapphires who caused Aunt Phoebe to throw us out of her house,' Josie said quietly. 'I've never really blamed you for that.'

He took several steps towards her. 'But the loss of your job on top made life so difficult, and I didn't know. Not until it was too late.'

'It's over now.'

Leo took a deep breath and sat down on one of the settees. 'Come and sit down. What about Freddy?'

'I suggested he went to Marseilles,' Josie replied, sitting at the other end of the settee. 'He wants to find a job on a yacht, but being Freddy he'll almost certainly end up on a tramp steamer!'

Leo chuckled and nodded. 'And Matthew? He's more dangerous. How he holds grudges!'

'From what Freddy said they appeared to fester, especially when Mabel was sacked and he wasn't able to steal any more of William's designs. I don't believe he meant to kill us, he was just desperate to spoil our chances by stopping us reaching Monte Carlo, and there'd been no opportunity since he tried to ditch us in Sweden.'

Josie was silent, thinking of the times she'd imagined she was in love with Leo. During the days they'd just spent together she'd come to appreciate many of his qualities that she hadn't seen when she worked for him, and she was bemused. Then he'd been cautious, she'd often been impatient with his careful, slow acceptance of new ideas for the business. On earlier rallies she'd seen the daring, risk-taking boy she'd heard about from the days when her mother had first been married to George. On this one when he'd been sliding round on the icy roads he'd laughed in sheer jubilation. He'd been calm and trustworthy, and decisive enough when he'd driven off the attackers. This new Leo was even more attractive than the old one. A man she could love. A man she *did* love, she realized. She simply hadn't allowed herself to believe it before, but now she knew she'd been in love with him for a very long time.

He spoke again. 'Freddy's out of reach. How can we stop Matthew trying again?'

Josie dragged her mind away from considering Leo's newly demonstrated qualities. 'William's taken the paper — I suppose it's a deposition — Freddy wrote. He'll lodge it with his solicitor with a covering letter. He'll write to Matthew and Bob Jenkins, and warn them against trying anything, with the threat that if they do he'll prosecute. I don't know, but William seemed to think it would be enough to frighten them. Matthew's not especially brave, always has to get others to do the risky bits.'

'William will put the fear of the law, if not of God, into Matthew. I've never known a more dependable fellow.'

'No,' Josie said with a reminiscent smile. 'Ann's so lucky!'

Leo stretched out a hand to grasp hers. 'Do you love him?' he demanded harshly.

Josie laughed, blushed, and shook her head. 'No, of course not! I'm not envious of Ann. I like him, very much, but I've never loved him.'

'Yet if he'd proposed to you, wouldn't you have accepted him?'

Josie, unexpectedly, giggled. 'I refused him,' she said, and then gasped as Leo's hand tightened on hers. 'He asked me, but it was more of a business proposition than a declaration of undying love. We both knew that, although we were friends and got on remarkably well, we weren't in love. I told him he'd regret it if he ever met the girl of his dreams. And practically the next day he met Ann and fell head over heels.'

'And you?' he asked softly. 'Don't you have dreams? I know I do. Josie, I've been in love with you for a very long time. Could you love me enough to marry me?'

'But I've been so unforgiving! I've held grudges. I would never listen to you, I blamed you for what Mother suffered, and it wasn't your fault. I know that, I think I always did.'

'I was the first one who wouldn't listen. But I promise I will from now on.'

'Do you mean it? Really mean it?'

'To listen?' he asked, grinning.

Josie laughed tremulously. 'No! That you love me.'

Sliding along the seat of the settee he pulled her into his arms. 'I'll have to show you, my darling Josie,' he told her, and she relaxed as he bent over her to kiss her until they were both breathless.

'Leo,' she whispered when she could breathe again. 'Leo, I've been so lonely without you! I don't know why, but nothing has so much sparkle, or is so exciting if you're not there. I'm enjoying running my business, but when it's just for me there doesn't seem much purpose in it.'

'Then you will marry me?'

'Yes.'

'Soon?'

'As soon as possible.'

'What a pity we can't have the rest of the journey home as our honeymoon, and stay in Paris,' he said. 'Shall we announce our engagement at the ball tonight?'

'Two celebrations?' Josie asked.

'We didn't win the Rally but we finished! And we won something even more important, my darling Josie! Come here, I need to kiss you again.'

Josie surrendered herself to the delights of being in his arms. Some time later he groaned and drew away from her. 'It will be sheer hell being with you, alone, and having to behave like a gentleman!' he complained, sweeping his hands through his dishevelled hair.

Josie giggled. 'Surely you wouldn't treat me differently from the *principessa*? Or am I less attractive than she is?' she asked provocatively.

Leo groaned. 'Wretch! Do you mean to hold all my failings over me?'

'I didn't get the impression you'd actually *failed* with her,' Josie said judiciously.

'I was crazy, losing you, and half of me wanted to make you jealous,' he confessed. 'Will you ever forgive me for the way I've treated you?'

'Only if you begin to treat me properly now. And you can start by telling me why you think I'm so prim and proper. I don't think I am, so why do you think you have to behave like a perfect gentleman? I don't see why we can't have two honeymoons. One in Monte Carlo now, and one after the wedding. After all, we both have thriving businesses, we can afford it!'

Leo stared at her, then gave a shout of delighted laughter. 'My adorable Josie! Then we'll keep this suite for a few more days, try and win at the Casino, and make a *very* leisurely journey back home. Come here, I want another kiss to seal the bargain!'

There were so many kisses necessary that in the end they almost missed the ball, arriving just in time to make their announcement to the many people who had become friends during the Rally, and to dance the last waltz together.